A KING UNDER SIEGE

Book One of
The Plantagenet Legacy

Books by Mercedes Rochelle

Heir to a Prophecy

The Last Great Saxon Earls Series
Godwine Kingmaker
The Sons of Godwine
Fatal Rivalry

The Plantagenet Legacy Series
A King Under Siege

A KING UNDER SIEGE

Book One of
The Plantagenet Legacy

Mercedes Rochelle

COVER ART: The Death of Wat Tyler from John Froissart,
Chroniques, Vol. 2., Royal 18 E. I, f.175
Reproduced by kind courtesy of the British Library

SKETCH MAP OF LONDON:
Drawn by Marjorie B. Honeybourne, 1945
Reproduced by kind courtesy of the London Topographical
Society

CAST OF CHARACTERS

AGNES DE LAUNCEKRONA, Lady in Waiting to Queen Anne, lover and second wife of Robert de Vere

ANNE OF BOHEMIA, QUEEN OF ENGLAND, First wife of Richard II, d.1394

ARUNDEL, RICHARD FITZALAN, 11th EARL OF, 9th Earl of Surrey, Brother of Thomas Arundel, One of the Appellants in 1387-88, d.1397

ARUNDEL, THOMAS, BISHOP OF ELY, later Archbishop of Canterbury and Lord Chancellor of England, Brother of Richard Arundel, d.1414

BOLINGBROKE, HENRY, DUKE OF HEREFORD, Earl of Derby, future King of England (Henry IV). Son of John of Gaunt, One of the Appellants in 1387-88, d.1413

BREMBRE, NICHOLAS, MAYOR OF LONDON 1377 and 1383-5, Wealthy magnate and chief ally of Richard II in London, d.1388

BURLEY, SIMON DE, Vice-Chamberlain, Lord Warden of the Cinque Ports and Constable of Dover Castle, Tutor and close friend of Richard II, d.1388

GAUNT, JOHN OF, 1st DUKE OF LANCASTER, Third surviving son of Edward III and uncle of King Richard, d.1399

GLOUCESTER, THOMAS OF WOODSTOCK, 1st DUKE OF, 1st Earl of Buckingham, 1st Earl of Essex, youngest son of Edward III and uncle of King Richard, One of the Appellants in 1387-88, d. 1397

HOLLAND, THOMAS, 2nd EARL OF KENT, 3rd Baron Holand, half-brother of Richard II through his mother Joan of Kent, d.1397

JOAN OF KENT, (also Fair Maid of Kent) Mother of King Richard and wife of Edward the Black Prince. She was known as Princess Joan because her husband was never king d.1385

JOHN BALL, Lollard "Hedge Priest", spiritual leader of the Peasants' Revolt, d.1381

MARCH, EARL OF, see Mortimer, Roger

MICHAEL DE LA POLE: see POLE

MORTIMER, ROGER, 4th Earl of March and 6th Earl of Ulster, grandson of Lionel of Antwerp (3rd son of Edward III) through his mother Philippa. Thought by many to be the heir presumptive to the throne after Richard.

MORTIMER, THOMAS, illegitimate son of Roger Mortimer, 2nd Earl of March, associated with the Lords Appellant. Uncle to Roger Mortimer.

MOWBRAY, THOMAS DE, 1st DUKE OF NORFOLK, 1st Earl of Nottingham, 3rd Earl of Norfolk, 6th Baron Mowbray, 7th Baron Segrave, One of the Appellants in 1387-88, d. 1399

NORTHUMBERLAND, SIR HENRY PERCY, 1st EARL OF, 4th Baron Percy, d.1408

PERCY: see **NORTHUMBERLAND**

PERCY, SIR THOMAS, 1st EARL OF WORCESTER, younger brother of Sir Henry Percy, later Vice-Chamberlain to Richard II

POLE, MICHAEL DE LA, Lord Chancellor of England, 1st Baron de la Pole, later 1st Earl of Suffolk, close friend of Richard, d.1389

RICHARD II, KING OF ENGLAND, son of Edward Plantagenet the Black Prince and John of Kent, d.1400

RICHARD ARUNDEL: see ARUNDEL

ROBERT DE VERE: see VERE

SUDBURY, SIMON, ARCHBISHOP OF CANTERBURY, beheaded during Peasants' Revolt 1381

THOMAS OF WOODSTOCK: see GLOUCESTER

TRESILIAN, ROBERT, Chief Justice of the king's Bench between 1381 and 1387, d.1388

TYLER, WAT, Leader of the Peasants' Revolt, d.1381

VERE, ROBERT DE, 9TH EARL OF OXFORD, Duke of Ireland, Marquess of Dublin, close friend to Richard II, d.1392

WARWICK, THOMAS DE BEAUCHAMP, 12TH EARL OF, One of the Appellants in 1387-88, d.1401

WALWORTH, WILLIAM, Mayor of London 1374-75 and 1380-81 during the Peasants' Revolt. d. 1385

WOODSTOCK, THOMAS OF: see GLOUCESTER

YORK, EDMUND OF LANGLEY, 1st DUKE OF, Fourth surviving son of Edward III and uncle of King Richard, d.1402

Map of
England

Map by Gregg Sollisch

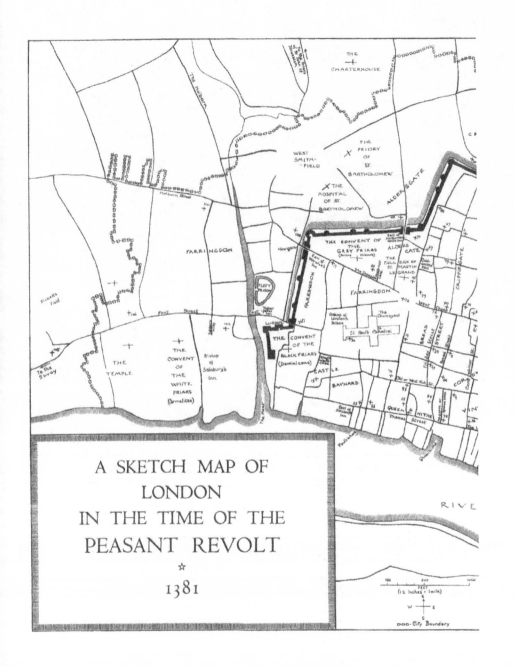

A SKETCH MAP OF
LONDON
IN THE TIME OF THE
PEASANT REVOLT
✯
1381

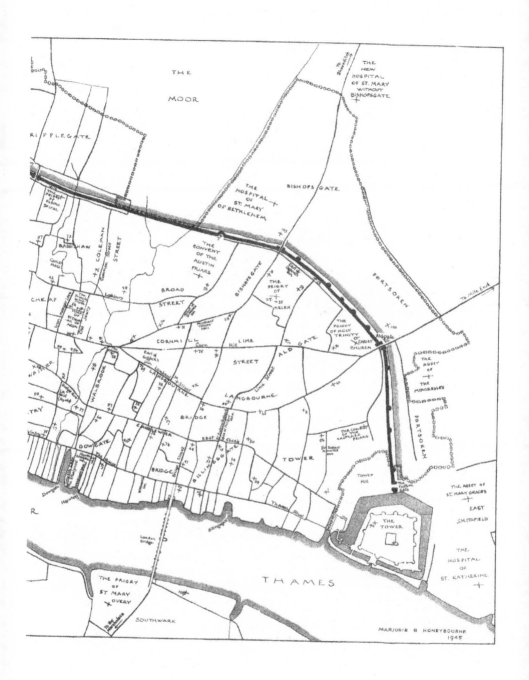

THE MOOR

RIPPLEGATE

THE NEW HOSPITAL OF ST. MARY WITHOUT BISHOPSGATE

BISHOPS GATE

THE HOSPITAL OF ST. MARY OF BETHLEHEM

THE CONVENT OF THE AUSTIN FRIARS

BASSISHAW

COLEMAN STREET

GUILD HALL

BROAD STREET

CHEAP

BISHOPS GATE

THE PRIORY OF ST. HELEN

PORTSOKEN

To Mile End

THE PRIORY OF HOLY TRINITY CHRIST CHURCH

Aldgate

THE ABBEY OF THE MINORESSES

CORNHILL

Corn Hill

LIME STREET

ALDGATE STREET

LANGBOURNE

WALBROOK

LANGBOURNE

Lime Street

PORTSOKEN

BRIDGE

CANDLEWICK

THE CONVENT OF THE CRUTCHED FRIARS

DOWGATE

EAST CHEAP

TOWER

THE ABBEY OF ST. MARY GRACES

EAST SMITHFIELD

BRIDGE

BILLINGSGATE

Tower Hill

The Postern Gate

THE TOWER

THE HOSPITAL OF ST. KATHERINE

Dowgate

Thames Street

London Bridge

THAMES

THE PRIORY OF ST. MARY OVERY

SOUTHWARK

MARJORIE B HONEYBOURNE
1945

PART 1

REVOLT

CHAPTER 1

Ten thousand or more crowded the banks of the Thames near the king's manor of Rotherhithe, shrieking and howling like the demons of hell. The royal barge, hung with the Plantagenet lions, floated safely in the middle of the river, while King Richard gripped his sword, trying to emulate his royal forefathers. His elders would agree that the fourteen year-old monarch looked every bit the Plantagenet successor; he was tall for his age, with delicate features and red hair like his father. Richard was born to be king and now he must prove it—though at the moment he felt more like a lamb than a lion.

He waited for the frenzy to exhaust itself. "Why are you here and what do you want?" The young voice, clear and shrill, reached its listeners who broke out once again into a clamor, shaking their farm tools and rusty old blades.

"Come to the shore!" One voice carried over the din. "Speak with us in person!"

Standing under a large red canopy with his counsellors, Richard glanced upriver at the four smaller barges serving as his escort. The boats had hung back, not daring to come any closer. This was a sorry plight his advisors had led them into! Sighing, Richard turned to Archbishop Sudbury; he could see the terror in the prelate's face. This wasn't helping.

"I p-promised I would speak with them," the king said uncertainly. "I must at least try."

Bristling under two great banners with St. George's cross and forty pennons, the mob continued its uproar while the king turned to his other advisors. Sir Robert Hales, England's treasurer, stepped up beside the archbishop. "We can't expect any mercy from them. They are out for blood." Richard frowned, dissatisfied. Hales might be Lord Grand Prior of the Knights Hospitaller, but today his courage seemed to have fled. The man's eyes were almost bulging from his head.

3

Richard then turned to the Earl of Salisbury, the most experienced soldier on the barge. "And what is your advice?" he asked, trying to keep a brave face.

"You cannot go ashore. They might restrain you—hold you hostage, or worse. This is an undisciplined rabble."

This was the best counsel they could give him? He had to do something, though his advisors would probably criticize him for making the wrong choice—with the utmost courtesy, of course, and polite language. Taking a deep breath, Richard turned back to the crowd. He hoped he could control his stutter. "What is it you want from me?" he shouted. "Tell me, now that I have come this far."

He stood, arms crossed, while the men closest to the river conferred with each other. Finally, coming to a decision, the apparent leader got into a boat with a couple of rowers. They brought their craft as close as they dared. "Here is what we want," the man called. "We demand the heads of John of Gaunt, Archbishop Sudbury, Treasurer Hales, Chief Justice Robert Belknap, Robert Plesington Baron of the Exchequer, John Legge and Thomas Brampton."

"Why, you seek to deprive me of my chief ministers," Richard cried. Behind him, he could hear Sudbury calling down God's curses on their heads.

"We seek to save you from corrupt officials," the rebel shouted back.

"By killing them all? How would that help me?"

"They are destroying the country with their dishonest administration."

"This is too dangerous," Salisbury spoke in Richard's ear. "We must leave."

Nodding in agreement, the king tried one last time. "If you wish to continue negotiations," he called, less sure of himself, "you may do so at Windsor on Monday next." While he was speaking, the barge was already turning around. Stunned at losing their advantage, the crowd howled in anger and the rebel boat fell back in confusion. But Richard no longer cared. He was headed for the safety of the Tower, though for the first few minutes they were at the mercy of any archer who might choose to draw his

4

bow. Fortunately, nothing happened aside from the shouts of "Treason! Treason!" that diminished as they gained speed.

The king stared at the receding mob, biting his lip, until they were out of range. He had never felt so alone. This debacle was not of his making, yet everyone was looking to him for a solution. It just wasn't fair. Even though he had been king for four years, he was in leading reins just as assuredly as any young horse. He sat in council meetings—even presided at Parliament—but his opinions were politely dismissed. They said he was too young, too inexperienced to make decisions. He was expected to watch and learn while his chief ministers made a mess of things. Well, they certainly taught him what *not* to do! And now, with half the country in an uproar, all they could do was dither. No one had taken the rising seriously enough to gather a force to confront the rebels, and now that the angry multitude was at the gates of London, no one had a suggestion what to do about it. Obviously, this attempt had failed disastrously. But at least he had tried.

How could all this have happened? We need to step back a couple of weeks, though I suspect this had been building ever since the Black Death created a labor shortage. First, the government imposed laws to hold the workers down. That was bad enough, but lately they started experimenting with a poll tax—in other words, a price per head—to raise money for the French war. Every person over the age of fourteen was taxed, though the rich man's portion was a pittance while the poor man was bled dry— especially if he had a big family. It just wasn't fair. And by the third poll tax, the government demanded even more money per head. It was too much, and who could blame the king's overburdened subjects for falsifying the tax returns? As a result, the head count came in suspiciously low and officials were dismayed by the shortfall. So what did they do? The fools sent out commissioners to collect the difference—probably the worst decision they could have made, considering the widespread resentment.

It all started in Essex—more specifically, in Brentwood—a town on an old Roman road between London and Colchester. By then, the townsfolk were already disquieted by the rumors of the commissioners, for bad news always traveled fast.

That impudent, loutish Thomas Bampton rode into town and made himself at home in the guildhall, accompanied by three clerks and two of the king's sergeant-at-arms. Brentwood's bailiff, Jack Straw, met them at the door of the building but they pushed past him, demanding tables and chairs to do their business. Grudgingly, the Straw ordered his clerks to oblige.

"We need to reexamine your accounts," Bampton growled. "I don't believe your numbers are correct. Bring out your tax assessments and lay them before me."

The bailiff shrugged. "It's all there," he muttered. "You can gauge for yourself."

"Oh, I intend to," the commissioner said, pushing him aside as he went back outside to his horse. Retrieving a bulky pack, he passed it on to a scrivener. "Meanwhile I intend to visit every one of your townsmen."

While Jack watched helplessly, he proceeded to do just that. The tax commissioner bid one of his men to follow and strode down the street, throwing open the door to the first building he came upon, which happened to be the blacksmith's shop.

Bent over an anvil, a burly man with a leather apron pounded a glowing bar of iron. Sparks flew across the room as the rhythmic bang, bang, bang shaped the metal under his sure hand. Noting movement at the door, the blacksmith stopped mid-stroke and stared at the intruder. "What can I do for you?" he asked, looking from the commissioner to his assistant.

"We have a shortfall on the king's taxes," the man said, "and need to make up the difference. How many in your household?"

The smith put down his hammer. "There is my wife and myself and my mother," he said, annoyed at the interruption. "We paid your levy."

"So you say. What is your name?"

"Edward Smith."

"Write that down," the tax collector said to his clerk. "Smith, let me see your family."

The blacksmith glared at the bailiff, who was grasping the hilt of his sword. Straw nodded briefly, and the other opened the rear door to his shop. "They are inside."

Slapping his hand against the door and forcing it all the way open, the stranger stared at the inhabitants of the room then came back into the shop. "Where is the rest of your family?"

"There are no others."

"You have no children?"

"None. I had a son and he died of a fever."

"When?"

"August last."

"August last," the tax collector snorted. "If I find he has come back to life, I will take it from your hide." He jerked his head and left the building. Frowning, Jack Straw followed him to the porch and watched as the man pounded at the door of the next house.

The owner was forced back as the commissioner pushed his way in. People were beginning to notice and a small crowd was gathering in the street. A few minutes later, the unfortunate victim was hauled outside, arms bound. Bampton faced the witnesses.

"I will arrest any of you caught trying to evade your taxes. This man will remain in prison until the money is found." He glared at the townsfolk, daring them to object. "Tomorrow, I expect every one of you to appear before me with the reckoning of this year's taxes. Pass the word."

The villagers watched him quietly as the poll tax collector went back to the guildhall. Then they started talking amongst themselves.

On the morrow they were ready.

Bampton sat behind the table, waiting; he was flanked by clerks, and the king's sergeants stood against the wall, obviously bored. As the door opened, a score of men crowded inside. They were not poor, shabby serfs; these men were craftsmen, merchants, priests, and idle soldiers, by the look of them. Their demeanor was more surly than intimidated.

"One at a time," Bampton said, pointing at a bench before him. "I want to see what you have declared."

7

The men crossed their arms and stood still while more filed in. Soon, the room was filled to capacity and others waited outside. Bampton stood up.

"What is the meaning of this?"

"Can you not see?" said their spokesman. "We will not deal with you. Nor will we give you any money."

For a moment the commissioner was shocked. But his natural bluster soon took over. "I am here on the king's business—".

"You are here on your own business! The king is badly served and you seek to fatten your own pouch."

Bampton pointed to the sergeants. "Arrest these troublemakers," he ordered. "Detain them all!"

The townspeople moved forward as one, pushing the table out of the way. The planks fell off the trestles. Bampton and his followers backed against the wall.

"You had best be on your way," the spokesman snarled as the men parted, presenting an escape route to the door. Bampton decided not to argue and trod on top of the planks as he made his way forward. He turned before he left the room.

"Don't think this is the last you've heard from me," he started, when all at once the company let out a growl, as ferocious as it was spontaneous. Bampton's sergeants shoved him out the door but they suddenly stopped, holding each other back. In the street before them, a hundred angry men shouted and waved makeshift weapons. As one, the mob rushed toward the intruders.

"This way," shouted one of the sergeants, pulling Bampton by the arm and dashing to the side. They almost broke free before a shower of sticks and rocks nearly drove them to the ground. Even a couple of arrows hurried them on their course. They helped each other forward and ran as fast as they could, followed by the vengeful throng, howling with glee.

At the edge of town everyone stopped, watching the fleeing officials. The crowd fell strangely silent, looking at each other.

"There's no stopping it now," said Jack Straw, who had been watching from the steps. "We've started something big and now we'll have to finish it." His companions grumbled in agreement. "You have a day or so," he added. "Those who can, ride out and send the message to the other towns. The king's men will return, and we'll need all the help we can get if we are to stop their reprisals."

There are times when action—even desperate action—invigorates a man. You couldn't find a soul who regretted his resistance to the hated tax collectors. Over the next three days, Brentwood's hundred disgruntled rebels swelled to two hundred, and more were coming all the time. Finally, as expected, on the 2nd of June Robert Belkmap, Chief Justice of the Common Pleas, rode into town to put things back in order. He brought with him three jurors who were supposed to identify the original rioters, and three clerks. They didn't get very far. As soon as the little party rode down the main street, from out of nowhere a shrieking crowd charged at them, pulling his assistants from their horses, kicking and punching and knocking them across the ground.

Jack Straw seized the reins of Belkmap's mount. "Take his papers. Burn them!" he shouted. As the bewildered Justice twisted around in his saddle, somebody grabbed his saddlebags and threw the contents into the street. Belkmap was the lucky one; while this was going on, angry men dragged the three screaming jurors into the center of town where the rioters had set up a makeshift executioner's block. The first victim struggled and kicked at his tormenters, until they forced his head sideways onto the stump.

"Here, John Blackhand," the strongest agitator shouted. "You are good with an axe. Finish this man off." A stocky yeoman, well-known for bragging about his battlefield exploits in France, stepped forward and rolled up his sleeves.

"Any last words?" he quipped, laughing.

"I've done nothing to you," the juror screamed. "Let me go!"

"You would have if we gave you the chance," his captor growled. He struck quickly and a spray of blood showered his face, though it took two blows to sever the man's head. "Bring the next one," he shouted, shoving the juror's corpse aside. Willing hands hauled the next wailing victim to the block, then the third. "A spear, a spear!" cried the mob, and the severed heads were soon shoved onto poles, bobbing over the crowd like gruesome pennons. The clerks fared no better; they were beaten to death before their heads, too, joined the raucous procession. Only Belkmap was allowed to live.

"Swear!" shouted Jack, pulling the commissioner off his horse. "Send for a priest! Tell him to bring a crucifix!" Belkmap struggled to get away but someone hit him on the side of the head with a stick. He fell against Jack, who pushed him to the ground. "You are a traitor to the king!" Jack shouted, then hauled the justice back to his feet. "You would hold court against us out of greed and malice!" Finally a cleric ran up with a crucifix and Straw took it, holding it out flat. "Swear on this cross that you will never again hold a *trailbaston* commission! Swear that you will never again act as a judge in a poll-tax inquisition!"

Belkmap spit out a tooth. Someone thrust a cudgel into his back, knocking him forward. Turning, he watched as the rioting townspeople added his papers to a growing bonfire. He grimaced, putting his hand on the crucifix. "I swear," he grumbled.

"Then let him go," Jack directed the others. They had already taken the horse away, but Belkmap was glad to get out of there alive. He started walking, not looking back.

Standing in a group, the villagers shouted curses and brandished their weapons as he stumbled down the road. Satisfied, Jack turned to his followers. "You have done well," he said in a loud voice. "We must gather more support and march to London, where we will lay our grievances before the king!"

The mob had already lost interest in Belkmap; they surrounded Jack and listened to his instructions. "Edward, John, and Robert," Jack called. "Go to the hackney stables and take three horses. Make your way to London and spread the word." He worked his way through the gathering, slapping men on the shoulders. "Come. Gather whatever food and drink you may find. Let us ferry across the Thames at Tilbury so we can share the good news with our friends in Kent." He raised his voice again: "Sound the Bell! Now is the time to make ourselves heard!"

They all knew what he was talking about. For the last twenty years, itinerant preachers had been spreading words of hope and defiance. Their leader, John Ball, had wandered across the land, sleeping under hedges, preaching in the woods by moonlight, avoiding the authorities whenever possible. The friar swore that all people were equal in the eyes of God and one day they would

10

rise up and shake off the yolk of servitude. Well, the day had finally come. The people's rising had begun.

It made sense to strike boldly at the nearest symbol of oppression: Rochester Castle stood only eight miles away along the Roman road to Canterbury. As they passed through villages, the clamorous rebels gathered more enthusiastic supporters. The unfortunate jurors' heads on poles led the way as the organized mob cried out their support of King Richard and death to all lawyers and corrupt ministers. They sang their songs of rebellion, pushed too far by the poll tax:

With spades and hoes and ploughs, stand up now, stand up now.
With spades and hoes and ploughs, stand up now.
Your houses they pull down, to fright poor men in town,
The gentry must come down and the poor shall wear the crown.
Stand up now, poor soldiers, stand up now.

The lawyers sit on high, stand up now, stand up now.
The lawyers sit on high, stand up now.
Arrest you they advise, such fury they devise,
But the devil in them lies, and hath blinded both their eyes.
Stand up now, poor soldiers, stand up now.

By the time the rebels reached Rochester, the district surrounding the castle was already in an uproar. The Norman fortress stood tall and square and solid, with a view of the surrounding countryside that gave its meagre garrison scant reassurance. On one side the Medway River protected its walls from the horde, which spread out over the fields. But in Rochester town, a swell of human bodies threatened to break against its curtain walls like a storm wave, inexorable in its power. A roar from thousands of throats carried threats of death and retribution, and the poor soldiers inside had little heart to resist the force of righteous anger.

Archers fresh from the war in France practiced their skill against any soldier brave enough to show himself. Townspeople brought ladders, and just like greedy ants reckless yeomen scaled the crumbling curtain walls—undermanned by soldiers putting up

11

a half-hearted resistance. It wasn't long before they breached the outer defenses. Terrified defenders retreated toward the keep while successful attackers opened the gates from inside.

Cheering, the rebels rushed toward the keep, though this would be much more difficult to overwhelm. The entrance was one full story up a single exterior staircase. King John had trouble taking the castle in 1215 with all his vast resources; what could a rabble expect to achieve?

The constable Sir John Newton was confident they could hold out indefinitely. But that didn't last long. He lost his complacency when he came upon a soldier leaning over the parapet, watching the rebels; his crossbow was propped against the stone wall.

"Knave!" he exclaimed. "Is this how you keep watch? Go back to your post at once!"

The soldier turned to the governor, scowling. "What it is you want from us?" he retorted. "I will not fire on my friends."

Newton was aghast. "Michael," he shouted to his next in command. "Seize this man!"

Michael did as he was ordered, and as he led the soldier away others came forward to replace him. The constable drew himself up. "We can defend this castle against that horde," he urged. "Look at them." He pointed to the unruly crowd. "They may succeed for a while, but they will pay dearly in the end."

The soldiers did not move. One of them stepped forward. "This is not our fight," he said. "We will not kill our countrymen. Nor will we be taxed again!" Many of his fellows grumbled in agreement.

"Have I no men loyal to the king?"

"You mistake us," someone else shouted. "Those men are loyal to King Richard and seek to protect him from his greedy self-serving ministers." The agreement was even more vociferous this time.

Newton turned his head, listening to the uproar from below. "All I hear is clamor. There is no order to this throng." He was about to continue when he heard shouting inside the castle. Someone had forced their way in while he was arguing with his men. A door on the rampart crashed open, spewing a succession

12

of ragged, bristling attackers. They grabbed Newton roughly and pushed him against the parapet.

"Open the prison," their leader shouted over his shoulder. He pushed his forearm against Newton's throat. The crash of wood splintering and carts pitched to the ground was enough to convince the constable that the fight was over before it started. He gritted his teeth while men shouted with glee, enjoying the destruction. "We want you to speak to the king for us," his captor said threateningly. "We will have our freedom, or my name ain't Jack Straw."

Almost choking, Newton shook his head. Then his eyes opened wide as a ceorl dragged two children up the winding steps. The man held the terrified boys by the back of their tunics. Jack turned around. "Are those yours?" He released his pressure on the throat somewhat.

"Please, don't hurt them," the constable said. "I'll do your bidding."

"That's more like it. Keep those boys safe and secure. We want no trouble from our knight."

Newton watched helplessly while they took his sons away. His own soldiers had already joined the sacking of their own castle—some willingly, some not so willingly. Horses were brought into the bailey, tugging at the reins held by unfamiliar hands.

"That white horse," Jack Straw shouted, pointing. "Save that one for me. The rest we'll hook up to wagons; we will need all the supplies we can carry. Sir Newton, we require your assistance." He bowed in mock respect and gestured for his prisoner to precede him.

Defeated, the constable obliged. His only concern was his children, and he hoped he would be relieved of his onerous position once the rebels found someone else to amuse them.

After the initial elation wore off, Jack Straw's followers went to work—that is, until they found the wine casks. Whooping in triumph, someone knocked the spigot off and his friends crawled over each other trying to catch the stream of bubbling red vintage—some with their mouths, some with their hands, the lucky ones with cups they found on shelves. Rochester castle was a great prize; everyone was determined to make the most of it.

The next morning they were well on their way. By now, the press of determined yeomen, villeins, shopkeepers, alewives, innkeepers, laborers, clerks, and craftsmen, to name a few, had grown so large that no one could pass them on the road. As they marched through villages on the way to Canterbury, they surrounded the town halls and ransacked the buildings for documents that could be burned in the middle of the road.

Anyone that dressed like a lawyer was confronted by threatening men. "You must take an oath of loyalty to the cause," a spokesman declared, "to be faithful to King Richard and the true Commons, and accept no king called John," meaning John of Gaunt, Richard's hated uncle. This was not the time to object, for surely a man must swear or die. Some poor souls were dragged along with the rebels whether they would or not.

The mob followed the Medway River to Maidstone, where they heard that John Ball was languishing in the Archbishop of Canterbury's prison. The jail was easy to find; dark and squat, it was attached to the Norman palace with its windows facing the road. Sudbury's tall and beautiful residence—topped with steeply conical roofs—turned its back to the ugly appendage as though embarrassed to be associated with it.

As they approached the prison, the Essex rebels slowed in confusion. Directly in front of them, a similarly armed group of rebellious citizens blocked the road. Pacing back and forth at their head, a short, stocky workman in well-worn garb stopped and let out a shout. He had a swarthy face, bushy eyebrows, and a red nose, brought on by a serious liking for ale. Luckily, there was no mistaking his welcome.

"There you are, my friends," he bellowed. "We've been waiting for you. My name is Wat Tyler and I represent these fine citizens from Kent. We are all here to join forces with you for King Richard and the Commons of England! Eh, my mates?" His followers let out a cheer, and Wat patted a few on the back. "Now that we are all properly introduced, let us break down the doors to John Ball's prison!"

14

Wat walked right up to Jack Straw and held out an axe. "I give you the first blow," he said jovially. "Let us forge our friendship in the blood of Archbishop Sudbury!" He leaned toward Jack's ear. "Though I think he is in Canterbury," he said in a lower voice. "No matter!"

Jack took the axe and proceeded to ply it against the thick wooden door studded with iron nails. The first few blows did little damage, until Wat came up beside his new accomplice with a lever. "Let me help," he called, and went to work, thrusting the tip into cracks and pushing with all his strength. Others crowded up next to them, prodding and shoving and chopping, and after a few minutes of energetic toil it appeared that their efforts were having an effect. "Give it your all, boys," Wat shouted, stepping aside, and with a great heave they broke open the door. Not hesitating for a second, the victorious attackers poured into the prison and wrenched doors open, freeing everyone inside. Minutes later, the leaders reemerged, arm in arm with John Ball.

Excited, the crowd cheered as John held up his hands, blinking rapidly as he got used to the daylight. Tattered sleeves slipped down his thin arms. He was tall and big-boned with a ring of unkempt grey hair around his bald crown; his face was smudged and his feet were bare. But the people's preacher didn't care about filthy clothes or an empty stomach. He had a mission to accomplish.

"My brothers," the friar called, "in the name of the Trinity, Father, Son, and Holy Ghost, let us stand together manfully. No longer will we see Rich and Poor, nor Lords and Serfs. The wicked in high places shall be punished. Covetousness and pride will be chastised and ended! Well should you ask: When Adam delved and Eve span, who was then the gentleman?"

They had all heard this message before, and the mob went wild, for they knew that this time, there would be no stopping their spiritual leader. Undeterred by his three months in prison, John turned to Wat Tyler.

"We cannot tarry; if we keep moving the government will not be able to gather its resources against us until it's too late. But first, I need quill and paper so I might write letters to our other spiritual leaders in Essex and Kent."

15

"Of course, father," said Wat. "I have men ready to do your bidding." Tyler had already anticipated Ball's release, for he led the priest into a local public house and set him down with dinner and ale and a pile of blank papers.

Watching from the doorway, Jack Straw realized that he need only step back and let this pair of leaders take over the movement: people were already calling them the captain and the prophet. Well, that was all right with Jack. He was not sure he had the vision to see this rebellion through to the end.

As Wat Tyler handed the preacher a quill and a bottle of ink, John Ball threw back his head and thundered to the room: "Let everybody know. John Ball has rung the Bell!"

CHAPTER 2

Wiping the sweat from his forehead, King Richard leaned against the wall in the practice yard while his friends Thomas and Robert exchanged sword blows, weighed down in full armor despite the summer heat.

"Keep your arms in front you, Robert. Don't pull back." Michael de la Pole, Richard's resident advisor and arms instructor, moved to the side so he could see better. "Don't let him come too close," he urged.

Richard could see that Robert was getting tired. He was having trouble holding up the point of his sword, and Thomas was sure to take advantage of any opening. As soon as Richard thought it, Thomas burst upon his sparring partner with a spurt of energy, knocking his sword aside and assailing him with a succession of blows to the head. Overcome, Robert fell onto his backside and the bout was over. Thomas drew off his helmet and shook his head, sending a shower of sweat over his prone rival.

And rivals they were, in more ways than one. Richard pursed his lips, watching as their instructor strode forward and offered a hand to help Robert off the ground. Thomas dismissed his opponent with a jerk of his head and walked over to the king. The three youths had spent much of their time together in Edward III's day while Thomas Mowbray and Robert de Vere were wards of the court. Now that Richard was king, they continued their training under the firm hand of Michael de la Pole, an old companion-in-arms of Richard's father the Black Prince. Windsor castle offered the best equipped and most expansive yard for jousting exercises as well as foot training. Though Richard wasn't excited about all this physical activity, he recognized the necessity of it. A king was expected to wage war and that was that.

There was no doubt that Thomas showed more aptitude for knightly skills than the other two. That was all right with Richard, though he was slightly annoyed when Thomas went to great lengths to humiliate Robert. De Vere, on the other hand, secure in

17

his friendship with the king, shrugged off any insult as beneath his dignity. That served to aggravate Thomas even more. It was a constant cycle of competition that Richard found tiresome, though at the same time he was flattered. Being king did not remove the need for reassurance.

Richard took a sip from a water bottle and handed it to Thomas. "That was a good move. He couldn't stop you."

Thomas poured the water on his head before drinking. "It was too easy," he said. "Robert needs to pay more attention."

"I will from now on," the other interjected from behind. Thomas scowled at Robert, apparently unruffled despite his embarrassing spill. Robert was a full head shorter than him but better looking, with a thick, curly shock of brown hair and high cheekbones, whereas Mowbray was cursed with a hook nose and crooked teeth. But he was the stronger of the two, which he thought was more important. Good looks were useless in a fight.

Coughing to hide his amusement, Richard grinned at his friend. Robert de Vere, earl of Oxford, came from one of the oldest but poorest aristocratic families in England. He was five years older than Richard and married to the king's cousin Philippa. Richard had taken a liking to him right away and it wasn't long before others tried to undermine their relationship, calling Robert greedy and grasping and not terribly stouthearted. But people were always jealous. They could complain all they wanted; Richard wouldn't listen.

Michael de la Pole approached, pulling on a set of gloves. "Are you ready, sire? It's your turn, though for now I'm going to attack and you can defend." Richard nodded reluctantly; he wasn't particularly anxious to start another workout, but it was too early to stop for the day. Thomas tightened the king's straps and Robert picked up his helm.

Michael waited patiently. Richard was a competent if unenthusiastic fighter; nonetheless, he was a clever lad and showed ingenuity. His skill with horses was impressive, and he could already control his mount with knees and thighs while handling a cumbersome lance and shield. He just needed some more practice with his swordplay.

Handsome and cultured, Michael came from a long line of successful merchants; his father had lent King Edward money to pay for his many French campaigns. But he was trying to rise above all that; Michael's recent appointment to Richard's council attested to his skill at diplomacy and political maneuvering. He was pleased that the young King showed more interest in the business of government than the swagger of combat. He had much to teach his young charge.

"Sire!" The single word echoed off the stone walls with such urgency that everyone turned. The king frowned as his other advisor approached. He could never overcome a dislike for Richard, Earl of Arundel, assigned to his council since the day he was crowned. The man always trying to control him and tell him what to do. Short and stocky, Arundel had a low forehead and pale blue eyes that bulged from their sockets, reminding Richard of a dead fish.

"No time for weapons training now," Arundel said, handing a message to Michael. "I've called a council meeting. We've had a serious disturbance in Essex that demands our immediate attention."

Michael glanced up from the paper. "They've assaulted a tax collector," he said. "They are up in arms."

"Worse than that," Arundel growled. "They are marching on London."

"Help me with this," Richard muttered, tugging at a strap. His friends hurried to unbuckle his armor as his advisors strode away.

"I can only assume this isn't an ordinary commotion," Arundel said to Michael. "Do you think it's the poll tax?"

The other nodded. "I argued against sending out commissioners, but I was overridden." He sighed. "Let's hope we can contain the unrest."

Events were soon to prove that matters had already gotten out of hand. As soon as Richard entered the council chamber, the first eyewitness was called into the room. The king took his place, assessing the council; they were a mix of prelates, barons, and knights. They all rose briefly to greet him then quickly sat, not even looking at each other. The tension in the room was palpable.

19

The door opened and a tall, slightly bent man in a black robe was ushered in. Arundel gestured for him to stand at the end of table. "This is Robert Belknap, chief justice of the common bench. He is here to tell us what happened."

Belknap touched his hat. "Sire, your Graces, I have come to report that Essex is already aflame with revolt. They must have been prepared for this..."

"Tell us what happened," Arundel repeated impatiently.

"Hmm. Well, as directed by the council after commissioner Thomas Bampton was driven from town, I went to Brentwood with three jurors and three clerks—"

"Driven from town? Who was driven from town?" Richard interrupted.

"Commissioner Bampton," the chief justice answered.

"Why was he driven from town?"

Belknap frowned in confusion at Arundel. "They refused to pay him the additional taxes they owed."

"And you were sent to impose order?"

Clearing his throat, Belknap nodded. "The council sent me."

"Why wasn't I told?" Richard turned to Arundel.

"Sire, it was a minor matter. Too small to bother you with."

"Too small." Richard repeated slowly. "What happened then?"

"We were attacked. My companions were slain. Decapitated."

"And you couldn't be bothered to tell me?" Richard's voice rose as he glared at Arundel. "When did all this start?"

"A week ago," Arundel muttered. "At the time, we deemed the chief justice and his clerks sufficient to deal with the situation. Since then, we have relied on local officials to quell the unrest. Sire," he added with annoyance, "we needn't trouble you about every small disturbance."

"Men were decapitated and you think this is a small disturbance? And now that you have seen fit to enlighten me, what are you doing to quell the situation?"

Arundel gestured to the guard at the door, trying to avoid answering. "Bring in Sheriff John Sewale. Chief Justice Belknap, you may wait outside."

The sheriff entered as the other left. Apparently the new witness was more than an onlooker; he had a bandage tied around his head and limped, leaning on a crutch.

"What happened to you?" Richard asked, unable to hide the frustration in his voice.

"Sire, I was attacked in my home by the rebels. They beat me and my servants and stole the proceeds of the recent tax reassessment. They took all my documents and burned them."

"How much did they steal?"

The man hesitated. "About 1000 marks."

"1000 marks. Gone. Where are you coming from?"

The sheriff hesitated again. "Cressing, sire."

Richard was shocked. "Cressing? Cressing Temple? Are you telling me that the rebels attacked Cressing Temple?" His voice slipped into its upper register but Richard was too upset to care. Cressing Temple was no mean estate; it was one of the largest possessions of the Knights Hospitaller. Sir Robert Hales was its prior, and as acting Treasurer, Hales was the same man who ordered the poll tax reassessments.

"Sire, they broke into the Temple and stole armor, vestments, gold and silver, and burned books and manorial records. They set fire to the preceptory buildings."

"Enough!" Richard slapped the table with the palm of his hand. "What you doing about it?"

His question was directed at Earl Arundel who sat in his chair, impassive. "Sire, that is why we have brought the matter to your attention."

Richard turned from him to Michael. "We must summon a f-force to put down this r-rebellion," he said. *Damn this stutter! Get a hold of yourself!* "Why hasn't this already been done?"

Michael shook his head. "Duke John, who has the largest retinue at his disposal, is in Scotland. Your uncle Thomas of Woodstock is in Wales with his army. Your uncle Edmund of Langley has just sailed for Portugal. We have no one at hand to call upon."

Richard was speechless. *How could this be?*

"We understand," Arundel explained, "that every town has opened its arms to the rebels. Many have crossed the Thames and

21

have joined forces with the people of Kent. Their numbers are growing by the day, and those that stayed on this side of the river are headed toward London."

The enormity of the problem drained all the anger from Richard's voice. "What are we to do?"

Arundel stood. "The first thing we must do is get you to safety. Tomorrow morning, we will move to the Tower for protection. With God's will, we will get there in time."

CHAPTER 3

Richard could be forgiven for not knowing that rebellion had been brewing before he was even born. For many years the impoverished, the downtrodden, the oppressed villeins had waited for this moment, and John Ball had an army of vengeful disciples. However, this was not to be a disorderly rabble. The friar proclaimed to his followers, "You will not take into your partnership those who will plunder and pillage for self-seeking!" Under his and Tyler's direction, the growing multitude would have their very specific targets: the lawyers, the royal officials, rapacious landlords, and John of Gaunt's servants. No one was to harm the common man or the simple village priests. It was all right to ask for food and contributions but not to demand them unless an undeserving lord fell into their power.

Of course, things didn't necessarily go that way. Still, a man could only do so much.

Once Ball's messengers were on their way, the confident rebels took the road to Canterbury; it was the weekend of the 8th and 9th of June. The road was black with marching men and women, shoulder to shoulder across the hard sunbaked ground that skirted hills and meandered through forests. Along the way, hungry rustics begged food from farms and villages that barely had enough to feed themselves. They spread like locusts over fields and orchards, plucking edibles ripe and unripe to fill their empty stomachs. When they approached a manor, no matter who it belonged to, they plundered the house and set it afire; the inhabitants were lucky to get away with their lives.

Just before noon on the 10th, Wat Tyler and his following arrived at Canterbury. They headed straight to the cathedral, surprising a group of priests who were in the middle of mass. All praying stopped as John Ball entered the church. The tall friar walked up to the altar and held out his arms.

"We seek the archbishop," he spoke confidently.

One of the priests stepped forward. "You interrupt the Lord's prayer," he admonished.

Ball nodded briefly. "I regret that. Where is Archbishop Sudbury?"

"He is in London, with the king."

Coming up beside him, Wat Tyler let out a brief laugh. "Then I suggest you elect a new primate," he shouted, "for Sudbury is a traitor and doomed to a traitor's death!" He raised his sword. "To the archbishop's palace!"

Cheering, the mob turned and ran out of the cathedral, leaving the bewildered priests to thank their maker that the church was undisturbed. The marauders had no interest in destroying God's house. But the nearby archbishop's palace was another matter.

The citizens of Canterbury were more than willing to demonstrate their support, and many lawyers lost their lives in the disturbances that followed. However, now that Sudbury had escaped, Wat and his followers had little reason to dawdle. Leaving the townspeople to finish their work, the rebels headed to London, by now at least 10,000 strong. Some chroniclers numbered them at 30,000, but how does one count a crowd like this?

The road was thick with marching revelers, some singing, some laughing, all of them enjoying their newfound freedom. Wat Tyler confronted every newcomer they passed, asking for the watchword. "With whom do you hold?" he would shout, encouraged by the others. By now, if they knew what was good for them, the strangers would have to answer: "With King Richard and the true Commons," or something in that vein. And at that they were obliged to join the parade whether they wanted to or not.

Nearing London, the marching renegades came across a curious sight. Sunk axle-deep in the mud, an odd-looking bright red wagon—or whirlicote—was surrounded by a handful of men-at-arms. The canopy was painted with the royal white hart. Servants strained mightily to budge the wagon, to no avail. Tyler dismounted and gave his stallion over to a helper. Then he strutted up to one of the soldiers.

"Who does this whirlicote belong to?" he asked, peeking around the guard to get a closer look.

"The king's mother rides inside," the other said, holding out an arm to discourage any familiarity. "She is returning from pilgrimage."

"Ah, the Fair Maid of Kent," Tyler cried out, turning to his followers. "It is the Princess of Wales, going to meet her son. Let us help her, lads! The wagon is too heavy for her spindly servants."

Joking with each other, many of the villeins put their shoulders to the stout whirlicote and grunted and heaved until the wheels started turning; with a yell, they gave one great push and the wagon broke free. Wat chuckled, rubbing his hands together, and gestured for a few men to approach. He leaned toward the soldier.

"Can we pay our respects to Princess Joan?" he asked, not expecting a refusal. After all, they had just helped her on her way.

The soldier raised a corner of the curtain under the canopy and spoke to the lady inside. He listened respectfully then dropped the drape, turning to Wat.

"Her Grace has no wish to speak with you," he said almost apologetically. "But for our part, gramercy for your help."

For a moment it seemed like Wat would object, but thinking twice he shrugged his shoulders. "No need to upset the king," he said to one his followers. He bowed and threw out his arm in a mock salutation. The men-at-arms surrounded the whirlicote again and the horses threw themselves against their harness. The contraption picked up speed, creaking and swaying.

"For King Richard and the true commons!" shouted Wat Tyler, and his men took up the salutation as they watched the whirlicote move away. It would soon pull far ahead of them, since Wat intended to visit more manors along the way to London.

By Wednesday the 12th of June, the rebel force had reached their destination. Blackheath was a scrubby, sandy, barren stretch of land near Greenwich. Adjacent to the Thames riverbank about four miles east of London, Blackheath proved a useful meeting place. It was large enough to have served as a long-term encampment for the Danes back in 1011, and this day tens of thousands of rebels settled down to rest. Here Wat and his fellow leaders planted their two banners with St. George's cross. Until needed again, the gruesome heads lined up along the bank on their lances, grinning vacantly upriver toward the Tower. Merchant cogs and hulks plied their way up and down the river, slowing in their course to gawk at the growing crowd.

"Where is Sir John Newton?" Wat bellowed. He paced back and forth until finally the reluctant knight was prodded forward.

"Ah, there you are," Tyler nodded. "Are his sons secure?"

"Aye, we have them," one of the guards volunteered, showing a gap-toothed smile. "They won't be going anywhere."

"Good. Sir John, serve us well and we'll return your children unharmed. We need you to go to the king with a message for us."

Newton pursed his lips but nodded briefly.

"Tell him this." Wat adjusted his belt, threw out his chest and started pacing back and forth. "Tell him that everything we have done and everything we will do is for his honor and the honor of the realm. Tell him that for a long time the realm of England has not been governed well by his uncle that scoundrel John of Gaunt, by that traitor Robert Hales, and most specifically by the Archbishop of Canterbury his chancellor; whereof we, the people, will have account! Have King Richard meet us here at Blackheath and listen to our grievances. Go now, Sir John Newton. We have a boat standing by, as you see. They will row you to the Tower and bring you back, or by God you shall see your sons no more."

There was no time to waste. Sir John boarded the vessel and as they rowed upstream, the waiting rebels shouted their encouragement. It was a fine day and for the first time in their lives—or their parents' lives, or their grandparents' lives—they would have the ear of the king.

"This evening," Wat said, turning to John Ball, "you shall give the finest sermon of your life, without having to hide or fear or pretend that you are other than the voice of the people."

The mud-encrusted whirlicote belonging to Princess Joan squeaked across London Bridge, pushing its way as best as it could. It was slow going; the street was only twelve feet wide since buildings lined both sides of the bridge. Each house only occupied four feet of the stone platform; the rest of its foundation cantilevered over the edge, supported by huge wooden struts. But that meant the twenty-foot-wide bridge was already reduced by eight feet. Two and three stories high, the houses blocked out the sun like a tunnel, especially since many of the top floors were connected by an enclosed walkway.

The bridge accommodated a world all its own, populated by every conceivable business except taverns—for they had no cellars. The shops occupied the ground floor with their colorful signs nine feet from the ground so a horse and rider could pass underneath. Every sign displayed an image representing a trade so it could be identified by anyone, literate or not. The noise was constant, at least until the last curfew bell was rung and the bridge gates locked. Hawkers shouted their wares while draymen argued with one another as they tried to pass their wagons through spaces too narrow for both. Children squealed, dogs barked, mules complained, while the din of the blacksmith shop mingled with the hammering of the carpenters. There was no getting away from the stench of excrement, rotten meat, fish, and human sweat.

In addition, people standing in front of counters at the local shops blocked the road, allowing even less space for travelers moving both ways across the only bridge to London. No wonder the princess's contrivance stalled many times, much to Joan's vexation. But they finally made it across and headed directly for the Tower.

Watching from the London side of the bridge, Mayor William Walworth nodded to himself in relief. He had already heard reports of the great uprising from Princess Joan's outriders, as well as frantic deputies sent by local sheriffs. Now that the long-awaited princess had safely arrived, he could order the drawbridge raised. Stroking his beard, Walworth gave another cursory look downstream before breaking into action. He was a big, strapping man, wealthy fishmonger before he was elected Mayor of London, and he was well-known amongst his peers as a champion of merchants' rights. Walworth never exhibited any hesitancy when there was a fight to be had, and in this growing crisis many Londoners relied on him for reassurance.

"You there, Henry Yevele," he shouted to the waiting Bridge Warden. "Now is the time. Pull up the chains and lift the drawbridge." He didn't wait to see if his command was followed, for his trust in Yevele was complete. Of course, he knew that raising the drawbridge wouldn't stop people from crossing by boat, but they wouldn't be coming in great numbers.

Walworth knew the old bridge intimately; it required constant attention, and many a time he had to raise funds for repairs. But it was solid; none could gainsay that. Built from grey Kentish ragstone, the nineteen piers were so massive they blocked almost half of the river, causing the water to gush dangerously between them like a millrace. The watermen had a name for every opening; the arch south of St. Thomas Chapel was called Long Entry, while the arch on the north side of the Chapel was Chapel Lock. You had Rock Lock and Gut Lock among others, and of course below the drawbridge was Draw Lock. The piers were not all built the same size, nor were they spaced equally far apart; their irregular placement was determined by the firmness of the river bed.

On the Southwark end, the bridge entered through the Great Stone Gate, tall and deep. In the portal, a portcullis and wooden gates provided the first line of defense. The Drawbridge was over the seventh arch, but first you must pass through Drawbridge Gate—called by some the Traitors Gate, surmounted by decomposing heads on long staves.

For the moment, at least, everything was quiet. Walworth turned to the aldermen who stood behind him waiting for instructions. "For now, we must secure all entries into the city," he said in a loud voice. "Aldermen, close the gates and double the watches. I have heard that the Essex rebels are gathering at Mile End. I'm sure they will try to force their way through Aldgate." This was the easternmost entrance through the London Wall, just above the Tower. "Hold your positions until you hear further from me."

Satisfied, Walworth went to meet with former Mayors Nicholas Brembre and John Philipot, and a former sheriff Robert Launde. They were all men he could depend on and they waited for him at the Billingsgate wharf, halfway between the bridge and the Tower. As he approached they quietly talked amongst themselves, pointing to activities across the river.

"The drawbridge has been lifted and we are closing all the gates," Walworth said as they turned to greet him. "Now we must help the king's council grow some ballocks." They laughed obligingly at his snide remark.

"Why they haven't raised a royal army during this last fortnight confounds me," Brembre said, shaking his head. "All they have done is talk."

"Well," Walworth said sadly, putting a hand on Nicholas's shoulder, "there will plenty of talk tonight, I assure you. They are much more courageous safely behind the Tower walls." Walworth had escorted the king to the Tower earlier that day when Richard came back from Windsor, agitated by news of the revolt. He may be king, but at fourteen years old Richard couldn't be expected to do much more than agree with his councilors, such as they were. And their lack of action did not bode well for the country.

CHAPTER 4

Richard sat at the head of the council table and watched uneasily as his advisors argued and bickered. He almost wished his uncle John was here, for although Gaunt didn't have much luck on the battlefield, at least he could command with some authority. Since the death of Richard's father, John of Gaunt was the oldest living son of the late King Edward III. He jealously guarded his prestige, which admittedly made him lots of enemies—especially in London. People listened to him because they had to; he was the only duke in England, and his wealth rivalled the crown. But now, Richard thought, the rebels wanted to murder him and all his followers. Maybe, after all, it was best that he was far away in Scotland.

Gaunt had left his eldest son Henry of Bolingbroke with the king; there he was, leaning against a pillar gnawing on an apple. But he gave small comfort. Even though they were only a few months apart in age, Richard and Henry were miles apart in temperament. Whereas Richard loved reading and the arts, Henry was all about jousting and boisterous games with his passel of friends. Having been raised alone in his sickly father's household, as a child Richard had not been exposed to boys his own age, and he felt a grudging envy of Henry's easy manner—though he would never admit it to anyone.

Richard always felt a twinge of discomfort when he thought about the day he first met Henry and his two sisters at his uncle's Savoy palace. Richard's family had just moved from Bordeaux where he was born and had spent the first five years of his life. He didn't know a word of English, and his mannerisms were, well, very French. Henry swaggered forward and tugged on the scalloped sleeves of his short voluminous velvet gown, belted at the waist; the sleeves were so long they almost dragged on the ground. "What is this?" he asked in French, then turned around and said something to his sisters in English. The girls giggled.

"It's a houppelande," Richard said haughtily. "Don't you wear them here?"

"A houppelande, a houppelande!" the girls squealed, clapping their hands. They ran in a circle around Richard, observing his gown from every direction, while he turned, following them. Soon they tired of their cousin and went back to their game, sitting on the floor facing away from him. Mortified at being ignored, Richard sat down in a corner and watched. He didn't know what they were playing anyway, yet it stung that they didn't invite him to join in. It didn't help that they spoke English to each other. Later he asked his mother not to bring him back there anymore.

Richard shook his head, ridding himself of the memory. Sighing, he rearranged his sleeves. This wrangling could go on all night. If only his father were still alive! He would know what to do. The Black Prince had been bred for the throne; according to everyone he was the flower of chivalry and the greatest warrior in Europe. It would always be Richard's deepest regret that he had never known his father when he was healthy and hale and magnificent. Alas for poor England, he caught dysentery while on campaign. It took years for Richard's father to die; he wasted away to nothing while the old king sank into decrepitude. More often than not, the Black Prince shut himself away in his dark, smelly room while Richard was ordered to play quietly so as not to disturb him.

In the middle of all that sickness, Richard's five year-old brother, Edward of Angouleme, died of the plague. He was two years older than Richard, and they would have been such good playfellows. *He* should have been king after the Black Prince. Not Richard. An heir and a spare, the old saying went; Richard was the spare. His parents were so worried about his health that he was never allowed to do anything that might put him in danger. He lived inside a tiny household with minimal exposure to the outside world until they moved to England. But at least he had Sir Simon Burley, a pillar of strength in a court that needed a strong administrator.

Oh, how he missed his tutor's guiding hand! But today, Burley was in Bohemia negotiating for Richard's new bride. It was a commission the king would trust to none other. He had been

31

with Richard all his life after having served the Black Prince for many, many years and now he was the king's trusted vice-chamberlain. If truth be told, Burley was closer, emotionally, than Richard's own sickly father had been. Instead of the Black Prince—or the infirm Edward III—Burley was the one who taught Richard the ideals of kingship, and instilled in him a sense of his prerogative. If he were here, Richard could draw on his strength and act with more resolution.

His mother Joan, sitting quietly at the end of the table, was his other pillar of strength—or at least, she usually was. Today, she was still shaken from her experience with the peasants, and Richard felt less secure as a result. He needed her to be strong.

Joan had been practically incoherent when she rumbled into the bailey of the Tower, only a couple of hours ago. As she was helped from her whirlicote, Richard came out to meet her and his poor mother fell into his arms, sobbing hysterically now that she was safe. He wasn't used to seeing her this way, and he had trouble suppressing his own tears. She was the strong one. She was the one who always comforted him, not the other way around.

Richard was surprised at his own emotions. His hands shook as he patted her on the back. "What happened?" he asked as soon as her sobs subsided into hiccoughs. He tenderly put her hand on his arm and slowly walked with her as they approached the stairs of the White Tower, the name given to the Norman keep. No longer lithe and graceful, the Fair Maid of Kent still retained her dignity and summoned a maid to straighten out her headdress which had fallen slightly askew.

She grabbed Richard's hand with cold fingers. "It was terrible," she said. "Those filthy, ragged, screaming peasants..." She breathed heavily for a moment. "I was returning from Canterbury when my carriage got stuck in the mud. I thought I would never be free."

Richard pursed his lips. "Then what happened?"

"Before I knew it, we were surrounded by a legion of rustics, singing and shouting. Peeking through my curtain, I saw that they were carrying poles topped with bloody heads!" She shuddered. "There were thousands of them, all marching on London. They were saying the most threatening things, about killing lawyers and traitors to the crown. I thought they were going to kill *me* in their bloodlust."

Richard rubbed her hand, trying to warm it up. "They didn't hurt you, did they?"

She shook her head. "No. No, I must admit. They helped my servants push my carriage out of the mud."

"Well, that's a relief."

"But Richard, they wanted to look into my carriage. They wanted to touch me. They wanted to lay their hands on me!"

"Surely not, mother!"

"Well, I wouldn't let them near me. We were fortunate to get away." Richard could see that she had had a good scare and as he slowly walked her into the council meeting he hoped she would quickly regain her composure. She was no stranger to affairs of state and he needed her advice.

Sitting in a place of honor, Joan's hand shook while she sipped a chalice of wine, but aside from that she seemed calm enough. "There were many thousands behind me," she finally said with a slight quiver to her voice. "They seemed to have had a leader. But they already murdered some victims whose heads they carried on poles. They cannot continue unrestrained."

No one spoke for a moment. The only men at the table who had any experience in battle were the earls of Warwick and Arundel—both of whom served in the French wars but did not particularly distinguish themselves—and the Earl of Salisbury, an older knight who fought by the Black Prince's side at Poitiers. The only significant commander left in London was the old *condottiere* Sir Robert Knolles, still at his headquarters in town marshalling his 120 soldiers and archers. The king felt somewhat reassured knowing that at least the Tower was protected by 600 retainers, but this didn't make up for the lack of leadership in the room.

Richard shifted in his seat. He turned his head and raised his eyebrows at the Earl of Warwick, who suddenly felt the need to whisper something at Arundel, sitting by his side. The king suppressed a surge of anger; those two were ready to defend their own patrimony at the mere hint of a threat, but now that he needed them, they were strangely taciturn. "Well, my Lord Earl. What do you advise?"

Warwick cleared his throat. "Sire, if we had our forces at the ready, all would be different..." His voice trailed off.

Richard frowned. "Yes. That much we know. What else?" No one answered. He swept the room with his glance.

At that moment, William Walworth, Nicholas Brembre, and John Philipot were announced, and Richard sighed with relief. At least they would have something conclusive to say in the face of all this vacillating. A year as mayor of this turbulent city was enough to toughen any man, and these three had all proved themselves during difficult times. Richard leaned forward. "I trust you have closed the gates," he said.

Walworth bowed briefly then stood with his feet slightly apart, hands on hips. "Sire, we have secured the city. There are many loyal men in London. I tell you, I can summon up 6000 men, arm them and throw them into action. Right now. They just wait for your word."

The other men in the room regarded Walworth doubtfully. Warwick cleared his throat. "Do you really think your citizen soldiers will follow you?"

"Of course they will. I have no doubt."

Warwick leaned over and spoke into Salisbury's ear. They both shook their heads. "I fear there are many in the criminal population that can't wait to join the rebels," Salisbury said. "I think there is an undercurrent of dissatisfaction within the city."

Walworth was about to answer when Archbishop Sudbury appeared behind him, obviously shaken. For a moment the prelate stood with his hand on the door jamb, scanning the room. *Was he searching for enemies?* Richard wondered. Everyone stared at the newcomer. Although Sudbury had been Archbishop of Canterbury since 1375, he had only been Lord Chancellor for one year—and it was financially the worst year anybody could remember. Learned, eloquent, a patron of the arts, Sudbury was nevertheless ill equipped for the stressful post of chancellor.

Taking a deep breath, the archbishop entered the room. Reaching into his sleeve, he pulled out the Great Seal and placed it on the table with a shaking hand. "I beg your leave to resign my chancellorship. My position is no longer tenable." He bowed his head, unable to look at Richard. The others shifted uncomfortably, but no one spoke up to contradict him and the archbishop took a seat next to Treasurer Hales, who was busy chewing on his fingernails. It was no secret that the rebels held both of them responsible for the hated poll tax that started this whole calamity.

Sudbury should be ashamed, Richard thought, pursing his lips. *Now is not the time to abandon his post.* Still, there was little point in berating him. At least not now. "I am most disconsolate at your decision," the king said, keeping his voice even. "We must discuss this further on the morrow." Sudbury hung his head even lower, if that was possible.

After a long pause, Walworth cleared his throat to continue speaking, then turned as a guard stepped into the room. "Sir John Newton," the man announced, "come from the rebel force with a message." This was a surprise. Almost everyone in the room knew Sir John; he had been one of the king's officers for years. What was he doing with the rebels?

Newton came forward and knelt before the king.

"What has happened?" Richard asked. "I expected you to be holding Rochester Castle for me?"

"Sire, I was unprepared for what happened. Without warning, we were surrounded by a throng of rebels. Thousands of them. The townspeople joined their movement—in truth, they were already showing signs of unrest. We could have held out except for the betrayal of my own garrison." He hung his head, just like Sudbury. "They behaved abominably, letting in the rebels before even a blow was struck."

"See what I mean," interjected Salisbury. "It happened at Rochester. It could just as easily happen in London."

Walworth grunted in disgust.

"My noble lord," Newton went on, "please do not take it amiss, the message I must deliver. They hold my sons hostage, and sent me here against my will. I must do their bidding else risk my children's lives."

"Stand, Sir John, say what you will. I hold you excused."

No one else said a word. John stood, his head still bowed.

35

"Sire, the Commons have sent me to desire that you come and speak with them on Blackheath. They will have none but you. You need not doubt for your person, because they swear they will do you no harm. They profess loyalty to you, sire, and want a chance to lay before you all their grievances. Your councilors, they declare, have mismanaged the country." Newton paused while grumbling filled the room. "If it please you, I would beg an answer so they know for truth I have spoken with you."

"Thank you, Sir John. You may tarry, for we shall have an answer shortly."

Newton stepped back against the wall and sat on a bench, exhausted. Richard pointed at Salisbury. "Sir William, what say you?"

The knight stood. "I have no faith in these rebel promises. If they seize your person, we are all lost."

Richard didn't want to think about this possibility, though he hid his uneasiness beneath a frown. "I trust their complaints are not against me. Would you agree, Sir John?" Newton nodded in acquiescence. "Perhaps a word with them will somewhat dispel their foolishness."

Most of the men shifted uncomfortably. "If you go, sire, you must be well accompanied," spoke Robert Hales.

Richard grunted. "You will be with me, for sure, Sir Robert!"

More grumbling. "I do not like it," the Earl of Warwick muttered.

"Nor do I," said Richard, running out of patience. "But I don't see where we have much of a choice. Did you not say there are 60,000 men just waiting for a chance to overrun my city? I will not have it!" His voice was slipping again and Richard took a deep breath. "Sirs, I have d-decided. I will venture forth tomorrow and address this gathering."

The Earl of Salisbury picked up his gloves. "Sire, I suggest we approach them on the river. You can speak to them from your royal barge. This would be the best way for us to assure your safety."

Richard nodded. "Very well. Are there any objections?"

No one spoke.

Salisbury bowed. "Then I ask your permission to depart so I can arrange a small fleet to escort us down the Thames."

"Granted. And Sir John, you may return to the assembly at Blackheath and inform them that I shall meet with them early morn at Rotherhithe." This was about two miles closer to the Tower.

Now Richard had to sit and listen to arguments about meeting the rebels at Rotherhithe, though he wasn't really paying much attention. He just couldn't accept that he was in any personal danger. Time and again the Londoners proved that they loved him. Even while his grandfather was still alive, they held a mummers' parade in his honor, with over 130 fabulous costumed figures parading over the Bridge to Kennington where he lived at the time—not far from Lambeth Palace. It was near nightfall, and their torches cast wild, flickering lights over the colorful masks; Richard would have been frightened except that his mother laughed in delight. Then he understood.

The mummers were invited into the great hall, where the fanciful knights sang a clever ditty. Two of them threw some dice on a table before the king, beckoning him closer. "Go on," his mother encouraged, giving a little push. As Richard sat before them, a man dressed like an emperor cast the dice, showing him what to do. "Give it a good throw," he said, and Richard obliged, squealing with delight when the dice rolled in his favor.

"A win for the prince!" cried the Mummer, and with a flourish he presented Richard with a gold cup. "Try again!" So once again, Richard threw the dice, and a second time he came up with a win. "A most fortunate triumph!" the Mummer exclaimed, and with another flourish he gave Richard a gold plate. "Dare you try it a third time?"

"Oh, yes," Richard laughed, clapping his hands. He shook the cup and cast the dice again. Another win!

"Oh, thrice lucky prince! You exceed all expectations!" This time, the Mummer presented a gold ring, exquisitely wrought.

"Look mother!" he cried, carrying his new prizes and dropping them in her lap. "I'm the luckiest prince of all!"

"You are indeed," she said, smiling. Then she leaned over and whispered in his ear. "Offer those lovely people some wine and maybe they will play for you."

"Ah!" Richard turned to the servants who were watching from behind his mother. "Bring wine for our guests!" he ordered in a high, clear voice. The Mummers applauded in appreciation while the minstrels pulled out their horns and pipes and began a merry tune while Richard danced to the enjoyment of all.

As the discussions continued amongst his counselors, Richard smiled at the memory. Of course, he later discovered that the dice were loaded and it was all an elaborate gesture from the city of London. No, it would be impossible. Why would they hate him now?

Wat Tyler and Jack Straw stood on a rise overlooking the Thames at Blackheath. From their vantage point, they could view the great Tower, rising majestically above a jumble of lower dwellings. Beyond it, the soaring spire of St. Paul's reached heavenwards. Although he couldn't see it, Wat knew that London Bridge stood between him and the cathedral and the way to the city would be blocked. But he wasn't too concerned. Theirs was a righteous cause, and he was confident that most city dwellers were sympathetic.

Behind him, the vast, level field of Blackheath bore a great human harvest, all ripe for the gathering. And he was the reaper. Wat nodded to himself, considering his options. In their excitement to join this great movement, many of these people came only with the clothes on their backs. They weren't prepared for a long wait; quite a few of them had no food or water. With luck, their neighbors would share what few provisions they brought, but either way they weren't likely to hold out more than one day. They would have to get some quick answers from the king.

In time, he finally saw what he was waiting for. Coming down the Thames, their boat was returning from the Tower. "Here they come!" Wat shouted, and many of his supporters ran up beside him. They could hardly contain their enthusiasm as Newton stepped on shore.

"What tidings? What tidings?" The rebels surrounded the little group.

"The king promises to speak with you in the morning," said Newton. "He will come down the river and meet you at Rotherhithe." The rebels cheered, not worrying too much that they would have to wait until the next day. The king was coming, just for them. They would be heard. Everything would be better.

More and more people were gathering at Blackheath all the time. The newcomers picked their way across the prone bodies of exhausted comrades—and who wouldn't be exhausted after walking seventy miles in two days? There was room for everybody, and tonight they waited in anticipation to hear the fine words of John Ball.

Finally, the moment came. Dressed in a long black robe, John Ball raised his hands and his listeners quieted down.

"When Adam delved, and Eve span, who was *then* a gentleman?" he started. Most of the crowd had heard this many times before and they cheered with vigor, knowing where this sermon was heading. "If we all sprang from a single father and mother, how can the lords claim that they are greater than us, except by making us cultivate and grow the wealth which they spend?" Ball was heating up now, and his voice rang out, flying over the heads of thousands. "They are clad in silk and velvets lined with squirrel and ermine, while we go dressed in coarse cloth. They have the wines, the spices, and the good bread: we have the rye, the husks and the straw, and we drink water. Things cannot go right in England and never will, until goods are held in common and there are no more villeins and gentlefolk, but we are all one and the same!" Ball spoke like this for more than an hour, convincing his congregation that they were on the verge of a great overthrow of both church and state. "Tomorrow, on Corpus Christi day, let us go to the king," he concluded, "and show him how we are oppressed. And we shall tell him that we want things to be changed, or else we will change them ourselves!" He stopped, waiting for the noise to die down. "The time has come for us to cast off the yoke of bondage, and live as free men!"

Wat grabbed John Ball's hand—the one holding his staff—and raised it up. They turned back and forth, acknowledging the hoots and shouts from their exhilarated crowd, for John Ball had outdone himself this day and all were infected with a righteous zeal.

Nothing more would happen until morning. All night people crowded into camp. Some took a few hours' sleep; others shared their modest provisions and the air rang with their inharmonious ballads. Regardless, by dawn most were up and about, heading toward their leaders who waited atop the berm alongside the river.

"It is time!" cried Wat Tyler. "Follow me to Rotherhithe, where we shall meet the king!"

Wat seized one of St. George's banners and John Ball took the other. Together they led a lively crowd, singing their war songs brought back from the fields of France. Not everyone would fit into the peninsula of Rotherhithe, but thousands chose to follow their leader anyway, confident that he would reason with the king and gain their freedom from the savage constraints of the old manor system.

As they waited for the king, the rebels shouted watchwords to each other, repeating themselves louder and louder and waving their swords and clubs or whatever they'd picked up along the way. They were ready for anything. When they saw the barges start out from the Tower, two miles away, their chanting turned to cheering. Though not all were happy; rising above the cheering you could hear howls for the heads of John of Gaunt, Hales and Sudbury.

Those in the back of the crowd continued to cry out, not noticing the activity in the forefront. Eventually, word worked its way back: Wat Tyler was rowing out to meet the royal barge. He would present their grievances to the king. Their mood swung from excited to apprehensive; the king's majesty was almost a tangible thing, and even at a distance the common man was overawed. But they didn't have to wait long; like a storm wave coming from front to back, the temper of the mob suddenly changed again. Curses and wild shouts of "Treason!" took hold.

"What happened?" people were crying.

"The king wouldn't listen," someone shouted.

"We've been betrayed!" cried another.

"It's time to take matters into our own hands!"

"To Southwark!" "To London!" "Kill the lawyers!"

After much shoving and shouting, the rebel leaders pushed their way to the road. Wat grabbed a spear from a man walking next to him and brandished it in the air. *"With spades and hoes and ploughs, stand up now, stand up now."* he bellowed, *"With spades and hoes and ploughs, stand up now."* Pointing the spear forward, Wat led his willing accomplices toward London's suburb, connected to the city by the great bridge.

Even though he'd never been there, Tyler knew that Southwark was a disreputable town. Fugitives from justice found anonymity there. Craftsmen and merchants moved across the river to avoid the city guilds. Taverns and inns lined major roads, while prostitution flourished under the protection of the Bishop of Winchester. Southwark was the center of vice and corruption; they were bound to attract many more followers.

The rebels surged down High Street, surprised at the number and variety of establishments. Here was the Boar's Head, over there the Bell, the Cardinal's Hat, the Tabard; someone counted twenty-five inns on High Street alone. Three and four stories high, the gables projected out over the road, blocking the sun and taking advantage of every inch of space. Cheek by jowl with the inns, shops of every kind advertised their wares to the hungry travelers. Men paused to buy meat and fish pies, hot pea pods, sheep's feet, puddings, flans and griddle cakes. Wat Tyler insisted that they pay for everything. The merchants weren't their enemies—only the lawyers, jurors, and those paid informants, the questmongers, whose only business was to give information and benefit from the misfortune of others.

Ignoring those who scattered—mostly interested in food and entertainment—Wat continued to lead his rebels down the main street. Soon, a fresh band of malcontents approached from the other direction, shouting their greetings. Their chief, a tall raffish individual, waved to Wat and held out both hands in greeting.

"Thomas atte Raven, at your service!" the leader said. "We're here to show you the way to the Marshalsea. We will free all the debtors, all the prisoners who will join our cause!" The two groups merged, clapping each other on the back. Turning, Thomas led the determined mob toward Southwark's infamous prison. More disgruntled citizens of Southwark joined them, armed with swords and knives and clubs and hammers.

Marshalsea Prison was a tall stone building set back a little from High Street—a frowning reminder of the power wielded by the king's ministers. Still, it was no match for determined yeomen. Shouting encouragement to each other, Tyler and his men started smashing gates and fences, and before long they forced their way inside. They released state prisoners before setting fire to the building and moving on to nearby King's Bench prison, then the Clink. But the rebels weren't finished; adjoining the Marshalsea, the residence of the hated jailer, John Imworth, stood empty and vulnerable. The Marshal had already fled the city, so they proceeded to demolish his house before going after the dwellings of the jurors and questmongers.

Wat was satisfied with their progress, but their real destination was across the river. However, there was one more prize on this side. He pulled Jack Straw aside, pointing upstream. "Thomas atte Raven told me you'll find the Archbishop's Palace directly across from Westminster. They say there is much to be had at Lambeth—more than you could ever dream of. The king's Chancery is there, full of documents that need to be burned. Burn them all! Take your men there while I get us across the bridge. Afterwards, you will know how to find us. Just look for the Savoy palace!"

CHAPTER 5

Mayor Walworth cursed under his breath as he hastened from the Tower landing. He had been on one of the barges and witnessed the pathetic showing of the king and his courtiers. Like a burst dam the angry rebels surged toward Southwark, and he barely had time to inspect their defenses. He prayed to God that the drawbridge hadn't been lowered.

But he was well aware that this wasn't his only problem. "I know, I know," he muttered to John Philipot, who was struggling to keep up with him. "The Essex rebels have been gathering at Mile End all day. They only have Aldgate to contend with." He grunted. "I can only hope that Alderman Tonge has matters in hand. I sent him extra guards to secure the gate."

"And yet," Philipot managed between pants, "if we try to keep them out and fail, they may take even greater revenge."

"Not if we can stop them from joining the Kentish rebels." Walworth pushed his way through the growing crowd blocking the road. "We must keep them out at all costs," he shouted over his shoulder.

That was Walworth's plan. Since the day before, the drawbridge had been raised; the 28-foot gap of churning water was enough to stop anybody. If he could keep the rabble out, they were bound to get hungry and disperse. At least this was as good a plan as he could formulate. But when he reached the end of the bridge, its keeper Alderman Walter Sibley only had a handful of armed men to help him.

"Where is everybody?" The mayor didn't even try to keep the annoyance from his voice. "Where are the burgesses? Where is Yevele?"

"I sent them home. This is my ward, under my protection."

Walworth was beside himself with fury. "You have disobeyed my orders! Your job was to guard this ward!"

"And so I have," Sibley shot back arrogantly. "But look there. Can't you see? It's useless to resist!" He pointed toward the

London bank upriver from the bridge; then he pointed downriver. It was obvious that the crowd was none-too-friendly, waving their clubs and shrieking support for the rebels. Walworth knew that many apprentices and cutpurses, petty thieves and troublemakers were among that gathering. This was nothing but trouble.

He approached the drawbridge and climbed to the side, showing himself to the Kentishmen. They were a huge crowd, filling the platform and beyond, so that all Walworth could see was a writhing mass of humanity.

Wat Tyler saw the mayor at once. "Let us enter," he shouted. His voice carried across the gap. "We are here to present our grievances to the king. We're not interested in plundering your fair city! We will buy provisions at market price! The people of London have no reason to fear us!"

Walworth scanned one side of the river then the other. Behind him, the Londoners were jeering and shouting. He had no militia—no way to impose order; he had no support from anybody. Gesturing to Tyler, he shouted, "Do I have your word that you will not destroy our property!"

Tyler turned to his followers. "What say you, lads? We will behave like guests of the king!" His mob cheered in response. "Tell everyone," he went on, gesturing for silence. "We are here for justice, not thieving. There is to be NO looting of goods, NO damaging the houses of our brothers. We are here to make things right and destroy all the lawyers and traitors. Anyone caught stealing will answer to me." As Tyler surveyed his multitude with a stern gaze, the nearest yeomen cheered and passed on his instructions to the ranks behind them.

Walworth watched this touching little scene before climbing back down. He turned to Philipot. "This is madness. I don't believe that man. If they get in, this city is doomed."

Frowning at Alderman Sibley, Philipot leaned close to the mayor's ear. "We may have no choice." He gestured to the growing mass of Londoners. "How can we hold them back?"

Walworth rarely felt uncertainty; it was an emotion he scorned. At the moment he had control over the drawbridge. But if the London agitators took matters into their own hands, what could he do to stop them? As he regarded the London crowd, one

44

of his captains pushed through, headed his way. Agitated, the man broke into a run when he saw the mayor, shoving people aside in his haste. Walworth and Philipot ran to meet him.

"They're through," he gasped, trying to catch his breath. "Aldgate. They've breached our defenses."

Walworth gasped. "The Essex rebels?"

"Yes. They're in the city. They are headed this way."

Taking a deep breath, Walworth put his hand on Philipot's shoulder. The other nodded resignedly, making a sign to Sibley.

The alderman didn't need to be told twice. He gave his orders while Walworth and Philipot turned back to the city. Behind them, the creaking drawbridge sounded like the gates of hell opening.

"God save us," said Walworth. "And God save King Richard."

The wooden span settled into place with a loud thud. Wat Tyler led his men onto the drawbridge, watching his footing for it was obvious the wooden platform was in great need of repair. At his side, John Ball gestured to their followers, and together the two leaders passed under the painted and gilded timber gate on the eighth pier. The rebels must have recognized the importance of the moment, for they arranged themselves into companies representing their home towns. Four abreast, they marched in a solid procession, row after row of feet thumping on the wooden deck. What a scene they must have presented in their ragged tunics, wearing the medals of pilgrimage they had purchased in Canterbury and carrying their cudgels and weapons on their shoulders! Some people said that the very bridge rumbled beneath their feet, though it may have been the Thames booming in turbulent eddies through the tight stone arches. The marchers trod past uneasy merchants who peered from the inside of their window-counters. Should they close up shop, or trust the integrity of the endless stream of new customers? After all, they were on the same side of this argument—all victims of corrupt royal officials.

So far, the insurgents were remarkably well-behaved. As promised, many paid for a quick bite to eat, though others were perfectly happy to accept an offering from an anxious merchant. At first they walked in ordered ranks—row upon row of them. But how many thousands could maintain such order? Those in the rear were impatient to move forward, and they started crowding each other in their efforts to get through.

Mayor Walworth and John Philipot followed the last travelers hastening toward the London end, pulling their carts and herding their squawking geese to get out of the way. Shoppers, workmen, even beggars were reluctant to be caught up in the crush. Walworth had done all he could to minimize the danger, but as he passed into the city the mayor turned a worried eye to the apprentices and artisans and unemployed Londoners. They stood at the end of the bridge in front of St. Magnus the Martyr—just waiting to welcome the newcomers. The mayor stepped into a doorway to watch as the rebel leaders reached the end of the bridge.

This was Wat's moment. He raised both arms, a weapon in each hand. "We are all brothers here! From city to country, we all suffer from corrupt leadership. Men and women are torn from their homes and locked away because they can't afford to stuff somebody's purse. Let us free our unfortunate friends. Where are your prisons?" he shouted. The Londoners got the idea right away and turned sharply to the side, leading the rebels past St. Paul's and straight to the western gate in the city wall. Ludgate it was called, built of stone and decorated with statues of England's ancient monarchs. The throng surged past houses and shops, closed up and quiet, their owners peeking out through upstairs windows. For the moment they were safe; Wat Tyler's orders were sacrosanct.

But on the other side of Ludgate, the rebels set themselves free from restraint. Immediately to the right stood Fleet Prison up against the river of the same name; the sluggish water stank with the refuse from butchers that plied their trade upstream, as well as human waste from the prison itself. This notorious debtors' house of detention was their first target. Shouting with glee, the rioters went after the gates with a vengeance. The thick outer walls were impenetrable against their makeshift weapons, but the prison gates were no match for determined jail-breakers. Rushing in, the horde pitted their axes against stout doors and tore down any barrier that stood in their way. They ransacked stores of food and released the prisoners before setting fire to many of the buildings. But most didn't linger; the big prize was yet to come.

Outside the city limits, after Fleet Street became the Strand, a row of grand ecclesiastic mansions lay along the riverside. But they paled in comparison to John of Gaunt's Savoy palace. The Savoy was the jewel in Lancaster's crown, the most opulent, most expensive palace London had ever seen. And now, it was the symbol of oppression. Gaunt was hated everywhere in England, but nowhere was he detested more than in London. Luckily for him, he was far away in Scotland. Unluckily, his fabulous palace was undefended.

By the time Wat Tyler prodded his followers to march toward the Savoy, the Londoners had already gotten there ahead of him. The few servants left in charge of the building had already scattered, taking what treasures they could carry in their haste. Before the Kent rebels reached the walls protecting the palace, they could see wisps of smoke rising into the afternoon sky. Wat groaned in disappointment when he saw that the gates were smashed open and broken objects lay everywhere. A fire was burning in the south wing.

"Well, there's still much for us to do," he shouted to his followers. "We won't leave here until we've taught Duke John a lesson. Remember. No plundering. We are here to destroy, not to steal! Anybody caught thieving will answer to me!"

Satisfied with his warning, Wat led his fierce company into the duke's prized possession. Pouring into the great hall, the newcomers dashed past broken benches and torn banners. They scattered in every direction, running from room to room—shouting and pointing to treasures they never dreamed of handling. And handle they did; furniture was hacked to pieces and thrown out the window; carpets were torn to shreds; wall hangings came crashing down in a cloud of dust, soon ripped apart with the help of rusty swords. John of Gaunt's privy suite was the favorite target of the rebels; men rolled on top of the red velvet bedclothes before slashing them apart.

"Look!" someone shouted. "The duke's gambeson." The man held up a quilted arming doublet, much to the amusement of his fellows. "Target practice!" someone else yelled, and a large group found this exercise most amusing of all. They dashed outside with the doublet and raised it up on a lance tip so the archers could symbolically slay their absent enemy. In short order the gambeson was pierced though with dozens of arrows, before they lost interest and tore it apart.

"To the State Chamber," Tyler shouted, leading the way. Passing through tall double doors, the rioters whooped and pointed at the fabulous marble mantle carved with intricate acanthus leaves before they took their pickaxes to it. "Help me up!" someone shouted, and his friends boosted him off the floor so he could reach spears and halberds mounted high on the walls. One by one he dropped the precious weapons to the ground; they were quickly snatched up and put to good use, knocking treasures over and tearing tapestries apart. Every room yielded up more prizes to destroy. Laughing and shouting, the rebels dragged pieces of shattered furniture into the great hall, followed by fabrics, heraldic shields—anything that could burn—and threw it all into a big pile.

The contents of Gaunt's office were gathered by the armful and dragged outside to start a new pyre. Wat followed, thrusting a burning torch into the center of the heap and stood back in satisfaction as the flames caught greedily. Hearing his name called, he scowled, turning on his heel.

"What is this?" he growled as four yeomen hauled up a man who was struggling to get away.

"We caught him stealing. Look!" One of the yeomen pulled out a silver goblet from the thief's jerkin.

Wat rolled his hands into fists. "I gave strict orders," he roared. "No pillaging! We are here to demand justice! We are not a collection of thieves!"

Terrified, the man started babbling his defense. But Tyler would have none of it. "Tie him up and throw the knave on the fire! We must have discipline!"

The man started shrieking but his captors paid no attention to his distress. Together they picked up the thief and heaved him onto the bonfire. For a few minutes his screams could be heard even above the clamor of the rioters. The keen scent of burning flesh wafted over the crowd, nauseating and sweet, permeated by the sulfurous odor of burning hair. Tyler took a deep whiff, pointing at their captive. "Anyone caught stealing will suffer the same fate!" he shouted over and over, until his followers started making a wide berth around him. Convinced he had made his point, he went back inside.

Wat passed men who were hauling more armfuls of treasure. "Whatever won't burn, toss it in the river. All of it," Tyler called, pausing to make sure they were not stealing. Another heap of rubbish had been growing in the great room and someone was throwing stacks of linens on top of it. Yeomen rolled barrels into the great hall and tore them open, throwing gold and silver plate onto the floor. By now, they no longer even looked at the beautiful objects they hurled on the pile, eager to purge years of hardship in an excess of destruction. The more they smashed, the more they wanted to smash.

Wat pointed to the growing mound. "Go ahead, it's time."

His companions knew what he wanted. One of them selected a couple pieces of wood and ran outside, setting them alight from the pyre of the dead thief. Ignoring the roasting carcass, the man ran back and thrust the burning faggot into the waiting stack. Wat stepped back, crossing his arms.

"It's a great sight, isn't it? Helping John of Gaunt's riches turn into a heap of cinders!" As they watched, the papers lighted first; then the torn wall-hangings caught with a great whoosh, shooting flames toward the ceiling. Growing tongues of fire worked their way across the floor, devouring splinters and slivers of furniture, jumping from one piece of rubbish to the next. Soon flames crawled up the wall.

Wat slapped his companion on the shoulder. "My job is done here. Make sure everyone knows to get out." Not waiting for an answer, Tyler moved outside, calling greetings to other Kentish men. There was still a little daylight left, and he wanted to plan their next move. Spotting Jack Straw near the gate, Wat waved at him, moving to join his fellow instigator. He held out a wine bottle which Jack took gratefully, tipping it so that the contents gushed over his beard.

"Thirsty work this is," Jack said, drawing his arm across his mouth.

"Aye, but satisfying!" Wat was reaching for the bottle as windows suddenly shattered. He whirled around, gratified as they watched flames curl out toward the sky. "I wish I had the lead from that roof," he started, when they were blown back by a huge explosion that flung chips of masonry across the courtyard. The fire took on a new intensity.

"Gunpowder!" Wat exclaimed, momentarily stunned. Rioters fell back howling. "Come on, lads! Someone might need saving!" He started back toward the palace and the others soon recovered their nerve and followed him. A few men staggered out of the door, still on fire, and frantic hands threw them to the ground, trying to smother the flames. Wat stopped at the doorway. The great hall was already consumed; pieces of the ceiling thudded to the floor.

"What happened?" he cried, spinning around.

"We brought some barrels in," spoke up a man with a face covered in soot. "We thought they contained gold and silver, like the rest, and someone threw them on the fire."

"And they contained gunpowder. Damn! Only a madman would go in there now." As they hesitated, they were chilled by the shrieking of terrified men. Wat twisted around, trying to locate its source.

"Sounds like they are below," Jack panted, having just come up. "In the cellar!"

"The wine cellar," someone else yelled. "I saw them go down there!"

The screaming grew louder. A few men started forward but Wat spread out his arms, holding them back. "We can't go in," he insisted. As if in answer, a beam crashed in front of them sending up a shower of sparks. "You'll be killed."

They slowly backed away from the building; the heat was becoming uncomfortable. "If they live, perhaps we can get them out later," Tyler said doubtfully. His followers muttered their assent. Suddenly their sport was no longer amusing. Wat could see that he had to do something fast or his movement might lose its vigor.

"Come on lads! Remember Hales? That traitor? We must pay a visit to the Temple. The Knights Hospitaller and their cursed parchments are the ruin of honest men!" That did it. All within earshot cheered with enthusiasm and he led them away from the burning palace. A few glanced back, reluctant to leave their companions, but they followed anyway.

Wat grabbed Jack Straw by the arm. "Jack, there is more to do. Take some of your men to Westminster Gaol and have them release the prisoners there. They can pass Newgate Gaol on their way back into the city."

"Fine idea." He leaned toward Wat's ear. "My cousin in London gave me the word. This evening there will be a meeting at Thomas Farringdon's house to draw up our plans for tomorrow. He's the man leading the London rebels. You'll find his house next to St. Alban Church, on the way to Cripplegate." Wat nodded in response and Jack gestured to his own followers. "Let's go!" he shouted, and soon a large number of eager men streamed toward Westminster, upriver from the city. But a larger crowd stayed with Wat, and they marched back to Fleet Street, brandishing their tools. Although they had passed the Temple on the way out and needed to backtrack, Wat was all right with that. Their real business was in London.

The Temple was just inside the city boundary—though still outside the wall—with six acres of prime real estate stretching down to the Thames. It had grown from a church into a whole collection of buildings for lawyers, containing their dwellings, inns, schools, and of course bureaucratic offices. The sun was setting as they entered the gates, and the inhabitants had already fled, leaving doors wide open. The more enterprising ruffians had already clambered atop the roofs and were busy tearing off shingles, while others competed with each other, seeing how high they could throw rocks through the church windows.

"Show them, boys," Wat shouted, holding up a flaming brand. "Show them how good we are at destroying government property." They streamed into the church, breaking open chests, throwing books on the floor, smashing statues. Archives and state papers, books and manuscripts flew into bonfires, as one pile turned into two in the middle of the road. The rebels danced and shared their drink and sang obscene songs while their London accomplices took especial aim at houses of informers. The bonfires cast a wicked glare on the surrounding buildings.

Wat was wiping his face with his sleeve when he spotted John Ball coming up Fleet Street from Ludgate. The friar dragged his feet, tired and disconsolate as he walked slowly forward, staring at the ground. Wat noticed that he neglected to observe any of the activity around him. But as Ball came closer the friar raised his head and locked his eyes on Wat, catching the leader in a deadly snare with his fiery gaze. He lifted his staff aloft and Tyler could not break away, though he tried to step backwards.

"Look what we have done!" John Ball declaimed. "We have unleashed the demons of hell on this poor city."

Wat blinked in surprise. Was this the man who preached such a fervid sermon the night before? "We have chastised our enemies. The king must listen to our demands!" he said defensively.

"Nay." Ball shook his head. "We have erred and shall pay the direst price. The innocent suffer alongside the wicked. We cannot control what we have started. This is not what I wanted at all."

Wat shook himself loose from John's gaze and put an arm around the priest's shoulders. "You are tired. You need rest, for we have yet to bring the king to heel."

"Nay, I say!" Ball pulled away. "No good will come of this. You are doomed, you and all your henchmen. I am leaving this den of iniquity." He turned his back on Wat, but the other wouldn't give up so easily.

"Look what we have achieved," he cried, following after the preacher. "See how far we have come!"

"Too far, I say! You will rue the day you fancied yourself God's spokesman! I will have no more of it."

He threw out an arm in dismissal and left a puzzled Wat Tyler standing alone in the roadway. But not for long. It had been a profitable day but the night was young and Wat wanted to see what this Farringdon was planning. They still needed to confront the king, and he wasn't exactly sure what to do next. He searched out one of his helpers and took him by the shoulders.

"I see that much remains to be done here," he said, trying to be heard over the roar. "But I am headed back to the Tower. We shall spend the night there so King Richard doesn't forget about us. Bring your men when you have finished."

Putting his little fingers in his mouth, Wat let out a shrill whistle. "Anyone for the Tower, follow me!" He waved his arm, pointing to Ludgate. A surprising number of rioters dropped what they were doing and followed him. That was good; the more, the better. The king's treasonous counsellors would have a hard time escaping his net.

Like the Pied Piper of Hamelin, Wat led his troops across London to the Tower, singing for all they were worth. By now he had total confidence that he could get exactly what he wanted. Look at how his men hung on his every word! They marched past St. Paul's where many of the merrymakers gathered around bonfires in the churchyard. They continued down Candlewick Street, shouting greetings to their fellows walking the other way, who were searching for food and easy liquor. They passed Bridge Street, where some of the latecomers joined them from Southwark. Before them, the Tower dominated the countryside, built by William the Conqueror in 1078 as a symbol of oppression. It was designed to keep the enemy out, but Wat had no doubt they would find their way inside.

Surrounded by a moat and flanked by the Thames, the Norman keep may have been easily defended, but no food was going to find its way inside. The insurgents made sure of that! Next to the Tower, a hill stood naked of trees, though tonight it was clothed by human bodies, for it was a good place to encamp, surrounded by bonfires, liquor, food, and lively company. Self-appointed sentries paraded back and forth, and the drunken rabble kept up a constant barrage of insults, shouting "Traitor" and threatening to storm the fortress as soon as first light. On the other side of the Tower, just outside the city walls, the Essex rebels had gathered by the Hospital of St. Katherine on a huge open field. Their uproar competed with the Kent rebels' clamor, for sometimes one side then the other assaulted the ears like a surging ocean of noise.

Once he had safely seen his followers to the Tower, Wat Tyler slipped away. He needed to make the acquaintance of this Thomas Farringdon who promised to be a powerful ally—as long as he didn't try to take over. Wat had to ask for directions to Cripplegate, but he had no trouble getting help; Farringdon's house was well-known. The crowd in front of the goldsmith's three-story mansion showed him that he had reached his goal. Wat was greeted by several of his adherents and finally Jack Straw, who waited for him outside the door.

"Did you reach Newgate?" Wat asked.

Jack threw down his half-eaten meat pie and wiped his hand on his trousers, ignoring the beggar who dived onto the remains of his meal. "We did indeed. The conditions were terrible. It was good to let those poor bastards out of that hell-hole."

"And you added many more followers to our cause. Well done!"

"Happy to help in any way I can. Come in, Wat. We are all here."

As Tyler entered the splendidly arrayed dwelling, he regarded the two-story great hall, fighting a surge of envy. Of course he had seen the Savoy, but that didn't seem like a real home. But this... Farringdon was truly a lucky man.

"He's a goldsmith," Jack whispered in his ear. "Works for the king, or something."

Wat turned as his host entered the room, gesturing for his visitors to take their place at a long table. Farringdon was a mountain of a man, and he had the bearing of someone used to authority. A cluster of secretaries followed him into the room, just like a little retinue. The man's eyes moved past Wat without even pausing to acknowledge him. His attitude told everyone that this was Farringdon's meeting; it was Farringdon's opinions that mattered and everyone else had just better behave. Although the rebels needed people of his standing, Wat disliked him from the first moment.

The London leader sat at the head of his table and took a deep breath. "As many of you already know, two days ago I led an attack on Cressing Temple in Essex. That traitor Robert Hales will miss his manor there, for the few hours he has left to live!"

"That's more than fifty miles north of the city!" Jack Straw exclaimed.

"Indeed it is, and it was well worth the visit. The Knights Hospitaller yielded many treasures and charters, not to mention enough livestock to feed my hungry troops. But don't worry; we left the barns alone. I'm not totally ruthless." He looked around to see if anyone appreciated his humor, though no one was smiling. He shrugged his shoulders. "After that, on the way to London, we stopped by the Hospitallers' Priory at Clerkenwell, which of course is their headquarters. We did a thorough job sacking all the buildings; I daresay they will burn the rest of the weekend. And we took more than a few heads to adorn our spears."

Wat was getting impatient. When would this man stop bragging and move on to business?

"This afternoon we plundered the Savoy," Farringdon boasted. "It was the jewel in our crown."

"You had some help," Wat interrupted.

"Yes, well—" He gestured for a servant to hand him a parchment. "As I was about to say, there are many here in London who deserve killing. I have a list..." He smoothed the paper on the table. "Starting with Richard Weston and John Knot, who have personally offended me and my family. And especially that Master of the Hospitallers, Treasurer Hales." He bent over, peering at the parchment. "Here, notary. I want you to add the names John of Gaunt, Archbishop Sudbury, Bishop Courtney—"

"What use is this list to us?" Wat interrupted. "We know who our enemies are!"

"Oh, and let me see," Farringdon continued, ignoring the intrusion. "We need John Fordham, Clerk of the Privy Seal, Chief Justice Belknap, John Legge, the king's sergeant, Thomas Bampton, and Sir Thomas Orgrave, sub-Treasurer of England." He stopped suddenly, turning to face Wat as if he noticed him for the first time. "If we don't give our supporters instructions, they will not help us achieve our purpose. Tonight, the chaos serves our aims. Tomorrow, not so much."

Wat pursed his lips, frustrated. He needed to get his authority back. "You carry out your own personal feuds. That is no matter to me. Right now we need to get the king out of the Tower and into our power."

55

The contemptuous sneer Farringdon gave him was enough to make Wat jump to his feet. He didn't need this aggravation. As their leader stood up, his men stood with him. "Come on, lads," he announced, "we have heard enough." United, the Kent rebels withdrew, reducing the conspirators by half.

As he reached the door, Wat turned. "You will see. We shall have your Archbishop Sudbury at our mercy, and Hales too!"

CHAPTER 6

King Richard stood quietly atop the turret, watching the fires burn in the distance. No one needed to tell him that his uncle's beautiful palace was reduced to ashes, or that the Hospitaller's fine temple had seen its last sunset. Below him, Tower Hill was covered with teeming rebels, intent on staying the night. They were setting bonfires with refuse torn from abandoned buildings. From his vantage point, the din was frightening and undecipherable. Richard felt like he was peering into the depths of hell. He leaned back against the stone wall, grateful for its solid support. At least the fortress was impenetrable.

What would William the Conqueror have done if faced with such a sight? Kill them all, probably. Of course, the Norman king had an army behind him. Richard had nothing.

Sighing, he went down the spiral stairs, keeping a hand on the center support. This wasn't the only view he favored. Another tower on the southeast corner of the fortress—next to the Hospital of St. Katherine—stuck out into the moat. From there he could observe the growing hoard from Essex camped out on the far side of the city wall.

Crossing over to the outer rampart, Richard walked inside the arches along its length, ignoring the soldiers who bowed as he passed. He was glad everyone respected his wish to be alone, for he needed time to think.

Ever since the day he was crowned four years ago, he had felt pretty useless. He was still recovering from the coronation when the first crisis arose. Just three days into his reign, a long truce with France ended and their King launched a powerful fleet against the southern coast. They landed at Rye and worked their way west, looting, plundering, and destroying every port all the way to Plymouth in Cornwall.

It was terrible. The royal council met at Westminster and Richard sat at its head, elevated on a pillow and uncomfortable in an oversized robe. Even at his age, he could see that the members were nervous and uncertain. Bishop Courtenay of London opened proceedings.

"I am told that the French fleet numbers at least 40 ships," he began after clearing his throat. "Possibly more. I understand they have been preparing for some months."

No one at the table had anything to add. Richard wondered if he was expected to take charge.

"We must speedily resume our plans for the naval expedition that had been interrupted by the king's funeral," the bishop added.

That sounded promising. Richard decided to speak up. "How many ships do we have?"

Courtney frowned. "Sire, our naval force is composed of five ships."

"Five?" Richard looked at the others around the table. "Why don't we have more ships?"

The Earl of March stopped writing for a second and glanced up. "They are still collecting the poll tax raised for that purpose. But for now, the exchequer is short of funds."

"Well then we must borrow the money," Richard insisted.

"Of course, sire," Courtenay said patiently. He turned to the others. "We shall dispatch orders for the detention of merchant vessels and impressment of mariners."

"But that will take too long," Richard insisted.

"We will send the fleet under Buckingham's command," the bishop continued, ignoring Richard's objection. The message was clear. He wanted the king to stop interfering. Richard closed his mouth and sat back in his chair. A smoldering dislike for Courtenay rumbled in his stomach. At the same time, a little bit of his confidence had crumbled; it was easier to lose it than to build it back.

Tonight, he needed to keep his composure more than ever.

Climbing the stairs to the Devlin tower, Richard gasped at the vast mass of people, extending as far as he could see. He hid behind the battlements, not sure if someone in that crowd might be tempted to draw a bow. He listened for a long time to snatches of laughter and an occasional crude ditty, sung by drunken carousers. They called to each other and shouted slogans they probably picked up along the way. Richard made a face, finding their rude language unpleasant to his ear. But the longer he stood there, the more certain he became that he was in no danger, and finally he stepped into an embrasure, just as a ray from the setting sun washed over him and lit his red hair from behind—though he couldn't know the effect of his appearance on his simple countrymen. They saw a halo around his head.

Almost at once, someone saw him and shouted. "The king. There he is!" A man stood and pointed at the tower and a hush briefly fell over the assembly. Richard bit his lip then raised a hand in greeting.

"The king! The king!" The words were taken up by more of them, until Richard was quite unsettled by the noise. Many stood up; a few of them cheered, some hooted, though most shouted words he couldn't make out. They didn't seem too threatening, but he just didn't know how far he could trust his regality to shield him. He stepped back a pace.

Robert De Vere came up and stood beside him. "It's you they support," he said. "I can imagine what your uncles are going to say when all this is over."

Richard frowned. "If they were here to help me, maybe I would listen to their counsel," he grumbled. "Otherwise, they had best keep their mouths shut."

Robert put a hand on his shoulder. "It matters not what they think. You are the master."

The king looked askance at his friend. He felt like no one's master. No one took him seriously, except for his tutor Burley, his chamber knights, and of course Robert. He sighed. "Well, maybe now is the time for me to prove myself."

Nodding his head in agreement, Robert went down on one knee. "You are not alone. I pledge my word as Earl of Oxford, that I will be your champion. I will support you in every dispute, challenge every disagreement, be it from Parliament or the common people. I am your man until the end."

Richard smiled. They both knew this wasn't necessary, but Robert had a way of making him feel more regal, more princely than any of his uncles did—or indeed, any of the great nobles. Ever since Robert joined his grandfather's household as a young ward, Richard depended on his friend to back him up in a squabble with his cousins. He rarely let Robert out of his sight.

"I will not forget," the king said solemnly. Then, at a noise from the crowd, both king and earl peered over the battlements.

"They are moving!" Robert exclaimed.

Richard leaned as far out as he dared while many of the rebels started filing through the Postern Gate onto Tower Hill. Stunned, the king and his friend ran back across the bailey to the other turret, where they watched the Essex mob mingle with the insurgents from Kent. They all seemed to be reinvigorated. Many shouted encouragements while others lit torches from the bonfires and ran back into the city, ready for more action. Before long, Richard could see new flames devouring buildings near the docks. He groaned, leaning against his friend.

"Take me back to the council chamber. We must find a way out of this trouble."

Putting an arm around the king's shoulders, Robert gave him a squeeze. "You will prevail, sire. I am sure of it." They walked slowly back to the White Tower, trying to ignore the shrieks and screams from the other side of the moat. Guards bowed as the king passed, averting their eyes, and Richard suspected they wished he was older and more able to command. Oh, how he wished the same thing!

As Richard suspected, many of his advisors remained in the council chamber, though the most important men were missing. "We must find Mayor Walworth," he said, turning to an attendant. "And I need Archbishop Sudbury; I require his advice." The men inside the chamber stood up and waited for Richard as he pulled out a small cloth from his belt and brushed the throne before gathering his robe and sitting down. He did not relax. Robert de Vere stood behind the king in his usual place.

Sudbury entered as others in the room took their seats. Sir Robert Hales remained standing. The Treasurer looked very pale—as well he should, for he had just heard word that his manor of Cressing Temple had been sacked by the Essex rebels. "Sire," he said, leaning on the table with bowed head, "we must do something by tomorrow or London might be brought down about our ears." Richard almost felt sorry for Hales; he had only been appointed Royal Treasurer four months ago. His predecessor resigned the post after Parliament decided to impose the third poll tax, leaving Hales the unsavory job of collecting it. There was no doubt he had gotten a bad bargain!

"I am ready to hear your suggestion," Richard said to the Treasurer. He waited. Sadly, nothing was forthcoming from Hales who shifted uncomfortably then sat down. *Another useless gesture!* Suppressing a grimace, Richard glanced around, trying not to move his head much; he wanted to maintain a regal pose. It didn't matter; most of the people in the room were staring at their hands. The moments drew on and the room stayed quiet.

Suddenly there was movement at the door and Mayor Walworth strode in. Relief! Richard knew he could depend on him to come up with a plan.

"What is the state of London right now?" Richard asked Walworth.

"No better, sire. Many of the rebels seem to be pursuing private feuds, and I've heard of sanctuary being violated."

"But they are showing signs of slowing down," Nicholas Brembre said, pulling up a chair. "It's drawing late."

The mayor took his place at the table. "It's true," he nodded. "By now, many of them are dead drunk, or will be in another couple of hours. They've been at it all day. I think we should go after them while they are most vulnerable."

As he was speaking, Salisbury joined the counselors. Due to his experience, most of them gazed at him expectantly. "What is your plan?" he asked Walworth.

"I say we issue out of the Tower and enter London by four different streets. We can slay these miserable wretches where they lie. While they are sleeping."

"But surely, mayor, they outnumber us terribly."

"That may be so, but out of twenty there's scant one wearing a bit of armor. We could kill them like flies."

Salisbury shook his head.

"Listen to me," Walworth insisted. "We have 600 good men with us in the Tower. Sir Robert Knolles has six score ready at his command. We may never have a better chance to gain control of this rabble."

Salisbury slammed his fist on the table. "This isn't like a field battle. Our soldiers will be attacked from all sides—even from above. They are not trained for street fighting."

Nicholas Brembre stood up and leaned on the table. "There are many good Londoners just waiting for someone to lead them. They know what to do."

"And how many more are in sympathy with the rebels?" shot back Salisbury. "We cannot gauge their loyalty. I say we can't take the chance. If we launch an attack tonight and fail because we are outnumbered, we are finished and England will become a wasteland."

Walworth stood too. "We cannot just sit here and do nothing!"

"We can and we should, I say! I have fought side-by-side with many of these so-called ceorls in the French wars. They are formidable foes. Your one in twenty make up for the rest."

"Gentlemen, gentlemen, let us keep a cool head," Richard reasoned. The others sat down, breathing heavily.

Taking a heavy sigh, Salisbury continued. "As I see it, a surprise attack would start out well. But what if the rebels rally and are joined by the populace of London? Our battle will degenerate into a riot, and who knows how that would end? They could overwhelm us and destroy us piecemeal."

There was grumbling in the room at that. No one wanted to think about such a terrible consequence. Archbishop Sudbury cleared his throat. "Surely we can come up with something less intemperate."

"Yes!" Salisbury nodded his head, turning to Richard. "We only need to disburse the rabble. If we can find a way to give concessions they will agree to, we might solve this problem without too much violence."

The king frowned. He saw where this was going.

"Sire," Salisbury continued, "if you can appease them with promises, perhaps they will go home. Grant them everything they desire, and so disarm them."

"How should we offer these concessions?" Richard asked the room. "You wouldn't let me do it from the barge."

Sudbury cleared his throat again. "Your life was in danger, sire."

"Was it?" Richard raised his chin as if to look down on the danger. "I was w-willing then and I am willing now. They claim they are my loyal subjects. How could they harm me?"

"It only takes one troublemaker to turn the tide against you. I don't like it," Walworth said. Many of the others agreed with him.

"But listen." Richard got up and approached the window. They could all hear shouting from the unruly crowd camped on Tower hill. "We don't have much choice."

The Earl of Warwick stood. "Of course we will accompany the king." He turned around with an arm out, taking in the council. "We have many warriors among us. He is right. They demand his presence; nothing else will suffice."

Walworth leaned over to his companions, talking in a low voice. Richard stayed by the window, crossing his arms. "Where shall we meet them?"

"We must lead the rebels outside the city," the mayor said, resigned. "If we take them through Aldgate to Mile End, there's enough room for all."

Everyone had been to Mile End, just northeast of the city on the London to Colchester road. Surrounded by fields on all sides, it was commonly used as a gathering place; fairs were held there, and citizens indulged in various summer sports. All week the Essex rebels had been using it for their camp, so thousands were already waiting. It just remained for the royal party to draw the besiegers away from the Tower.

Richard wrapped his fingers around his pouch, comforted by the Great Seal nestled inside. It was his now, at least for a short time. Sudbury should never have given it up like he did, right before the crisis. There he was at the table, staring at his crossed hands, his shoulders hunched and his lips pursed. He was still Archbishop of Canterbury, but his usefulness was at an end. For now, the king's word was law as long as he held the Seal to enforce it.

"Then let's have an end to this discussion," Richard stated decisively, annoyed when his voice slipped back into his childish timbre. Oh, when was he going to be a man? "Mayor Walworth, have the sheriff and aldermen of London announce to their wards that whosoever would speak with me should leave the city and go to Mile End. I will meet them tomorrow at seven of the bell." Walworth stood at once and bowed, leaving without a word.

Turning, Richard beckoned to Robert. "Make sure we bring my household clerks. I may need them." Suddenly exhausted, he took his leave. The others started discussions among themselves, but the king no longer cared. He knew tomorrow was going to be difficult, and he needed his rest.

At first light, Richard took a bath, clothed himself impeccably, and ate a full breakfast with his mother. Between them they decided that Joan would stay in the Tower; she had little desire to expose herself to the rebels once again. Thus refreshed, he made his way back to the council chamber. Many of the others were already there; he suspected they had spent the night in discussion, for they looked drawn and unhappy. There was a scraping of benches when he walked into the room, but he waved for everyone to sit down.

"How many are coming with me to Mile End?"

The Earl of Salisbury remained standing. "All the earls will be with you, of course. Thomas and John Holland, Sir Thomas Percy, Mayor Walworth, Nicholas Brembre, John Philipot, Sir Aubrey de Vere—" Aubrey was Robert's uncle— "and Sir Robert Knolles will be bringing a host of knights and squires..." His voice trailed off.

Richard lifted his eyebrows at Archbishop Sudbury and Sir Robert Hales. Sudbury took a deep breath. "Sire, they are after my blood. And the Treasurer is in similar straights. We do not dare show our faces."

Richard frowned, but he couldn't deny the facts. There would be no way to protect these sacrificial lambs. He switched his glance to young Henry of Lancaster, who had moved to stand behind the archbishop. Henry stared boldly back.

"I suppose you should stay behind also," the king said. "Your father seems to draw the most fury of all. He never could get along with the Londoners." Richard couldn't suppress a sense of gratification, ignoble though it was. His uncle Gaunt was overbearing, arrogant, and imperious; even Richard had not been spared his indifference.

Sudbury nodded anxiously. "Yes, sire. By all means. Leave Henry with us."

"But will they be safe here?" Richard asked the Earl of Salisbury.

"The Tower has never been breached," the other said uneasily. "But I can't guarantee the loyalty of our garrison." Gasps were heard about the room. The thought was unheard of. "Perhaps," the earl went on, "it would be better for the archbishop and any others who are in danger to get as far away as possible. While we go to Mile End, they can slip down to the water-gate, take a boat and save themselves."

"Yes, that is a good plan. Let us proceed."

The castle bailey was crowded with horses and grooms, dogs barking and men shouting, but as the king and his knights emerged from the White Tower order was quickly imposed. Richard wanted to lead the procession, but he finally agreed that Aubrey de Vere would go first, holding up the sword of state. Warwick and Arundel insisted on riding directly behind him, followed by Robert de Vere, Salisbury, and the rest of the knights. Richard would ride next, extravagantly dressed so his subjects would look up to him; he was not one of them, and he wanted to remind everyone of this. The king's steed was equipped with the finest saddle covered by a padded cloth; the halter was studded with jewels, his stirrups made of silver. Richard wore an elaborate tabard of blue and silver and his little hat, buttoned under his chin, bore a white plume. Despite the heat, he insisted on wearing his jeweled gloves. The outriders carried spears mounted with pennons, though the flags hung limply in the thick humid air.

Richard emerged from the Tower gate with every expectation that the populace would appreciate his efforts. After all, didn't they declare themselves his loyal subjects? As planned, Aubrey went first, but stopped immediately, causing everyone behind him to jerk to a halt. Craning his neck, the king was surprised that the road in front of them was clogged with dirty, rowdy, drunken peasants, shaking sticks and rusty weapons, trying to outshout each other. From behind, the king heard Sir Robert Knolles bark an order for twenty soldiers to come forward and force a way through the crowd. Ten men on each side trotted past and lowered their spears, shoving recalcitrant provincials out of the way.

Shortly thereafter, Aubrey moved again, holding up the sword. Shaking off his uneasiness, Richard nudged his horse forward, lifting his chin. As he passed, the rebels struggled against the arms of the soldiers.

"Give us the traitors," shouted one man.

"We want the head of the false prior!" howled another.

"Justice to all the people!"

"Kill the lawyers!"

Listen though he did, Richard never heard one person say *God Save the king*. What happened to his loyal subjects? Suddenly, a man broke through and grabbed his reins. "Thomas Farringdon!" cried Walworth. "Get rid of him!"

Farringdon ignored the mayor. He didn't let go the reins. "Avenge me," he shouted at the king, "on that false traitor Hales, who has deprived me of my tenements by fraud. Do me right justice and give me back my own, for if you do not, I will take justice into my own hands!"

Richard's mount stepped aside in alarm and he struggled to calm the animal. "You shall have all that is just," he answered uncertainly, while Walworth urged his own horse between the king and the perpetrator. Farringdon dropped the rein and slipped back into the crowd. "I thank you," Richard said to the mayor, grateful for his presence. "Stay with me, if you would." Robert de Vere pushed over to his other side and the king gave up any more thoughts about leading his party.

Their progress was slow. "To Mile End," shouted Aubrey, encouraging the rebels to follow them. Ten more of Knolles' soldiers flanked the retinue and the crowd finally began to move, though the clamor never ceased. Grubby hands reached toward the king; men fell to the ground, pushed by those behind them. The guards kicked them back into place. At one point, someone else dashed forward, seized the reins of Nicholas Brembre's horse and almost assaulted him, but he too was driven off. It was the longest quarter-mile Richard ever rode.

They finally passed through Aldgate and the king's party breathed freer. Unbeknownst to Richard, his half-brothers the Hollands took advantage of the moment to pull away and dash north. They were the lucky ones; the king had no such option. It was up to him to gain control of his unruly subjects.

The crowd had thinned but by no means did Richard find it reassuring. He couldn't help but notice that many of the rebels had chosen *not* to follow them out of the city. Still, there was hope; soon enough, word would travel fast and everyone would learn about his magnanimity.

Mile End was so called because of its distance of one mile from Aldgate. The closer they approached, the thicker the throng. Thousands and thousands of men sat and stood in various postures. Some had obviously camped out for days; others, not as disheveled, had apparently just arrived. All were noisy; nonetheless, these people had a purpose and they gave way before the king's party. Apart from the multitude, a small group of armed men sat astride horses, waiting for them. Richard turned questioningly to the mayor.

"Yes," Walworth said, "yonder is their Wat Tyler."

Richard had not noted him in the boat at Rotherhithe; too much had been happening at the time. If he had paid attention, he would have seen that today Tyler had grown in self-importance. His posture was arrogant; he had managed to appropriate finer clothing. He awaited the king like an equal, ignoring those around him who held back, intimidated by the royal company. But as the king stopped in front of them, even Tyler dismounted with the rest and went down on one knee.

Richard studied his adversary for a moment, then swept his gaze over the multitude; they were a sordid sight after two or three days in these primitive conditions. He held a handkerchief over his nose, trying to get used to the stench. Some of the rebels had removed their hoods in respect, some waited for the king to speak. Richard saw much to and fro at the fringes of the crowd, though the movement was too far away to deserve much attention. Pennons attached to spears fluttered here and there, trophies were borne aloft—Richard even saw books stuck on the prongs of pitchforks—while the occasional bloody head or body part

67

reminded the king of the rebels' untrustworthiness. As though he needed reminding!

Composing himself, Richard spoke as soothingly as possible. "Ah, good people, I am your king. What is it you would say to me?"

Wat Tyler stood up, hat in hand. "We welcome you, King Richard. We are here to convey our grievances."

Richard nodded benevolently. "What lack ye? What is it you want?"

"My lord, it is our wish that villeinage be abolished all over the realm." He paused, but as Richard did not respond, he went on. "All feudal services must disappear, so that serfs would become free tenants, and pay rent to the landowner rather than forced labor." As the king still said nothing, Wat continued more confidently: "In addition, all restrictions on free buying and selling of our goods shall be swept away." Richard waited. "And we request a general pardon for any irregularities committed during this rising."

Wat waited. He didn't know how far he could go. The king sat astride his horse looking neither to the right nor the left. He consulted no one.

"Sirs," said Richard finally, "I am well agreed thereto. Withdraw to your homes and leave behind you two or three men from each village. And I shall make writs and seal them with the Great Seal, which they shall bring home containing everything you demand."

There was a long wait while the king's declaration was spread back into the crowd. During this delay, Wat went down on one knee again. "There is one thing further, my liege. The Commons declare that you must let them deal with all the traitors who have sinned against you and the law."

For a moment Richard had to fight against rising panic. This is what he feared the most. But taking a breath, he suppressed his alarm. "Any traitors shall be prosecuted as the law demands," he said, temporizing.

But Wat would have none of it. "We insist that the traitors pay for their crimes!"

They were telling their king what to do! *Insist* was not a word Richard tolerated from anyone. He took a deep breath, reminding himself that anger could turn them against him. Finally he spoke, moderating his voice.

"Let me say this. If you find traitors in my realm, arrest them and bring them before me. In safety. And justice shall be done as the law demands. Now, let the men who wait upon my charters form two lines before me. You shall have the first. And so that all shall be better assured, the good men of Kent shall have one of my banners, and those of Essex another, and you of Sussex, of Bedford, of Cambridge, of Yarmouth, of Stafford, and of Lynn, each of you shall have one. I pardon everything that you have done hitherto, so that you will follow my banners and return to your houses." He turned to his clerks. "Go back to the city and bring forth my banners, and thirty more clerks prepared to write pardons." Once again, his hand strayed to his pouch, where the great seal sat ready to perform its duty. He would stay there until every last parchment was penned and sealed, until every community had a chance to present their specific petitions. For the first time in his life, Richard felt like a real king. There was no turning back.

He sat upon his horse, ignoring the heat, ignoring his thirst, and watched the rustics mill about, repeating to one another what he had just said. The handful of scribes he had brought were unloading tables and supplies from a wagon. At first all was a jumble, but eventually some of the rebels came forward and started forming lines to receive their pardons, while others gathered up their belongings. A few were actually leaving! While the king and his party waited, it became clear that many of those gathered were content and anxious to return home.

In all the activity, Richard neglected to notice that Wat Tyler had slipped away, leaving one of his followers to collect the pardon and a royal standard. The leader of the revolt had some traitors to hunt down, and he needed to reach the Tower before that renegade Thomas Farringdon took all the glory.

CHAPTER 7

Archbishop Sudbury and a few lonely followers watched the king leave the Tower. For the moment they felt safe inside the royal apartments. Sudbury looked out the window first before stepping aside for the treasurer. "Our young King takes after his father," the archbishop said. "He is much braver than I would expect for one so young."

Robert Hales said nothing, watching as the king's guards pushed their way through the crowd with great difficulty. It was disappointing, though not surprising, that almost none of the rebels moved from Tower Hill to follow Richard out of the city. Several hundred strong, the filthy, noisy crowd satisfied themselves with chanting "Kill the Traitors! Kill the Traitors!" over and over. The treasurer stepped aside, letting Henry of Bolingbroke observe the activity. Gaunt's physician, William Appleton, moved up beside him and rested a hand on the boy's shoulder.

"Let us not waste any time," Sudbury stated. "Let us take Walworth's advice and escape this prison while everyone is distracted."

Gathering up his robes, the archbishop went back down the stairs, followed by the others. It was a quiet little group that hurried across the open bailey, for everyone was absorbed by his own thoughts. They stopped before the large, low arch that encompassed the water gate in St. Thomas's Tower.

"We are in God's hands now," the archbishop said, making the sign of the cross in the air. Hales, Henry and John Legge, the king's sergeant-at-arms crossed themselves, then the four of them descended the steps to the water. Hales climbed in first then took the oars, trying to brace the boat while the others stepped in slowly. He grimaced as the vessel tipped uncomfortably, but the boat had a wide hull and it was relatively stable. Hales pushed them toward the gate which opened inward. Up close it was quite large, and it took some tugging and maneuvering to raise the bar

70

and get one side open. Finally, they nudged the boat through and into the Thames.

For a moment, all appeared quiet. Hales glanced over his shoulder and dropped the oars into the water when a shriek assaulted their ears.

"There they are!" shouted a woman, watching from a nearby wharf. "The traitors! Stop them! The traitors!"

Sudbury let out a large groan, putting his face into his hands. But Hales had no time for such dramatics; he quickly turned the boat around and they went back the way they had come. Together they pushed the water gate shut again, and forlornly climbed the stone stairs.

His shoulders bent under the weight of despair, the archbishop led his followers back into the White Tower. They passed the guardroom and climbed up a spiral staircase inside the middle of the wall; it led them straight to St. John's chapel which had been used by royalty all the way back to the Conqueror. Despite his agitation, Archbishop Sudbury marveled once again at the simple peace and tranquility he felt when entering this venerable house of God. Twelve thick columns representing the apostles supported a second floor gallery under a tunnel-vaulted roof. He took a deep breath and turned to his companions.

"I will pray for God's forgiveness. Who will join me?" He walked to the altar, lit by a shaft of light from the window in the curved apse wall. Gathering his prayer book and chalice from a table, he lifted his pallium and kissed it before placing it around his neck.

The comforting sound of Latin liturgical phrases filled the chapel and Treasurer Hales took the lead in kneeling in the first row. He knew, as well as any of them, that the walls of this fortification—never breached in its long history—were the only barriers between him and certain death.

Wat Tyler pulled on the reins as he saw the crowd gathered before the gatehouse—the only access into the Tower aside from the water gate. A short stone barbican was the first barrier they must pass; beyond it, a walkway crossed into the battlemented half-circle Lion Tower—a huge structure crowded with soldiers who casually regarded the intruders on Tower Hill. Wat wondered why they didn't just scatter the mob with their arrows; the rebels were an easy target from that vantage point. But the guards' apparent lack of interest was good for the cause.

He needed to get up to the gatehouse and nudged his mount forward. "Clear the way," Wat shouted. "Clear the way for your leader!" Some of the laggards glared at him, but once they saw his determined band of yeoman they drew aside. Wat kicked at a couple of idlers as he squeezed past; they barely ceded enough room for him to move. Once he saw who was haranguing the crowd, he became even more insistent. "Farringdon," Tyler growled. "That bastard. This is my territory."

Ignoring complaints, Wat forced his way up to Farringdon. The big man turned with a scowl. "What do you want?"

"How do you plan to get in there?" Wat said scornfully. "Do you expect them to roll over and play dead?"

The grumbling grew louder. Apparently that was what they had just been arguing about.

"As you can see, they haven't raised the drawbridge," Farringdon said, pointing.

Wat had been too busy fighting the crush to observe the long causeway over the moat. But he wasn't about to admit his ignorance. "And you see that as an invitation? How kind of the king."

"The king was too busy getting his arse wiped to worry about the drawbridge. We should have no trouble getting in."

"Pah! You can defend this castle with a handful of men. Any child could see that!"

If a man could bristle, Farringdon would have done so; he resembled a boar more than a goldsmith. "You can just stay right there and watch us bring out the traitors!" he growled.

"Foolish chatter!" Wat stood up in his stirrups, turning around. "No need to expose ourselves to unnecessary violence. I have a man coming with the king's own banner. And a pardon, too, stamped with the Great Seal!"

Farringdon frowned but held his tongue; even he couldn't contain his curiosity. Wat settled back into his saddle. *There, that was better*, he thought. "I just came from Mile End. King Richard has agreed to all our demands!" That came out as a shout. Wat smiled, looking back and forth benevolently as the rebels cheered. "At this very moment his clerks are writing pardons for every county in Kent. He wants your Essex men to go home, too," he sneered at Farringdon before turning back to the crowd. "But don't worry, boys," he yelled. "We won't be bought off so easily. There are twenty thousand of us and only a few of them. There will be no laws in England saving those we declare! With my own mouth I will declare them!" This is what the rebels wanted to hear, and another great cheer followed his words. Wat Tyler had retaken his place at the head of the revolt.

Farringdon crossed his arms. "Say what you will. The traitor Hales is mine."

Wat dismounted, handing off his horse to one of his captains. "You may have your treasurer. I want the archbishop. But we must wait for the royal banner."

The delay was difficult for the leaders. The noise was so loud you couldn't hear yourself think. Wat and Farringdon glared at each other, walking back and forth all puffed up with their own importance. Wat called for ale to be brought forward; his thirst could not be quenched that day. The crowd cheerfully passed around what victuals they had appropriated along the way. They amused themselves by jeering at the Tower guards, who shifted around nervously. Wat started singing his battle songs and they joined in enthusiastically. But they were growing restless; Wat insisted that his messenger would be back soon, slapping men on the shoulder and promising a good time. Finally, from the back of the crowd, a new cheer announced the return of his long-awaited captain. Rising above their heads, a banner with the Royal arms bobbed up and down, and this time the crowd parted willingly.

The proud message-bearer handed over the pardon with a flourish and Wat unrolled it. He raised his arm in the air, turning around; you couldn't miss the six-inch Great Seal. Even Farringdon was impressed. "And now, my good man," said Wat, showing the warrant to the first guard blocking the entrance, "as you see, we bear the king's authorization to seize the traitors residing in the Tower." The man had been watching their behavior for some time and was not convinced. However, it wasn't his place to disobey the king.

The guard made a show of studying the document, though judging from the blank expression on his face it was apparent he couldn't read. He straightened up and thumped his spear on the ground. "You must wait here while I summon my sergeant," he said before gesturing for someone to take his place. Two men stepped forward, crossing their spears before the opening.

Wat knew they were going to get through. He stepped up to one of the soldiers. "You are one of us," he reminded him. "We are brothers. We are not here to fight with you. We just want to slay the traitors!" He laughed unpleasantly. "It's time we stood up for our rights!" He turned, grabbing a cudgel from one of his followers. "Come, join us." He poked the stick into the guard's chest. "We are moving forward!"

The man-at-arms hesitated, looking at his mate who shrugged his shoulders, stepping back. The way was clear! Encouraged, the rebels shoved forward in their eagerness to get through.

"Wait!" Wat shouted, holding the others back with a grand wave of his arms. This was his moment; Wat took his time strutting under the archway. Then Farringdon squeezed past him and he started to run. Shouting in glee, the first knot of rebels charged over the moat, their feet booming across the hollow drawbridge which lay flat, chains slack. Two guard towers flanked the next archway and soldiers stood on the battlements, holding their bows halfway drawn. A line of troops blocked the entranceway.

The half-crazed rebels stopped so suddenly that those behind them collided into their backs. They raised their weapons threateningly. "Let us in. Stand back! Kill the traitors!" Imprecations resounded one on top of the other. Wat stepped forward, brandishing his pardon. He gestured for his followers to calm down, then faced the soldiers.

"Who is your captain?" he shouted.

The line of guards parted and their leader stepped forth. "What right do you have to disturb the king's peace?"

Those within hearing guffawed. "What peace?" someone bellowed.

Wat ignored them. "I have the right. Do you not recognize the king's Great Seal?"

The man glanced briefly at the parchment. "Why would the king give his seal to the likes of you?" he said with a sneer. Wat was shocked into silence.

But not for long. Farringdon stepped forward. "We are not all ceorls. I am the king's goldsmith." He was exaggerating his importance, but a common soldier would never know. "King Richard gives his command." His voice rose in volume, loaded with authority. "The king has authorized us to seize the traitors in the Tower. Let us pass." Farringdon stood a head taller than the captain of the guards, and he pushed the man's spear with a hand the size of a wooden mallet. Wat wondered once again how this artisan could master such delicate work; then again, he probably let someone else do the finer stuff. Regardless, his dominance served to intimidate the captain who involuntarily stepped back.

"Do you dare reject the king's orders?" Farringdon pursued. For a moment the man seemed to be arguing with himself, but of a sudden he shuddered when a distant building in the city crashed to the ground, throwing up a huge plume of smoke.

That was enough. "Let them pass," the captain yelled. Clicking their heels together and thumping their spears, the other soldiers retreated. Finally! Cheering, Wat and Farringdon led their followers through the archway; few bothered to look up at the sharp points of the portcullis, suspended above their heads. However, there's no doubt that the castle builders knew their defensive techniques; once through the barbican the rebels found themselves in the outer ward, facing a blank wall. White Tower rose majestically inside the bailey, though it wasn't easy to see how to get there. "This way!" Wat called, pretending he knew where to go. And luck was with him; after a short run they turned left and passed under an arch that connected with the inner ward. The White Keep was before them!

On the closest wall of the edifice, a short fore-building appeared to be the way in. The rebels streamed toward the keep, oblivious to the men-at-arms who moved back, anxious to stay out of their way. Farringdon grabbed Wat by the arm. "Remember, the traitor Hales is mine!"

Wat gave him a scowl and pulled away. He wanted to be the first inside. Pulling the door wide, Wat whooped his elation. It was the staircase. Taking two steps at a time, he burst into the first chamber and kept going, running past stacked bows, coats of mail, helmets and shields. The armory didn't interest him. Where was the staircase to the upper levels?

His followers were not so discriminating and the huge room was filled with shouts of glee as they helped themselves to the king's generosity, snatching whatever they could get their hands on. "No swords here!" someone shouted. "Where are the spears?" Halfway down the long wall in the middle of the room, a series of arches opened to the next large chamber filled with all kinds of tools, equally stacked. Workbenches filled the space, and in a corner, four cannons surrounded by stone balls. Wat dashed through and spotted the staircase in the far corner tower.

"There it is, lads!" He ran for the stairs, ignoring the few soldiers still in the rooms. Overwhelmed, the guards did their best to shrink into alcoves, flattening themselves against walls. The rebels kept pouring into the Tower like a burst dike.

Princess Joan had taken refuge in her bed when the shouting in the bailey confirmed her worst fears. She wasn't alone; she had invited young Henry of Bolingbroke to keep her company and her handmaidens clustered about her bed. Henry was pacing back and forth, frustrated though he knew that John of Gaunt's son could expect no mercy from the mob. On hearing the commotion he dashed to the window.

"They are here," he announced, shocked. At that instant, a knocking on the door elicited a squeal from one of the maids.

"Hush," the princess scolded. "They would not knock. See who is there."

That was not necessary; the door opened on its own and Joan sighed when she recognized the newcomer. "John," she started, then swallowed a sob. "John Ferrour. Thank God you are here."

John Ferrour, whose business dealings with the Tower gave him privileged access, strode into the room carrying a bundle of clothing. "Here," he shoved a coarse tunic at Henry. "Put this on.

We need to get you to the kitchens where you can mix with the servants."

At first Henry stepped back, offended. But John wouldn't accept any argument. "Make haste. We don't have much time." The youth wasn't happy about it, but he saw the sense in John's demand. He quickly undid his belt and pulled off his short garment, handing it to the older man before yanking on a pair of leggings. The tunic soon followed, then a cap, and Henry was transformed into a common boy.

"Good. Come, Henry. Your grace, make sure the door is firmly latched." John took a last look at Joan and pulled the door shut. Then he led Henry through the passage that ran all the way around the building—only one person wide—just inside the outer wall. The state apartments were on the third floor, as well as the council chamber and the kitchen. In the latter, John felt, they might disappear amongst the servants, and he sighed with relief to see that they arrived ahead of any disturbances. Although many of the cooks had disappeared, a few staunch servants remained at their posts. Disregarding the boy's rank, John took Henry's arm and placed him next to a cutting table. He pushed a cooking knife toward Henry, then grabbed a tray of onions and slid it in front of him. He gestured to one of the scullery knaves. "Show him how to cut them," he insisted, "or by God we are all in trouble." He tugged off his own tunic, threw it in a corner and knelt by the open fire, taking a turn at the crank. He was not a moment too soon.

Even from the third floor they could hear shouting, and then the unmistakable tramp of feet on the spiral staircase. Some of the intruders surged out on the second floor; others continued to the top, scattering into every room. When they burst into the kitchen, Henry lowered his head and concentrated on his cutting.

"Victuals," called a particularly dirty peasant, sauntering across the floor. He plunged his hand into a bowl of figs, throwing a couple at his companion. More of them pushed their way in, handling the utensils, pulling down dried herbs. The first rustic came up to Henry and snatched the knife from his hand.

"'Ere's how you do it," he said, placing an onion on the table and severing it with a swift chop. He cut it again and held up a

77

piece, taking a bite. "Now that's good and sweet, but you have to cut it right. You better pay more attention, boy." He brandished the knife in Henry's face then decided to keep it, slapping the youth on the shoulder before turning away. Henry gritted his teeth and leaned on his hands, bent over the table. He didn't look up until the laughing adventurers moved on.

But the danger wasn't over; more shouting could be heard from below and the next wave of rebels was sure to come into the kitchen. John found another knife and handed it to Henry. "Well done. They didn't suspect a thing." At that moment a new racket signaled more trouble: the far-away pounding of metal against wood. "The royal apartments," cried John in alarm. He couldn't decide who needed his protection more, but he knew that Henry's life wasn't worth a farthing if the rebels discovered his identity. On the other hand, hiding in plain sight seemed the best way to escape detection. "I need to attend the princess. Stay here until I return."

Meanwhile, Wat stopped before a locked door on the third floor; this was just too promising to pass up. "Come, help me with this," he called to his followers. A burly axeman moved forward and pushed the others out of the way. Taking a big swing, he sunk his weapon deep into the wooden panels; jerking it loose he aimed for the lock. Three more blows and the door gave way, opening up a vision that stopped them in their tracks.

"The king's bedroom! It must be!" Wat pushed the broken planks aside and stepped through. For a moment his followers held back, then someone gave a holler and dashed in, throwing himself on the bed. "Now I can say I slept like a king!" he shouted, and those around him guffawed. "You look more like a giant rat," someone laughed, hopping up with both feet.

"Oh yes. And this is for you, traitors. Take that from Thomas of Gravesend!" A red-headed man pulled a sword from his sheath and stabbed it into the mattress, making the others jump out of his way. He stabbed three more times when Wat interrupted him.

"Put that sword to better use," he exhorted the man. "Sweep it under the bed so we know there are no cowards hiding there! Then look behind the arras." Thomas liked that idea; he ran over and started plunging his sword into the tapestry, checking for resistance. The others started digging into chests, tearing up the bed curtains for souvenirs, ripping holes in the pillows. But Wat had lost interest; he had commanded his axeman to assail the next locked door.

The first thwack elicited shrieks inside the room. "Ha! Now it's getting interesting. Could they be hiding our traitors?" This door gave way easier than the other one, and the rebels whooped at the assortment of women inside; three servant girls huddled around Princess Joan, who still sought to protect herself with covers.

"It's the princess," Wat called. "I remember you from the Canterbury road, when we pushed your wagon out of the mud. Look boys! She still owes us her thanks!"

Joan nodded slightly but couldn't seem to find her voice. Several of the uninvited guests called to each other, thinking this was great fun and sitting on her bedside. "Give us a kiss," one of the older yeoman grinned, reaching out his arms. The princess shrank into the embrace of her handmaidens. "Oh come," another man said from the other side of the bed. "We are your good subjects and have earned your reward." He leaned over and she drew back the other way. Other rebels were more interested in her velvet curtains and soon started tearing them apart. Men tucked precious objects under their arm and dashed from the room. It was too much; Joan finally found her voice.

"Leave this room at once! Leave me alone!" Everyone was ignoring her. Wat pulled up the edges of her mattress, trying to see if anyone was underneath. Wall hangings came down. Men poked under the bed. Finally, they were satisfied.

"Let's go, boys. We need to find the traitors before they escape!" Pushing a few of his followers, Wat started the exodus from the princess's bedchamber. Joan put her face in her hands; this was no time to lose control. But she lost the battle; before long, her sobs became wails while her maids tried to dress her. Someone was making noises at the door again and the servants tried to block the princess from view. But they heaved a sigh of relief when John Ferrour pushed his way in.

"God save me, is she all right?" He ran across the room. Joan took one look at him and fainted. The ladies tried to prop her up, but John gathered the princess in his arms. "Come, we need to get her out of here." Alas, Joan was almost more than one man could carry, for she had gained much weight since the Black Prince died. John staggered and braced himself against the wall before moving forward. The maid-servants were more than ready to leave the Tower, and they did their best to support their mistress until Joan recovered her senses. "I can walk," she said unsteadily. With a sigh of relief, John lowered her to the floor and kept his arm around her waist.

Ignoring the few rebels busy ransacking the state rooms, they made their way down the spiral staircase to the first floor. A few peasants started toward them then decided to stick with their treasure hunt. "Come on," John urged. They picked up their pace, escaping without interference. Once on firm ground, the little group crossed the open area and made their way to the water gate, not realizing this was the same exit the archbishop attempted a short time ago. But this time, they were luckier. No one cared to stop a cluster of frightened women.

As they approached St. Thomas's Tower, John observed a soldier watching them from one of the windows just above the archway. "Come down here, man," he called, hoping not to call too much attention to himself. "Princess Joan needs your help." The man checked both ways and withdrew. John cursed to himself, but no, there he was in the doorway at the bottom of the stairs.

"She needs to leave this place before something happens. Take her up river."

Used to a lifetime of obedience, the soldier didn't hesitate. He helped Joan into the boat and the rest of them squeezed in. Taking the oars, the man maneuvered the boat to the gate and, as John watched, managed to get them through and into the river. John crossed himself; it was an ungainly vessel and they had a long ride to safety. But he had another concern. He had left poor Henry stranded inside the kitchen. Would the boy still be there when he returned?

Wat Tyler led his men into the outer passage. "This way," he shouted. Passing through a doorway and down a couple of steps, they found themselves in a viewing gallery which overlooked the royal chapel. A hush fell over the group as they spread out, leaning against tall piers that supported the roof. They couldn't help it; this was a house of worship unlike anything they had ever seen before—light and airy, hung with gold-embroidered banners. Those in front shushed the men behind them, for one good push and they would be shoved off the edge.

Even Wat stopped for a moment, but he could barely contain himself. There was no mistaking the man below, making the sign of the cross over Treasurer Hale's head. "There he is," sputtered the rebel leader, almost overcome by excitement. He pushed his way past a few incautious companions and ran to the far turret, taking the staircase down one flight. They had to backtrack through the banqueting hall, joining forces with Farringdon as he was leading his men, weighed down with ill-fitting helmets and shiny new weapons. Wat pointed toward the chapel. "The traitors are inside."

That was all Farringdon needed to know. He forced the door and stopped just inside the room as the archbishop finished his prayers, trying to ignore the interruption. The doorway filled up with gloating predators, ready to pounce on their victims.

Finally Sudbury straightened and crossed himself, saying "All the holy saints, pray for us". Then, taking a deep breath, he reached for his crosier. William Appleton, a friar and Gaunt's physician, handed it to him.

The rebels could wait no longer. "Where is that traitor to the kingdom?" shouted Wat Tyler, enjoying the way his voice echoed from the vaulted ceiling. "Where is the despoiler of the common people?"

Archbishop Sudbury stood still, projecting a calm he did not feel. "Good, my sons, you have come; behold, I am the archbishop whom you seek, but not a traitor or despoiler."

Shouting in glee, the rebels surrounded him, grabbing his sleeves, his hood, his arms—anything they could get their hands around. William Appleton was next. As the mob dragged the priests from the chapel Farringdon pointed to Treasurer Hales, who was trying to sneak out a postern door.

"Stop him," he bellowed. "Don't let him get away!" Two men threw themselves on the treasurer, knocking him to the ground. He started yelling but someone punched him in the side of the head, shutting him up. They pulled Hales off the floor and shoved him after the archbishop, through the banqueting hall and down the turret stairs. Hales tripped on the top step and fell on the men before him, but such was the glut of bodies that he didn't fall far. Farringdon took a strong grip on the neck of his tunic and pulled him back onto his feet before thrusting him forward again. No one in the chapel escaped their wrath: they captured John Legge, the king's sergeant-at-arms and a lawyer Richard Somenour, who just happened to be in the wrong place at the wrong time.

By then, Tyler had reached the main door and his men goaded the prelate down the exterior stairs. They burst into the inner bailey and drove their prisoners back the way they had come—over the drawbridge, through the gates and out onto Tower Hill. The assembled rebels shrieked their elation—sounding, a later chronicler said, like the devilish voices of peacocks. On and on the ruffians dragged the archbishop until he was in the midst of the vast assembly on Tower Hill. Someone had brought up a stump, and it was to this spot that the victims were drawn.

Sudbury knew he was doomed, but he tried one more time. "What is it, dearest sons, what is it that you propose to do?" He knew that only the ones nearest to him could hear above the uproar, but the clamor dimmed somewhat when he spoke. "What sin have I committed towards you? Beware lest, if you kill me, who am your pastor, prelate and archbishop..." Someone shoved him and he fell to his hands and knees. But he pushed himself up again, rubbing his bruised hands. He raised his voice, trained to fill the space of a cathedral: "The fury of a just vengeance shall fall on you; certainly for such a deed all England will be laid under an interdict!"

But the rebels were beyond caring. "We fear neither you nor the pope!" someone shouted. "You have no choice but to submit to the will of the people!"

"You are a traitor and deserve to die!"

The cries became unintelligible again, and Sudbury ceased to resist as strong arms grabbed him by the shoulders and pushed him to the ground, stretching his neck onto the log.

The headsman was one of their own and his axe looked like it had seen plenty of tree trunks. Laughing at a joke from someone behind him, he spit on his palms, took the axe and swung it heartily at the quivering archbishop's neck. "Ohhh," groaned the crowd when he missed the mark, gashing the neck but not severing it. Sudbury shrieked and put his hand on the wound. "Ah, Ah! This is the hand of God," he cried, but the axeman took no pity. The blade came down again, severing the tops of Sudbury's fingers and sinking deeper into the neck. Blood spurted over the executioner, but still the job wasn't done. Sweating now, the axeman struck again and again, this time hitting the head, next the shoulder. At least his victim was insensible by then. Finally, on the eighth blow, the head rolled away from the body and the archbishop's corpse hit the ground with a thud.

They were just beginning; the headsman had more victims to dispatch. As Wat dragged the body away from the stump, Farringdon pushed down the treasurer who was already half-dead with fear. Luckily for him, the executioner paid more attention and Sir Robert Hales quickly followed his fellow victim, his head severed in one stroke. The last two men were also decapitated, almost as an afterthought because the rebels on Tower Hill were busy jumping up and down, congratulating each other, and drinking to their success.

Sudbury's head lay on the ground, face up. The eyes bulged and the mouth gaped open in a perfect expression of terror. Wat Tyler stood contemplating the archbishop's face, when suddenly he had an idea. "A hammer," he shouted. "Bring me a hammer and a nail." There was some scrambling around, and while he waited Wat pointed to the other bloody heads. "Put these things on poles so we can show the world we are free from these traitors!" As his followers complied, someone handed him a hammer. "Good. Bring that traitor's skull over here." Everyone knew whose skull he meant, and a willing accomplice plucked the still-bleeding head from the ground, its neck shredded and ragged. Wat picked up the archbishop's mitre. "How can people recognize you without this?" he laughed, brandishing the red hat. He put it on Sudbury's head, stepped back, straightened it, and held out his hand for the nail. It only took a moment to hammer the archbishop's mitre onto his head, then Wat shoved the skull onto a spear.

As the four grizzly trophies rose into the air, the crowd howled even louder, if that was possible. "Go ahead. Make our archbishop give our treasurer a kiss," Wat shouted. The pole-bearers obliged, smacking the two heads together to the great entertainment of all. "And now, our triumphal procession!" Some of the makeshift musicians banged their drums and two shepherds came forward with their bladder pipes, making a shrill and demanding screech. Leading the way, the players started down the hill and back into the city, followed by the leaders, the pole-bearers, and the executioner who hung the fatal axe from his neck in front and a dagger down his back, boasting about his exploits. A large number of Wat's followers, came next, ready for more violence.

The four corpses lay where they fell, still seeping blood. No one dared touch them.

Making its noisy way down Thames Street toward Westminster Abbey, the procession gathered more merrymakers as it progressed. "Here is the predator's head" they shouted in glee, bobbing the pole bearing the distinctive red mitre. They passed before St. Paul's Cathedral and through Ludgate, ignoring the smoking manors they had destroyed the day before, and continued all the way to Westminster before they turned back. Many citizens of London joined the fray and others dropped off along the way to pursue their private vendettas. Runaway criminals broke into storefronts, helping themselves to whatever they could find. Debtors decided to do away with their creditors. Apprentices killed their masters. Drunken rioters set fire to buildings, just for fun.

By now, Wat Tyler and his Kentish followers had forgotten their earlier resolution. This was no longer a crusade for justice against lawyers and judges. Like any other mob, they were carried away by excitement. Violence begat violence. Rules no longer applied. Though even Wat was surprised at the violence toward foreigners. A mob of Londoners blocked the procession in the Vintry as they dragged Flemings out of St. Martin church, where the frantic merchants had taken refuge. Already a pile of corpses lay haphazardly in the square, and crazed Londoners yanked their screaming victims around and beheaded them without mercy. Many of the Kentishmen roared their encouragement, though only a few joined the fray. After all, this wasn't their argument.

By the time the grisly procession made it across London Bridge, they had amassed nine heads. Since time immemorial, or at least as far back as anyone could remember, heads of criminals and traitors were displayed on poles atop Drawbridge Gate. Like sentries they gazed south at anyone entering the city from Southwark. None of the locals paid them much mind unless they were fresh, and Wat joked with the Keeper of the Heads as he presented his precious acquisitions.

"Take good care of them now," he chortled, handing over the first two poles. "These are the most eminent skulls you will ever see. We'll keep the rest; they are not important. See here; that's the archbishop. Make sure he is higher than the rest."

The Keeper considered his new charges; he held a lance in each hand. "Send a man up with me," he said. "I'm right full at the moment. I'll need some help, then."

Wat gestured for a man to follow the Keeper as he mounted the stairs inside the timber gate. Waiting with the other poles, the rebels jostled each other as they filled the road, blocking all access across the river. No one dared argue with them. "There they are," Wat pointed. The Keeper seemed almost lost in a tree of lances, and someone counted thirty heads as their man lowered two that had been mostly picked clean by ravens and crows. The Keeper carelessly plucked a rotting skull from the spear and tossed it into the river, then moved some others away from the center to make room for the new stakes. He located a pike and transferred Sudbury's head so that it would stand above the others; thrusting the pole firmly into place, he turned it to face south. A roar of approval greeted his actions.

By the time the Keeper finished with Hales, the crowd had diminished. He held out his hand for payment and Wat rewarded him generously, offering a bottle of wine in the bargain. "No, thank you my good man," the other said. "I have much tidying up to do here and I need to keep my head clear."

That was a great joke and Wat laughed heartily, slapping him on the shoulder. "Keep your head clear," he roared, pushing his followers back toward the city. "The Keeper of the Heads has to keep his head clear. That's good. That's very good!"

CHAPTER 8

It was a long afternoon at Mile End, issuing pardons and patiently speaking with petitioners. Most of them were not peasants at all, Richard discovered much to his surprise. A few even had legitimate complaints, mostly concerning wrongs inflicted by unsympathetic manor lords. The hated Statute of Laborers prohibited them from demanding wages that would keep up with the rising costs of food and everything else. They were underfed, overworked, denied the opportunity to better their situation—and overwhelmed by the last poll tax which pushed them beyond the breaking point.

King Richard returned to the city exhausted but thoughtful. Many things had gone wrong in his kingdom, none of which he'd ever thought about before. Most of the problems remained left over from his grandfather's rule. That was easy to see. What to do about them was not so easy.

At least for now he hoped he'd made a difference. Without any guidance from his elders he had taken it upon himself to make promises. Would he be able to keep them? They listened to him, his subjects who only wanted to be heard. For the first time he actually acted like a king; he was proud of himself—proud that he faced a dangerous situation and didn't flinch. But oh, he had so much more to do before he could rest. Although many of the rebels left Mile End clutching their precious banners and pardons, there were still countless more writs to compose.

As they approached Aldgate, he was pulled from his thoughts by the clamor inside the city walls. If anything, it was more unruly than before.

Mayor Walworth, riding before the king, drew his horse to a stop. He turned to Nicholas Brembre. "I don't like the sound of this. Something is very wrong."

The whole royal party halted, waiting as the guard at the gate hastened toward them. The man bowed briefly toward the king then turned to the mayor. "I just heard the report. The rebels have murdered the archbishop and the treasurer."

Richard kicked his mount forward. "What is that you say? They are safe in the Tower!"

"Sire, the drawbridge was never raised. The rebels forced their way in and seized Archbishop Sudbury and Treasurer Hales and dragged them to Tower Hill, where they were beheaded. As we speak they are swarming through the city with the heads on poles."

"That's not possible," Richard muttered, shaking his head in disbelief. But in the distance they heard the discordant sounds of inharmonious music.

"That's them you hear," the man nodded. "They have taken over the city."

Any feelings of mercy Richard may have felt had already evaporated, leaving a deep, simmering indignation. His entourage surrounded him protectively.

"You can't return to the Tower," Walworth decided. "Lord knows what is happening there."

"But where is my mother?" the king asked. "I can't leave her alone with those fiends." His horse sidestepped.

"It is not safe for you. Take heart; I still have a few men I can trust. We will go there and find out what is happening. If she managed to escape, where would she go?"

"The Great Wardrobe. I'm sure of it."

"Then you must go there, sire. If your mother is still in the Tower, we will find her and bring her to you."

It was a logical choice. Nestled in the shadow of Blackfriars and across from St. Paul's, the Great Wardrobe was accessed by river at Puddle Wharf and would be a convenient place for his mother to disembark. It was a fine building that Edward III had bought for Queen Philippa decades ago. His mother often used it as her London mansion but it was also a storehouse for money and arms, and many of the king's personal items were kept there. Although the Great Wardrobe was not as safe as the Tower, they had just seen ample proof that strong walls were not necessarily protection enough.

Brembre leaned forward in his saddle. "How will we get the king across the city?"

Richard gripped his reins. "They say they are for me. How could I not be safe?"

No one had an answer. They listened to the hubbub in the city.

"No, I will trust to God," the king decided. "I will bring my entourage and we will travel forth. No one will dare attack my person."

Walworth took a deep breath. "Very well. Instead of Thames Street, perhaps you should go through Cheapside, where there is less commotion."

It was an unhappy party that accompanied the king through the city. Richard, Earl of Arundel led the entourage. For once, the king was happy the earl was in his party; his strong arm went a long way toward discouraging unwelcome attacks. The king rode in the middle of a tight retinue, and his attendants did their best to hide him from view. He tried to ignore the plundering and ransacking that went on right before his eyes. At least the perpetrators veered away from the bristling cavalcade, searching for easier prey.

As they passed through the gates of the Great Wardrobe, Richard sighed with relief. Only two guards stood at the entrance and Arundel was quick to assign more sentinels. As the earl turned toward the king for instructions, Richard reached into his pouch and withdrew the Great Seal. He held it out, reluctant to relinquish it but eager to let someone else finish the onerous task of signing petitions.

"I temporarily assign you control of the Great Seal," he said, trying to sound official. "We have many more writs to deliver to the sheriffs and reeves of local shires. Will you undertake this charge?"

Arundel couldn't repress a grimace as he bowed, accepting the Seal. "I will do your bidding, sire, though I suspect this will prove to be a waste of our efforts."

Richard frowned. What he didn't need right now was criticism. "It is no matter. We must do what we can to save the city."

Not waiting for further argument, Richard practically flew up the stairs to the privy chambers. Knocking quickly at his mother's door, he didn't wait for an answer before lifting the latch. A little shriek greeted him, quickly hushed. There she was next to the fireplace, her three ladies gathered around her—one with her hands over her mouth. Joan stood up unsteadily then ran to her son, arms outstretched; she nearly collapsed against him, groaning her relief. Richard took her into his arms, breaking into tears. He was almost taller than her by now, but at the moment he felt like a child again.

They both sobbed for a moment before he took his mother's hand and led her to the bed. They sat on the edge, staring at each other. The crisis was by no means over, but at least they were both safe.

"I was afraid they had hurt you," he said, "after what happened."

Her eyes grew wide again. "What happened?"

"You don't know?" She shook her head. "They k-killed Archbishop Sudbury and Treasurer Hales."

"Oh no." She closed her eyes. "I fled by the water-gate after those dreadful people broke into my rooms. Oh, it was terrible. They climbed onto my bed, stole my possessions; they ransacked my room. Maybe they were looking for the archbishop."

Richard tightened his grip on her hands. "Did they touch you?"

"They tried to kiss me. I was so frightened. But their leader made them move on."

"How did you get out?"

"That man... John Ferrour. Do you remember him?" Richard shook his head. "He supplies me with my silks and velvets. He helped us out of the Tower and into a boat."

"Then he shall be rewarded," Richard assured her. "Things could have been so much worse for you. Poor Sudbury. In a way he gave his life to save yours."

Joan wiped her eyes. "I shall pray for him. But tell me: what happened at Mile End? I was so worried about you."

Richard bit his lip. "They were very respectful once we got there. But they made many demands which I granted."

"What kind of demands?"

"Nothing less than the abolition of villeinage." He grunted. "That should upset my uncles. But really, mother. I heard their grievances. There was some substance to their plaints."

"Nonsense. There have been villeins from time immemorial. Or serfs. Call them what you will. How else would the land be worked? They were born into that condition. God willed it so."

Richard shrugged. "Perhaps you are right. But there is more. They demanded a pardon. My advisors—" he said that word with a twist of sarcasm—"told me to promise them anything. So I did. We spent the whole day issuing writs and sending some of them home with a royal banner. And yet, when we returned to the city, we found that the rioting was worse than ever! I feel that our labor has been a failure."

He stopped to listen, for the shouting and laughter was getting louder, as though a crowd was gathering in front of their building.

"Not again," she gasped.

Richard stood. "We must be brave," he told her, not feeling brave at all. "Let us go to the roof and see what is happening."

Hiding behind the chimney, Richard and his mother observed the street below without being seen. Before them, the tower of St. Paul's stood stark against the smoke from burning buildings in the distance. Joan grabbed her son's arm. "There." She pointed toward Ludgate, through which a festive crowd cavorted. Some played instruments, many were drinking. Following the musicians, a number of men carried heads on poles, bouncing them up and down to the tempo. Even from a distance there was no mistaking the red mitre atop Sudbury's head.

"My God, it's true," she said. They watched, shocked by the gruesome procession passing below them. "Your father would never have believed this day."

Richard glanced hard at her, all too aware of his own helplessness. No matter how hard he tried, he could never begin to achieve the awesome renown of the Black Prince. He took a deep breath, squaring his shoulders. "This must end. I must end it."

The next day, Saturday the 15th of June, the sun was past midpoint when Richard rode out with 200 retainers who had been gathering all morning. The rioting had continued with barely a pause. Unruly men got up from the streets where they fell the night before in a drunken stupor and picked up where they left off. By now the king had settled into a somber determination; one way or the other, something had to be done. He had sent town criers to every corner of the city, bidding the rebels to meet him at Smithfield to negotiate further. At the same time he sent messengers to the London aldermen to assemble their forces and be ready for his command.

But first, Richard decided to go to Westminster Abbey and make confession. He would pray to Saint Edward the Confessor and prepare his soul for the upcoming confrontation. Little did he know that just an hour before, John Imworth, Marshal of the Southwark Marshalsea Prison—known as the Tormenter Without Pity—had been attacked by the mob as he hung on for dear life to a pillar in this very chapel. By now, the rebels cared nothing about Sanctuary. They dragged their screaming victim out the Abbey and down to Cheapside, where his head was struck from his body while his assailants celebrated his demise.

Richard would find out about this later. That morning, as he rode down Fleet Street, the king glumly observed the battered Temple and other damaged buildings along the riverside. Once the pride of London, they were now empty shells. Richard put a cloth to his nose, slightly overcome by the dust and smoke. They somberly passed the smoldering ruins of the Savoy, and Richard thought—not for the first time—that his uncle John was still a fortunate man, for he was far away in Scotland. Then, with a start, he remembered his cousin Henry of Bolingbroke. Leaning toward Robert de Vere, he asked if anyone knew what happened to him. Robert shook his head and turned to Walworth.

"Ah," the mayor said, "he is well. Somebody disguised him as a servant and the rebels didn't recognize him. I found him when I was inquiring about your mother."

"My thanks to you for taking matters in hand. Did you have trouble getting into the Tower?"

92

"The rebels abandoned the grounds, at least long enough to carry their wretched trophies around the city. We secured the gates and the raised the drawbridge. They reoccupied Tower Hill overnight, but they couldn't get into the castle proper."

"And the...victims?"

"We managed to bring their bodies to the chapel."

Richard sighed. He knew where the heads were.

But his gloomy thoughts were interrupted when he saw the prelates from Westminster coming to meet him halfway, all in procession. Dressed in their finery, they nonetheless walked with bare feet to demonstrate their humility. At least here was some sense of normality. His heart lightened as he entered the church and was led to the high altar. He knelt in prayer along with his followers, then gave himself over to confession before leaving a precious offering. Now he was ready to face his misguided subjects.

Just north of the city walls, Smithfield was an open space so large it would take about ten days for a yoke of oxen to plow it. Every August since the time of Henry I, the famous Bartholomew Fair brought people from all over the country. Otherwise, Smithfield was most often used as a horse market, though sometimes it hosted sporting games, tournaments, and even executions. The Scottish rebel, William Wallace, was hanged, drawn, and quartered in this very spot, under the elms in the far northwest corner. Richard wondered if that event drew an ever larger crowd than this one.

Accompanied by his large and colorful group of retainers, he ordered his heralds to announce their approach. They made their way past St. Paul's, skirted the Convent of The Grey Friars, and processed through Aldersgate. All wore armor beneath their long gowns. They drew rein before the Priory of St. Bartholomew on the east side of the square. Already the rebels waited for them, standing on the opposite side of the field in orderly bands like a little army; a constant flow of newcomers augmented their ranks. For a time, both sides stood and watched each other as the afternoon sun threw shadows across the empty space between them.

Richard looked around, thinking this was a good site for their purposes. If a disturbance was to break out, they needed to direct the rebels away from the city. There was only one way they could go: further North. At Richard's back, the Priory with its solid Norman church blocked access to the east. To his left, St. Bartholomew's Hospital butted up against the city walls. Behind the rebels, the River Holborn widened into the Fleet, reeking with the stink of refuse from the butchers and tanners. This left the north open, toward Clerkenwell Fields and Essex, where many of them came from in the first place.

The king's horse bumped into Walworth's mount. Richard turned to him, ignoring the shouting and taunts from the mob. "I think it is time," he said. "Go forth and summon Tyler to appear before us."

Richard and his retainers sat astride their horses while Walworth crossed the distance between the two groups, stopping just outside of rock-throwing range. He wasted no time.

"Wat Tyler," he bellowed. "The king commands you to present yourself and submit your petitions in person." Wheeling his horse around, the mayor trotted back to the royal party.

The rebel leader was standing in the second rank, and he puffed his chest out when his name was called. "Imagine that," he boasted to his neighbors. "The king calls me by name." He couldn't stop himself from bouncing up and down in excitement. "Look at them, cowering over there like so many sheep. They know we are the rulers of this city." He stepped out and gestured for someone to bring his horse. "What say you, lads? Shall I go and address the king?"

"Yes, Yes!" the rebels clamored their support. Wat mounted his hackney and rode into the open field, accompanied by a single follower carrying the king's banner given them the day before. He glanced up at the sky, wanting to remember this moment. The horizon was slightly hazy in places from the smoke of burning buildings. The sun warmed his back; his followers cheered him on. Today, Wat Tyler would make his mark as England's champion. Across the square, the king waited for him. For him alone. He rode right up to the unsympathetic lords and quickly dismounted. Just as quickly he bowed, then seized Richard's hand and roughly shook it, to the astonishment of everyone.

"Be of good cheer," Wat declared. "For you shall have, in a fortnight, forty thousand more commons than you see right now, and we shall be good companions."

Richard suppressed a shudder. Pulling his hand away, he asked, "Why haven't you gone home, since I gave you what you asked for?"

All elation fled. This wasn't what he wanted at all. "Upon my soul I will not go home. Not until we have a charter more to our liking." He unsheathed his dagger and pointed it up as though to emphasize his declaration. "There are many different points that need clarifying. And if you don't you will bitterly rue the day you opposed the commons of England!"

Sitting behind the king, Robert de Vere grunted in anger. But Richard held up a hand, silencing him. "And what points are these you need clarifying?"

Wat started tossing his knife from one hand to the other. Back and forth the knife went, while he proclaimed each carefully rehearsed statement. "Well, sire. It's like this. First, we demand that all game laws be abolished. Every man should be able to hunt his own food without worrying about getting killed, trying to feed his family. Secondly, there should be no outlawry in any process of the law." He paused, waiting for a response but none was forthcoming. Again. Wat took this as encouragement, resuming his knife toss. "Thirdly, the goods of the Holy Church should no longer remain in the hands of the religious. Let the clergy have sufficiency to support them, but let the rest of their goods be divided among the people of the parish. Lastly, we demand that there should be no more lordships. All the lands should be divided among the people, except what belongs to the king. There should be no more villeinage and no more serfdom, but all men should be free and of one condition." He stopped, wiping his forehead.

Richard nodded briefly. "You shall have all that I can legally grant, saving the regality of my crown. Now go. Go back to your own home."

The king and his men sat unmoving on their horses. Not another word was said. Even the rebels had quieted down, though they were too far away to hear any speeches. Wat stared at the king; this was not going right.

Jerking his shoulders, he turned around. "Water," he shouted to his follower. "Bring me water." He stared at the king while he waited, then held out his free hand as he heard someone run up behind him. He took a deep draught from a jug, swished it around his mouth and spat on the ground in front of Richard's horse. The animal stepped away but Richard nudged it back into place. The king held up a warning hand once again. He waited. He could tell that Wat was losing his self-control.

"Ale," shouted Tyler. "Bring me ale!" Once again he waited; once again he quaffed the contents in one long gulp. Handing the mug to his companion, he remounted his horse, turning his back on the king.

"You are a common thief and a liar," someone shouted.

Wat spun around. "What! Is that you John?" he growled, recognizing the voice of Sir John Newton, his old captive from Rochester. "Come out here." He shook his dagger threateningly.

"I will not! You are naught but a knave and unworthy of my sword!"

Wat couldn't believe that his authority was slipping away so fast. "By my faith," he hollered, "I shall never eat meat again till I have your head!" Blinded with rage, he pushed his horse into the royal entourage, intent on striking his challenger.

But Mayor Walworth expected something of the sort. "False stinking rascal," he shouted, and interposed his own horse between Wat and Newton. "I arrest you for drawing your blade in front of the king's face!"

Momentarily distracted, Wat swung around and thrust his dagger at the mayor's stomach—only to see it turned aside. The steel breastplate had done its job. He struggled to disentangle his blade from the fabric, but Walworth was faster; he drew a short sword and slashed it down on Tyler's shoulder, driving him onto his horse's neck. One of Richard's squires plunged his sword twice into Wat's side.

The rebel leader was incapacitated but he had enough energy to pull out of the crush. "Treason!" he cried, urging his mount toward his followers. The horse took a few running steps, but slowed to a stop and Wat slipped out of his saddle, hitting the ground with a thud.

Nobody moved. From across the field, a groan went up, rising in volume as though the heart was rent from thousands of breasts. Louder and louder the cries grew, until shrieks of rage shook the multitude. "Our captain is dead! Our leader has been killed!" Many of them reached for their arrows and bent their bows, intent on slaughtering everybody they could reach.

As soon as Walworth had dealt his blow, he turned his horse and charged away from the king directly toward the city. Richard's followers were in a panic; everything was happening too fast. They broke their close-knit ranks; a number of them followed the mayor. Others milled around the king when, without notice, Richard spurred his horse and galloped across the field toward the rabble.

"Men," he shouted. "What aileth you? Ye shall have no captain but me. I am your king! I will be your leader. Follow me into the fields without!" He pointed north to Clerkenwell and slowed his horse to a walk.

Bewildered, they hesitated, gawking at each other. All of a sudden, everything had changed for the worse. From the beginning they had claimed their support for the king, and now the king commanded them to follow. What else could they do? The rebels lowered their weapons and obeyed for lack of better leadership. Still standing in a semblance of battle order, they kept their formation as one and followed Richard toward the fields around Clerkenwell.

Robert de Vere shouted to the men of Richard's retinue. "Stay! Don't leave. We must protect King Richard!" Although some had dispersed, enough loyalists remained to join in a frantic effort to reach the departing King. Pushing through the crowd, they were slowed by the crush of people. "Let us pass. Give way!" Robert shouted to no avail. For the moment Richard was alone and he didn't dare look back.

Forgotten, a handful of Wat's closest henchmen approached their fallen leader, hopeful that he wasn't dead yet. The turned him over, encouraged when he let out a groan.

"What shall we do?" asked one.

"There. We'll take him to St. Bartholomew's hospital. Between the four of us, we can carry him." Bending over, taking Wat carefully into their arms, the men brought their captain to the hospital, just a few steps away from where he fell.

Meanwhile, Walworth rode through Aldersgate, shouting to one and all as he searched for his aldermen. "Most noble citizens, go and help your King without delay, for he is sorely threatened. Now is the time to save your city! Meet us at Aldersgate."

His words did not fall on deaf ears. Men ran into the streets, armed with swords and bills and bows. The aldermen, waiting for the signal, mustered their citizens. As he rode through Cheapside, Walworth was almost overwhelmed with relief when he saw Sir Robert Knolles riding toward him at the head of 120 soldiers. He embraced the old *condottiere* from horseback.

"You are the most welcome sight to my poor eyes! Make haste, Sir Robert. Take charge of this sortie and go save the king! By now you will find him at St. John's Fields in Clerkenwell."

Thousands of men gathered at the foot of St. Martin's Street before Aldersgate. Some carried banners belonging to their wards. Nicholas Brembre and John Philipot were among them, helping Robert Knolles organize the men into columns. "Follow me," Knolles shouted, leading the determined citizens of London through the gate and across the now deserted field.

Less than an hour had passed since Wat Tyler fell from his horse. It was a miracle that so much happened in so short a time!

Walworth was worried about the king, but he knew Knolles was more than capable of taking care of the situation. The mayor had other things on his mind. Assembling a company of lancers, he returned to West Smithfield, only to discover the rebel leader gone.

"Where is he?" Walworth exclaimed, kicking up a dust cloud next to the bloody patch of ground that marked the spot where the rebel leader fell. "What happened to him?"

"There it is," one of his men exclaimed, pointing to a trail of blood that started several feet away and led to St. Bartholomew's Hospital.

"He's not getting away that easily. Dead or alive, we need his head."

The mayor and his stalwart followers were a formidable sight, marching up the steps and pushing through the wooden doors. Spotting a young monk carrying a bowl of water, Walworth grabbed him by the sleeve and spun him around. Water splashed all over the floor.

"Where is he?"

The novice glanced around for help.

"I'm not here to hurt you. Where is Wat Tyler?"

The monk pointed to his right. "The master's chamber."

Walworth led his men past others who shrank away. They opened first one door, then another, then turned a corner and saw a small band of men guarding a room. "That must be it."

At first, the men blocked the door, but they were outnumbered and it was obvious their task was useless. They stepped aside as the others pushed forward. Walworth threw open the door and grunted with satisfaction. Wat lay insensible on the bed.

"We must do this in public. Let's bring him out."

One of the burlier lancers bent over and slung Wat over his shoulder. As they were leaving the building, Walworth pointed to a stool. "Take that," he said to one of Wat's men who was following from a distance. "It will serve." A small crowd followed them to the center of the field and groaned when the lancer threw the body to the ground.

"Is he dead?" someone asked.

"No matter," Walworth grunted. "Remove his head."

The lancer grasped his victim by the shoulders and pulled him up while another grabbed the stool and shoved it under Wat's head. "Go ahead," the lancer said, leaning back and supporting the body. "I'll hold him for you." Nodding in agreement, the makeshift executioner pulled out his sword and swung with all his might. His aim was true; the head dropped to the earth, rolling over until it stopped at Walworth's feet. The mayor glared at his witnesses, daring them to object. No one said a word.

"Mount it on a spear," he growled. "Let's see what the rebels do now."

Richard didn't turn around as he rode his horse past the burnt-out ruins of St. Johns Priory and into the fields at Clerkenwell. It would have been hard for him to describe how he felt; this was the closest he had ever come to leading an army, and look at his rag-tag horde! But they belonged to him, at least for the moment. They were following him, trusting him not to betray them. As they spilled into the open fields, he directed them to stand in their battle arrays, just as they had at Smithfield.

A few of the more irascible rebels surrounded the king, vexing him with questions.

"Where are our pardons?" the loudest yelled.

"My clerks are still sealing pardons as we speak," Richard assured him. "They will be sent by messenger to all the shire reeves who haven't already received them."

"Where is John of Gaunt?"

"He is in Scotland."

"What about the poll tax?"

"There will be no more poll tax. I promise you."

Richard held his patience. The longer he kept these insurgents busy with questions, the more time would be given to his rescuers. If he showed enough forbearance, perhaps he could restrain them from any more violence.

"Where are you from?" he asked the man closest to him.

"Fobbing, sire." Suddenly chastened, the man removed his hat.

"That's near Brentwood, isn't it?"

"Aye, sire."

By now even Richard had heard that this was the starting point of the revolt. He narrowed his eyes. "What is your name?"

The man looked around for support but saw none. "William Tanner," he mumbled.

"William Tanner. Have you a wife and children?"

"Aye, sire. I have three little ones."

"Who is taking care of your business while you are here?"

Clearing his throat, William stared at the ground. "I trust my wife is capable, sire."

"You had better hope so. She is doing both your work and her own. Hadn't you best be getting home?"

"Aye, sire." Bobbing his head, the tanner backed away.

Richard smiled wearily, noticing that some of the other instigators were slipping away, not wanting to draw attention to themselves. But oh, he felt so tired. How much longer could he keep up this pretense?

Suddenly with a scramble Robert de Vere appeared at his side followed by a handful of retainers. "Are you all right, my Lord?"

Hiding his relief, Richard nodded. "D-do you have something to drink?"

Fumbling around, Robert untied a water bottle. "This is the best I can do," he said apologetically. Richard rewarded him with a smile. He took a long draught then paused, staring down the road toward Smithfield. Somewhere in that direction he could hear the regular stamp of marching feet. In a moment, just poking up over a slight rise, the city banners came into sight and at their front, the standard of Robert Knolles.

Ignoring the rabble who stubbornly lingered near his horse, the king leaned toward Robert. "We are saved."

Under the banners, rows and rows of grim Londoners came into view, well-armed and organized and ready for violence. The rebel host shifted restlessly, suddenly vulnerable. As Richard watched, Knolles divided his force right and left, totally surrounding the insurgents. They were caught in a trap of their own making, regretting their trust in the promises of their sovereign.

Just as the last of Knolles' soldiers reached the fields of Clerkenwell, Walworth and his lancers followed, carrying a trophy high for all to see. The rebel leader's dripping head was mounted on a spear—a bloody, gruesome mockery of all the skulls he had harvested along the way. A collective groan rose

101

from the devastated host and many fell to their knees, begging the king for forgiveness.

Richard summoned the lancer and bid him stand beside him. "Hold it high," he said. "This is the moment we kill the revolt." Drawing his sword, Richard pointed it in the air, looking back and forth across the pathetic host. He ignored the voices of his own people who muttered that now was the time to wreak revenge— that he had the rebel host at his mercy. Robert Knolles pushed his horse forward and leaned toward the king's ear. "They would kill us if they had the chance. I can destroy them right now."

Richard shook his head decisively. "No, Sir Robert. Many of these rebels were brought here by fear and threats. I will not let the innocent suffer with the guilty."

As the mob continued to plead for mercy, the king raised his other hand. "Henceforth, you must promise to be my loyal subjects. Lay down your arms and I give you leave to depart."

At first, the rebels were reluctant to trust the king's promise, though some of the men on the edge of the crowd dropped their axes and their spears, their staffs, bows and arrows, and dashed for safety. After a brief hesitation, others followed, until the crush resembled a landslide, with the Essex rebels heading for home. But not all of them followed. The Kentish men were stranded on the wrong side of the city, and as their more fortunate brothers dispersed, they stood uncomfortably among the discarded wreckage of their hapless uprising.

Richard sat triumphant on his horse, heedless of the grumbling of his followers. "Sir Robert," he said, leaning toward the old *condottiere,* "assign some of your soldiers to escort these men through the city and over the bridge. Proclaim throughout London that no citizen should have communication with the rebels, nor shall any of them be permitted to stay in the city this night." He could see that Knolles was angry and frustrated. "Be patient, Sir Robert. They will be punished by and by." He put a hand on Knolles's arm. "Mind you, take that evil thing," he added, pointing to Wat's head, "and erect it on London Bridge in place of poor Sudbury and the others."

He turned back to the rabble. "You men of Kent," he shouted, pointing toward Smithfield with his sword. "Form yourselves in ranks there, on this road. You must leave London this very day or your lives will be forfeit."

Nothing loath, the remainder of Wat Tyler's ragtag army obediently formed a column, flanked by Sir Robert's grim men-at-arms.

"Mayor Walworth, you have my leave to arrest anyone still attempting to plunder or blackmail my Londoners." Walworth bowed, anxious to get to work. "But wait." Richard turned to one of the mayor's lancers. "Give me your helmet," he said, holding out a hand. The puzzled guard obliged, then Richard in turn offered it to Walworth. "Put this bascinet on your head."

Accepting the helmet, Walworth obeyed. "For what reason, my liege?"

"I am greatly beholden to you for your services. And for this reason you are to receive the order of knighthood."

Shocked, Walworth hesitated. "Sire, I am not worthy. I do not have the means to maintain a knight's estate, for I am only a poor merchant and must live by my trade."

Richard shook his head, dismounting as he handed his own sword to Sir Robert Knolles. "I will grant you the means to support your knighthood. Kneel, William Walworth. Do you swear by all that you hold sacred, true, and holy that you will honor and defend the Crown?"

Lowering his head, Walworth said "I do."

Richard took back the sword in both hands and tapped it on William's shoulders. "Then I do dub you with this sword, and by all that you hold sacred, true, and holy... Once for Honor... Twice for Duty... Thrice for Chivalry... Arise, Sir William Walworth."

Overcome, Walworth stood and removed the bascinet. Richard was so pleased he almost forgot about the departing rebels. "I also summon Nicholas Brembre and John Philipot." The astonished aldermen also came forward and were initiated into the knighthood order as well. If there was any doubt about Richard's favor toward these Londoners, it was put to rest that day.

The new knights bowed to the king. "We are beholden to you for your generosity," Walworth said. "But we cannot pause to celebrate. We have much to do before this day is over."

"Do whatever you must to keep the peace," the king said, "even it means beheading the offenders."

Satisfied, Richard led his tired retinue back to the city, followed by Sir Walworth and his band of lancers. The king returned to the Great Wardrobe and his waiting mother, while the newly revived loyalists spread out through the city, arresting malefactors so busy at their looting they failed to notice the rebellion was over. Wat Tyler would have been gratified to know that Thomas Farringdon was one of those unlucky incendiaries caught demolishing the house of yet another enemy—and thrown into prison. But Farringdon was much luckier than Wat; a year later he obtained letters of pardon and escaped with his reputation intact.

On the other hand, Wat had achieved immortality.

PART 2

RESISTANCE

CHAPTER 1

Although London had been saved from the wicked plots of Wat
Tyler and his accomplices, the Revolt was far from over.
However, Richard's relief and his newly-acquired pride were well
deserved, and no one could fault him for telling his mother, back
in the safety of the Great Wardrobe, that he recovered his lost
heritage that day, and the realm of England also. What could not
be hoped from a young king who had so remarkably faced a
throng of murderous rebels, all alone, fearlessly? Whether they
liked it or not, his detractors must agree that Richard showed the
courage of his formidable father, and this day he had won his
spurs, so to speak, against perilous odds.

It was Sunday, the day after the terrible events at Smithfield,
and Richard and his mother sat in their privy chamber at the Great
Wardrobe. A side table was laden with fruits and nuts and
cheeses, but Richard showed little interest in food.

"You haven't eaten a bite," Joan said.

Richard absently took a fig between his fingers, twirling it
around.

"Speak to me," she urged. "I've been so anxious for you."

Richard sighed. He took a little bite. "I am troubled. Look
what I have p-promised."

"Promised? To whom?"

"To them. My subjects. They have gone home now, clutching
their pardons and sealed writs promising to abolish their wretched
villeinage. Yet I know what is to come."

She leaned forward, stroking his velvet sleeve. "Surely you
don't intend to fulfill those promises."

When Richard turned to her, Joan was surprised to see the
struggle in his face. "That's just it, mother. They could have killed
me, but they trusted me instead. And when my great nobles force
me to revoke my promises—which I'm sure they will—I will be
seen as an oath-breaker. My honor will be stained."

"No, no. You were forced to write those pardons. It was the only way."

"Was it?" Richard pursed his lips. "It was the easiest way. Could I have done something differently?"

Joan shivered at the memory of those last minutes at the Tower. "They were animals. There was no controlling them."

"And yet, they believed me. At least, the ones at Mile End believed me. They went home, directly after I promised them. Not all of their complaints were unreasonable."

He stopped at a knock on the door. A squire opened it and Robert de Vere slipped in.

"There you are. Sit with us." Richard gestured to a chair at his other side. "We were just talking about my pardons."

"Yes," Robert nodded, reaching for an apple. "We solved one problem and created another."

Richard laughed shortly. "As usual, you go the heart of the matter. I'm not sure what to do next."

Robert sat back in his chair, taking a bite. "I can imagine that you will hear nothing but complaints from your council."

"Oh, my council." Richard grimaced. "They were a lot of help."

"Sire," Robert leaned forward suddenly. "Perhaps they did you a favor. Never, never again will they be able to treat you like a child." He glanced at Joan for support.

"He's right," she said. "You have proven yourself. They must take you seriously."

Richard nodded in thought. "I can be my own master. I *am* my own master." After a moment, he slumped again. "Still, there is only one of me. Against all of them."

"Ah, but you have demonstrated your regality," Robert reminded him. "They cannot take that away from you."

Was it really so easy? Richard doubted it. He had no one to show him the way—to demonstrate how to act as king. As he was growing up, his old grandfather had spent most of his time sequestered with his self-serving mistress, leaving Gaunt to represent him in Parliament. That didn't go well; once again, his uncle had demonstrated what *not* to do. Richard saw how the commons, when united, forced his uncle's hand, and how a year later Gaunt turned the tables on them and reversed all their unfavorable rulings. And look how despised he became!

There must be another way. Richard knew his grandfather was popular in his prime, but he didn't exactly know why. Or how. Did it have everything to do with winning the war in France? Was there something special about how he made laws? Or was it because he surrounded himself with trustworthy retainers?

Richard turned to his friend. "At least I have you behind me."

"And William Walworth. And Nicholas Brembre. And John Philipot."

"And Simon Burley. Oh, I wish he was here."

"So do I," sighed Joan. He had been with them for so long he was almost part of the family. Simon had fought with her husband for years, then became a member of Joan's household before serving as Richard's tutor. If truth be told, Burley was more of a father to Richard than the Black Prince.

Collecting herself, Joan perked up. "Just wait and see. He will bring back a beautiful bride for you."

Richard smiled warmly at her. The marriage negotiations had been long and drawn-out but at last they were nearing the end. Who else would they send if not their most trusted friend?

On Tuesday, while Walworth and his fellow commissioners were still arresting malefactors in London and enforcing their rough justice, Richard's council gathered at Westminster to cobble together an interim government. So many officials had lost their lives! Richard sat at the head of a long table while his customary advisors took their places; this would be a larger gathering than normal, for many decisions needed to be made.

As usual, one of the first attendees was Richard, Earl of Arundel. Apparently he wasn't at all embarrassed about his ineffectual performance during the Revolt, because he strode arrogantly into the room and took a seat next to the king, barely acknowledging him. Next came Thomas Beauchamp, the Earl of Warwick—another who was unaccountably incapable when Richard needed him the most. Although he was a great nobleman, Warwick bore himself like a man bent under the burden of an illustrious ancestor. He would never live up to the reputation of his father, hero of Crecy and Poitiers—much like himself, the king had to admit.

Richard was mildly relieved that his uncle Thomas of Woodstock had just arrived from the Welsh marches, for his strong arm would be needed in the upcoming reprisals. Yet the grimace on Thomas's face as he sat down at the king's other side did not inspire much confidence; Richard couldn't remember any time he was not disagreeable. Youngest son of Edward III, Thomas never benefitted from lands and titles like those bestowed on his older brothers. As a result, he was a bitter, disappointed man, and to make matters worse he never had a chance to prove himself in foreign battle. Easily goaded into quarrels, Thomas showered abuse on everyone around him—especially Richard, whom he always treated like a child.

The king caught himself frowning. He couldn't help but notice that everyone in the room was unfriendly to him. This was going to be business as usual, and to these self-important despots his courageous behavior at Smithfield didn't matter a fig. Richard didn't know whether he was annoyed with them for not recognizing his bravery—or was he annoyed with himself for expecting more? He stood, looking around the room.

"Thank you for coming. With sadness, we need to appoint an acting chancellor and treasurer, and a new chief justice among other officials. I am hopeful that we can keep the daily administration running until next Parliament."

Arundel opened his mouth to say something, though for once he restrained himself. The king held out his hand. "Sir Richard," he said slowly, "I am grateful to you for your assistance during this terrible time. But now, I think it would be best to relieve you of the burden of the Great Seal."

His frown deepening, Arundel pulled out the Seal and placed it on the table. Richard picked it up, tapping it against his palm. "For now, I will place it in the custody of the steward of my household until we appoint a permanent chancellor." He sat down, resisting the impulse to put the Seal in his pouch.

There was some shuffling but no objections. Arundel cleared his throat. "Sire, there continues to be great unrest among the

110

populace. The rebellion may have been crushed in London, but reports are coming in hourly about disturbances elsewhere in the country, all the way north to York and even Scarborough. Instigators are using your *alleged* pardons—" he emphasized the word, glaring at the king—"to attack officials and landowners. The rascals seem to think they have your sanction to kill anyone they deem a traitor." He paused as others in the room grumbled their accord. "We need to act quickly and put them down by force."

Thomas of Woodstock stood, adjusting his belt. "I will lead the first army in reprisal. We will go to Brentwood in Essex, where, I am told, this rebellion began." The others nodded uncertainly, unwilling to contradict him though some feared that armed reprisal might spark further rebellion.

Exchanging a glance with Thomas, Richard of Arundel faced the king. "Concurrent with your uncle of Woodstock's foray, I believe it would be wise for you to lead a commission of inquiry to Essex. Only you, sire, can repair the damage done by these pardons."

Richard felt his face turning red. *Again! This was unjust!* Without his charters, the peasants may have burned the city to the ground. He had done what needed to be done—and at their advice! No one else had come forward with a better idea.

Seeking to calm the king, Bishop Courtney stood, leaning over the table. "Let us appoint Sir Robert Tresilian as chief justice," he said smoothly. "He will accompany King Richard and pass judgment on the wrongdoers." Courtney was a tiresome, preachy busybody and Richard found him annoying. He was about to say something when the bishop hurriedly added, "King Richard will overawe his disobedient subjects with the majesty of royal authority. Tresilian will restore order."

Richard wasn't fooled by the flattery but Arundel turned in his seat, pursing his lips. The king suspected the earl wasn't finished castigating him, but Courtney seemed to have shut him up for the moment. Somewhat mollified, Richard took a deep breath. The bishop's suggestion was sound; Sir Robert Tresilian was the perfect choice to replace the murdered John Cavendish. Staunch and unyielding, he would impose justice.

The Earl of Warwick spoke up. "I understand that Essex is in your jurisdiction," he said to Thomas, "and you have your own retainers to call upon. As for Kent, I recommend that we send commissioners accompanied by five or ten lances each. That should be sufficient." This suggestion met with a more positive response.

Thomas grunted, satisfied. As long as the council didn't obstruct his plans, he wouldn't interfere with theirs.

Earl Arundel shortly recovered himself, gesturing for the bishop to sit. "Before we send out the commissioners we need a proclamation authorizing the sheriffs to enforce the law in their counties. They must be allowed to use whatever measures they think are necessary."

"Legally necessary," Richard interrupted. "According to the law and custom of England." Arundel nodded absently and called for a clerk. After much back and forth, the councilors finally agreed on the wording. Satisfied, Arundel passed the proclamation to the king.

Picking it up, Richard proceeded to read the document out loud. "We hereby notify you—sheriffs and justices—that risings and assemblies against our peace did not derive from *our* will or authority. They displease us immensely as a source of shame, of prejudice to the crown, and of damage to our entire kingdom. You must command each and every of our liegemen to desist completely from such assemblies and return to their homes to live there in peace, under penalty of losing life and limb and all their goods. Witnessed by myself at London, 18 th of June."

Richard affixed the Seal to the document. "With God's will, I hope this proclamation will settle things down." In his heart he doubted it would be so easy. He looked around the table, and every face reflected his own.

Seven days after Smithfield, King Richard rode out from London with an imposing army; his uncle Thomas of Woodstock had already gone ahead. There was no mistaking the royal authority; Richard was preceded by thirty sergeants-at-arms and twenty-four foot archers marching in solemn procession. His household knights, esquires, and clerks surrounded him, along with Chief Justice Tresilian and Bishop Courtney. Thousands of loyal countrymen had rallied to the king's call for arms, and his army marched at a good pace reaching Waltham, just northeast of London, by the 23rd of June. The king and his immediate household stayed at the abbey while his troops camped out in the fields.

Richard expected to meet local sheriffs and justices. What he wasn't expecting was the glut of petitioners waiting for him—too many to fill the room. The king scanned the crowd, surprised— though he shouldn't have been. The rebellion might have collapsed but their grievances remained. Richard's sergeants attempted to nudge the attendees into some sort of order when a particularly aggressive man stepped forward waving one of Richard's pardons. The wax seal imprint dangled from its cord, swaying back and forth as though to emphasize its importance.

"Sire," he called, "we have come to confirm the privileges you granted us at Mile End."

Despite himself, Richard gritted his teeth. This is what he had feared would happen—what he knew would happen. No one was going to believe that for a short time, he actually wished he could give them their freedom. No one would believe that King Richard wanted to ease their burdens. He really did. He sympathized with their grievances at Mile End. But that was before they murdered his archbishop and treasurer—before they terrorized his city with riot and slaughter. How dare they throw back his promises in his face, thinking there would be no consequences for their savage rampages!

Irritated—he wouldn't admit to chagrin, even to himself— Richard motioned for someone to take the nuisance away. But the man would not be so easily removed. "You promised us relief from the Forest Law. Relief from the Statue of Laborers." He waved the document again.

Richard leaned over toward Robert de Vere. "Am I to be plagued by every villein in England?" he muttered. "They will drive me mad."

"Sire," the man called more desperately as the guards pushed him back, "you promised that all Feudal services would disappear."

"Promised!" Richard growled at Robert. "P-p-promised!"

Other voices were raised in the man's support. The justice's marshal pounded his staff on the ground for quiet, though the more he pounded the louder the complaints rang out. Men stood up and shook their fists. Justice Tresilian called for more guards, who dashed into the room, striking those closest with batons.

Richard couldn't stand it anymore. He leaped to his feet, breathing heavily. Like magic the room fell silent. "Oh, you wretches!" he shouted. "How dare you think you are equal to your masters? Rustics you were and rustics you are still; you will remain in bondage, not as before but incomparably harsher. Go now! Deliver my message. I will spare your lives but only if you remain faithful and loyal. Choose now which course you want to follow."

The king clenched and unclenched his hands as the sergeants escorted the troublemaker from the room. He did not appreciate the look of satisfaction Tresilian turned in his direction and sat down heavily, biting his lip. Robert put a hand on his arm.

"That was well done, sire."

"No. No it wasn't," Richard grumbled. "I lost my temper. Why did they push me so hard?" He frowned as the Chief Justice started interrogating his first prisoner. "From now on, I'll be the king who broke his word to his people."

Justice Tresilian's voice cut sharply through the murmuring in the hall. "You have been accused of tearing down the Abbey's fences," he said to the man. "How do you declare yourself?"

"It's like this," the accused responded, standing straight and proud, "we have a signed document from the Abbot giving us permission to graze our herds. I only did what I needed to do."

"And how was this document procured?"

"He gave it to us as a community."

"During the Revolt?" The man didn't answer. Why bother? "This document and your actions are illegal. I order you to give the names of your allies." Again the man didn't answer. "Sergeant,

114

take this man away and hang him. Maybe his example will loosen other tongues."

As they dragged the man out, Richard watched sullenly; the prisoner turned at the last moment and glared at him so accusingly that Richard was torn between anger and shame. That man was punished unfairly, but anything less would be seen as weakness. He didn't know whether he was vexed at Tresilian for his harshness, at the prisoner for blaming him, or at himself for allowing this travesty to go on. Was this the only way to impose order?

But he knew, without having to be told, that his father would have done the same thing. So would his grandfather. So would his uncles. Kings were expected to be forceful. Centuries of warfare turned men into beasts and there was only one way to force submission. Disgusted, he got up and left the room with Robert behind him.

He knew this was only the beginning. Let Tresilian enforce his rough justice; the man was good at it. Richard didn't have to sit and watch every day. He stayed away from the court as often as he could; fortunately he had much else to do. His chamber clerks passed in and out of his cabinet all day, for ordinary business still needed his attention. Payments had to be made to his captains still putting down the rebellion elsewhere in the realm. Complaints had to be dealt with. Administrators, great and small, had to be assigned to fill vacancies.

However, there was no getting away from Tresilian, who would not let things rest. After a particularly arduous day, the justice accosted the king in his cabinet, where he was working with Robert. "Sire," he exhorted, sitting down heavily without asking permission. "You must officially revoke your charters. Every day that you delay, more people are rebelling, thinking that they are acting on your authority. It makes my task so much more difficult!"

Richard glared at him, biting back his objections. Revoke his charters? So painstakingly written while the rebels waited respectfully for their own turn, safe in their conviction that the king was on their side? Tresilian didn't understand. Richard had purposely delayed annulling them, knowing this was his last fine thread to the boy king who could do no wrong.

The chief justice took advantage of the pause and hurried on. "Think of how far some of them traveled back to their home, trusting that they held a pardon in their hands. They don't know any different. I've already heard reports that new disturbances are breaking out in Norfolk. Fortunately for us, Bishop of Norwich has taken a hand in suppressing the violence. You must revoke those charters."

For a few moments Richard considered rebuking him for his impertinence. But Robert put a hand on his arm, conveying caution.

The king took a deep breath. "I will consider what you have said," he conceded, seeing in Tresilian's face that the justice was losing patience with him.

"Well, we are nearly finished here and I suggest we move on to Chelmsford." Tresilian pushed himself out of the chair. "Shall I notify your purveyors?" At Richard's nod he went to the door, then stopped and turned back. "Please think on what I have said. We have no choice."

Richard frowned as the door closed behind him. "This is not what I planned at all," he muttered. "My subjects had some weighty concerns. They did not rise up for no reason."

Robert nodded. "That may be so. But their subsequent behavior annulled any concessions you made to them."

Thoughtful, Richard scratched his cheek. "You mean like killing Sudbury."

"I mean exactly that. And the plundering, and the rioting. They deserve no mercy from you."

Richard had already come to the same conclusions, but he needed more reassurance. "And yet we continued to write their pardons throughout the night."

Robert gestured his dismissal. "You had no choice. We had to get them out of London."

"Yes, yes. That's true. Still, they went home in good faith. They will see me as an oath-breaker."

"They went home because they lost their leader. No, a man of your majesty need not concern yourself with such trifles."

116

Another clerk knocked and entered the room, laying a small pile of parchments in front of the king. Richard fidgeted with his ring. "Nonetheless, I hate to succumb to Tresilian's pestering." Frowning he picked up the top letter. He glanced at Robert. "Though perhaps he is right. Here's another sheriff begging us for help against the rebels." He flipped to the next page. "And another. And another." He pushed the pile away and gestured to his valet for some wine.

"Have you considered," Robert said, leaning forward, "that Tresilian is a man you might want by your side, if we have trouble in the future? He has strong resolve, and will not tolerate dissent. See how he accused the ringleaders? We may have need of a man like him."

Resignedly, Richard nodded. Robert was right. It wasn't necessary for him to love the men he depended on. He was surrounded by people he despised. At least the Chief Justice would never pretend to be his better, like his uncles. It was good to have people around him who relied on his patronage for their advancement. That was the strongest attachment of all.

Thomas of Woodstock yanked the reins of his war horse, turning it around and forcing it to quiet down. He knew how the stallion felt; he, too was ready to dash down the hill and teach those unruly curs a lesson. This was the first armed confrontation in the field between the rebels and the government, and Thomas was determined that it would be the last.

No one would deny his ruthlessness. Deep-set black eyes and a hairline which plunged to a point like a hood on a black snake— they were enough to unnerve the boldest of opponents. The creases beneath his stubby nose emphasized his heavy mustache and thick frowning lips. He rarely smiled, even with his friends.

Hundreds of unrepentant yeomen had gathered in Rettingdon Wood—just east of Brentwood, where it all began. He could see from the way they barricaded their flanks with ditches and carts chained together that their leaders, at least, had fought in the French wars. He promised himself not to fall prey to overconfidence.

Sir Thomas Percy, brother to the Earl of Northumberland, came up beside him. "The vanguard is right behind us. Let me have the honor of the first charge."

Thomas grunted. Percy had always needed to prove himself. "Do so, then. Once you break their ranks, we will surround the woods and kill the rabble." As he watched impatiently, Percy assembled a score of his best warriors. They mounted their destriers and pulled down their visors as squires waited to hand up their lances. This charge was undoubtedly for their own glory, but it would serve its purpose. Since no French campaigns were planned, this was the closest thing they would experience to real combat. Once again, Thomas cursed his nephew. A child when England needed a warrior king. Look how close they had come to complete destruction—from an army of peasants and journeymen. If only he had been in London...

He turned as the rumble of mounted soldiers grew from behind. Good. They were more than enough to suppress this disturbance. With a yell, Percy led his lancers at a canter down the slope and Thomas held his breath, captivated as always by the beauty of mounted chivalry, gaining speed as they charged the opposition.

There was no contest. The riders crashed through the stout line of poorly armed defenders, who fell back—flailing and trying their best to strike as the knights passed between them. Percy knew what he was doing and already there were more bodies on the ground than men on horseback. Pointing his sword into the air, Thomas shouted "En Avant!" and closed his visor, leading the vanguard down the slope. The king's forces crashed into the woods and chased the frantic rebels who had already scattered, leaving their camp to the tender mercies of the victors. Chroniclers later said that over 500 men were killed and 800 horses captured.

As Thomas suspected, his easy victory discouraged many of the rebels who disbursed after this dismal encounter. A few of the survivors tried to carry on, but in the end their warlike efforts were fruitless.

Moving the king's household was as routine as it was formidable; this was a way of life for everyone involved. Many of his sergeants, esquires, and servants had been doing this for years—often they inherited their positions from parents. For as long as anyone could remember, the court was itinerant; Richard and his ancestors had no permanent residence. Sometimes they stayed at a royal manor; sometimes they paid a visit to one of their nobles. Richard came to prefer stopping over at a monastery. He knew how expensive it was to sustain his household; if someone else could cover the costs for a couple of days, it would be a great help to his overburdened exchequer.

The purveyors went first; they were responsible for buying food and drink, hay, oats, and litter for horses, wood and coal for heating and cooking. Their authority extended throughout the verge—that is, within 12 miles of the king's presence. No one could refuse them, even though they often didn't get paid until much later—if at all. Then the harbingers went out to arrange sleeping quarters. Richard had a royal manor near Chelmsford, so he knew that at least his immediate officers and clerks would be comfortably lodged. As for the rest of them, houses in town would have to do or, failing that, tents. Transportation needed to be arranged and items had to be packed. By the time the king was ready to move on, over 100 servants had preceded him.

On the 2nd of July, Richard entered Chelmsford in state, and his first visit was to the old cathedral. Tresilian impatiently waited for the king to finish mass, for today was the day Richard finally agreed to revoke the charters of manumission—those absurd warrants giving villeins their freedom. A large batch of rebels awaited Tresilian's judgment, but he wanted Richard's proclamation to set the tenor for the day.

Richard left the cathedral and paused at the top of the stairs, waiting for the cheering to die down—not that there was much acclaim. Tresilian watched from a distance, exasperated. Ever since Smithfield Richard had become puffed up with his own importance. From now on he was going to be difficult to reason with—as if these trials weren't grueling enough. At least for the moment, Tresilian had prevailed. The boy could be sullen and petulant, but he was not foolish. Like it or not he saw the

119

reasoning behind this unpleasant task; the revolt had spread throughout the country with no end in sight. Revoking the charters was the only answer; too bad this act was so perilously late in coming. Wat Tyler may have started the depredations; it remained for the king's justices to end them. This was no time for leniency.

The city's council hall was filled to overflowing; as Richard entered the room all chatter died down immediately. The king and his entourage passed through the crowd without glancing either to the right or left, then seated themselves on the raised platform at the end of the room. Richard gripped the arms of his throne.

"On mature reflection and advised by my council," he started, "I realize that my Charters of Privileges and Pardons issued at Mile End have prejudiced and disinherited the crown and the State. I therefore revoke, invalidate, and annul them. All letters of manumission and pardon must be returned to the chancery so they can be destroyed. They have no legal authority. Every freeman and bondsman must go back to his usual works and services without complaint. Without resistance. As you are my loyal subjects, you will so remain in my good graces."

Richard could almost hear the groans, though none were uttered. He watched the faces before him; once so hopeful, they were suddenly crestfallen. It was over. His brief accord with his people—such as it was—had shattered in the worst possible way. When could he ever gain their trust again?

He raised his eyes above the crowd, wishing he was somewhere else. Is this what he had to look forward to, as king? He was beginning to realize how difficult ruling could be when one decision was as thorny as another. Not that he ever had any choices. He didn't necessarily want to be king; God had chosen for him, and it was up to him to meet his destiny. But that knowledge didn't make this any easier. Up until the Great Revolt, he chafed at restrictions imposed on him by the council. And now, how he wished his life was so worry-free!

Retribution would be inexorable and the trials began at once. Rigid, immobile, the king was forced to watch as rebel after rebel was tried and condemned; Tresilian was very thorough. Twelve men were drawn and hung for treason and a further nineteen hanged from a gallows. An uneasy peace settled over the region and the king's administration moved on to St. Albans.

Here, Richard was obliged to witness the trial of the Revolt's most notorious surviving instigator. By now, the king was thoroughly sick of executions. Still, this was John Ball and the king was expected to preside over the court. When the friar was brought before the judges, Richard halfway expected to see a big, strong bull of a man, spouting curses and foaming at the mouth or something equally imposing. Instead, they dragged forth a shriveled, half-starved hermit. The king almost felt sorry for him. So this was the man everyone was making such a commotion over? How could this wraith inspire anyone?

John Ball stood quietly before Justice Tresilian, his hands bound, eyes on the floor. Even in his reduced state the friar showed no fear.

Tresilian strode back and forth, waving a letter. "This was found in the tunic of a man we condemned to death," he said. "Let me read it to you: Beware of guile in the borough, and stand together in God's name. We shall chastise the robbers and force the king to remedy all the great evils besetting us..." Tresilian stopped before the friar and pointed a finger at him. "You wrote this letter, didn't you!"

John Ball looked up from the floor and stared at the king for a moment. His eyes were bloodshot and his beard was streaked with stains.

"Answer me!" shouted Tresilian.

Ball took his time removing his gaze from Richard. "Yes, I wrote that letter," he said finally.

"Any many more besides."

"Yes. I sent them to my flock."

"Do you know how much destruction you have caused? How many were murdered because of what you started?"

For a moment Richard saw a spark of passion in the friar's eyes. "I am not responsible for this. You have caused these people to rebel. Your oppression and bad government have forced good and loyal Englishmen to protest in the only way they knew how. Why do you let the fat and lecherous abbots force poverty on their own tenants? Why must you keep my fellow countrymen

121

enslaved?" Having spent his last bit of strength on his rebuttal, the light went out of John Ball's eyes and he turned his gaze back to the floor.

Tresilian rose on his toes. This time he was pointing at the ceiling. "There," he exclaimed. "In front of God, by your own words you have revealed your guilt to the world. I declare you a traitor and condemn you to death. Take him and give him a traitor's execution."

Wearied of this world, John Ball let the sergeant-at-arms drag him away. Richard had seen enough. While the justices prepared for their next inquest, the king removed himself from their presence. Everyone stood and bowed while he hastened from the room.

The king entered the abbey's chapel and knelt to pray. He stayed there a long time, and when he finally crossed himself and turned to leave, Robert was waiting for him.

"Are you ill, sire? You are very pale."

Richard put his arm through Robert's, walking slowly toward a side door. He leaned against his friend, happy to let someone else share his burden. Servants appeared out of nowhere to accompany them. When they reached the royal apartments, Richard took off his crown and handed it to a waiting valet, while another took his gloves.

"I weary of all these executions. All these reprisals. When will there be enough blood shed?"

"When they are all satisfied," Robert said.

"All?"

"Those who would advise you."

"Hmm. We shall see. You know, I didn't think I'd ever say this but I wish my uncle John was here. He would know what to do with these people. Tomorrow I shall send to him commanding his return from Scotland. I need him here."

If only John of Gaunt had known how Richard felt, he would have been saved much grief. By the time hysterical rumors had reached Scotland, he didn't know whether he was the enemy of the people, the government, or both.

CHAPTER 2

John of Gaunt could pride himself on having negotiated a prolonged truce between Scotland and England, all the while refusing to acknowledge the panicked rumors flying across the border. In fact, he managed to keep the news from the Scots until negotiations had finished; they were entirely unaware of opportunities springing up as England fell into anarchy.

Preserving a calm facade, Gaunt quietly sent messages to his garrisons in Yorkshire and the Welsh marches, ordering them to prepare for a siege. The reports were appalling: some said that all his castles in the south lay in ruins. Others said that an army of peasants 10,000 strong were marching north to murder him. He was well aware that the king was undefended, and once the parley was over he was anxious to get back to London.

Gaunt's fellow commissioners found him in a state of high annoyance the evening before they planned to leave Berwick for the south. Normally phlegmatic and self-possessed, under the best of circumstances the duke was not a man to underestimate. His curved eyebrows and long straight nose, thin lips and stiff beard all contributed to the aristocratic pose that lent him such an air of superiority. He held up a rolled document and slapped it against the table.

"Damn it. This is from the earl of Northumberland. Listen to this." He unrolled the paper. "Percy tells me that due to the situation in London and letters of privy seal he received, he advises me to stay in the royal castle of Bamburgh until he is better informed of the king's intentions." His eyes shot fire. "Who is he to give me orders?"

The others stepped back, uncertain. One of them, the Bishop of Hereford, cleared his throat. "How old are his tidings?"

"Newer than mine, I suppose, and more reliable. One of Sir Percy's valets was in London the day the rebels entered the city and he brought the news posthaste. That was on the feast of Corpus Christi."

"They entered London! Dear God." The bishop crossed himself. "What are we to do?"

Gaunt paced back and forth, folding his arms over his chest. "We must recover our supply wagons anyway, which I left at Bamburgh. We will make our dispositions then."

Their destination was one day's ride away. Gaunt's large retinue stretched farther than he could see—in fact, they disappeared into the mist. The road lay flat and straight until it reached the ridge next to the ocean; the castle perched upon its brow, brown and gloomy. Tired from the ride, Gaunt and his bodyguards pushed their mounts up the steep, windy path next to the curtain wall. Reaching the gates, he was annoyed to see them closed against him.

"Announce us," he growled at his trumpeter who sounded a shrill note. No one answered his call.

"This is outrageous. Bang on the door."

The trumpeter drew his sword, striking the wood with his pommel. The hollow boom echoed against the walls. For a moment longer there was no response, until finally the captain showed himself on the barbican above.

"Duke John," he barked, his voice arrogant. "Word from the south is not good. We fear that the king has declared against you. Sir Henry Percy has ordered that you must be refused admission to any castle in his charge until he receives the king's license."

"What! That is disgraceful. There is no conflict between us. I am the king's lieutenant!" Gaunt roared.

"That may be but I have my orders."

"Who initiated this order? Was it Percy or the king?"

The captain hesitated. "I know not."

"I must have my supply wagons!"

"We will hold them for you, Sir John. I cannot open the gates."

"Who has spread these lies about me?"

The captain spoke to someone over his shoulder. "We had reports that you set your bondsmen free and they swore to make you king. We heard reports that you are marching south with an army of Scots to seize the kingdom."

"Reports! As you can see, I have only my retinue!"

"My lord Duke, I cannot help the rumors. I must obey my master."

"Whoreson! I will not forget this affront!" He jerked his horse around, facing his appalled followers. "Find me lodging in town. Tomorrow we will move on to Roxburgh." As his men turned their horses around, he muttered to himself. "Tonight I will write to the Earl of Douglas. He'll give me safe conduct back to Scotland."

At Roxburgh, Gaunt was greeted by his own governor, but no one could inform him about the situation in the countryside. Ugly rumors followed each other with no official word from the king or his officers. Sadly, John dismissed his retinue—the ones who hadn't already deserted. Two knights, Sir John Marmion and Sir Walter Urswick, vowed to stay with him for good or ill. "We will travel north," Gaunt said. "The Earl of Douglas has professed his friendship many times, and I am determined to take him at his word."

Gaunt's instincts were correct. On the way to Melrose Abbey, the duke and his companions encountered the earls of Douglas and the Scottish King's son Carrick with 500 spears. The Scots greeted them as welcome guests and escorted them all the way to Edinburgh, where Gaunt was lodged at Holyrood Abbey. Then he wrote a letter to King Richard, though he did not know where to send it. As a result, he was forced to forward several copies under his seal, hoping that one, at least, would find its recipient. Many anxious days passed while conflicting reports reached his ears, until finally a letter came under the king's seal.

"Listen to this," John said to his knights, his voice filled with relief. 'Return at once,' the king states, 'for I have great need of you. I am sending out warrants defying any negative rumors and commanding my sheriffs to protect you on your journey south.' Dear God, I was prepared for the worst. I should have had more faith in my nephew." He spoke those last words with more sadness than regret, for Richard had done little to reassure him the last couple of years.

Gaunt wasted no time preparing to leave. He recalled as many of his retinue as he could, directing them to join him on his return to London. Douglas and Carrick, gracious as ever, accompanied the duke south with an escort of over 800 spears. They stopped at the border, where Lord Neville, Gaunt's retainer, waited with a body of soldiers. After taking leave of his Scottish allies, John continued south, gratified to see his forces swelled by levies provided along the way in response to the king's writs. They paused for five days at the duke's castle at Pontefract, then continued on to Reading, forty miles west of London, where the king waited.

Duke John had no complaints about Richard's greetings. Gifts were exchanged, kind words expressed; John was given the place of honor at Richard's table. Nonetheless, his patience had its limits; after all the preliminaries were attended to, Gaunt laid his grievances before the king.

"Sire," he said, bending his knee, "I accuse Sir Henry Percy of disobedience to your orders and contempt for myself, your representative. He deserves censure; his conduct was disloyal to both yourself and me."

Richard was nonplussed. "But uncle, I know you have been friends with Percy for years."

John's eyes momentarily filled with tears, much to Richard's surprise. "That makes his betrayal so much worse. He humiliated me and put me in grave danger by refusing admittance to any of his castles. I don't understand why he would drive me away like a common criminal."

Richard suspected that Percy's behavior had something to do with resentment. Perhaps the earl thought *he* should have been the king's lieutenant in Scotland, rather than Gaunt. Maybe he was wreaking revenge, and the revolt was a perfect excuse.

Feigning ignorance, the king shook his head. "We must bring this out in the open and reconcile the two of you. I cannot have my greatest lords openly hostile to one another. Come, uncle. Bring your grievances to our council at Berkhampstead in August. All the earls in the kingdom will be in attendance."

Richard watched as his uncle bowed in acquiescence and backed from the room. This was the first time Gaunt had shown any weakness, at least in his presence. The events must have shaken him badly. *As well they should*, the king thought. If the commons would have had their way, John would have gone up in

126

flames along with his precious Savoy. He may not have realized just how despised he was throughout the country. Added to that, he hadn't been sure whether the king had declared him a traitor or not. Richard laughed inwardly, despite himself. Perhaps there was more than a grain of truth to that assumption.

Henry Percy, Earl of Northumberland was summoned to Berkhampstead to answer John of Gaunt's complaints. He was a powerful man—the kind of man whose presence filled the room. As he strode into the council chamber, barely suppressed anger added ferocity to his normal rustic bearing. Like most of his countrymen in the north, he was solid and uncompromising. His right eye had a slight cast to it which some people found disconcerting.

The meeting started out badly. Percy drew himself up before the king's council, glaring at the seated men with his square jaw set. He swung around as Gaunt entered the chamber, his frown deepening.

Richard tried to sound conciliatory. "My lords," he started, gesturing to both. "There has certainly been a misunderstanding between you. Duke John of Lancaster had mistakenly been denied access to Bamburgh—"

"There was no mistake!" John interrupted. "His orders were deliberate, and his captain was most insolent! I did not think you were so great a lord," he said contemptuously, "that you would dare to order your fortifications shut against the Duke of Lancaster."

"You overreach yourself. Sir Matthew was only acting under my orders, and I was acting under the king's orders." Percy briefly glanced at Richard. "I was ordered under pain of death not to suffer anyone to enter towns or castles under my jurisdiction. Anyone!"

"And you didn't think to exempt myself, uncle to the king and lieutenant in the North?"

"Why should I? You were not mentioned specifically in the warrant."

"That shouldn't have mattered. Sir Percy, you have impugned my honor by giving credit to rumors that I committed treason. You withheld my supplies and exposed me to unnecessary dangers."

"From what I can see, you had allies enough among our enemies."

"Disloyal man!"

Percy leaned back, momentarily stunned. "Disloyal? Who took refuge with the Scots?"

"You drove me to it! Does our kinship and friendship mean nothing to you?"

"I am your friend only as long as I am useful to you!"

"Scoundrel!"

"Traitor!"

"Enough!" The king leaped to his feet. "Be silent, both of you!"

For a moment the two lords glared at each other. But John, ever aware of his dignity, broke off with a grunt and turned away. Not so with Percy.

"Who are you to think you are above the law?" he shouted at John. "What makes you so important that you can trample over the rights of others? I am Lord of the North. My family has been there for generations. We are the law in Northumberland! I dare you to say differently!" He pulled his glove from his belt and threw it on the floor before Gaunt.

Lancaster controlled his temper, infuriating Percy even more. But this was too much for the king. Still on his feet, Richard pointed at Percy, his finger shaking. "How dare you quarrel in my presence? Arrest this man! I accuse you, Sir Henry Percy, of *lèse majesté*." The room fell into a hush. This was a grave offense, and the punishment could be severe.

When two guards approached and took Percy by both arms, the earl shook them off. "I will go with you," he spat, throwing one last angry glance at Gaunt. Luckily for the earl, he had many friends. Before the end of the session, the earls of Warwick and Suffolk stood surety for him and guaranteed that he would show up at the next Parliament to answer the charges.

128

This was a terrible state of affairs! The country was still unsettled from the Great Revolt, and here the two most powerful magnates were at each other's throat. Their quarrel had taken on a life of its own, and Richard didn't know what to do to keep it from escalating.

The next Parliament was scheduled to be held at Westminster. As November 3 loomed, the situation was grave; John of Gaunt raised 500 men-at-arms though he knew better than to bring them into the city. He garrisoned his troops at Fulham, west of London, and kept them ready for action if called upon. The citizens of London took no chances; would Gaunt wreak revenge on them under the guise of his dispute with Percy? They erected barricades at vital points and posted guards at every gate, just in case the duke decided to advance on the city. Percy, on the other hand, was welcomed with open arms. He was given gifts and offered hospitality; the Londoners even offered pastures for his horses and cattle, which he had brought to feed his vast entourage.

The great hall at Westminster Palace was noisier than usual; voices rose in argument, some favoring Gaunt and others Percy. Richard sat on his raised chair, wishing for once that he could wander through the room incognito. But that was of course impossible. He beckoned to Thomas Mowbray, who was talking with Archbishop Courtenay. Mowbray was friendly with many in the crowd and shouldn't have trouble engaging some in conversation. Nodding, Thomas approached, lending an ear.

"I need you to discover what they are arguing about," Richard said, gesturing to a particularly outspoken cluster of lords. "Or them." He glanced at another. "Insinuate yourself; they will talk to you."

Mowbray straightened up. He studied the room thoughtfully before bowing to the king. Richard held out his hand for a goblet of wine as he watched his friend move through the attendees. "Archbishop Courtenay," the king called. "Come tell me about the effigy they are building for my father's tomb at Canterbury."

Courtenay smiled in pleasure; this was one of his favorite projects. "It's extraordinary, made of bronze gilt which glows even in the candlelight. He wears his full suit of armor with the heraldic arms emblazed on his jupon like embossed gold. His gauntleted hands are held in prayer like this—"Courtenay demonstrated—"and his helmeted head is graced with a jewel-studded crown."

Richard sighed while he continued to watch Mowbray. "It will be a worthy monument. Do tell me; when will it be finished?"

"We hope to see it ready by next Michaelmas. We will host a high mass and invite all the prelates in England to attend." They talked more on the subject until finally Mowbray wound his way back to the king.

"I thank you, Archbishop Courtney," Richard said in dismissal and the other rose, ceding his place to Mowbray. He already noticed that the king had been watching Thomas closely.

"I've never seen such bickering," Mowbray muttered, leaning toward Richard. "I swear these men would draw their swords if they were a little more drunk. That one there," he pointed at a bear of a man with bristling whiskers, "threatens to challenge anyone who dares accuse Gaunt of disloyalty. And that other..." he pointed to a short man with a big chest, "he says that Gaunt's truce with the Scots weakened Percy's authority as defender of the north."

Richard nodded. "It was my decision to send my uncle to Scotland. Did they say anything against me?"

"Not in my presence. I think the old antagonism against your uncle is still alive and strong. Many never forgave him for lording it over the Bad Parliament in '77."

"I remember, though I was too young to understand it all." Richard said. "He reversed all the decisions of the Good Parliament from the year before. It was quite an outrage. He acted like a king, and many worried that he would take the crown from me." He bit his lip, recalling his uncertainties. "After all, my father had just died and the old king was too infirm to protect me."

Mowbray gestured to the room. "And look at them all, ready to tear your uncle's throat out. It didn't take much for people to believe he was marching south to use the rebellion in his favor."

Richard sighed, frowning. "His arrogance knows no bounds. On the other hand, Percy seems to think he is lord of the north. He, too, needs a lesson in humility." He leaned back, crossing his arms. "I almost wish I could leave them alone to fight out their differences. But we've had enough violence for now."

Richard stood, followed by Mowbray. "Let it be known that no one will be permitted to carry arms to Parliament tomorrow," the king said. "We'll have enough problems without worrying about that."

It was a wise precaution; the next day's session started out even more tense than at Berkhampstead. It was obvious that no business would be attempted until this crisis was dealt with.

After the opening remarks, Gaunt was given the floor. Once again, he recited all the insults and humiliation he sustained. When Percy made ready to respond, the king told him to be silent. "Tomorrow," Richard said, "you will give your answer."

The following day it was Percy's turn. Standing before the assembly he pulled out a small batch of letters from under his arm and held them up for all to see—four letters, all stamped with the privy seal.

"Let me read to you the contents of these missives. Here is the first: 'Richard, by the grace of God King of the England to Sir Henry Percy, Earl of Northumberland. Let it be known that on this day, the feast of Corpus Christi, London has been beset by rebels numbering in the tens of thousands. They have caused great damage to our city and for now we do not have the means to bring them under control. Since the disturbances started in Essex, I have cause to believe that the unrest will spread to the North. Therefore I command you to secure all castles under your care and do not permit entry unless under my license.'"

Percy stopped reading and glared at John of Gaunt, who was preparing to stand up then thought better of it. They both regarded the king who sat expressionless.

"Very well," the earl went on, "here is the second letter written the next day. It says 'The situation with the rebels has not been brought under control. Word has reached us that an army of 10,000 rebels is marching on the north. Until we learn otherwise, my orders remain in place.'"

Without pausing this time, Percy read the other two letters, which related more of the same. When he finished, he took a deep breath. "Therefore, my lords, I acted under the king's command. I

131

felt it was not under my discretion to exempt anyone from the mandate."

Very few men, even Gaunt, were prepared to object to Percy's defense. It was solid. But everyone knew that the real issue was his behavior at Berkhampstead, which insulted both Gaunt and the king.

It took five days to discuss every angle of slander and justification, until finally Richard was ready to move on. "Sir Percy, what do you have to say for yourself?"

Was the Earl of Northumberland worn down by incessant debate, or did his supporters—the earls of Warwick and Suffolk—convince him that his futile argument was likely to get him imprisoned, or worse? Whichever it was, Percy resigned himself to swallowing his pride. He knelt on one knee before the king.

"My most honourable liege lord, whereas in your presence at Berkhampstead, without leave or license from you, I offended you by disparaging the Duke of Lancaster and by throwing down my gage before him. I submit myself to your grace, and pray that you pardon my offence."

Still on his knee, he faced John of Gaunt. "In offending you, Sir John, and in throwing down my gage before you, I submit myself to your grace and ordinance, and pray that you pardon my offence."

And then, just to make sure they were appeased, he continued. "My liege lord, God knows that it was never my wish nor my intention to disobey in any way your royal majesty. And if I acted so through ignorance, I submit myself to your gracious will. My Lord of Lancaster, if any disobedience was done to you through ignorance or otherwise, that was not my intent and I pray that you will pardon me your anger."

Such a humbling of this imposing man! Even Gaunt was surprised. Almost embarrassed for his former friend and ally, John stood and turned to the king. "For myself, sire, I am prepared to accept Sir Henry's apology." Richard nodded his acquiescence.

Was Gaunt reconciled with Percy? Probably not. But after such a public airing of their dispute, there was little point in continuing their open animosity. With the king's approval, Parliament was finally permitted to move on to its real objective:

restoring order and confidence to the country devastated by the great upheaval.

However, this, too was cut short. In the middle of the next session, a herald entered the chamber with great fanfare.

"The princess Anne of Bohemia has landed safely at Dover."

Richard stood, everything else forgotten. "This Parliament is adjourned," he called, his voice ringing out through the room. It wasn't his place to announce a postponement—that was the chancellor's job—but for once he could be forgiven.

King Richard's betrothed had finally come to England.

CHAPTER 3

The afternoon sun was shining as the modest fleet bearing Anne of Bohemia approached the Dover harbor, dominated by stark white cliffs with a castle on top. She turned to Burley, who had spent so much time at her side she treated him like a favored uncle. "Is it true that the Romans originally built a castle here?"

Burley smiled at her, scratching his chin. Although Anne was tall for her age, he towered over her like a protective eagle with its chick. Broad at the shoulders, bearded and balding, his heavy eyebrows shadowed a kindly glint that gave away his better nature. "From what I learned, the Romans built a fort on top of an even older earthworks."

"And this castle?"

"William the Conqueror built it, but I think it was expanded by Henry II."

"It is impressive." She turned to watch as the mariners furled the sails. "I never thought we'd get this far," she added, pulling her cloak tighter. "I am so happy we're in England."

They had been traveling for well over two months with her fifty knights and a score of ladies. They had a long stay at Brussels because of the Norman privateers trolling the Channel; it took her uncle the Duke of Brabant's intercession to guarantee her safe conduct. Then they rode off to Bruges, Gravelines, and eventually Calais where they had to wait again for a change of weather.

Finally, all that was behind them. Anne and Burley stood on the upper deck watching the activity below. The anchor was dropped and the boat tied off to the wharf; some of the more restless knights immediately jumped ashore. Burley went to main deck and verified that everything was in order before returning. "I believe we can disembark now, your Grace," he said, holding out a hand. Anne was grateful for the help, since this was the first time she ever travelled by ship.

Once ashore, she exchanged greetings with officials and lords who surrounded her curiously. They wouldn't have called her a great beauty—her chin was a little too long, her face a little too narrow. But Anne had a way of listening when spoken to, and showing genuine interest that people found agreeable. Her smile was warm and her voice was melodic. Burley could tell that those around her were favorably disposed toward her.

They moved slowly away from the ship when unexpectedly the cog started rocking; a few ladies clung to the rope on the narrow ramp and men ran over to help them. Suddenly the rocking turned violent and the boats lurched dangerously to the side, their contents sliding over the deck and pitching into the water. One of the boats—the one Anne just disembarked from—gave a loud crack and the mast came crashing down onto the deck. Women screamed but their voices were drowned out by the splintering of wood and the clash of ship against ship. Floorboards jutted up, knocking people over; planks split apart; horizontal yards tore loose and dropped to the deck in a tangle of rigging.

Shocked into action, Burley scooped Anne into his arms and dashed away from the shore, trying to protect her from the terrified crowd that ran alongside them. By the time they had reached safety and he put her gently on the ground, the water-shaking diminished. Some of the boats were leaning, others were sinking. The Bohemian entourage had been distributed among several ships and the one Anne sailed on took the most damage.

"My ladies," Anne gasped.

"Are you all right?" Simon examined her, turning her around.

"Yes, yes. My thanks to you."

"Then I will go and see. Stay here, if you would."

Well-wishers surrounded Anne while Burley and other men ran back to the wharf. Some of the seamen were helped out of the water; fishermen jumped into little boats to aid those on the other side of the wreckage. A few of the ladies sat on the ground crying; Simon went from one to the next, bending over them to ensure they were unharmed.

Anne was still trembling when he came back. "What happened?"

He observed the Channel which had calmed down already. "I have heard stories of times when the water shook. They say it comes from deep in the ocean, but I've never seen it before."

It was later said by Anne's detractors—and she had many, since she came with no dowry—that this was a bad omen. What it was a bad omen *for*, they never specified. One thing is for sure; the incident was so unusual that everyone remembered it.

After two days everything was put back together, and the glittering cortège started out for Cambridge. By now, word had spread that the long-awaited princess had arrived, and she was gratified to see a welcome in everyone's face. It was evident they were impressed by the fancy new sidesaddles employed by the ladies; women in the crowd pointed at the little benches strapped to the horses with a footrest for satin shoes. Each lady's palfrey was led by a footman who managed the bridle-rein while the lady held onto a pommel; this meant that they could proceed at no faster than a walk. But this was no matter; the sidesaddle was merely used for ceremonial purposes. Once outside of town, Anne and her ladies climbed into two gaily painted wagons, lined with scarlet cloth and fitted with cushioned benches.

Late that afternoon they approached Canterbury. Burley nudged his horse next to Anne's wagon, pointing at the walls. "They are in the process of refortifying the defenses," he said. "The old Norman walls fell into disrepair, and King Edward ordered them to be rebuilt. By the time it is finished, we'll have twenty-four towers around its perimeter. In the cathedral rests the shrine of St. Thomas Becket of sacred memory. Would you like to see it?"

"Most certainly. I look forward to leaving an offering there."

They were interrupted by a sharp blow of a trumpet. A large cavalcade came out of the city gates and approached, led by a magnificently arrayed knight on a white horse. Behind him rode his trumpeters and several ranks of knights, carrying lances topped by gaily fluttering pennons.

"That is the king's uncle, Sir Thomas of Woodstock," Burley said. "He brings you formal greetings."

Anne remounted her palfrey and her retinue walked slowly toward the procession before halting. She was relieved that the sun chose this moment to come out from behind the clouds; everything glowed with color. Sir Thomas dismounted and knelt before Anne, bowing. She held out her hand.

"I am so very pleased to meet you."

Thomas stood and kissed her fingers. Tall and imperious, he bore himself like a true aristocrat; his black eyes stared unwavering at the princess. "Your Grace, we welcome you to England."

Her smile was genuine. "I am happy to be here. You are most kind."

Prepared to dislike her—since he was one of the advisors who argued against the costly marriage—his face softened and he took the reins of her horse, chatting amiably as he led her into the city.

Their stay at Canterbury was a short one because Christmas was approaching and the king was to meet them at Leeds, his royal castle near Maidenhead. Sir Thomas and his knights went ahead at a gallop, anxious to make sure all was prepared. As Anne's entourage set out on the morning of the 23rd, the sky was heavy with grey clouds but the bleak scenery did nothing to dampen their mood. Anne and her maids rode in their wagons; they were urged to proceed as fast as their carts would permit, for it was a full day's journey. Musicians played at their pipes, courtiers laughed and joked amongst themselves. Burley rode next to Anne, pointing out landmarks and recalling memories about Richard's childhood.

"On coronation day, young Richard was only ten years old. He was a bonny lad, with curly red hair and the sweetest smile you ever saw. The ceremony took place eleven days after the funeral of his grandfather, Edward the third of that name. On the eve of the coronation, a grand procession wound its way from the Tower to Westminster: first the commons, then the esquires, after them the knights and the aldermen, the dukes and earls and finally Richard, riding all by himself. They were all clothed in white."

He smiled, remembering. "He looked so proud on that big white horse. Even though it took hours to pass through the city, he sat straight and tall in the saddle. They proceeded across London and through Cheapside, where the conduits ran with wine. The next morning, they bathed Richard and dressed him in heavy robes. The clergy led him in procession to Westminster Abbey—that's where you will be crowned as well—while the representatives of the Cinque Ports carried a cloth-of-gold canopy. And with them came all the uncles holding swords of state. I was honored with carrying Richard's personal sword.

"The ceremony was so long. It must have been terribly wearisome for the lad, but he bravely stood tall and noble while the archbishop anointed him with oil, and he acted most kingly during the taking of oaths. He sat through the prayers and the hymns, until finally they put the crown on his head and the scepter into his little hand, and after that they gave him the orb and the sword and buckled the spurs onto his feet. The poor child was buried under his regalia, and then he had to sit through more prayers and hymns!"

Burley laughed briefly. "By then, Richard could hardly hold up his head, he was so exhausted. When the ceremony was finally over, I took him up in my arms and carried him out of the Abbey, regardless of the disapproval I could feel all around me. Alas, the boy was so tired he didn't even notice that he lost one of his sacred slippers, until we heard the crowd fighting over it. By then I had put him in his litter and off they went, under the golden canopy." He sighed. "That slipper caused me so much trouble."

"And why is that?"

He grunted. "Only that it had once belonged to Alfred the Great! He wore them at his consecration in Rome in 853, and they have been part of the coronation ceremony ever since. You can imagine how loose they hung on those little feet."

Anne was shocked. "What a terrible loss!"

"I was blamed most bitterly. But I don't regret carrying the young king out of the church. Not for a moment."

"No, Sir Simon, it wasn't your fault. Someone had to look after Richard. He must have felt very much alone, even in the midst of all those people. I wonder if he understood all that ceremony."

"It was too much for most of us." He gave her a sly smile. "You will fare much better, I trust."

The afternoon was almost over as the travelers reached the castle of Leeds, not quite halfway to London. Surrounded by water and spanning three islands, the castle was formidable and beautiful at the same time. They crossed the stone arched bridge, passed over a drawbridge, through fortified gates, and into a large inner bailey. On the far side, a newer stone building with turrets and crenellations glowed in the setting sun, and everyone knew that warm drinks and food would be waiting for them inside.

Sir Thomas of Woodstock came out through the door and strode directly up to Anne, bending and kissing her hand. "Welcome to Leeds Castle," he said. "The king has already arrived and awaits you in the privy chamber." He smiled politely, though his eyes were unreadable.

For just a moment Anne felt a tremor of anxiety. After so many months—nay years—of waiting, she suddenly felt unprepared. The king had taken on mythical proportions. All of a sudden she was to meet him face-to-face, and it occurred to her that he might not like what he saw. She glanced at Burley who smiled encouragingly.

"I'll let him know you are refreshing yourself after our long journey," he said. "I have much to tell him to fill the time between now and when you are ready."

Nodding, Anne turned to her ladies. "Agnes, you know where my jewel box is. Helen, I'll need my fine linens."

Thomas gestured to the servants who helped the maids down from the wagon and began lifting boxes to carry inside. An esquire led the way to the queen's apartments. Anne tried her best to shake off her weariness and followed with her head held high, lifting her skirts and acting as though she knew the way herself. An enclosed bridge led to the royal apartments in a three-storied keep on its own island. Anne's room had tall ceilings and a large fireplace; damask covered the walls and a platform supported the wide bed with matching draperies. Anne walked through the room and into an adjoining chamber lit by double windows topped with a quatrefoil. She let out a little gasp of pleasure to see a bath tub under a canopy and across from it another large fireplace.

"Too bad I don't have time for a bath," she murmured. Though tired, she was anxious to meet her bridegroom. She hoped to impress with her finery; that would take long enough to prepare! Anne's chamber maids rummaged through the first few chests until Agnes found what she was searching for. With a flourish she pulled out Anne's favorite sideless surcoat, a flattering blue brocade with white fur trim. Helen brought forth a white silk underdress that would show off Anne's slim, shapely figure.

"This will be perfect," said Agnes while one of the other ladies laced up the back of the underdress. "And we can use your tall horned headdress."

"No," mused the princess. "I think it's too soon to shock them with our continental styles. Let us wait until Christmas court. Tonight, I think we'll stay with my gold threaded caul under my garnet coronet."

"Very good, your Grace." Together, the two servants raised up the surcoat and pulled it over Anne's head. Agnes went right to work, brushing and rolling Anne's hair so it could be stuffed neatly inside the netting. A fine gauze veil hung down past the shoulders, and the coronet sat high on her forehead. Agnes stepped back, admiring their efforts. "You are beautiful. King Richard will fall in love with you."

Anne laughed. "I will be happy if he likes me. I dare not hope for love."

It was a short walk to the king's apartment and two household esquires stood ready to escort the princess and her ladies to the waiting royal party. Anne knew that the chamber would be full of curious strangers and she took a deep breath before they opened the doors. Many candles lit the room and a big blaze roared in the fireplace. Voices stopped talking when Anne stepped into the room, and she quickly looked around, hoping to recognize the king.

It wasn't too difficult! There he was, speaking with Burley— tall and thin with wavy red hair. Richard turned to look at her, a quizzical smile on his face. He was just about the same age as Anne, too young to support the little beard he was trying to grow. His eyes were brown with arching brows; his nose long and straight, and as she curtsied his smile broadened into a grin of welcome. He reached out as he strode forward to meet her. Lifting her up, he raised her left hand and turned, presenting his new

140

bride to his friends. They softly clapped while Anne's ladies slipped in behind her.

"Welcome to Leeds Castle, Lady Anne," he said. "I've been so impatient to meet you!"

"You couldn't have been more eager than I was," she answered, and was gratified to see he was happy with her response. The others in the room pretended to relax while Richard led her around from group to group. As part of her royal upbringing, Anne had been trained to remember names, but there were so many all at once that this was a whole new challenge. It didn't help that the English names were unfamiliar to her ear.

"You know my uncle Thomas," the king said while the other bowed. "And this is Sir Richard Arundel. He has been serving on my council since before I can remember." Arundel bowed also, though he didn't glance directly at either one of them. It was as though he wished he was elsewhere. Affecting not to notice, Richard moved on. "Here is my friend Robert de Vere, Earl of Oxford." Robert kissed Anne's hand, but his eye strayed to Agnes who was standing behind her. He caught himself and smiled at Richard. "They are a delightful addition to our court," he agreed. The king smiled indulgently before moving on to a seated lady surrounded by her own damsels. "And this is my mother, Princess Joan. She is the one I have to thank for bringing our negotiations to a successful conclusion."

Joan smiled at Anne. Although she was overweight, Joan still retained the beautiful face that made her an object of universal admiration. "I am so happy you are here. Once Richard is finished introducing you, come back and sit with me."

Anne was grateful for Joan's warmth. Never having left home before, she missed her own mother terribly. As they smiled at each other, a man quietly bent over Joan and put his hands on her shoulders. His hair was dark and thick and his eyes deep blue. Joan tilted her head, grinning up at him. "Here is my son, John Holland." His piercing gaze was unnerving, as though he was looking right through her. Anne suppressed a shiver.

Richard gave her hand a squeeze and moved on to the next group of courtiers. "This is my dear friend Thomas Mowbray. He comes from an old family that goes back to the conquest."

141

Mowbray bowed and gestured to his companion. "And this is Henry Earl of Derby, the king's cousin," he said. "We are all of an age." Henry bowed in turn. He was handsome and red-haired like the king, though more muscular. It appeared that he spent a lot of time training, for he glowed with vigor.

The king moved on, placing Anne's hand on his arm. There were more people to meet, but she was already beginning to feel overwhelmed by the time they reached Simon Burley. She sighed with relief. "Here is one who doesn't require introduction," she laughed. "And he has told me so much about you." She smiled at the king. "I have the advantage, for I already know you are nearly perfect!"

Richard grinned, relaxing his regal demeanor. "How will I ever be a match for Simon's honeyed words? Be careful. He knows me too well!"

Anne was charmed. This wasn't going to be so difficult after all. As Richard turned to answer someone's question, Simon bent toward her ear.

"You must be tired," he whispered.

"I am, but I'm happy too. I would love to sit with Princess Joan. Do you think you can arrange it?"

He whispered to the back of Richard's head and the king nodded, relinquishing Anne's hand. "Don't go too far," he smiled.

Joan moved aside as Simon brought Anne over. "How was your journey?" she asked.

"For a while I thought we'd never leave France," Anne said, looking at Simon. "Twelve vessels full of Norman privateers sailed back and forth between Calais and Holland. They seized and pillaged every ship that fell into their hands. We were told they were combing the Channel for me!"

Joan gasped. "How terrible!"

"We understood that the King of France wanted to stop my marriage and they had orders to abduct me. We didn't dare attempt the crossing."

"Absolutely not."

"When the duke of Brabant sent ambassadors to King Charles," Simon added, "he finally conceded—out of love, he said, for Anne—not for the King of England's sake!"

Joan laughed shortly. "That sounds so much like him. He is a sour man and very disappointed."

"Perhaps my marriage will smooth things between our two countries," said Anne timidly.

Joan took her hand. "I hope so. We have seen enough of war."

Simon grunted. "There are many in the room who would disagree with you."

"Because they crave the glory of their fathers." Joan frowned in the direction of Arundel and Woodstock. "They have no opportunity to advance themselves. Little do they realize the cost of that glory." She shook her head, remembering. "Richard's father was the most renowned warrior of his day, and see what happened to him. Cut short in his youth from that disease of the battlefield. Of the siege, rather! Bad food, bad water, bad air. Like so many others, my Edward was no match for the Grim Reaper."

She shuddered and for a moment a pall fell over them. "But this is no time for melancholy." She shook her head and lightened her tone. "So tell me, my dear. Where do your gentlemen find those shoes?"

Anne turned around, glimpsing some of the knights in her train. They had taken longer to dress and were just entering the room. The stir they created justified the effort. Many of the English courtiers were clearly amazed and couldn't help but stare at them. "Ah, those are called Crakow, and sometimes Poulaine shoes because they are originally from Poland."

"They are so long!"

Anne was so used to the shoes she stopped to stare at them. The pointed tips extended several inches from the toes, and some of them curled upwards. "I suppose they are. The men's are much longer than the women's. See?" She lifted her skirt and stretched her foot. Indeed, her toe also had an exaggerated tip though not enough to make walking difficult.

"How do they hold their shape?"

"Oh, they are stuffed with moss or some other soft material. I've seen some that were even longer, and attached to the knee with a little chain."

"Oh, they are frivolous," Joan laughed. "And so they must be fitting. I fancy our young men will need to have a pair themselves. What about you, Simon?"

He laughed. "Fortunately, I am too old to worry about such fashions. I leave it to them."

As Richard came over, he glanced around to see what they were talking about. Pursing his lips, he raised his eyebrows. "Well, I see I have rivals! I'll have to summon my cordwainer and put him to work."

"See? As I said." Joan enjoyed the jest. "Every shoemaker in London will be busy for the next year."

Anne may have been anxious to see London, but she was destined to be disappointed for a while. As she was soon to find out, Richard's government had to scramble to pay for her wedding and the coronation. It didn't help that the king had agreed to loan Anne's wily brother, the King of the Romans, the incredible sum of 10,000 marks for the privilege of her hand—just to guarantee the emperor's alliance against the French. A sizeable installment had just been paid in December and the exchequer was practically empty, not having had time to recover from the Great Revolt. She would just have to wait until the funds could be borrowed.

But Richard didn't seem to mind. After all, they had the Christmas celebrations to enjoy, surrounded by the most cultured, the most flamboyant courtiers—all dripping with jewels and velvets, bells and tassels. He was delighted when Anne and her ladies made their first formal appearance at their welcoming banquet. The newcomers swept into the hall wearing their most elaborate headdresses; wire forms and pasteboard horns extended two feet high and two feet wide, shaped like a wide-spreading mitre. Fine glittering veils draped gracefully to their shoulders. The room filled with excited chatter from men and women alike. Even Richard stood in amazement while Anne took her place beside him at the high table. He laughed and applauded before gesturing to a page who advanced and knelt before the princess, holding up a silk pillow.

Anne's eyes glistened as she carefully lifted a gold chain from the cushion, dangling a white-enameled ostrich with a diamond for an eye. "My badge! Oh Richard, it is so beautiful." Agnes came up and fastened the necklace while those nearby voiced their appreciation. Richard nodded his approval.

As the other guests took their seats on the *banquettes* along the tables, the *pantner* came forward, balancing loaves of bread and trenchers on his arm. While no one in particular watched, he trimmed the loaves to size for the king and guests. After him, the *ewerer* approached with an aquamanile shaped like a lion; water poured from the beast's mouth into a bowl for the king to wash his hands. As the others followed suit, a procession of servants emerged from the kitchen, carrying covered platters that revealed the most delectable creations. Anne had a choice of roasted swan, sliced venison, custard with dried fruit in pastry, roasted cranes, roasted herons, almond soup, roasted rabbits, Lombard stew; the plates went on and on. With a fanfare, two young squires carried out a large platter with a tall castle, its walls fashioned from deep-crusted pies. Even though she came from continental aristocracy, Anne had never seen such an extensive spread.

"This is so delightful," she said to Richard. "I wish I could taste every one of these dishes."

"Don't worry. Each one of the twelve days of Christmas will enchant you. My master cook has promised new creations for every meal." Richard nodded toward his butler who gestured to the master of the minstrels in the gallery above. A sweet melody drifted down while more platters were carried to the long tables below.

Dinner lasted until just before vespers, and the servants quietly cleared the tables while the courtiers moved into the center of the hall, waiting to be entertained. Richard took Anne's hand and led her forward as the others parted to make way for them. "We have a special guest tonight." He gestured to a man who appeared to be in his mid-forties, well-dressed and confident, with a full mustache and beard and a gentle face. "This is Geoffrey Chaucer, my court poet, diplomat, and Controller of the Petty Customs."

Chaucer bowed. "I am most honored."

"And he has offered to give us a reading of his new poem, Troilus and Criseyde. I believe he will read for us throughout the week, for it is very long."

The courtiers clapped their hands, for Chaucer was well known to everyone. Even Anne had heard of him. Three chairs were brought up for the king, his mother and Anne. Once they were settled, Chaucer began his great work:

Troilus's double sorrow for to tell,

he that was son of Priam King of Troy,

and how, in loving, his adventures fell

from grief to good, and after out of joy,

my purpose is, before I make envoy.

Tisiphone, do you help me, so I might

pen these sad lines, that weep now as I write.

Anne settled back into her chair, stealing a glance at Richard who sat, straight and still, as though conscious of his dignity. She had yet to see him relax, though she had only been here a couple of days. When would they find time to speak together, just the two of them, uninhibited by inquisitive eyes? Oh, she knew that some of the courtiers were already finding fault with their future queen. Absently, her hand wandered up to her jeweled collar. Here, at least, was a gift to demonstrate the king's favor. She smiled for a moment and he turned his head, smiling back at her and reaching for her hand. His face was infused with a warm glow, and Anne was certain it was not forced.

Anne needn't have worried. Once the story telling and subsequent dancing was over, a light supper of wine and spiced cakes was served. Afterwards, Richard invited her to join him in his solar. This upstairs chamber was private and comfortable, warmed by a large fireplace and lit by many candles which chased the shadows into corners. Entering the room, Anne was relieved to see the king accompanied by only a few close friends; his mother sat by the fire, Burley was standing at her side, and Robert de Vere was playing chess with Thomas Mowbray.

146

Richard came up and led her to a window alcove. They sat on a padded seat, gazing out; the moon was full and it glistened on the lake. A pair of swans glided across the still surface, leaving a wake that crisscrossed behind them. Anne marveled at the way the moonlight glowed almost blue on Richard's face.

"Are you content?" he asked. Even seated she had to look up to him.

"Oh, yes. Everyone has been so gracious."

"Hmm."

She could see he wasn't entirely convinced, so she hurried to reassure him. "Oh, my attendants are having a little difficulty finding a place for themselves. But one, at least, seems to be doing all right." She nodded toward her lady Agnes, deep in conversation with Robert—the chess game forgotten.

"Ah, Robert. He is married to my cousin Philippa, though I know it's not a happy union. I had better speak to him."

"Perhaps, though I know Agnes is very lonely."

"Away from home? I imagine you are lonely too."

Anne sighed. "I miss my parents. Though I wanted to come a year ago; I was so excited. Except..." She paused.

"The Great Revolt? A terrible business." He pursed his lips, remembering.

"I heard you were very heroic," she said tentatively.

"Heroic? No, I wouldn't call it that. They claimed they were my good subjects. You know, their watchword was 'King Richard and the true Commons'". He frowned. "But their leader went too far and my mayor of London was forced to kill him. I just took charge afterwards and they followed me."

Anne had heard the whole story from Simon who heard it from others. "They say that you were on a knife's edge, and things could have gone very badly."

"Yes." The pause was so long she was afraid she had annoyed him somehow. "But they trusted me," he said finally. "They trusted me, Anne. I promised them a pardon and, as soon as it was all over in London, we went into the country and crushed them one village at a time." He ran his hand over his forehead as if to wipe away the memory. "They said I was too young, too foolish to make those promises."

"They? Who are they?"

"My uncles. The council. The barons."

"Your advisors," Anne spoke scornfully. "It's easy to pass judgment afterwards. Where were they when you needed their help?"

"Helpless."

She laughed and he joined her; his tension eased away. "It doesn't matter that I am king. I gave my word and broke it," he finished sadly. "The worst part is I believed they had good cause for some of their grievances. I even queried Parliament last November to see if we should truly end their villeinage, as I had promised. Naturally, the answer was overwhelmingly no. They said I had no authority to free the serfs since those directly affected had not agreed to it, and that they would never agree to their dying day."

They contemplated the lake again as a cloud drifted over the moon.

"Are the worst of the reprisals over?"

"Yes, thankfully."

She hesitated again, not sure how much she should say. But she wanted to ease his sadness. "Perhaps you could issue a general pardon." He pursed his lips, considering. "Would this help to reduce the bitterness between you and your people?" she added.

For a moment a wicked smile crossed his face. "It might cause some bitterness between me and my council, but I think I can suffer through that."

"Well..." she took a deep breath, "perhaps we could announce it at my coronation. You could say I pleaded for mercy."

Suddenly Richard's face was infused with a glow of its own. "You are so wise! That's a perfect solution. No one would dare object. And it would be over, once and for all."

Awkwardly, Richard put an arm around Anne and pulled her into a hug, knocking her headdress askew. Embarrassed, she laughed, putting a hand to her head. "I'll put this away tomorrow. It keeps us apart."

"It will take more than that to separate us! I feel stronger already with you by my side." He gravely kissed her on the lips,

148

taking care not to bump into anything. It only lasted a second, but it was enough. Richard had found his helpmeet, and Anne was truly at home.

By mid-January, London was ready to welcome their new queen. It would take the slow-moving entourage three days to get there, giving time for the lord mayor and citizens to arrange a special greeting. After the disaster of the Great Revolt, everyone was in the mood for celebration. How ironic that they all gathered to meet her at Blackheath, the same site used by the insurgents before they invaded London. But now, all traces of the destructive crowd had been removed, and Anne would not have known the history of this location if Burley hadn't told her all about it.

Luckily, she had little opportunity to think about the past. It was all happening so fast! Once again, she and her ladies rode sidesaddle, their horses led by gaily bedecked grooms. As they approached Blackheath, a noisy and colorful cavalcade approached, led by the mayor in his robes of office. Next, the aldermen of the city and wealthy citizens walked, accompanied by seven minstrels. And next, Anne was honored by the whole goldsmiths' company—all seven score of them. The welcoming citizens stood aside while the king and his party passed, clapping and calling greetings, then joined the royal procession all the way to Southwark and over the Thames.

Richard leaned toward Anne; they rode as close together as her sidesaddle would permit. "This is your day," he said happily. "I've never seen such a reception!" As if to emphasize his words, the minstrels gaily sounded their chimes and broke into a song, making Anne laugh. They approached the gateway onto the bridge and Anne's smile faded as she looked up at the grinning skulls crowning its roof, stuck firmly on pikes. No one else seemed to notice, so she tried to suppress a shudder as they passed underneath. But she couldn't help straining back as they squeezed between the jumbled houses along either side of the bridge.

"What is it?" asked Richard.

"Those heads. They are a disturbing sight."

"As well they should be. Those heads belonged to the traitors who terrorized my city. They should serve as a warning to anyone else who harbors such thoughts."

Blinking, she turned forward. "Of course. So this is the famous London Bridge."

"Grand, isn't it?" He pointed to the banners and flags bedecking upper balconies. "They have tidied up, just for you, and put on their best adornments. Usually we must force our way through the crush, but today they have cleared a path for your entry."

The whole city was in a festive mood. As they processed through Cheapside, the royal party was honored by a wood castle built for the occasion. From all four turrets, beautiful girls dressed in white tossed slivers of gold leaf that fell like snow on Anne and Richard's heads and shoulders.

Two days later they were married in the new Royal Chapel of St. Stephen's in the Palace at Westminster. Two-stories tall, the chapel was graced by a beautiful vaulted ceiling painted blue with golden stars. Tall stained-glass windows ran the length of both sides, and below them, full-sized painted saints held tapestries with coats of arms. Richard and Anne walked down the center of the nave, divided by a carved wooden screen. The lesser nobility, on the lower side of the partition, bowed as they passed. On the other side of the screen, the dukes and earls sat in choir stalls, with larger seats reserved for Princess Joan and Duke John of Gaunt. The high altar displayed gilded scenes from the Passion and Resurrection of Christ; standing before it, the Archbishop of Canterbury and the Bishop of London waited for them. They took turns speaking the words of the ceremony as the happy young couple knelt on cushions. As Richard put the wedding ring on his bride's finger, sweet hymns filled the chapel, uttered by precious young voices.

Afterwards, all attendees moved next door to Westminster Hall, where the feasting was even grander than during the Christmas festivities. Trumpets announced the arrival of each course, a display of beautiful creations that seemed too perfect to eat. Anne was so excited she couldn't partake very much. She enjoyed the minstrels, followed by troubadours then jesters who climbed on top of each other, stacking bodies impossibly high from the floor.

Finally, that moment came. It was time to retire. From Richard's other side, Princess Joan leaned forward, eyebrows raised. Anne touched a cloth to her lips and nodded. Joan gestured to the waiting ladies who gathered as the bride rose to her feet. All the guests stood in response. "I thank you one and all," Anne said, knowing that few could hear her words. But that was enough. With a shy glimpse at her husband, Anne led her companions away.

The royal apartments were nearby, with the queen's chamber very close to the king's. Already Anne's servants had been busy preparing the room. Lazy flames crackled in the fireplace. Two curtain rods flanked the bed, suspended by ropes attached to ceiling beams; they were hung with embroidered red velvet cloths that draped to the floor. Atop a mattress filled with wool, the featherbed was plumped up under fine linen sheets, and another sheet was wrapped around the bolster which supported the pillows. A fur-lined silk coverlet was folded back just enough to display its silky texture.

Joan took especial pleasure in choosing the right garments for Anne and chatting about her own first husband while Agnes brushed the bride's hair and applied rose oil sparingly.

"Were you afraid?" Anne asked timidly when she mentioned her wedding night.

Joan paused, looking over her shoulder. "Afraid? Oh dear, I was too dazzled to know what to think. Thomas Holland was so handsome, so charming. He stole my heart away. I didn't have much time to think about what I was doing because we married in secret." An impish smile crossed her face. "Well, mostly in secret. We did have witnesses, though in the end I was forced to marry William Montague anyway."

Anne gasped, forgetting all about her trepidation. "You were married to two men at the same time?"

"Not willingly, I assure you. But I only spent a couple of days with Thomas before he went off to the French wars. I didn't hear anything from him for over a year. I wasn't even sure he was alive. My mother forced me to marry Montague; it was all

151

arranged. You see, I was too afraid to tell anyone about my secret wedding, especially the king. Of course, when Thomas came back there was quite a commotion."

"I would imagine so. What happened?"

"As you can guess, my feelings didn't matter. Montague had noble blood and was close to the king. Thomas was just a knight. As far as everyone was concerned, I was married to Montague, and that was that. I was very distressed, as you can imagine. Thomas comforted me as best as he could before going away again; he promised me he was going to make his fortune and petition the Pope. And you know, that's exactly what he did."

She helped Anne into bed, smoothing the coverlet as the ladies stoked the fire. Others were lighting candles, while Agnes poured sweet liquor into tiny cups, placing them on a tray. "When he heard that Thomas went to Rome, Montague was furious and tried to lock me away. But there was nothing he could do; according to the Church, if I agreed that I married Thomas willingly, as far as they were concerned the union was valid. I loved him dearly, you know. Thomas came back with the Pope's decree and Montague was obliged to concede. Thomas and I had a public wedding and we went on to have four children together. You met my oldest, John, at Leeds Castle." She kissed Anne on the cheek. "A year after he died I married Richard's father Prince Edward. We were close ever since we were children. I hope your life with the son will be as happy as mine was with the father."

Her words felt like a blessing, and Anne sighed in relief just as the king slipped into the room, accompanied by the Bishop of London, Robert de Vere and a few of his close friends. Richard climbed into bed next to his bride and clasped Anne's hand under the cover. The Bishop gave them a blessing. It was all very proper, and after a few pleasantries Richard bid his friends adieu. The ladies were the last ones to leave, closing the door gently. Richard smiled, admiring his bride, and Anne thought he never looked so handsome as at this moment.

Their first night together was a little awkward, a little careful, a little tentative. Neither one had much exposure to the outside world; both relied on delicate advice from more experienced confidantes. But they were young and curious, and by the time they fell asleep in each other's arms, the newlyweds were confident that practice would prove their best instruction.

Queen Anne's coronation followed two days later in the Abbey itself, using the text of the new *Liber Regalis*—an instruction book for royal services—compiled just for this occasion. The Archbishop of Canterbury performed the rites; as usual, the consort's ceremony was much shorter than the king's. She was anointed, then knelt at a small prayer bench while the prelate placed the coronation ring on her fourth finger. He put a bejeweled crown on her head, the scepter into her right hand, and a rod topped by an ivory dove in her left hand. As she got up and turned to leave, Anne's six ladies-in-waiting picked up her heavy ermine-lined train and escorted her from the chapel.

Once again the feasting was held in Westminster Palace; this time Richard stood and called everyone to attention before festivities started. "I have a proclamation to make," he said, smiling down at Anne. "My queen has earnestly petitioned me to forgive and pardon all my subjects in regards to the recent rebellion. Because of the great love I bear her and as a coronation present, I hereby grant a pardon to one and all."

For a moment everyone in the hall was startled into silence, but soon they applauded with relief. Anne noticed that Richard's uncle John of Gaunt was frowning and took a drink from his chalice instead. She knew he was still raw from the destruction of his Savoy palace. On the duke's other side, Arundel was speaking to someone behind him and pretended not to pay attention. Their reactions were pretty much what she expected; as for the other guests, Richard's declaration met with general approval. The king sat down and raised her hand to his lips.

"That was so well done," she whispered. "You cast both of us in God's blessed light."

With his lips on her fingers, Richard glanced slyly at his uncle. "Let him disapprove all he wants," he mumbled. "He forgets that I am king here, not him."

Richard was anxious to take his queen on a tour of his palaces. Immediately after the coronation they planned to visit Windsor, but Sheen was on the way and he decided to stop there first. It was an intimate party that embarked upstream on the royal barge; most of his entourage had gone ahead by road, and another two barges followed. Richard leaned on his red cushions, watching Anne and her ladies point at the landscape as they left the city behind. Robert de Vere sat next to Agnes, and Richard noticed that his hand strayed too close to her arm, her back, even her neck. He resolved to say something before things turned too serious.

The only discordant presence was his uncle John of Gaunt, deep in conversation with Richard's mother—especially as they passed the burnt-out ruins of the Savoy. Of all his uncles, John resembled King Edward III most closely, maintaining a steely-eyed stare that never ceased to send a surge of ice down Richard's spine. No matter what the situation, he always took command, whether he imposed on Richard or not. Still, common sense reminded the king that Gaunt could have easily gone after the throne when his father died. Everyone feared he would try, which is why Richard was crowned at age ten instead of having a regency. But, surprisingly, Gaunt was unfailingly correct in his comportment, proving that preserving the royal prerogative was more important than his own ambition. Nonetheless, it was obvious that Gaunt respected the rank of king rather than the person wearing the crown.

Richard grunted to himself. If his uncle had been in London during the Great Revolt, he wouldn't have fared any better than his precious Savoy. Did his humiliation at the hands of Percy teach him anything? Probably not. Gaunt's very public brawl in Parliament had nearly started another civil war. That was so like him!

Richard turned away, gazing upstream. They were nearing Sheen now, just a few miles west of the city. It was his grandfather's favorite palace; he had died at Sheen after having spent more than 2000 pounds renovating it. A sprawling collection of free-standing timber buildings flanked two courts, and King Edward had built special accommodations for his

154

favored courtiers. The postern gate next to Down Court stood ready to receive them.

Richard held out a hand for Anne and they disembarked together. "I'm glad you are wearing your traveling clothes," he said. "There's something I want to show you." While the boats were unloaded, the royal couple walked along the riverside. He pointed at an island in the middle of the Thames. "I used to go there when I was a child. I know every inch of that island." He turned, waving at Burley. "Come nearer, Simon." His old tutor joined them, smiling. "Do you remember my old adventures on La Neyt?"

"Ah, I remember when you played pirates with your cousin Henry and young Robert. You borrowed boats so you could row back and forth and chase each other across the island. Of course, you had help with your boat."

Richard laughed. "You helped, if I remember. I needed your strong arm to keep up with Henry." His face darkened momentarily. Henry was always ahead of him, especially in feats of strength. Simon would take the oars from Richard, letting the prince catch his breath.

The king shook his head, ridding himself of unpleasant memories. "Simon, I would like to show La Neyt to Anne. Would you get us a boat?"

Simon strode back to the dock, summoning help. He returned with Robert and Agnes while a small vessel was being prepared. "There you are, your Grace," Agnes said. "I was looking for you."

"Come with us," Richard said. "There is something I want to show the queen. And I need you, Simon."

Curious, the little party kept asking questions but Richard smiled, refusing to answer. "You'll see," he kept saying as they crossed the narrow span of river. The island was long and forested, had a natural beach and a shallow draught, perfect for their boat. Richard helped Anne step out of the vessel as she held up her skirt, trying not to get her feet wet. Robert just swept Agnes up into his arms, for her dress was much less cumbersome than the queen's; he grinned widely as he walked to the edge of the sand, placing her daintily on the grass.

155

There was an opening in the trees ahead; Richard took Anne's hand and led the way. They passed into a gentle mead, unseen from the boat. On two sides the trees stood straight and tall, while before them the foliage thinned, giving a long-distance view of the rolling countryside beyond the Thames.

"It's beautiful," breathed Anne.

"I intend to build a Royal Lodging here, just for you and me. We will use it to enjoy our solitude. I will build it out of the rarest timbers, with a fireplace in every room, and I have plans for a bath house lined with painted tiles." He turned to Burley. "Like my grandfather, I will renovate our royal palaces, make them more suitable to our current needs. We will start here, at Sheen. Tomorrow I will give orders to the Wardrobe for the necessary payments."

Anne adjusted her cloak, pulling it tight. She saw no need for improvements to the old palace, but she was pleased by Richard's excitement. As long as he was happy, she was happy.

"You are cold," Richard said, putting an arm around her shoulder. "Come, we will talk more on this after we warm up."

CHAPTER 4

After Richard's marriage, the continual council—imposed on him since his coronation—fell into disuse, which suited him perfectly. With a wife came more responsibility, and he was chafing to rule on his own. Although he was sometimes constrained by his interfering uncles, Richard often turned to his closest associates who were more than willing to do his bidding. He could look with pride on his growing affinity. Naturally he could rely on Simon Burley, his vice-chamberlain who attended him regularly and controlled access to the chamber. His steward, Sir Hugh, acted for him in Parliament and took over judicial capacities. Robert de Vere and Thomas Mowbray were his boon companions, as well as Sir Ralph Stafford, all of whom were raised as wards in Edward III's court. His ten chamber knights guarded him and attended him when they weren't needed to perform special duties. Nicholas Brembre, one of his heroes from the Great Revolt, had become quite useful in dealing with the tempestuous Londoners. His clerics of the chamber took care of his religious needs and gave him good counsel. His secretaries were adept at managing the administrative work that needed his attention. He had his signet seal to express his wishes to other officers.

By 1383, Richard had a new chancellor: Michael de la Pole. He was already comfortable with Michael as his advisor, and since the man had proven himself such a competent and exceptional administrator, it was a short step to the chancellorship. Better than that, Michael treated the young King with respect and showed a willingness to cooperate with his wishes. His appointment in Parliament aligned precisely with Richard's plans.

In fact, Richard was beginning to think that perhaps he could concentrate all the king's business within his chamber. Let the magnates deal with the war and foreign affairs; he had his own priorities and could build up the crown's power with his inner circle.

Alas, he reasoned without his barons. The young king was soon to learn that those magnates, denied access to his chamber, took great offense to his exclusionary behavior. Richard may have been building his own court faction, but there were those in the government determined to keep the upper hand.

At first glance, the Salisbury Parliament of 1384 started out fairly routine. Richard presided while Chancellor Michael de la Pole told the gathering that another temporary truce had been secured with France.

"Now that Duke John of Lancaster has enforced the peace with the Scots," Michael continued, "we may start negotiations for a permanent peace treaty with France." He turned to Richard as if to confirm his approval, then continued. "It only remains to decide on the terms. King Richard does not wish to conclude this business without your consent and knowledge, as far as it is possible."

The Commons grumbled uncertainly. A permanent peace was by no means agreeable to all. On the one hand, they would appreciate relief from war taxation. Things had not gone well for many years, and financial losses were exorbitant. But on the other hand, after the glories of King Edward III, it felt like cowardice to ask for peace. Richard moved around in his chair, fighting his impatience. Were they always to be like this, quibbling and squabbling about every little thing?

Michael de la Pole was relentless. "Put yourself in the king's place," he urged. "What would you do if faced by so many successful enemies and almost no recent victories?"

The Commons were unwilling to commit themselves. Let the Lords declare that they preferred peace to war and the Commons would not argue. Much discussion went back and forth, but it was clear they were not making any progress.

In disgust, the Earl of Arundel stood up. "We are in this situation with France because we have no leadership! Our kingdom lacks good government and is wasting away! If something is not done about it soon, our country will be in grave danger and collapse completely."

What was this? Richard couldn't believe what he was hearing. His reign began deeply in debt thanks to mismanagement in the last years of Edward III's life. And now *he* was blamed? Arundel was himself one of the captains who failed to distinguish himself in the recent French campaigns.

Shaking with rage, the king leapt to his feet and pointed a finger at the earl. "If you are saying it's my fault that England has suffered from bad governance, you are lying in your teeth! You can go to hell!"

Clenching his fists, Richard looked around him, sensing the crushing disapproval. Michael de la Pole dropped his papers on the table. Arundel's face had blanched and the muscles around his left eye quivered. All stared at the king except for John of Gaunt, who sat rubbing his forehead with his hand. Richard sat down.

The hush was deafening until Gaunt stood, pushing his bench away. "Sire," he said as soothingly as he could, "what the earl meant to say was that reform has been slow in coming. Since the beginning of your reign the Earl of Arundel has been committed to the economy of the royal household. He suggests that you be guided by the great magnates as well as your personal council, though of course the final decisions rest with you."

Richard knew that Gaunt was trying to cozen him, but he also knew he had gone too far before Parliament. He turned his head, gesturing for deliberations to proceed, and he could hear collective breaths released as one. There was little more business to be done this day anyway. Everyone was relieved when the Bishop of Salisbury announced that they would hold high mass that afternoon in the cathedral. All stood as Richard took his leave, trailed by de Vere and his other officers.

As the door slammed behind the king, Gaunt turned to the earl. "What possessed you to do that?" he growled. Gaunt had been thinking something similar, though he wasn't boorish enough to insult the king. Why did Arundel have to antagonize Richard at every opportunity?

The other sat down heavily. "I just couldn't hold it inside anymore." He sighed, licking his dry lips. "He's surrounding himself with those... knaves. Ignoring our advice. We deserve better than this, John!"

Gaunt frowned at him. "That may be, but attacking him is no way to get the king on our side. We need to gain his trust, not inflame his temper."

"I know. I know. But it had to be said."

"No, it did not." Shaking his head, Gaunt turned away. It was just as well; the scornful grimace on Arundel's face would have sparked another unneeded feud.

Later that day, quite a tumult was building outside Robert de Vere's town house. The king was staying with the Earl of Oxford, and the members of Parliament gathered there to wait for him; they were to stage a grand procession to the cathedral for mass. During the delay, bishops moved from noble to noble soliciting donations for their private charities. Priests were swinging incense holders; clerks tried to coax people back into line. Everyone kept watching the sky, for the clouds were thickening and no one wanted to get caught in the rain. An hour passed. Then another hour. The first raindrops fell.

The archbishop approached John of Gaunt. "I think it's time to cancel our procession. Perhaps you should approach the king," he said. "Something may be amiss."

John nodded in agreement, though had he known what was going on at that moment in Robert's chambers, he may very well have headed in the opposite direction. They had already survived one outburst this day; but that was nothing compared to what was about to occur.

Robert had his hands full trying to pacify the king. They were all in his receiving chamber; Queen Anne and her ladies, two clerks of his chapel, Simon Burley, John Montague, the king's seneschal, and a few of his esquires. The room was hushed as Richard paced back and forth, still seething.

"How dare he! How dare that man speak to me like that! And to think my uncle defended him!" Just to emphasize his words, he stamped on the floor.

"Sire," said Robert. "You know I'm not fond of your uncle. Nonetheless, I think he was just trying to bring order to the proceedings. Everyone knows that Arundel is a vindictive, jealous man. He would take any opportunity to malign you."

"He didn't even make sense," Richard fumed. "My ministers have only been in office a few months; many of our difficulties date back to my grandfather's reign. But make no mistake. I knew it was an attack on me, thinly veiled though it was. Oh, I despise that man!"

"His time will come, assuredly." Robert reached for a chalice of wine and offered it to the king.

At that moment, a knock on the door was followed by a knight, whose job it was to announce visitors. "Sire, a Carmelite friar asks to speak with you. He says it is urgent."

Richard raised his eyebrows to de Vere, who shrugged. "All right then. Let him in."

The knight moved aside and a friar entered confidently, dressed in the white robes of his order. Brandishing a staff, he strode up to Richard.

"I have the gravest information for you."

Richard frowned. "What is your name?"

"I am John Latimer." Judging by his accent he was apparently from Ireland. "Sire, there is a plot against your life. The citizens of London and Coventry led by Sir John of Gaunt have conspired to seize and dethrone you, or even put you to death, so Gaunt can take the throne for himself. Your life is in danger!"

Richard's face grew redder and redder until the friar stopped speaking. Then he stamped his foot again. "That's it!" he shouted. "Arrest my uncle Gaunt and execute him. At once!"

The room filled with objections. Simon was the closest to the king and he leaned toward Richard's ear. "You cannot put your uncle to death without a trial." Richard shook his head while others surrounded him, pleading for restraint. Even Queen Anne came up and took his arm though she didn't speak. Robert approached his other ear. "This is not the time for rash deeds," he cautioned. "Wait and see." The clerics came near and added their voices to the pleas for mercy.

The door was still ajar and at that moment John of Gaunt brushed past the guard. He stopped short at the sight before him. Richard stood with his hands clenched, trembling with rage or

161

fear—he couldn't tell which. The king was surrounded by courtiers who were trying to calm him down.

A friar spun around as he entered. "There is the villain! Seize him or he will cause your death," he shouted, pointing at John.

Gaunt was astonished. His mouth even fell open for a moment. But he was a man of action and he strode forward.

"Who is this man that accuses me?"

Richard was still upset. "This friar claims that you are plotting to kill me."

"What! This is an outrage!"

The door was filling with curious witnesses, when suddenly Thomas of Woodstock pushed his way through the crowd. He drew his sword, advancing on the friar. "Hold! I will cut down anyone who accuses my brother, even if it's the king himself!"

Richard looked askance at Thomas and willed himself to calm down. He was starting to feel foolish.

But Gaunt wasn't finished. "I swear my innocence before God. I never had any ill intentions against the king! Why would I do such a thing? Your enemies couldn't make me richer in lands and honors than I already am in your service." He surveyed the room. "I declare myself willing to prove my innocence by wager of battle!"

John's incredulity was too genuine to be disbelieved. Richard turned on the friar in anger.

"Take this man and execute him!" he cried. Burley and Montague grabbed the Carmelite by the arms.

"No. Wait." Gaunt raised a hand. "We need to find out who has instigated this plot against my honor. Who is behind this accusation?" He advanced on the friar who recoiled, bumping up against de Vere. He had lost his confident demeanor; involuntarily, he lowered his head and hunched his shoulders.

"Who is responsible for this allegation?" Gaunt repeated.

The Carmelite shifted his eyes around and stopped at the duke, captured by his black gaze. "Um, I was told that you were leading a conspiracy of Londoners and other cities to usurp and kill the king."

"Who told you?"

"It was...William Lord Zouche of Harringworth."

162

John straightened up, his spine stiff as a tree. "Lord la Zouche! Montague, summon Lord la Zouche. I know he is here."

The seneschal left the room. John turned to a clerk. "Get some writing materials. I would have this man record his story."

Burley led the friar over to a table and everyone stared at him as he started to write, though his script was unintelligible. Finally, Montague returned with Lord la Zouche, who had been abed with an illness. The knight knelt before the king.

"Sire, what is your will?"

"Lord la Zouche, this man has claimed that you have knowledge of a plot against my life?"

"A plot? Most certainly not."

"This friar tells us that you have instructed him to warn me."

"About a plot? I know nothing about a plot against your life."

"Do you know this man?"

"I have never seen him before in my life."

Richard could feel his temper rising again. "Are you certain?"

"Sire, I deny this man's story and am ready to defend my honor with my life."

Gaunt put a hand on his shoulder. "That will not be necessary, Lord la Zouche. I believe you."

"Thank you, my Lord." Glaring at the Carmelite, Lord la Zouche took his leave.

"What do you have to say for yourself," the king asked impatiently. "I warn you, Friar Latimer. My patience is at an end."

The Carmelite stared at the floor for a moment, then raised his eyes to the king. "I was also told by Peter, squire to the Earl of Oxford."

It was Robert's turn to step forward. "You lie!" he spat, raising an arm to strike him. Richard put out a hand to stop him. "I knew nothing of this," Robert assured the king. "This man is desperate to throw off the blame."

Richard noticed that the others were eyeing de Vere suspiciously. He took a step toward Latimer. "Who else are you going to blame?"

The friar was growing frantic, turning from one accuser to another. Suddenly, breaking loose from his restraints, he started running around the room searching for an escape. He shouted nonsense at the top of his lungs while dashing over to a window. He pushed open the shutters, threw his hat and cloak outside, then pulled of his shoes, hurling them after. He was about to climb onto the window sill when two men pulled him back.

Gaunt grunted in disgust. "He seeks to feign madness."

Exhausted, the friar slid to the floor. Richard waved his hand in dismissal. "Lords Burley and Montague, take this man to Salisbury castle. Perhaps a day or two in isolation will loosen his tongue."

Nothing loath, the two men roughly seized the Carmelite and pushed him from the room. As they were leaving the building, they ran across John Holland, the king's half-brother and four other knights.

"What conspires here?" asked Holland.

Burley tightened his grip. "This friar has accused Duke John of plotting to murder the king. We are taking him to Salisbury castle."

"John of Gaunt? He is many things, but never a conspirator. Who is behind this?" Holland bent his face close to Latimer, a fierce glint in his eye. "You seek to cause strife in our court. Someone has suborned you against Gaunt. Who is it?"

The Carmelite pursed his lips refusing to answer.

Holland scowled. "This is intolerable. We must make this man talk." He gestured to his companions and the whole group crowded together as they hauled the increasingly alarmed friar to the castle.

John Smith, warden of the castle, led the prisoner and his keepers into a large cell deep in the dungeon. While he lit torches Holland seized the friar and shoved him backwards; chains with shackles hung from the wall and the knights roughly snapped the iron bands around Latimer's wrists. Burley and Montague stood against the door and watched; this was a messy business and they did not want to participate. The others seemed more than capable of making the friar confess. Jerking his head, Burley dismissed the warden.

Latimer stood with his arms raised above his head, staring at the floor. Holland grabbed a handful of hair and forced the friar to look at him.

164

"Don't make this harder on yourself," he snarled. "Just tell us who is behind these accusations?"

Clamping his mouth shut, Latimer stared at his interrogator.

The other increased the pressure on his hair. "Who are you protecting? Why? No one is going to help you now."

Silence.

"I see you need a little more persuading. Thomas, start a coal fire in the trough." The room was well-equipped for torture. While the others got the fire going, Holland pulled out a dagger. "You must understand, Friar Latimer, that you are not leaving this room until you tell us who sent you." He placed the point on the prisoner's cheek and drew it slowly down. A thin red line followed the knife, dripping blood on the friar's white robe. "You must tell us," Holland reiterated, drawing a matching cut on the other cheek. Still no response.

One can only imagine what happened during the long night of torture. Even after several hours John Latimer refused to talk. Eventually, Holland was so exhausted by his efforts that he resorted to roasting the friar's feet over a coal fire. By dawn, the Warden of the castle—himself a hardened man—was so appalled that he finally intervened and demanded they hand the prisoner over to him. But it was too late; the friar slipped into a coma and died a few days later. It was said that both Richard and Gaunt shed tears when hearing of the friar's terrible end.

In de Vere's chamber, as the friar was dragged away, the air was heavy with suspicion. John of Gaunt faced the king, his face flushed and his eyes flashing.

"How could you possibly believe such nonsense? And from such a source!"

Embarrassed, Richard turned away.

"The man is obviously mad," John pursued. "How could I possibly even conceive of a plot to kill my own nephew?"

Richard blinked back at him, tears of frustration in his eyes. "You know I was already distressed from this afternoon. I was unprepared for the friar's accusation."

"And you acted like an unprincipled child! Sire, you must remember your rank." Not trusting himself further, Gaunt bowed and left the room followed by Thomas of Woodstock and their retainers. Thomas threw an angry look over his shoulder.

But Richard no longer payed attention to his uncles. Exhausted, he sat heavily on his portable throne. "Am I ever to be tormented by those old men?" He leaned toward Robert who shook his head. "They provoke me at every turn."

Taking Gaunt's withdrawal as their signal, others in the room started to leave. Robert acted the host and gracefully aided their departure with cheerful observations. Only the king's intimate circle remained. "You may go," Richard muttered, dismissing his pages. "Oh, bring some wine before you leave."

Anne sat by his side, taking his hand. "It all happened so quickly. You are not to blame."

Swallowing his anger, he smiled briefly at her. "My dear wife." He squeezed her fingers, comforted that Anne was next to him. But even she couldn't remove the sick feeling in his stomach—that feeling one gets having done something so wrong that no excuse will ever make it go away. How could he have condemned John of Gaunt to death without even a second thought? Did he hate his uncle that much?

He picked up Anne's hand, kissing it. "He scolded me and I deserved it," he murmured, so quietly no one else heard. "I was so quick to believe the friar. What is it about my uncle that makes me distrust him so?" He gazed into the queen's eyes but found no answer there. "Is it because he thinks himself my heir?"

"Surely not," Anne whispered.

"And yet, in the eyes of many, he is. At least until we have a son of our own."

Anne blushed deeply. So far, her monthly cycle had been all too regular.

"Don't fret, my beloved. We are still young." He kissed her hand again.

As the last of the servants finished up their chores and brought benches forward, Robert sat near the royal couple. "Your uncles behaved abominably," he declared. "How dare Woodstock draw a sword in your presence?"

Richard pursed his lips. "The situation was unprecedented. But you are right. He has always tried to intimidate me, especially in my earliest years as king. I needed g-guidance then, not scorn. Arundel, too, curse his black soul."

"And Gaunt. What a tyrant. The sooner he goes back to the continent, the better."

The king shook his head. "Parliament can spare no funds for another misadventure. We'll have to find a better way to diminish the power of those who seek to hold me back."

Thomas Mowbray sat next to Robert. "It seems to me that the great nobles are already finding common cause against us. Sire, I believe they are already convinced they are losing influence. How often do you call on them for help? How often do you heed their advice?"

"Never, if I can help it," Richard said emphatically, adjusting his sleeve. "They forget I am already seventeen years old. My grandfather was eighteen when he started to reign on his own."

The others stared at each other, suddenly abashed. They knew that Edward III's strength sprang from a close, tight-knit group of supporters who bolstered his throne. All sons and heirs of great houses, they were instrumental in his coup against the traitor Roger Mortimer, who tried to rule in his stead. Edward could depend on friends who were united in serving him—unlike Richard's combative courtiers.

Mowbray looked askance at Robert; the rivalry between them was well-known. Robert took delight in edging Thomas out of the way whenever possible. Mowbray had a tendency to pout whenever he didn't get his way, which didn't help matters. Richard tried to humor him, but his sullen temper ruined his chances of besting Robert. Now that Richard was king, he did his best to hide his rancor—but only with mixed success.

Pushing a shock of black hair out of his eyes, Mowbray cleared his throat. "What I fear is an alliance between your nobles that could threaten you. We must tread carefully..."

"And do what?" snorted Robert. "They are more protective of their rights than a bear guarding its young."

"Give them reason to support you. Give them titles. That should disarm them."

Richard pondered this. "Do you think so? Do you think I could win them over?"

At first no one answered, but finally Mowbray nodded his head. "If you raised your other uncles to dukedoms, they would be a bulwark against Gaunt. How could they not appreciate your recognition of their rights?"

Richard grunted. "And what *about* my uncle Gaunt, who has everything?"

"Except the crown," muttered Robert.

Mowbray overrode him. "He's interested in the crown of Castile, not England." He paused, considering. "If he were to go to Spain, however, that would keep him busy..."

Richard stood, gazing at Thomas thoughtfully. "Could there be any truth to the friar's conspiracy? I think my uncle hates me. He probably trusts me as little as I trust him."

"After tonight," Robert said, "he will assuredly be on his guard. I wonder who was behind that accusation?" He tried not to notice that many in the room regarded him suspiciously. Richard wasn't one of them; he was all that mattered.

After Salisbury, John of Gaunt went back to France to negotiate a new truce, while Richard returned to London, eaten up with doubt. For the moment, everyone maintained a steady and even course—that is, until the Great Council met at Waltham after Christmas. The meeting was well attended: Chancellor Michael de la Pole was present, as well as all three of Richard's uncles, including Gaunt, who had just returned.

Duke John got right to the point. "I met with four Dukes of France: Berry, Burgundy, Bourbon, and Brittany. Castile was there, and Scotland, as well as Navarre and Flanders. They were unwilling to consider a new truce, and merely extended the current one until May."

He paused while the councilors talked among themselves. "I do not feel that they are trustworthy," he went on. "At first I thought they were going to negotiate since financially they are in dire straits. However, my informants tell me that King Charles VI is planning an attack against our coast, and I discovered that he has already sent 1600 French lancers to Scotland commanded by Jeanne de Vienne. I believe their plan is to attack us simultaneously from the south and the north."

This was indeed bad news. Chancellor Pole leaned forward. "What do you suggest?"

Gaunt was ready. "I recommend a royal expedition to France, led by the king himself. If we do nothing, they will cross the Channel and crush us. Attacking is our best form of defense."

There was scant enthusiasm for his words. Richard Arundel stood. "I believe the king should stay in his own country. He would risk much going to France." Voices of agreement rose after this statement.

"An expedition to Scotland would serve our purpose well," Pole suggested. "If we remove the threat from the north, the French would be unsupported."

"The king has not been north of Nottingham," Archbishop Courtney said. "It would be good for his people in York to see his presence there, especially after the Great Rising. It would enhance the influence of the crown."

"He could go at any time," Gaunt said impatiently. "There must be no delay invading France. As you know, our Flemish allies have captured the port of Damme; they will not be able to hold it without our assistance. If they are pushed back by the French, their whole offensive will be overturned."

"Another risky venture! For many years our losses in France have been expensive and unproductive," said Chancellor Pole. "You and I have fought there together. Even with the Black Prince's leadership, our campaigns accomplished nothing. The Commons are clamoring to reduce taxes, and our government has not cleared our old war debts. I say we should continue to seek a settlement with France. I think we would have better results in Scotland."

The room filled with arguments. Richard stood, holding out a hand. "I am confident that we should go to Scotland."

Everyone had forgotten that Scotland sheltered John of Gaunt during the Great Revolt. He did not relish invading his former protectors. "I will not go!" he shouted, trying to be heard. "Expect no support from me unless we go to France."

169

Angered, many in the room shouted back at him, raising their fists in the air. But Duke John was adamant. He turned on his heels and stormed out of the room. The din quickly diminished to grumbling. The council members exchanged uncertain glances; no matter how unpopular, Gaunt was still the leading peer of the realm. Richard took several deep breaths, trying to control his temper. Once again his uncle had gotten the better of him. He stared at Robert de Vere, and his friend stared back, convinced that Richard was trying to tell him something.

Later that evening, in the shadowy corner of council chamber, a small group of men put their heads together. Robert de Vere led the discussion, and occasionally the opposing voice of Thomas Mowbray was raised in concern. Chief Justice Tresilian could be seen shaking his head, and Richard's chamber knights did little more than lend their assent.

"With Gaunt's resistance to everything the king proposes, our councils will be continually torn asunder. All of his concerns are aimed at the continent, where he can fight his private battles. Everything he does is to benefit his Castilian ambitions!" Robert dropped a fist onto his knee to emphasize his words. "He must be stopped."

Mowbray grunted. "And how do propose to stop him?"

"His actions against the king are treasonable. Justice Tresilian, I have called you here for a reason." No one spoke. De Vere considered each one of them in turn. "We must arrest John of Gaunt and have him tried for treason. Once he is convicted, his execution will remove the source of King Richard's problems. Would you agree that few men would object to his removal?"

More silence. Finally, Tresilian took a deep breath. "Treason. Well, there are precedents."

"True. Back in Edward II's day Thomas of Lancaster was executed. And he was much more popular than Gaunt."

"It will not be easy convicting him of treason," mused Mowbray.

"Chief Justice, can you persuade your associates to support your judgment?"

After thinking about it, Tresilian nodded. "As long as we prepare a suitable guilty verdict, I believe I can convince them."

170

"Good." De Vere crossed his arms, satisfied. "There only remains the question of where and when."

"At Westminster," Nicholas Bonde, one of Richard's chamber knights interjected. "On the 13th and 14th of February the king is holding a tournament."

"Ah, yes. We can arrange a council meeting and summon Duke John to attend. When he shows up, we can arrest him and arraign him for treason." De Vere glanced around, expecting confirmation. "It will be quickly done, and with the Chief Justice in attendance he will be even more quickly sentenced."

"Then the king can rule unimpeded," Tresilian said, coming to terms with his disagreeable task. He was no stranger to unsavory judgments. The Great Revolt had cured him of that.

They spent some more time working on the particulars and deciding who else to involve in their conspiracy. "Do we tell the king?" asked Thomas Mowbray.

Robert shook his head. "He is not to know, but he hopes we can do something to release him from this predicament. He trusts me to find a way."

Mowbray was satisfied. If something was to go wrong, Robert would bear the blame. Many people—high and low—resented de Vere for dominating the king's attention. It wouldn't take much for that resentment to grow into retribution. And he would be there to see its fulfillment.

February's Westminster tournament came and went yet John of Gaunt was nowhere to be seen. The council meeting was held as planned, though without the duke's presence nothing could be resolved. Robert de Vere did his best to pretend that nothing was amiss, and the king was too vexed to notice any backroom discussions between the co-conspirators. Richard sent out messengers and discovered that his uncle had ridden to his castle at Pontefract, far to the north.

Suspecting that something was wrong, Richard finally summoned Robert to meet him in his chambers, alone. He was of two minds; yes, he wanted de Vere to help him figure out what to do about his uncle. On the other hand he feared how far his friend would go. Murder was a common way of dealing with an enemy, but surely this was not one of his options. On the other hand, they had never had that kind of discussion.

Standing with his back to the fireplace, Richard nodded as his friend entered the room. "There you are. I think you have something to tell me."

Robert paced the floor uncomfortably. He didn't know where to start.

"It's not an accident that my uncle didn't show up for the council meeting."

Considering the implications, Robert shook his head. "No, sire. It was not an accident."

The king waited. "Well?"

"Well, we had hoped to solve your problem. With the duke."

"I concede he is a problem. What did you do?"

"He was to be arrested and tried for treason."

Richard gasped, despite himself. "Such audacity!"

"It could have worked. Tresilian was ready."

"I doubt it. Nothing my uncle has done falls within the Statute of Treason. My grandfather enacted it to avoid situations just like this one. Tresilian knows that." He pursed his lips, adjusting a sleeve. "But it doesn't seem to matter, does it? Someone obviously warned him."

Robert nodded, afraid to look at the king. "Evidently so."

"Hmm. You know that according to Edward III's entail, my uncle of Lancaster is heir to the throne. At least until I have children."

Surprised, the other blinked. "No, I didn't know that."

"Very few people do, except for the witnesses. My grandfather settled the order of succession in the male line, which excludes any heirs from my aunt Philippa—that would be the Mortimers. Anyway, there was not much point in publishing the entail, considering the unpopularity of my uncle Gaunt. I don't want it known, especially since I detest that clan." He scratched the back of his neck. "Well, detest might be too strong a word. But that's one reason I believed the Carmelite Friar when he said that Gaunt was plotting my death."

He started pacing back and forth before the fireplace. "You can see the difficulty if my uncle is killed—especially for a trumped-up charge of treason." He paused, sighing. "I would be held responsible."

Robert gulped hard, almost afraid to move. But Richard didn't seem too angry or he would have known by now.

"No more talk of killing my uncle, or arresting him, or God Forbid accusing him of treason. Now that I know what has happened, I'm going to have to submit to his scolding, which is sure to come."

Richard was not mistaken on that account. After the tournament was over, he moved his household to Sheen. Ten days after his arrival, Richard's sergeant-at-arms espied movement on the opposite shore of the Thames. Though the sun was setting there was still enough light to distinguish a large body of armed men led by John of Gaunt's unmistakable banner. He reported the duke's arrival but, considering the apparent stealth surrounding the newcomers, Richard decided not to acknowledge them.

John of Gaunt ordered the bulk of his force to stand guard where they were, ready to act if called upon. He wasn't expecting any real trouble, but he needed to be certain. The king's ferry was on his side of the river and he took a score of men with him, leaving ten at the water gate and taking the rest inside as an escort. All wore breastplates under their jupons. The royal guards politely asked him to wait while they announced his presence. Meticulously correct, John agreed.

They didn't have to tarry long. "Please come with me," said the sergeant, leading the duke and his retainers into the great hall. Richard was sitting on his throne next to Queen Anne. His favorite chamber knights stood beside them as well as a few courtiers that John didn't recognize. He ignored them.

The sergeant stood aside and Gaunt strode forward, his men in a tight formation behind him. He stopped before the king but did not bow.

Richard sat up straight in his throne. "Why do you dare bring armed men into my presence?"

The duke stared at him with those icy black eyes. "I was warned that there was a plot against my life. I feared for my safety."

"Another plot? Is that why you refused to show up at my council meeting?"

John said nothing, still staring.

"Why are there so many plots against your life?"

"You must ask those who surround you, who will let no one else into your presence."

"On my life, I know of no plot against you, uncle."

"I would that I could be reassured. It seems that I am beleaguered by men wishing me harm." He took a step forward. "I will tell you this: it is shameful that you, the embodiment of the law, would countenance such intemperate behavior among your own councilors. For shame, I say! It's time you learned the difference between right and wrong. Get rid of these scoundrels and find some wise and loyal advisors who would forswear lawless actions."

He stepped back again, waiting for Richard to show his temper. But much to everyone's surprise, the king relaxed in his throne. "Uncle," he said mildly, "your words are strong but just. I will concede that these have been difficult times for us all." He paused, silently amused at the surprise on Gaunt's face. "I promise you that I will act more justly in the f-future so that you will cease to find fault with me."

John waited, expecting Richard to say something more. "Well, see that you do," he finally said, nonplussed. Then his voice grew stern again. "Until I see signs of reform, you will not see me at the council again."

And at that, the duke whirled around and led his men from the hall. Once he was safely out of sight, Richard slumped into his throne. Anne gestured for someone to bring wine.

"He was very wroth," she said softly.

Richard took a goblet from his page. "I expected as much," he said, trying to sound reassuring, "after his absence at Waltham." He took a sip, knowing he should explain Robert's involvement while feeling a bit ashamed for his friend. "I wish mother was here," he said finally. "She would know what to do."

174

"Let us write to her. If anyone can reason with your uncle, it would be her."

The next day a messenger rode off with a sealed message to Princess Joan.

But for now, little more could be done to help the situation. Another council meeting was scheduled at Westminster the following week, and he had no choice but to attend. As far as Richard knew, the French treaty was on the agenda, though as soon as Archbishop Courtney and his pack of bishops lined up in their episcopal regalia, he saw they had something else on their minds.

"Your Grace," the archbishop droned in his most forbidding tone, "my colleagues and I feel compelled to speak to you about your reckless behavior. You surround yourself with sly and unscrupulous companions who will stop at nothing to attempt an assassination of anyone who stands in their way. Such plots undermine the laws and customs of this kingdom!"

Richard stood, trembling with ill-concealed rage. "Archbishop Courtenay," he growled, "this meeting is over. Next time we meet, if you value your position, you had better be prepared to discuss the business we have assembled for. Uncle," he said, turning to Woodstock, "I believe we have a meeting with the Mayor of London."

CHAPTER 5

Sir Nicholas Brembre and his wife Idonia lived in a grand
mansion in the Vintry, just upstream from London Bridge and the
second richest ward in the city. Their lifestyle was as elegant as it
was ostentatious and even the king appreciated an invitation to
dinner. Brembre did not disappoint. In between courses of swan
and salmon and stuffed capons, Richard and his uncle were treated
to samples from the mayor's renowned wine cellar, and
afterwards, figs and raisins pureed in sherry. All this was in
preparation for business, and Brembre was expecting another
request for a loan. This was all right, for he had a request of his
own.

"Sire," he began after the king's needs were taken care of, "as
you know, John of Northampton has been threatening the city
with riot and disorder as my reelection approaches."

"Northampton again," Richard murmured.

"I have learned that he has instructed his followers—the ones
not even eligible to vote—to congregate at the Guildhall that day.
They are to be armed and intend to attack anyone not belonging to
their faction, driving them away."

"We cannot have that. I do not want Northampton in charge
again. He has caused nothing but trouble."

"Then with your approval, I intend to take measures to stop
his disruptions. I will hide my own armed men in the back rooms.
If Northampton causes no problems, they will go home. But if he
tries to upset my election, I will order my men to drive them from
the hall, and take their argument to the streets if necessary. If
troublemakers are gathering and disturbing the peace, I intend to
arrest a few of them and chain them up in Newgate—just to make
an example of them."

Richard shrugged. "Do whatever is required. You have my
support."

Nicholas smiled, relieved. It was good to be one of the king's
strongest allies. Between them, London would be a more

manageable place to do business. If only they could keep it that way.

An excellent meal and new loan went a long way toward settling Richard's temper—that is, until they returned back to Westminster, taking the royal barge up the Thames. The king and his uncle were accompanied by Sir John Devereux and Thomas Trivet—more old campaigners of the Black Prince—whose company Richard liked. As they passed the mouth of the Fleet River the spring breezes brought with them a stench of excrement and muck. The king covered his nose with a handkerchief.

"This is outrageous," he grumbled. "There is such an abundance of dung and *laystalls* along the banks that it is surely a peril to everyone who must work on the river. We must bring the matter before the council, uncle." He was turning toward Woodstock when his face changed, becoming hard. "Oh, no," he said with a groan.

"What?" Thomas looked around. Then he saw it. Coming from Lambeth Palace, the archbishop's barge—smaller but gilded and painted like the king's—was approaching from upstream. No wonder Richard groaned; he was still irritated about the unpleasant council meeting earlier that day. Thomas thought for a moment. "Sire," he said carefully, "we cannot have you at odds with the Archbishop of Canterbury. Let us take advantage of this opportunity to reconcile the two of you."

Courtenay was the last person Richard wanted to talk to right now. *He's an interfering old goat and he always sounds like he's complaining.* The man's voice never failed to irritate. Still, he would never get anything done without the cooperation of the Church. Feeling petulant, Richard reluctantly gave in and Thomas flagged the other boat. The royal barge dropped anchor and the other pulled aside. Archbishop Courtenay was grasping a cloak around his shoulders. His discomfort was unmistakable.

"What is it?"

"Your Grace, come aboard and speak with the king." Thomas turned toward Richard. "I guarantee the archbishop's safety," he said loudly, more as an admonishment to the king than reassurance to Courtney. Richard nodded.

177

Some of the bargemen grasped the gunnel of the royal boat and pulled them together while others helped Courtenay clamber ungracefully over the side. He risked an exasperated glance at Thomas before regaining his composure.

"I thought I would take the air this evening," he said lamely. Richard didn't answer and Courtney decided to quit wasting time. "Sire. I consider this unexpected meeting a Godsend, for it gives me the chance to speak with you as a father to a son." He paused, waiting for a response and still receiving none. While he was talking the king had gradually turned, observing the far bank; the archbishop was so disconcerted that he opened and shut his mouth like a gasping fish. If he had seen the expression on Richard's face, he surely would have gone back to his own barge. But, deprived of that warning, he felt committed and pressed forward, hoping to make himself understood. "I know you are young and inexperienced in the ways of the world. I would recommend you follow the advice of those who are interested—nay, committed—to your wellbeing. A man of your authority should surround himself with—"

"With what?" Richard shouted, whirling around. "Who are you to correct me like a child? How dare you?" He was so angry that spittle flew from his mouth. Throwing back his cloak, the king tugged his sword free, pointing it at the archbishop's breast. If he had been closer, he might have followed through but Thomas of Woodstock was quicker, seizing his wrist. Sir John threw himself between the two while Trivit wrapped his arms around Richard's chest, heaving him back.

"Let go!" shouted the king, but no one obeyed. The archbishop scrambled over the side of the barge while Trivit disentangled the king's hand from his sword. He handed the blade to one of the household pages before releasing his grasp.

Richard turned on him in a righteous fury. "Traitors! Betrayers! You deserve to die for this! How dare you lay a hand on your sovereign! You shall answer for this!" His three guardians backed off and then, as one, scrambled into the other barge as the rowers pushed it away.

"Come back here! Stop those men! Traitors!" Throwing himself against the gunwale, he leaned over so far he nearly fell

178

into the river. No one dared interfere. Breathing heavily, Richard glared at the receding barge; his eyes practically bulged out of his head. Then he pushed himself up and turned around. Everyone on the boat was staring in shock, unable to move. He rearranged his circlet then held out a hand for his sword. Kneeling, the page returned it. Inspecting it for a moment, Richard carefully lined the blade up with the scabbard and pushed it in gently. "It's all right. Take me to the Palace." Breathing a sigh of relief, the bargemen went back to their business and raised the anchor.

Richard sat on a bench, annoyed with himself. Once again he had lost control of his temper. He knew that everyone would be talking about him, calling him young and foolish and much worse than that. He had heard all about his grandfather's temper—and Edward I—and all his forefathers back to Henry II. He was heir to their rage every bit as much as heir to the throne! But for some reason his wrath didn't seem to have the same effect on others. Maybe someday it would, when he was older. And stronger. Some day he would show them all he was a true Plantagenet.

As Richard had hoped, Princess Joan managed to convince John of Gaunt that it was in his best interest to forgive the king. They all met at Westminster and in a very public ceremony a formal peace was declared between the duke and all his adversaries. Meanwhile, it became clear there was not going to be a French offensive that year, though that didn't stop Jeanne de Vienne from raiding into Northumberland. He and the Scots were still a force to be reckoned with, even though King Robert II declared himself too ill to participate. It didn't matter; even without their king, plenty of Scottish nobles eagerly joined de Vienne, hoping for plunder. Resigned, Duke John agreed to join the English expedition, bringing a huge contingent.

Parliament agreed that it was time to throw all the country's resources at the north. This would entail calling up a feudal levy—for the last time in history, as events would prove. Richard would finally get a chance to lead an army in person, assisted of course by his great nobles. He put out a declaration that the whole baronage would assemble at Newcastle on July 14, 1385. This

179

was to be England's greatest show of strength, and the Scots knew from hard experience that a formal battle would be very hard-fought indeed.

Richard and his forces had reached the village of Beverly, just outside of York, when the first trouble began. As usual, lodging was in short supply and most of the army had to camp in the fields. Naturally, Queen Anne's Bohemian retainers were given priority though this raised much resentment among the rank-and-file. Crossing through the horse-camp that first evening, one of the queen's favorite knights, Sir Meles, was accosted by a pair of squires belonging to Sir John Holland.

"Where are you headed?" the first one protested, grabbing him by the arm. "The headquarters are over there, where my master resides."

Sir Meles pulled away. "It is no business of yours where I am going."

"But it is Sir John's business," the squire pursued. "Why are you quartered in town while good English lords must sleep under a tent?"

"I suggest you take your complaints to the king then. I must be on my way." Refusing to countenance any further impudence, Meles turned his back to the squires and strode off. They were discussing whether they should pursue him when two archers wearing the Earl of Stafford's livery interposed themselves between the squires and the retreating knight.

"We heard you just now," one of the archers said, pacing back and forth. "You did wrong to insult that knight. Don't you know he belongs to the queen?"

"What does it have to do with you?" the other retorted, spitting on the ground.

"It has plenty to do with us. He is a companion of our master, and I will not stand by and see him insulted."

"Rascal! If I thought you would help that foreigner against me, I would run this sword through your body!" As if to emphasize the point, the squire drew his blade and brandished it at the archer.

That was enough. The archer, who had already strung his bow, quickly pulled out an arrow and, without needing to aim, released the shaft. At that distance the arrow went almost all the way through the man's chest and he fell like a sack of grain, shot dead. His companion let out a yell and fled the way he came, leaving the archers staring at each other in consternation.

"What do we do now?" the other one said.

Unstringing his bow, the instigator grunted, his anger turning to vexation. "Let's leave the bastard here. He's no use to anybody. But we had better go to Sir Ralph de Stafford and explain ourselves before someone tells the earl his father."

The two archers reluctantly made their way back to the Stafford camp, agreeing on the story between themselves. Sir Ralph was comfortably seated before a fire when they came up, and he could tell from their bearing that something was wrong. He sighed, getting up.

"What happened?"

The archers exchanged glances and the first one stubbed his toe into the dirt. "Well, it's like this, Sir. Two of Sir Holland's squires showed disrespect to Sir Meles. You know, the queen's knight."

"Yes, I know Sir Meles. Did he have a hand in this, whatever you are about to tell me?"

"No, my Lord. He was walking away and they were about to follow him when we stopped them in their tracks. We exchanged words and before we knew it one of them drew his sword and I shot him dead with an arrow."

Sir Ralph frowned. "That was badly done."

"Well, Sir. I had rather I killed him than that he killed me."

Despite himself, a smile ran across Sir Ralph's face, quickly squelched. "Do this then. For now, go off where they can't find you. I will arrange peace with Sir John Holland, be it through my father or through others."

"Thank you, my Lord." They both bowed and ran off, getting swallowed up by the night.

Sir Ralph took a deep draught from his mug then placed it on the table with a thud. "I had better take care of this now, before it spreads all over the camp," he said to his squires. "Does anyone know where my father is?"

"The last I saw him he was with the king," one of them answered. "That was while it was still light."

"Stephen, Walter, come with me. The rest of you may enjoy your leisure." Ralph reached for his sword then shook his head, waving his hand in dismissal. "This should only take a minute," he said to Stephen. "He can't be far away."

Meanwhile, the surviving squire ran to Sir John Holland's pavilion, gulping for breath as he requested entrance. Sir John came out, himself, curious at the commotion. Seeing his squire's distress, his eyes narrowed. "Where is George?"

The squire bent over, steadying himself by his knees. "Killed," he gasped.

"What is this? My squire killed? Who is responsible for this deed?"

"One of Sir Ralph's archers was shot with an arrow. At the behest of Sir Meles."

"That Bohemian rake? Lording it over us like a pompous ass? Give me my sword," he shouted. "Never will I eat or drink until this be avenged!"

Holland's squires knew better than to dissuade him; every one of them had been the butt of his rage at one time or another. One ran for his sword, another for his belt and dagger. A third went for his horse.

"Make haste, you sluggards!" Striding back and forth, he kicked a piece of firewood into the flames; the flash on his face gave him the appearance of an evil spirit. "Come with me, all of you!"

Moving as fast as they could, John's squires dragged his horse forward and mounted their own. He leaped into the saddle, tugged at the reins and turned his horse around. "Where is that bastard Sir Meles?"

The others did not know and Holland kicked his mount into a trot. Every person he met he shouted the same question: "Where is Sir Meles lodged?" Most pulled away, shaking their heads, but finally a soldier pointed down the lane to the left.

"I think you will find him in the rear-guard with the Earl of Devonshire and the Earl of Stafford."

Without a word of thanks, Holland kicked his horse and his squires followed them. It was cloudy this night and they had difficulty telling where the camp was. Hedges and bushes hugged the lane and they had to ride single-file; more than once brambles caught against their garments. Finally they saw someone coming toward them.

"Who goes there?" the stranger called. "I am Stafford."

"And I am Holland," growled the other; one quarry was as good as another. "Stafford, I was searching for thee. Your archer has killed my squire who I loved best in all the world. You must answer for this!"

Ralph drew rein, alarmed. He reached for his sword then remembered he had left it in the tent. But he did not have time to withdraw. Without a moment's delay, Holland spurred his horse forward, drawing his blade. Roaring his rage, he slashed it down, catching Ralph in the neck. The blow went all the way to the bone and Sir Ralph Stafford crashed to the ground, dead before he could utter a sound.

Stafford's squire shrieked, falling back. "Holland, you have slain the Earl of Stafford's son! How am I going to tell his father?"

The men behind John milled around in consternation. "Sir, you have killed Sir Ralph de Stafford! He is the king's boon companion!"

"I can see that, dolt! So much the better! I would rather have killed him than one of lesser rank, for it gives more honor to my poor George."

Ralph's squires had already fled and Sir John sat for a moment, frowning at the corpse. "This will cause me a great deal of trouble. No doubt of that. I don't know how the king will react, even though he is my brother." He wiped his blade and resheathed it. "I had best find sanctuary at Beverly Minster." Holland's return was slower than his outward ride, for by now his rage had passed, leaving him with a great sorrow—not for the death of Ralph of Stafford, but for the trouble he had brought upon himself.

Sir John Holland went directly into sanctuary, heedless of the great turmoil that ensued once the Earl of Stafford learned of the death of his only son. Some of Ralph's dearest companions went to recover the body while the earl called together his friends and fellow nobles. He needed counsel on how he should avenge himself. His grief was overwhelming, especially when the mangled body of his beloved heir was laid out before him.

"Do nothing this night," he was advised. "We shall take care of Sir Ralph so that he is laid to rest as becomes his station."

The earl sobbed in grief, and his wise counselors did their best to comfort him who could feel no solace. He agreed to wait until morning so that he could recover his strength before confronting the king and demanding justice. All the bold and enterprising young knights bore great love for Sir Ralph, and in the morning all of his feudal levy came forward. Hundreds of soldiers poured out their grief as they brought him to a nearby village church and buried the youth with all funeral rites. Afterwards, the Earl of Stafford assembled sixty of his kin and retainers and rode to the king.

Richard had already been informed of the tragedy and was furious at his half-brother. He was surrounded by his uncles and great lords when the earl approached and dismounted. The poor man had aged overnight, and once again he burst into tears as he fell to his knees. "Thou art King of all England and thou hast solemnly sworn to maintain peace in the realm. You know how thy brother without cause or reason has slain my son and heir. Sire, you must do me justice, or else lose my friendship and support." He stopped for a moment, overcome. "You must know that the death of my son touches me so near that it's all I can do to restrain my revenge. I will not ruin this expedition to my lasting dishonor." He stood, looking up at the king for he was a short man. "For now, I will refrain so long as this expedition lasts, for I cannot suffer the Scots to rejoice at the misery of the Earl of Stafford. Otherwise, I would avenge myself so highly that men would talk of it for a hundred years to come."

The king put a hand on his shoulders; tears ran down his flushed face. "Earl of Stafford," he said, "I mourn with you because Sir Ralph was my dear friend and will be sorely missed. My queen will be disconsolate, for I know he was in her retinue. Be assured I will maintain your justice to the highest level, and not for any brother will I fail to do so. Sir John Holland is a murderer and shall be treated as such."

184

He turned to the assembled lords. "I hereby deprive John Holland of all his offices, confiscate his lands and declare him outlawed. Arrest him as soon as he steps outside of sanctuary."

Unbeknownst to Richard, one of Holland's squires was in the back of the hall. As soon as the king made his announcement, the faithful squire slipped away and rushed to the minster. He found Holland sitting at a table in the back of the church, sullenly dipping a piece of brown bread into a bowl of broth. On hearing the man's approach, he glanced up hopefully. "There you are, Piers. I hope you have some good tidings for me. Look at what they're making me eat in this wretched place."

Welcomed thus, Piers stopped short, suddenly unwilling to deliver his news. Seeing his face, Holland grunted. "The king did not take this well then, I assume."

The squire shook his head. "The old earl confronted him with threats of retribution. But King Richard was already most wroth and did not need further persuasion." He paused while Holland continued with his breakfast. "My Lord, the king has deprived you of all your offices and declared you an outlaw."

Sir John's hand stopped before he took another bite. He turned his head. "Me, an outlaw? My own brother has ruled against me?" Disgusted, he dropped the bread into his soup and pushed away the bowl. "My God, what am I to do?"

Neither spoke for a moment—Piers because he was afraid of the wrong reaction, Holland because he had expected to get away with murder. But he soon shook himself free of doubts.

"My mother will know what to do. She will write to the king." He pushed himself from the table. "Piers, I need you to take a message to her. She is in residence at Wallingford on the Thames."

As soon as he was equipped with money and a strong horse, Piers was on his way to Princess Joan. Sir John Holland had a long wait ahead of him, and he wrote his most eloquent letters to King Richard, begging for relief. No response was forthcoming.

On the 6th of August the royal force, almost 14,000 strong, crossed the Tweed into Scotland—a great day for King Richard, for he had finally led his own army on campaign. This should silence the nagging complaints that he loved peace over war. Now was the time to commemorate his accomplishment, and he chose this moment to stage a great assembly of nobles. The army spread out over a large field, with multi-colored pavilions and flapping standards. Knights tested their skills in tournaments while archers competed at the butts for a silver gilt horn. At midday, Richard called forth his uncles: Thomas of Woodstock, Earl of Buckingham, and Edmund of Langley, Earl of Cambridge. He also summoned Sir Michael de la Pole, Chamberlain.

Resplendent in a dark red houppelande and jeweled crown, Richard held a gold chain with a badge of office hanging from it. "Sir Edmund," he began as his uncle, fifth son of Edward III, knelt before him. "In recognition of your faithful service to the crown, I now declare you Duke of York along with the appurtenances belonging to your station." He placed the chain around York's neck. "Arise, Sir Edmund of Langley, Duke of York." Richard liked this uncle; he was the least troublesome of them all and could be relied upon to do whatever was expected of him.

The same thing couldn't be said for his uncle Thomas, youngest son of Edward III. Richard hadn't forgotten any of the indignities inflicted by this most unpleasant man. He may have disliked John of Gaunt, but at least Gaunt showed some respect. Not so with this one. Nonetheless, Mowbray was probably right; this new honor should make him more amenable. "Sir Thomas," he droned, putting on his most neutral face, "in recognition of your faithful service to the crown, I now declare you Duke of Gloucester along with the appurtenances belonging to your station." Robert de Vere gave him another gold chain and he placed it over Gloucester's head. "Arise, Sir Thomas of Woodstock, Duke of Gloucester." Thomas stood and bowed, his eyes resting on Gaunt rather than his nephew.

The next to step forward was Michael de la Pole, faithful servant of his father and even John of Gaunt before he became Chancellor. Now he was Richard's man. "Sir Michael," Richard said, smiling; this one was a pleasure. "In recognition of your faithful service to the crown, I now declare you Earl of Suffolk along with the balance of the Ufford estate belonging to this title."

186

Richard put the chain over Michael's head. "Arise, Sir Michael de la Pole, Earl of Suffolk."

Saving the best until last, Richard called forth Sir Simon Burley who ignored the mumbling of the attendees as he knelt before the king. "Sir Simon," the king announced, glaring at the loudest objectors, "in recognition of your faithful service to the crown, I now declare you Earl of Huntingdon along with the appurtenances belonging to your station." He knew this would be an unpopular move, but he hoped he could squeeze it in amongst the uncontroversial honors given the others. As far as Richard was concerned, Burley deserved recognition just as much as the others. He was well pleased with the ceremony and afterwards retired to his pavilion with a small group of intimates.

"I hope you were right about giving Gloucester and York titles to keep them quiet," Richard said to Thomas Mowbray, holding out his goblet for a refill. "The cost to the crown is not insignificant. Now we have three dukes instead of one."

Mowbray frowned; he didn't want to take the blame if something went wrong. "You did the right thing," he said, gesturing to a page.

"Gloucester is more powerful than before. If he chooses, he could cause me a great deal of trouble."

"Why would he do that?"

"He has ever treated me like a child who needs guidance. It will be hard for him to give that up."

"He will just have to learn," interjected Robert de Vere. He was about to say more when one of the king's squires interrupted him.

"It's from Princess Joan," said the messenger, coming into the pavilion with a letter. Richard put down his goblet and reached for it.

"I've been expecting this," he said, his face hardening. "She will beg me to forgive my brother."

Everybody watched while he read the letter, pursing his lips. Reaching the end, he crumpled the paper. "As I said. Robert, fetch my secretary. I must answer her at once. He may be a Holland, but this time John has gone too far and I will not pardon him."

Most of the king's friends sighed with relief. If Holland was allowed to go free, all hell would break loose. The Earl of Stafford had been remarkably restrained up to this point, though it wouldn't take much to create a fatal breach in their ranks.

Stafford was not Richard's only concern. As the army marched north, the Scots retreated before them, leaving a large wake of destruction. They would not engage. Farms had been burnt, livestock spirited away into the vast forests where peasants waited for the soldiers of both sides to leave. Already provisions had begun to run out and men fell sick along the way. Random troops of desperate mercenaries attacked the fringes of the royal army, killing stragglers and even taking prisoners.

Unbeknownst to the English, their French and Scottish adversaries had studied the advancing army from a distance. The English force was more than double their size, and the Scots were unwilling to meet them in a pitched battle. They talked the reluctant French into a different strategy. Instead of continuing their fruitless march, those willing to carry on would travel through less frequented mountain passes and cross west into Cumberland, where Carlisle and Penrith waited to be plucked like ripe apples. Richard wasn't destined to learn about this change of plans until they reached Edinburgh on the 11th of August.

They found the city empty; all inhabitants had fled, leaving the walls undefended. The streets echoed with the marching feet of angry invaders. "Burn this place to the ground," Richard fumed. "And the abbey of Holyrood as well. If they don't care enough to preserve their own capital, we will at least teach them to respect our wrath."

Let loose, the men spread out over the city, searching for food and drink, plundering shops before setting fire to them. Richard and the barons retired to Edinburgh castle; they could no longer delay a decision as to the next phase of the expedition.

It was a sullen group that gathered around a rough vellum map of Scotland. John of Gaunt ran his finger straight down from Edinburgh toward the Solway Firth.

"This is where they are headed," he said to Richard. "If we were to follow them, we could cut off their retreat."

"Through all those mountains? So we can be ambushed in the narrow passes?" Richard was not impressed. "We are nearing autumn and those areas will get the snow first."

"But sire," interrupted Thomas of Woodstock. Richard had to keep reminding himself that his uncle was the Duke of Gloucester now. "We would be marching south anyway, back home."

"How will we feed our army? If you remember, we are provisioned from the sea. I have no intention of extending our supply lines across the mountains." He swung back on Gaunt. "I don't need to remind you of your last campaign in France, where you lost half your army to starvation. You, and you, and you," he emphasized, pointing at the nobles, "you will be well fed from your private stores. But the common soldier perishes along the way. No, I will not subject my men to such deprivation. You may chase de Vienne if you want," he said to Gaunt. "You have a large enough force. I am going home."

He turned toward Robert who had touched the map with a pointer. "Could it be," de Vere suggested, "it is hoped by some that King Richard might lose his life in the wilds of Cumberland?"

Gloucester started forward but Gaunt restrained him. "Sire," he said calmly, "you have no more faithful subject than myself. Where you lead, I will follow."

"It is settled then," Richard said with a warning glance at Robert. "We will return by way of Berwick. I am satisfied that the threat from our northern neighbors has been countered by our march."

Not everyone agreed with him, though ultimately they had to admit the campaign was not totally ineffectual. They had ravaged the abbeys of Melrose and Newbattle, sacked the abbey of Holyrood, laid waste to much of Lothian and reduced Edinburgh to cinders. Best of all, Jeanne de Vienne took his lances and left the country in disgust, frustrated that he had never engaged with the English as he had so often boasted he would. Scotland was destined to be quiet for many years.

The army was not reluctant to return home. It was over forty leagues to York but the weather had not yet turned against them. Richard and his immediate household rode ahead, for Queen Anne was waiting for him and this was the first time they had been

189

separated. Even though the campaign was not a triumph, the city leaders insisted on decorating the streets with gay banners and flowers. The citizens turned out in great numbers to cheer when the king passed on his way to the cathedral. Beautiful young girls threw rose petals in front of his horse.

The archbishop waited with his priests in full regalia, as behind him a choir sang sweet tones of rejoicing. Anne stepped forward with her arms held out in welcome, her long silk-lined sleeves trailing on the ground. Richard dismounted, kissing her on the forehead and both cheeks.

"I have missed you so," he whispered, delighted at her blush. "You must tell me everything that has happened while I was gone." Her face fell and her mouth started trembling. Richard blinked in confusion. "What's wrong?"

Anne forced a smile. "After mass. Then we will talk."

Richard did his best to concentrate on the services, but the minute the archbishop said "Amen" he pulled Anne from the church. Everyone muttered in consternation; this was so different from his usual behavior. They made their way directly to the archbishop's palace, where the best chamber stood ready for them. As the servants quietly went about their business, Richard and Anne sat close to each other on the bed, holding hands.

"It's your mother," she whispered. "Oh my dear, she's gone."

"Gone." He started blinking back the tears. "G-gone, you say. My mother. When?"

Anne drew a ragged breath. "They told me she died six days after she received your letter. I am told that she was heartbroken about John. It was all a great shock to her."

"My mother. She died from a broken heart?"

Anne nodded. "It appears so. But how could you possibly have known? It wasn't your fault."

Richard shook his head absently. "No. There was no other way. He murdered my dear friend Ralph, thinking his rank would save him from punishment." Tears ran down his cheek. "What am I to do without her?"

He closed his eyes, desolate. His mother had always been ready to comfort him, no matter what the cause. The first time he fell from his pony, there she was, brushing him off and insisting

190

he get back into the saddle. When he lost his favorite toy she helped him look until he found it. She prayed with him for his father and together they lit candles at the cathedral. She was always the voice of reason when his temper got the better of him. She defended him when his uncles showed too much disrespect.

And now, she was gone. His last words to her had been cold and uncharitable.

Anne put her arms around him and he lay his head on her shoulder. She knew he had been a lonely child, and now that his mother was gone she was the closest confidante he had. She wished she possessed some of Joan's wisdom; perhaps she could make up for it by providing comfort, and solicitude. She heard footsteps and smiled thinly, seeing Simon Burley approach.

He knelt before the pair. "My little poppets," he said sadly. "I am here for you."

Richard pulled him close, a rare gesture for him. "Oh, Simon. She loved you so."

"And you, sire. Her every thought was for you."

Giving himself a moment of grief, Richard sighed and pulled himself straight. "Go to her," he said. "See that her wishes are followed. Not long ago she told me you would be one of her executors. Prepare her for me." He wiped his eyes. "My stubbornness has killed her. How can I go through with my brother's outlawry?"

No one dared answer. The tears came again. "Somehow I must find a way around this," he sobbed. "It's what she would have wanted." He pulled a small cloth from his sleeve to blow his nose, then wiped his eyes again before taking a deep breath.

Simon stood and the king took Anne's hand, playing absently with her rings. "I must confer with my uncles and the other lords. Perhaps there is a way for Holland to expiate his crime that would satisfy the Earl of Stafford. I will talk to my uncle John. He was close to my mother. He will understand."

Richard was right. John did understand and after much negotiation between the lords and Stafford, an agreement was finally arrived at. John Holland would obliged to pay for three priests who would celebrate divine services every day, to the end of the world, for the soul of Ralph Stafford. But that was not all.

191

Released from sanctuary, Holland rode, surrounded by a royal guard, to Windsor castle where the ceremony of public penance and remorse was to be held in front of all his peers—and, most importantly, the grieving father.

"By my troth, it feels good to breathe fresh air. How did they persuade the old earl to come?" Holland asked his squire. He took a deep draught of wine from a bottle.

The other looked askance at him. Sir John demonstrated none of the repentance one would expect after several weeks spent in a church. "From what I understand, Duke John convinced him no good would come of waging war against the king's brother."

"Good old Gaunt. I knew I could rely on him. After all, he is soon to be my father in-law. My dear Elizabeth would be heartbroken if her betrothed was outlawed."

"Nonetheless, I understand Stafford gave in very reluctantly. You will have to show great contrition to win his forgiveness."

"Oh, don't worry about that. I will know what to do."

When the time came, Sir John acted as convincing as anyone could have wished. He entered the chamber dressed in mourning, flanked by the Archbishop of Canterbury and the Bishop of London, and immediately fell to his knees. Hoping he portrayed convincing penitence, John crept forward, bowing, until he was before the throne. Still on his knees he straightened up, extending his arms and weeping.

"I humbly beg your forgiveness," he pleaded to the king. "I am a sinner and my rash temper has driven me to excesses. Dread King, I seek your mercy. I have done great wrong and committed a crime that will follow me for the rest of my days." He prostrated himself then knelt again, still sobbing. "I beseech your forgiveness. I am a poor sinner and beg God's mercy." He prostrated himself again, weeping even harder. Some of those around the king were impressed.

"Please forgive this penitent," he begged, prostrating himself a third time. Moved to pity, both bishops knelt beside him and clasped their hands. "Forgive him," they implored. "Great King."

The Earl of Stafford, standing beside John of Gaunt with his arms crossed, shook his head sadly. At the duke's other side, the Earl of Warwick wept on seeing the bishops kneel. "Can a mere man ask any more?" he said to Stafford. "Truly Sir John repents his wickedness."

This went on for several more minutes before Stafford approached the king. "Sire, as long as Sir John employs three priests to pray for my son every day, I cannot sustain my wrath. Though I tell you my heart is riven in two."

Richard stood, putting a hand on the earl's shoulder. "Your son was very dear to me and I mourn along with you. Alas, Sir John has much to answer for as has caused the death of our mother as well. But perhaps it's better to leave the matter in God's hands." He glared at Holland who made sure to keep his head down.

Stafford bowed and stepped back, subdued. Richard could tell he was not reconciled in the least. Still standing, the king turned to Holland, pursing his lips. The immediate crisis had been averted, but there was no telling what his tempestuous brother would do next.

"Stand, Sir John."

Trying to hide his relief, Holland got to his feet as gracefully as possible. He assisted the Bishop of London who was having trouble pushing himself off the floor.

Richard waited. "Sir John, I pardon you on the condition that you pay for three priests to hold mass every day for the soul of Sir Ralph. This is as we have already discussed. Furthermore, I release you on the condition that you accompany Duke John of Gaunt on his upcoming expedition to Portugal." The king knew this was exactly what Holland wanted to do, so this stipulation would benefit everyone. Holland would get his military glory, Stafford would see his son's murderer leave the country, and Richard would be rid of his disagreeable kin for years to come.

Gaunt's expedition to Portugal was a long time coming—ever since he married his second wife Constance, heir to the throne of Castile. He had been calling himself King of Castile and León since 1372, though it wasn't until now that circumstances and finances allowed him to bring an army and try to make good his claim. He was anxious for a crown of his own and Richard was anxious to see him go.

The king may have thought his troubles would be over once John of Gaunt was safely out of the country, but he was soon to learn otherwise. In fact, his troubles had nothing to do with Gaunt; if anything, it was his uncle who kept the wolves at bay. While John was busy preparing to leave the country, Parliament was arranging a demonstration of its own; and they were to prove far from friendly.

As usual, Richard sat on his throne with the higher clergy on his right, the lay magnates on his left, and the chancellor standing just below him. Michael de la Pole opened up the October Parliament with his usual request for taxation to ease the government's debts. Their reaction was unsettling. "Nay, nay," shouted a petulant Commons. Their Speaker stood up with a long list of objections.

"We bring to your attention, Lord Chancellor, the cost of royal largesse, which, if unchecked, will exhaust the king's personal revenues before he reaches his twenty-first birthday. In which case, Lord Chancellor, the burden will fall on Parliament to provide for the future. This cannot be allowed to happen!"

Richard clenched his hands but this time he knew better than to speak out. He couldn't risk alienating the Commons, especially before he got what he wanted.

Michael de la Pole hoped to circumvent the issue. He went on with his discourse, ignoring the objection. "My Lords, our first items to be discussed are the recent grants made by the king on the Scottish campaign. We seek to invest the new peers of the realm as follows: Sir Edmund of Langley as Duke of York, Sir Thomas of Woodstock as Duke of Gloucester." Pausing, the Chancellor nodded to the Deputy Speaker, who went on to say, "Sir Michael de la Pole has been raised to Earl of Suffolk, Sir Simon Burley has been raised to Earl of Huntingdon—"

"Nay, nay!" Shouting in the hall drowned out the Speaker, who sought to regain control. "We will not have the Earl of Huntingdon," cried a particularly outspoken member. "No Earl of Huntingdon." The chamber roared their agreement. Michael turned questioningly to a frowning Richard. It seemed likely that they wouldn't be able to force Burley's appointment. There was little the king could do at this point and they had hardly begun.

In the end, both dukes were approved as well as Michael's new title. But that was all; the Commons were united in their opposition to the king's financial policies. It was a long and grueling Parliament, lasting a month and a half; the whole time Richard felt like he was taking a thrashing. They insisted that the king make no grants from Crown revenues for at least a year. Reform would be enacted to increase the royal revenues, so the king could "live on his own". He was to appoint an annual Commission to oversee his household accounts. It was too much. Five days before the scheduled end of the sessions, Richard stood and declared "I will submit my accounts to no one! I will do as I please with my personal gifts and my ministers!"

This started another round of recriminations, until finally the king was forced to negotiate. "I will concede to your demands under one condition. I am raising up Robert de Vere, 9th Earl of Oxford as Marquess of Dublin for life, with Palatine rights over the Irish Pale. Once he is ratified, you will find me more amenable."

The silence in the room was more than gratifying. Finally, Richard had caught everyone by surprise. No one in English history had been given the title of Marquess. They all knew that in France, a marquis ranked between duke and count. By his sudden declaration, Richard would be elevating his friend above all the earls in England—his undeserving friend, as far as they were concerned.

The timing of Richard's proclamation couldn't have been worse. Already the Commons were disgruntled with his impulsive behavior—doling out wardships, escheats, annuities, and gifts with reckless abandon. And now this! It took three weeks to finally authorize de Vere's elevation, but both sides eventually compromised—at least on the surface. Richard got his marquisate while the Commons insisted on a committee of nine who would curb his spending, review his revenues and put royal finances on a firm footing. Whether or not Richard understood that he was on probation until the next Parliament, he loathed the idea of putting himself at the mercy of the same men who controlled the first years of his reign. He was too old for that now! Agreeing in principle only, Richard resolved to go on as before, while the Commons went home embittered and frustrated. The committee of nine never materialized.

Richard and Simon pulled their horses ahead of the royal entourage as they returned to London from Westminster. As expected, Burley was crestfallen after Parliament's refusal to ratify him as earl. Richard felt terrible; not only was Simon the most important officer in his household, he was a pillar of strength against the king's adversaries. The king's inability to impose his will on the Commons was humiliating; it wasn't right that Simon should be so singled out, just because he was a royal favorite.

Approaching Ludgate, Richard pulled out his handkerchief and held it over his nose while his horse picked its way through discarded entrails and organs left by the butchers along the Fleet River. "This muck is unacceptable," the king muttered. "This has been going on long enough! We must pass an ordinance commanding the butchers to cut up their offal and load it into boats. Let them can cast their filth midstream into the Thames where it can be washed away. Not here on the roads!"

Once they passed into the city, Richard nudged his mount closer to Burley. "Listen to me. I cannot force Parliament to sanction your earldom," he said, "but there something I can do. As you know, I have not appointed a constable of Dover since Sir Robert Ashton died. I intend to appoint you in his place, and Warden of the Cinque Ports as well."

Simon turned in astonishment, all sadness forgotten.

"Of course," Richard went on, "this goes along with the feudal honour of Dover and its courts, with all their revenue reverting to yourself—somewhere around 300 pounds a year, I am told. You may not be earl, but you shall be more than adequately endowed."

"Sire, I am honored!"

Richard smiled, satisfied. "I know you will serve me well. Who else can I trust to guard the coast in these dangerous times?"

He laughed briefly. "Considering what the French have in mind, you may not thank me for long!"

CHAPTER 6

On July 7, 1386, John of Gaunt sailed from Plymouth with his wife, his three daughters, Sir John Holland, and 10,000 men to gain the crown of Castile and surround France with hostile neighbors. Richard and Anne gave them a royal send-off, presenting Duke John and Duchess Constanza with gold crowns. They dined on the duke's flag ship with Henry of Bolingbroke, who was to stay behind in England to manage the family estates.

As the great flotilla left the port, noisily followed by many smaller boats packed with well-wishers, Richard and Henry sat on their mounts side-by-side, silently watching. Each one of them had something different on his mind. Richard could barely suppress his glee to be finally rid of his overbearing uncle, while Henry was brooding over the responsibility thrust upon his shoulders. He alone would represent the great duchy, weeks and even months away from his father's advice should something go awry.

Richard turned to his cousin. "Do you think your father's expedition will discourage the French from attacking our shores?"

Was this a trap? Henry hesitated; he never knew whether the king was being straightforward or not. "I understand King Charles is determined to invade us. I am told he is building a mighty armada at Sluys. It may take more than my father to stop him."

"Hmm. My council is urging me to send troops to the coast for our defense. But there's no money left to pay their wages. All the taxes we collected for the war effort have been dedicated to your father's enterprise."

Henry said nothing. This was too dangerous. Besides, he would not be drawn into his father's affairs.

"Well, at least he will return the ships when they have disembarked. It only remains for us to recruit more mariners to man them." Richard let out a long sigh. "The funds will have to be collected somehow." Again Henry said nothing and Richard shrugged, tiring of the conversation. "We are off to Sheen. Would you like to join us?"

Henry was not the least tempted. He shook his head. "I thank you for your kind invitation, sire. But my wife is due to deliver our first child within the fortnight, and I am off to Monmouth to be present at the birth of my son and heir." He smiled crookedly. "At least I hope it's a son. If I say it enough times, perhaps it will come true."

Richard had to suppress a surge of envy—altogether too common when comparing himself with his cousin. Henry was stronger than him, better educated, more successful at arms, free to come and go whither he wanted without the weight of the world on his shoulders. And now he was to be a proud father while Richard and Anne remained childless. How unfair it all was!

"Well, I wish you the best and will pray for a safe delivery," he said, trying to sound sincere. Then he turned his horse and rode away without a backward look.

Henry watched him leave, bemused. There was no secret that they barely tolerated each other. Often and again his father remarked that he would be best served to stay as far away from the king as possible, and watching recent events he heartily agreed. Gaunt struck fear into everyone's heart; Henry hadn't yet learned how to do so. He could hold his own—and even excel—on the tournament field, which he had so recently proved at Smithfield. But on the political field, he was untried. It took years for his father to learn the skills of diplomacy, and even so he was helpless when Richard's temper provoked attacks the king surely must be ashamed of. At least Henry hoped he was ashamed of them. But there it was; if Gaunt couldn't stand up to the king's erratic behavior, how could Henry expect to survive? How many times had his father been the target of assassination attempts, allegedly planned with the king's approval? How often had he withdrawn to his distant estates, just to escape the turmoil of court? What would Henry do in similar situations?

It had been two years since construction began on Richard's lodging on the island of La Neyt across from Sheen Palace.

Although the buildings were not yet finished, the king's receiving chamber and bedchamber were declared habitable and he was excited to see them. Once everyone was settled in and dinner was gotten through, Richard encouraged Anne to cross the river and explore their new getaway. "Just the two of us," he whispered in her ear. Anne smiled. She knew he was discounting the small army of servants already working hard to prepare the chambers for them. But the courtiers, clergy, secretaries, and officers could stay in the main buildings. They could amuse themselves without Richard's regal presence.

They stepped gingerly into the small ferry-boat and watched, holding hands, as the island came closer. The walkway to the lodging was laid with rushes and Richard gallantly helped Anne step from the boat, leading her slowly while savoring the charm of their private cottage. It was everything he expected; the entrance way was finished in loving detail. Delicate carved vines climbed posts flanking the double doors. The roof was thatched, and diamond-shaped pieces of glass—held together by strips of lead— peeked out at them from small window-frames. The door opened and the royal couple stepped inside. Anne turned and smiled at the esquire holding the latch.

"Welcome to La Neyt," he said, bowing.

They admired the ceiling with its hammer beams already shadowed in the afternoon light. Richard put Anne's arm through his own and they followed the esquire into their sleeping chamber with a canopied bed and its own fireplace. Six cushions and four diapered pillows—used for their seating during the day—graced the coverlet.

"Come, I've been waiting to show you this." Richard pulled Anne into the adjoining room and she gasped in appreciation. All four walls—and ceiling as well—were covered with hand-painted tiles, placed together to form a continuous picture of flowers and birds. "I bought 2000 tiles in all," he said proudly. But, even so, the luxury of the walls paled in comparison to the bath in the center of the room with large bronze taps for hot and cold water. He went over and turned the hot water spigot; after a moment water flowed freely into the tub.

"We'll try this later. For now, I want to take a walk through the bowers behind the rose garden. Ah, here is the privy." He pulled aside a curtain, exposing a toilet with padded seat. "It is even heated from the chimney when we need it."

Anne was charmed by Richard's enthusiasm. In a world where men were often brutish and violent, her husband appreciated the finer things. In this lovely, secluded cottage he could relax and just be himself: loving, quiet, curious, and best of all, attentive.

The afternoon light was starting to fade, but there was enough time left to explore. The rose garden was in full bloom, and Richard frequently bent over to smell the fragrances. "This is my favorite." He held his hand around a large deep red blossom and she obediently bent over to sniff it.

"Ah." She inhaled deeply then sneezed.

Laughing, Richard pulled a handkerchief from his sleeve. "Here, take this. I have found it quite useful."

Anne sneezed again and accepted the cloth, turning her head aside as she blew her nose. "Better," she laughed. "Must have been the dust from the flower."

Putting her arm through his again, they walked down the garden path and into the bower. Suddenly they stopped, hearing a rustling noise to the side. Richard lowered his head and saw a splash of blue.

"What is this?" Without hesitation he stepped forward, pushing aside a leafy bush. What he saw made him stop short with an intake of breath. Anne leaned over his shoulder and gasped as well.

Lying on a cloak in a state of undress, Robert de Vere and Agnes de Launcekrona both jumped up in fright and scrambled to cover their nakedness. Shaking his head, the king let go the branches and turned to his wife, shrugging his shoulders. "I should have known," he said, mostly to himself. "We saw them too much together."

Anne had her hand in front of her mouth. She, too, felt like an accomplice. "What are we to do?"

"What are they to do?"

201

Neither moved from the spot. Finally, after much shuffling around, the guilty pair stepped onto the path. The reached for each other's hand.

"This is a shameful breach of discretion," Richard chided, though his heart wasn't in it. He wanted Robert to be happy and this was only going to get him into trouble.

Robert lifted his chin proudly. "I love her," he said simply. "You know my wife despises me."

Richard sighed. "That doesn't matter, does it? She is my cousin."

Pursing his lips, Robert squeezed Agnes's hand. "I can't live without her."

Anne reached for her lady-in-waiting and pulled her away. "Is this how you repay me?" Agnes blinked back her tears and the queen shook her by the shoulders, pushing the girl back toward the cottage. "Go. You have done enough damage for one day."

Taking two steps then breaking into a run, Agnes fled. Anne and Richard both stared at de Vere. "This can't go on," the king said.

Robert turned a trusting eye on his friend. "We have pledged ourselves to one another."

"Foolish man. You can't betray your marriage vows."

"I have no marriage. It can be annulled."

Anne gasped. "You cannot!"

"No? Let us think on it." Robert bowed, turning on his heel and leaving the other two staring at each other.

"We were so happy," Anne murmured.

"No, ma chère. We are still happy. This is a trifle. Robert is a sensible man. He knows his duty."

Alas, for once Richard underestimated his friend's tenacity. In the face of love, duty pales. As far as Robert was concerned, now that the king knew he might as well do his best to persuade Richard to countenance his affair. This would take some time, but he did not doubt his influence over his royal friend.

Court business went on as usual. The next day Richard surrounded himself with his clerks of the chamber, his knights, his treasurer, his Keeper of the Signet. They were going through a pile of writs and pardons which the king was anxious to finish.

"Seal this one, and this one," the king said to the keeper. "I'm sure the chancellor will warrant these. And here, I promised John of Knyghtley the lands and tenements in Appeley to hold during the minority of John atte Wolde." The keeper dripped his wax and stamped the writ with his signet. Richard handed him another. "Here's a pardon, at the supplication of Nicholas Slate, for Andrew Bruton. He was indicted for breaking into the house of Thomas Berkeley and taking goods and chattels to the value of 20*s*. Yes, seal this too." This went on for the whole afternoon before the Keeper of the Signet gathered up all the documents and prepared them for Michael de la Pole.

As Richard stood, stretching, de Vere came into the chamber.

"Ah, Robert. There you are. Come, walk with me." The two of them passed into the great hall hung with new tapestries just imported from Arras. "Look, this is my favorite." Richard pointed to a colorful scene portraying a hunting party, crowded by so many men and women with brocaded houppelandes that you could hardly see the animals being skewered.

"That horned lady there reminds me of the queen," Robert laughed. "And there, the dogs look like they are ready to step on her train."

"Ha! You are right. I'll have to show her."

They walked along the wall in companionable silence until Robert felt brave enough to speak what was on his mind. "Sire, I have been thinking."

"Oh?" Richard straightened his sleeve. Robert recognized the gesture; the king usually made it when expecting something unpleasant. It was a shame; he had gone too far to stop now.

"It's about Agnes." Richard sighed in annoyance but Robert pushed on. "I want to marry her."

"Robert, I thought we talked about this already. Do you know what this will do to your reputation?"

"I don't care. I need her by my side."

"This is all wrong. Your wife is sister to the most powerful nobles in the land. Are you mad?"

"We were children when we wed. We never cared for each other."

"And you want to petition the Pope for a divorce?"

"With your consent, yes."

"No. I know you will do whatever you want. But you do not have my consent, nor my approval." He paused, moved by his friend's stricken face. "I will not stand in your way, either," lowering his voice.

Robert knelt, kissing Richard's hand. "Thank you, sire."

"Pah." The king gave him a crooked grimace. He could refuse Robert nothing. Yet he knew that no good would come of this whim of his. Perhaps Anne could talk Agnes out of it.

Between the two of them, Richard and Anne prepared an argument for her favorite *femme de chambre*. That night, as Agnes was brushing Anne's hair, the queen soon realized she could have saved her breath. "Robert spoke with the king today," she started.

Her maid inhaled sharply but continued brushing.

"He is causing the king great distress."

Agnes stopped and knelt before the queen. "You must understand, your Grace. He is the kindest, the most considerate man a woman could ever hope for. He will be a loyal husband."

Anne reached out and touched Agnes's hair. "That may be so, but what happens when the Duke of Gloucester turns on him? Or Lancaster? They will be furious at the way Robert treats their sister."

"Robert has the king to defend him."

The queen frowned. Even Richard had his limitations before the law. "I wouldn't depend on that," she said. "He is very unhappy with Robert. Look what your behavior has done to our household propriety. We have a scandal under our very noses."

"Oh, your Grace, we are forsaken." Putting her hands over her face, Agnes broke into sobs.

Anne could not bear to see another person miserable. "Shh. It's not as bad as all that. I will speak with the king."

Wiping her eyes, Agnes rose. "You give me hope. I do love him so."

Shaking her head, Anne gestured for her continue brushing. "We shall see. Whatever the king says, we must abide."

As the summer progressed, tidings of France's invasion preparations followed one upon the other. It was said the King of France made himself a ship painted red to signify the blood he was going to spill. People started to get frantic and there was much disorder. Sir Simon Burley tried to persuade the abbot of Canterbury Cathedral to move the shrine of St. Thomas Becket to Dover for safekeeping. But the abbot and all his monks feared he was trying to despoil them of their treasure and they forcefully refused. People on the Isle of Thanet were ordered to evacuate, but they refused to go. Forced loans were raised for the defense of the maritime counties. In London, Mayor Nicholas Exton proclaimed that all citizens who left the city must return by September 19 so they could be on hand for its defense; he also ordered the aldermen to lay in a stock of provisions for three months. All knew that the only thing keeping the French on their own side of the Channel was adverse winds. How long would that protect England?

Finally, desperate for money, the king called a Parliament to be held at Westminster on October 1. All the great lords were there, and Richard could see that the Commons were in a surly mood. Michael de la Pole opened the session with the usual official notices. He saw that everyone was anxious to get down to the real business, so the chancellor didn't waste any more time.

Michael waited until the noise died down. On the floor, behind the railing, the Speaker of the Commons glared at him while he cleared his throat. "As you know," Michael began, "we are threatened with the most serious invasion since the Norman Conquest. The French have assembled a large fleet amounting to nearly 1000 ships. Our coastal towns are at the highest risk, and our defensive capabilities need to be strengthened. The king is obliged to ask for sufficient aid to ensure that protective measures can be ordered."

As expected, the chamber filled with grumbling. Finally the Speaker raised his voice. "How much taxation is the king asking for?"

Michael made a show of consulting his papers. "We have determined that four fifteenths and tenths, payable in a year, and the same number of tenths from the clergy, are necessary, or else the king could not be relieved of his debts, both of war and his household." By the time the chancellor reached the end of his sentence he was shouting to be heard. Men shook their fists in the air. "Impossible!" "Unheard of!" Both sides of the room exploded in anger and Michael could do nothing to make it stop. He banged his fist on the lectern, shouting for order. Nobody listened.

The king glared at the room. Who was guiding this disruption? Gloucester? Was he somehow directing the Commons behind his back? Between Gloucester, Arundel and Warwick they controlled many of the counties represented here. Naturally they all stood together. Finally, after much too much time had passed, the Speaker gestured for order and the members complied.

"Sire, we are of the opinion that before we concern ourselves with external enemies, something should be done about our internal enemies." He paused as the room burst into cheers. "The realm is in danger. There is much mismanagement in your great offices. We demand that you dismiss the treasurer John Fordham and chancellor Michael de la Pole. We have certain business to do with the Earl of Suffolk which we cannot transact so long as he remains in office."

Amid more acclamation, Richard stood, fists clenched. How dare these low-ranking burgesses and knights presume to order his affairs! Presumptuous upstarts! As he pointed his finger at the house, the shouting faded to a murmur.

"I will not dismiss so much as a scullion from my kitchen at your request! The French could be sailing up the Thames at any moment. This is no time to be removing ministers! Return at once to your proper business and drop this matter!" His voice rang out and silenced the room. Not for long; angry voices rose again.

Richard directed Michael to bang his pole on the floor. "This session is over!" shouted the king. Drawing himself up haughtily, Richard marched out of the room followed by la Pole, Burley, de Vere, Fordham, and other members of his household. No one dared try to stop him, but members shouted their objections as he disappeared. Richard was deaf to their pleas.

"I'm going to join the queen at Eltham," he said to Burley. "I will not stay here a minute longer."

It was an unhappy little group who assembled at Eltham. Forlornly sipping their wine, they dallied with their new Spanish playing cards. Michael de la Pole had stayed in London to keep an eye on the proceedings; Simon and Robert traveled with the king who was still fuming from that afternoon's disaster.

"This defiance cannot continue," Richard muttered, holding his cards up to Burley for advice. "Simon, I remember well the lessons you taught me about the royal prerogative. Parliament is trying to reduce me to a puppet. I know that my grandfather's last years have tarnished the kingship. But there is no reason why I should let this go on."

Burley plucked a sword card from Richard's hand and placed it on the table. "I fear your uncle Gloucester hopes to take Gaunt's place as dominant peer of the realm. This would be his first opportunity."

Squinting at the queen as she stacked her coins, Richard threw down a groat. "You may be right. With Gaunt across the sea, Lancastrian influence has waned. At least my cousin Henry shows scant interest in governing in his place."

"Let us hope so," said Robert, placing a chalice card on top of Richard's. "One less Lancastrian to worry about. But I think Simon might be right; now we have a new faction to worry about."

"A new faction? You mean Arundel and Gloucester? And Warwick? Do you think they are strong enough to challenge the crown?"

"I think they are very strong," said Burley. "They keep making statements that you are badly advised by your counselors."

"They are talking about you." Richard grumbled. "And Michael. And of course you, Robert. They think I have no mind of my own."

"They say you are young," Robert said. "They want to pretend that you are still a child. They think that because they are peers, you have to listen to them."

"Hmm. We shall see about that."

207

Later that evening, Richard pulled Robert aside. "Come into my closet. I've been thinking about what you said and it's high time we did something to strengthen my position." Robert closed the door and they sat close together, lowering their voices.

"Listen," Richard started, "I have no dukes who are loyal to me. I have no retainers I can call my own. What if that new faction, as you call it, decided to challenge me? What would I do to defend myself?"

"Pah," snorted Robert. "They wouldn't dare."

"And what do we call that little demonstration in Parliament? First they ask me to dismiss my treasurer and my chancellor. What comes next?"

Frowning, Robert reached for a pitcher of wine. "I don't know. What are your thoughts?"

"I'll tell you my thoughts. I need you to recruit a loyal army. Royal retainers. I think we should concentrate on Cheshire, where my father enlisted so many of his archers."

The other nodded. "It certainly makes sense. But under what authority do I recruit these Cheshiremen?"

"Ah. I intend to make you Duke of Ireland. We will tell the world that you'll be raising troops for my expedition."

Robert's eyes glowed. "Expedition?"

"Oh yes. No English king has concerned himself about Ireland since John, and that was two hundred years ago. Since then, it has become a drain on the exchequer, thanks to those petty chieftains who think they are in control. I have every intention of going there. But not yet. You will retain loyal troops until I need them, under the auspices of going to Ireland. Our real purpose, which shall remain hidden, will be to buttress my throne. And I will have a loyal duke on my side."

"My lord, I am overwhelmed."

"No, Robert. I haven't had much opportunity to reward you. This is well deserved."

"I will do my best to serve you."

"I know you will." Richard held out his cup and Robert poured more wine. They tapped their chalices together. "To our mutual endeavor."

The next day, King Richard made a formal entry into Eltham's receiving chamber, where many of his knights and courtiers waited. "I have had it on my mind to remind Parliament who is king here. Robert de Vere, Earl of Oxford, I hereby raise you as Duke of Ireland. I do this by royal charter as of this day, 13th of October 1386. To support your station and pay for your upcoming expedition to Ireland, I grant you the ransom of John de Blois, pretender to the duchy of Brittany. I also grant the estates of James, lord Audley, recently deceased." As Robert knelt to receive the collar of office, the others murmured in surprise. Richard's gesture was daring but provocative; it would not go unanswered.

As expected, Parliament wasn't long in responding. The next evening, while the court listened to a new poem recited by Richard's chamber knight Sir John Clanvowe, an usher came in and leaned over Richard's shoulder. After listening intently, the king nodded then waited for John to finish. He joined in the polite applause before turning to Burley.

"It seems that Parliament has sent a messenger. Go, Simon, and see what they want."

Simon nodded and left the room with the usher. He wasn't long in coming back, and by then Richard had moved to the fireplace, rubbing his upper arms to warm up.

"It's cold tonight. So how goes it with my seditious Parliament?"

Burley bent down and poked the fire with an iron. "They have instructed their man to tell you they will not assent to any grants and cannot attend to normal business until you return to Westminster and show yourself in person."

Letting out his breath in a burst of annoyance, Richard started pacing. "I would pull their teeth! How did they get so overbearing?"

"Once they discovered they held the purse strings, the Commons became insufferable. Your grandfather flew into a rage on more than one occasion, I remember!"

"I do not wonder." Richard strode to the window and peered out. Anne came up next to him with a cloak. "That moon reminds me of our first Christmas," he said, kissing her on the forehead.

209

"You were so helpful to me then! What do you suggest, dearest Anne?"

She slipped the cloak over this shoulders. "If you won't go to them, let them come to Eltham," she said simply. "They are the supplicants, not you."

"My wise and worthy wife." He put an arm around her shoulders and turned her around to face Simon. "All right, send the messanger back. Let Parliament put together a delegation of forty of their most experienced members. They can come to Eltham and we shall discuss their demands." He kissed Anne again. "What would I do without you, my turtle dove?"

Smiling at the pair, Simon went to do Richard's bidding. When the king and queen acted like this, they were sure to disappear from the room.

Two days later they received another messenger, this time from Michael de la Pole. Once again, Simon interviewed the knight; once again, he came back with a disagreeable response, interrupting Richard's breakfast of bread and fruits. "We must be prepared for the worst," he told the king. "Your request for an embassy was taken as a trap. Somehow a rumor started in London that we were planning to arrest the delegates, or even kill them in ambush. The assassins would be led by Nicholas Brembre."

"Fools!" Richard threw his napkin on the table. "Why must I always be surrounded by rumors of murder?" He gestured for a servant to take his food away.

"There's more. In place of an embassy, Parliament is sending your uncle Gloucester and Bishop Thomas Arundel."

Richard glanced worriedly at Burley. He disliked the wily Bishop of Ely—brother to Richard Arundel—but not nearly as much as he disliked his uncle. Simon knew how intimidating Gloucester was; the man was ambitious and jealous of his nephew's position.

"I'll be with you, sire. So will Robert. So will the rest of your household. Whatever they have to say will be done before witnesses."

Witnesses or no, Gloucester had his attack well prepared. Unbeknownst to Richard, before the pair left Westminster, they ordered that the records of Edward II's deposition be produced and read before the House. This way they might discern what strategy they might use against the current king. Whether this was merely an exercise in precedent, or with something altogether more drastic in mind, it didn't bode well for Richard's position.

When Gloucester and the Bishop of Ely arrived, an usher showed them into the receiving chamber where they were obliged to wait while the king prepared to receive them. Finally, after much pacing, they were alerted by a pair of trumpeters announcing Richard's entry. The chamber doors swung open and Burley strode forward, followed by the seneschal, the steward, the rest of the royal household. Finally the king entered, resplendent in a red ermine-lined short cape on top of a floor-length dark-blue gown sprinkled with gold stars. His crown was studded with jewels and he held a golden sceptre. As his visitors bowed, Richard swept past them and seated himself on a throne, surrounded by his officers.

Gloucester stepped forward, pretending not to notice all this magnificence. He was no mean presence, himself, never forgetting for a minute that he was the son of a king, not a grandson. His face showed no tolerance—only an incontestable will to have his way.

Trying not to be intimidated, Richard stared over his head. "What is it you want?" he asked, hating the shrillness of his voice.

Thomas Arundel, Bishop of Ely appeared diminished at Gloucester's side, even in his full regalia. But Richard wasn't fooled; Thomas was every bit as dangerous as his uncle. The bishop was clever and extremely well educated; he could turn an argument on its head by sheer use of words. He was the first to speak. "Sire," he started, his voice expressionless, "I bring greetings and salutations from the Lords and Commons of Parliament. I am instructed to tell you that because they support the financial burdens of the exchequer, it is only fair they have a say in how, and by whom, the taxpayers' money is spent."

He paused for breath and Richard leaned toward Simon to whisper in his ear. Frowning, Gloucester took his turn.

211

"Furthermore, we have it by ancient statute that if the king wantonly absents himself for forty days, as though not caring about the harassment of his people, they have the right to dissolve Parliament and go to their homes. No taxes to be raised, no concessions to the king. No confirmations of the king's appointments." His voice was much more contemptuous. Richard knew his uncle was trying to get a reaction, and despite himself he obliged, jumping to his feet.

"I know of no such statute," he objected. "Now I can clearly see that the Commons intend to resist everything I do. Against such persecution, I would be better off going to the King of France to seek advice."

Gloucester and Arundel were momentarily taken aback. They gaped at each other in dismay, but then the duke made a gesture of dismissal. "Have you lost your reason? The King of France is your enemy! If he were to set foot in England it would be to expel you from the eminence of your royal position." He put special emphasis on the word *royal*. "No, you are too much aware of your father and grandfather's labors to conquer the lands in France that belonged to them by right. And now, our country is all but impoverished, their efforts wasted."

Chastened, Richard sat back on his throne. He knew Gloucester wasn't finished.

"These ills spring from evil counsellors that surround your Grace. Which brings me to my last statute of old—and one that was used not very long ago. If ever the king, through evil counsel or wanton ill will, alienates himself from the people—if he does not wish to be ruled by the laws of the land..." The slow words came out almost as a growl. "Then it is lawful for them by common consent to remove that king from the royal throne, and substitute another close relative of the royal line in his place."

It was as though the force of those words pushed Richard back against said throne, for his head pressed against the wood and his chin pulled into his throat. He gripped the arms of the chair and his eyes opened wide while he gritted his teeth. None of his supporters knew what to do and they all drew in their breath.

Poor Richard wasn't to discover until very much later that the supposed statutes never existed at all, and Edward II's

212

deposition—for this was the reference—was not a Parliamentary law establishing precedent. At the time, no precedent was intended. Nonetheless, the threat was all too real. Once again Gloucester and the bishop exchanged glances, this time in triumph.

Waiting for the king to relax, the duke took a step back. "Will your Grace be returning to Parliament with us?"

This was the last thing Richard wanted to do. But his stubborn resistance was not helping; the king nodded reluctantly in acquiescence. Taking belated charge of the situation, Simon Burley banged his staff on the floor. "This session is over," he thundered, gesturing for the sergeant to throw open the doors. Gloucester and Bishop Arundel bowed and left the room, followed by the king's knights and other witnesses.

Richard sat in his throne, chin in hand. "Sit, Simon," he said absently.

Burley sat on the step below the throne.

"That did not go well," Richard said, letting out his breath in a short laugh. "We just witnessed an act of treason," he added pensively. For once, he was not saying it as a direct accusation; even he knew he had used that word carelessly too many times in the past. "But there comes a time when even the king's majesty will not protect him against rebellion." He glanced at Burley, tears in his eyes. "Has it come to that?"

Frowning, Simon's heart went out to the king. "I don't think so," he said slowly. "I think Gloucester was testing his limits. Still, none of us will know what he is planning in Parliament unless we are there. It is good that we are going back."

"I know. Yet I fear what will happen. Simon, outside of my household, I have no supporters. I have no power except for m-my royal prerogative." He sighed, taking off his crown. "I may have to do their bidding once again, for how can I refuse? But there will come a reckoning, I promise you. I don't know how long it will take, but there will be a reckoning."

CHAPTER 7

On October 23, Richard entered Parliament. The Commons were ready for him and wasted no time in demanding the dismissal of Michael de la Pole. Yielding to his weak position, the king had lost all his will to fight. He meekly agreed to a panel of judges— including Gloucester and Arundel—who passed judgment on his chancellor, his treasurer, and his keeper of the privy seal. Everyone sighed with relief at the king's mild words, though his enemies might have quailed had they seen the rage in his heart. But Richard was a fast learner. He saw how ineffectual his temper had proven. In the future, he would find a way to strengthen his position. For now—the rest of this session—he would quietly watch. And learn.

The day after Michael was dismissed, Bishop Thomas Arundel was elected chancellor in his place. Richard considered the bishop his enemy, yet still he maintained his silence. He watched as the Lords and Commons launched impeachment proceedings against his friend and counsellor; now that Michael was no longer chancellor, he was fair game. To no one's surprise, Michael defended himself eloquently against seven charges, comprising dereliction of duty, misuse of his powers of patronage, and lining his pockets at the king's expense. But it was to no avail; they were after his blood. Not only was he impeached, Michael was fined, condemned to forfeiture of his properties and imprisoned at Windsor Castle. Under Burley's custody Michael was immediately hustled off before the king could do anything to protect him.

Richard knew he was being attacked through his faithful servants and was helpless to do anything about it. And this was just the beginning. By the end of November, he was saddled with a new commission known as the Great and Continuous Council. They were to reside permanently at Westminster and take complete charge of the government. Determined to enact financial reforms, they exercised full control of the Great and Privy Seals;

the king's signet had already been discredited and would no longer be recognized. They had the right to inspect his household at any time. The council took over the exchequer leaving Richard with a small allowance—too small to support his lifestyle. Even his jewels were out of his control. He was completely at their mercy.

As if this wasn't enough, Parliament compelled the king to swear that he would obey the commission's decisions. Standing before his collective enemies, Richard took his oath. "Let it go on record," he added, "that I sanction nothing that affects my prerogative and the liberties of my Crown." There was some mumbling but apparently they thought they had gone far enough with the king's humiliation; Parliament could afford to ignore his powerless objection. However, his next demand caused a bigger stir: "Also, I insist that this council only last for twelve months, expiring on the 19th of November, 1387."

The speaker of the house immediately protested. "It is our request that the council continue, after its expiration, until the next Parliament meets."

"Absolutely not!" For once, Richard's voice rang out with conviction. "The council will not be extended even one day beyond its expiration. On this I insist."

He felt like a stubborn child while they debated in low voices. But this was no time to show weakness. They had already stolen his pride, his dignity, all of his privileges. In addition to removing his great officers, they had even dismissed many of his minor administrators, including his favorite poet, Geoffrey Chaucer. By now, Richard had nothing left except his resolve. He was determined not to let them touch that. He straightened his back, narrowing his eyes at the Commons. Finally they conceded, giving him a tiny bit of satisfaction.

"One last matter: the confirmation of Sir Robert de Vere as Duke of Ireland, with income awarded by the ransom of John de Blois so that he might recover my dominions so recently lost." Richard knew this grant was wildly unpopular, since it would rank Robert an equal with the sons of Edward III. De Vere was not of royal blood! *Well, that was too bad; they would have to get used to it.* The king watched patiently as the Commons debated the matter among themselves. He knew that their desire to be rid of

215

his friend outweighed their objection to his elevation. Eventually they agreed to his terms on the condition that Robert would cross the sea before Easter.

Consenting, Richard smiled to himself. They probably hoped Robert would meet an untimely end on that savage island. Many a good man—and not so good men—had left their bones on Irish soil. As far as the Commons was concerned, it was worth Richard's price to be rid of him. As far as Richard was concerned, considering what they put him through, he was justified in stretching the truth to get what *he* needed.

This was the first time the king deliberately practiced deception. By no means was this to be his last.

No sooner had Parliament ended than Richard gathered his greatly reduced court and moved on to Windsor castle, where he intended to spend the Christmas holidays. He took with him his queen and Robert de Vere, and just as soon as he arrived at Windsor he released Michael de la Pole from confinement.

Since the king's allowance was now at the mercy of the Council, celebrations were conducted on a greatly reduced scale. Richard didn't care; he was determined to enjoy himself. It was a small gathering that celebrated Christmas dinner, and Richard smiled in satisfaction at his former chancellor, who held the place of honor at his left. Michael's lenient confinement at Windsor had done him no harm, and he looked resplendent in the king's livery—a red-and-white velvet gown Richard had gifted him just that morning.

The king's server placed a thin portion of rabbit in sauce on his trencher. Richard took a taste and briefly closed his eyes in contentment. But he couldn't keep his mind away from his troubles for long. "Gain access to my household, indeed!" he muttered. On a sudden thought, Richard turned to Michael, a malicious smile on his face. "Are they not obliged to stay in Westminster? So why don't I just take my household with me into the provinces where they can't follow?"

Michael took a sip of wine from a gold enameled cup. He gestured for the server, eyeing the rabbit appreciatively. "There is

216

much merit in your idea, sire. Since they insist on running the government without you, then you would be free to go on a royal progress to learn the humor of the rest of the country."

"Since the French have dismantled their invasion force, we have one less thing to worry about. It's amazing how quickly it came to nothing." Richard crossed himself superstitiously. In October, the threat was terrifyingly real. But by the end of November, delays and late season gales forced the French to disband. "Do you think they will be back next year?"

"The French?" Michael shook his head. "King Charles spent an enormous amount of money raising his fleet. He cannot afford to do it again. I think the danger has passed."

"Thank God for the Channel and bad weather. We must ask the archbishop to deliver a thanksgiving mass, don't you think?"

Anne was tugging his wrist. "My ladies have been practicing this carol for days, just for you. It's quite beautiful."

Richard took the hint and leaned toward Michael. "Tomorrow then," he said with a wink.

The next day proved more expedient for everyone. Richard surrounded himself with his most trusted advisors; though this was an informal meeting, no one mistook the gravity of their situation. His friends' fortunes rose and fell along with his own.

The king's eye passed from one of them to the other. "I appreciate each and every one of you," he started. "We have worked long and hard to consolidate my administration. And now, enemies among the Peers of *my* realm seek to interfere. They aim to hold the power amongst themselves. For the moment they have won. But with your help, I will take back the initiative." He sat back, waiting for their thoughts.

Robert was first. "You have every right to fight for your prerogative," he insisted, standing up and pacing. "I say we raise an army from the provinces. Without armed support, your position will continue to be weak."

Richard nodded at his friend; on the way to Windsor they had planned to take this up with his followers. This was a good time to assess their feelings. Even Burley wasn't aware that Richard and Robert had already discussed raising support, though the king was certain his old tutor would be pleased to know how well he had absorbed his lessons. "I hope it doesn't come to open warfare. As you have seen, they are striking at me through Parliament. Curse them, I don't know how they found a way to bring the Commons to their side."

"It won't last," Michael assured him. "Their real goals are not the same."

"I agree," said Burley. "Nonetheless, there is good sense in what Robert is saying. If the Lords do choose to raise an army, you have nothing to defend yourself with."

"Except my dignity," Richard said bitterly. "Which seems to be diminishing."

"Never!" Robert insisted. "They may seek to bring you down, but your regality outshines them all."

"How can I doubt?" Richard muttered absently.

"Nonetheless," pursued Burley, "it wouldn't hurt to follow the lead of your magnates and start distributing livery badges to new retainers—men we could call on in case of need. The more people see you, the more likely they will rally to your cause."

"Your earldom of Chester has always been favorable to you," mused Robert as he continued pacing. "This would be a good region from which to raise support."

The others murmured their agreement. Crossing his arms, the king turned to Michael; he knew his former chancellor had the best political instincts of everyone in the room. "What are your thoughts?"

"Hmm. I see the value in this," he said slowly. "As it stands, you are like a lion whose teeth have been pulled. You need to build your strength. On the other hand there is much to be said for attacking Parliament on their own terms. On legal grounds, I mean."

His words were met with considered silence. This was covering territory that few military men understood. "Perhaps we should consider both plans," Michael went on. "As secretly as possible, we could muster armed assistance from the provinces. And in even more secrecy, we could summon the finest judicial minds in the country and challenge the legality of this last Parliament."

Richard followed him. "We must bring Justice Tresilian into this undertaking. He would help determine how we could go about this challenge."

"And if we approach it the right way, perhaps we can even overturn their rulings—"

"And make you chancellor again," Richard concluded. He turned to John Beauchamp, his new steward. "Naturally I will travel with a greatly reduced household. How will we pay for this?" Richard smiled wryly at him; John's was an unenviable position. "We won't be entirely without funds," the king added, trying to reassure him, "I believe the exchequer will release an allowance to me throughout the year. Eventually."

Simon leaned forward. "Sire, everything I have is yours."

Richard sighed. "I thank you, old friend. I knew I could rely on you."

"And I am certain that Nicholas Brembre will be willing to make loans," Michael added.

"We will arrange to stay at abbeys along the way," Beauchamp said. "They will be more than willing to offer shelter."

"Especially with the promise of future largess." Richard nodded. "I learned that from my uncle of Lancaster. So, when do we begin?"

By February, Richard and his small retinue started their long trek to York, pausing along the way to converse with local sheriffs and mayors. At first, the king did little more than listen, for this was the first time he had appeared in public since the terrible retributions after the Great Revolt; he wasn't entirely sure whether the hostility had worn off. He found them to be cautious and noncommittal, which was something he could build upon. As they neared his northern capital, he stopped at Royston to settle a dispute between the canons of Beverly and Alexandre Neville, the Archbishop of York. Since the archbishop was currently serving on the hated council, Richard thought it wise to secure his gratitude.

Once joined by Justice Tresilian, the king's advisors began deliberating just how they would challenge the last Parliament.

After a short visit to York, they went back to Windsor for St. George's Day ceremonies—where the king distinctly snubbed his uncle Gloucester—then off to Reading where he held the first of many Great Councils in an attempt to gather local support. Alas, enthusiasm was lukewarm.

"I think it's time we went to Chester and north Wales," Richard said to de Vere. "Let us make our military preparations. We'll satisfy the Council that you are gathering an army; only you will not embark for Ireland. Not yet."

Robert was ready to take on the duties of his new office, for Richard had promised to make him Justice of Chester. But first, he had an interest much closer to his heart. A courier from Rome had caught up with Richard's itinerant court at Berkhamsted Castle, bearing a letter Robert had been anxiously waiting for. Then he had to plan for the right moment. Finding the king and queen at a private dinner in their chamber, Robert entered the room leading Agnes by the hand.

Anne turned, frowning, as the two of them knelt.

"Sire. Your Grace," Robert spoke, lowering his head but glancing up with his eyes. "We have joyous tidings to share with you. The Pope has authorized my divorce and I am free to marry Lady Agnes."

The pause following his announcement demonstrated just how joyous the others found his news. Richard put down his spoon, clearing his throat. "You plan to go through with this. Now, while I am in the midst of such turmoil."

Robert beamed at his beloved. "We have waited long for this."

The queen turned in her seat. "You are leaving my service?" It was more of a statement than a question.

Agnes blushed deeply. "Perhaps I can serve you as well," she stammered.

"Absolutely not. I do not consent to this marriage, nor will I permit such scandalous behavior in my presence. You have insulted the king by this divorce and will bring the wrath of his uncles down upon his head."

This was not what Robert anticipated; Queen Anne was normally so accommodating. But one peek at Richard and he

220

knew he would get away with it. The king leaned back in his arm-chair, picking his teeth with a silver toothpick. He studied the queen, saying nothing. After all, Agnes was her hand-maiden. It was her concern.

Anne glanced at him angrily. *All right*, Richard thought. Maybe it was both of their concerns. He knew when it was time to support her.

"The queen is right," he said mildly. "Agnes must go. How do you propose I tell my uncle Gloucester?" He grimaced at the thought. "He will take this as a mortal insult."

"I don't care. This is not his business."

"Oh, it is very much his business. Your dear wife Philippa would normally go to Lancaster with her complaints, but since he is in Portugal she will turn to Gloucester. Think hard before you do this." Richard shook his head; he knew that his words fell on deaf ears. Picking up his knife again, he took a deep sigh. "Do what you must. I will meet you in Chester in a fortnight." At this, the queen turned her back on her maid. Wiping her tears, Agnes bowed and withdrew from the room.

They must have planned this day well, for that very evening Robert de Vere, his beloved, and a small entourage rode hard from the castle without fanfare. Richard accompanied Anne to the queen's rooms, for he suspected she would need company. When she opened the door to her receiving chamber, she interrupted the other maids frantically trying to straighten the disarray. They knelt as she entered, and Anne broke into tears. No one was as organized as her dear Agnes, and already she could see the difference. Richard put an arm around her shoulders and drew her near.

"She was so dear to me," Anne sobbed into his shoulder. "I can't believe she left me for...him."

Despite himself, Richard shrugged. "They love each other. Not everyone is as fortunate as I am."

She raised her head, smiling through her tears. He kissed her cheek. "I don't know if I am strong enough to protect him," he mused. "He has chosen his course. He might as well have a few weeks of happiness before my barons strike back."

By the middle of August, Richard's advisors had finally put together a series of questions. It was not at all unusual for judges to answer queries from the king, or the council, or even the lords in Parliament. So if anything, this was business as usual. Richard knew enough about the law to assert that the last Parliament had overstepped its authority. He just wanted confirmation. They would be advising him only; he would retain their answers for future use when he was strong enough to act upon them. A future trial, perhaps? Richard allowed himself to gloat, if only for a moment.

A summons was sent for a conference at Shrewsbury, scheduled for the 21st of August. Just nine miles from the Welsh border, Shrewsbury was built inside a loop of the River Severn. The old castle was still in use though just barely. But Richard liked the proximity to Wales where he felt safer than London. The conference was attended by the king's usual advisors plus the Archbishop of Dublin and the bishops of Durham, Chichester, and Bangor. Also Archbishop Alexandre Neville had made a special trip from London with Nicholas Brembre.

On the judges' side, Robert Tresilian, Chief Justice of the king's Bench, sat among his venerable fellows including Chief Justice Robert Belknap and Justice Holt, along with three others from across the country. Of course, Tresilian knew the questions, since he was instrumental in composing them; he was well positioned to encourage the others to give the correct answers.

"I thank you for coming," Richard started, knowing full well they couldn't easily refuse. "I have questions of legality concerning last year's Parliament. We have much at stake here, notably my royal prerogative, the establishment of the Commission and the impeachment of my former chancellor. To this end I am consulting you all, given your integrity, your knowledge, and your respect of the law. I enjoin you to silence. You are absolutely forbidden to discuss the contents of this meeting with anyone, outside of this room. Do I have your solemn promise?"

One by one the judges acquiesced, noticing that the doors were all being closed and guards placed in front of them.

"Very well. I would have you swear an oath to respond as the law and custom of the realm demands." He sat patiently as they proceeded to do so. "And now, Archbishop Neville will read you the ten questions, which we will proceed to discuss."

The archbishop stood, holding his parchment. "Question number one." His voice was appropriately sonorous. "Was the Commission that was established at the last Parliament derogatory to the regality and prerogative of the lord King?" He stopped and observed the judges over the top of his paper. They glanced at each other.

After observing their reactions, Tresilian got up and walked back and forth in front of them. "You may consider this question logically and with a clear conscience. By forcing him to defer to a Commission appointed by Parliament, are the rights of the king being threatened? We are considering the very position of the monarch in relation to the government. With this in mind, I repeat the question. Was the Continual council derogatory to the king's prerogative?"

All of these men had been present at the Parliament of 1386. There was no question that they knew the issues. There was also no question that they had sanctioned the actions of the Commons—or at least made no objections. This made them very nervous. Then again, perhaps they had not been in total agreement with Parliament. This would be a good time to redeem their guilty consciences.

Tresilian retraced his steps and stopped before each judge, waiting for an answer. One by one, they replied in the affirmative. After all had responded, Tresilian said "Aye" in a loud voice, asserting his own answer. At that point, Neville moved on to question two.

"How should those be punished who procured the statute and established the Commission?"

The justices looked at each other again. Again Tresilian started his pacing. "If it is derogatory to the king's prerogative, then it is against his will. Is it not?" Reluctantly, they nodded. "Then is it not a grave offense to constrain the king to give his assent against his will?" Again, they nodded. "Then those offenders should be punished! I ask you again: how should they be punished?" He stopped before John Holt, who he knew was the least forceful of the group.

Holt scribbled something on his paper before looking up. "I would say they would be worthy of the extreme penalty of the law." Satisfied, Tresilian nodded before moving on to the next. "I would agree," the second judge said after a pause, "unless the king of his own free will wishes to extend his grace to them." Frowning, Tresilian stood before Belknap. "See here," Belknap said, "yes, I agree the offense is derogatory to the king's regality. But it is not treasonable!"

"Ah." Tresilian turned his back to them, regarding King Richard for guidance.

The king leaned forward in his throne. "You are my officers," he said. "My position would be the same as any of my magnates if *their* entitlements were threatened. There is not one among them who would refrain from upholding their own judicial rights in the most severe manner possible. Surely the king's prerogatives rank higher than theirs."

Sustained by Richard's conviction, Tresilian turned again. "I ask one more time. How should these offenders be punished?"

Belknap had lowered his face into his hands. As the others waited, he straightened. "I cannot."

"Cannot what?" Tresilian had lowered his voice.

"I cannot declare this treasonable."

Tresilian stood with his hands on his hips, glaring at Belknap. The other did not return his stare. "If you value your life you will."

The other judges exchanged glances for a third time. The Chief Justice had just crossed the line and there was no turning back. Belknap let out a sound somewhere between a sigh and a groan.

"As the king wills."

The Chief Justice pointed up in the air. "And?"

"If the king wills it, they should be punished by death."

Nodding, Tresilian went on to the others until he had the same answer from all six. Then they were ready to proceed to the next questions. One after another, the judges were queried as to whether the king's prerogative was violated when Parliament ruled on matters without Richard's permission or even his knowledge. Parliament punished royal officials without his permission; Parliament hindered the king from exercising his will. By then, the judges knew what was expected of them; every time Tresilian asked how the offenders should be punished, the unanimous answer was that they should be punished as traitors.

The king had three more questions: *What should we do with the person who proposed that the statute should be consulted concerning the deposition of King Edward II?* Without a doubt they all knew his anger was directed against the Duke of Gloucester, who dared raise the menace of abdication. Unhesitatingly, the answer was the same. Yes, he should be punished as though he was a traitor. *Can the king dissolve Parliament at his pleasure?* Assuredly yes, and if anyone acts contrary to the king's will, he should be punished as a traitor. And lastly, *was the judgment against Michael de la Pole, Earl of Suffolk, erroneous and revocable?* Yes, it was erroneous in every respect.

Satisfied, Richard nodded graciously to the judges. "I understand this has been very difficult for you. Hence, I have decided to give you one week to consider the questions and your responses, so no one will suspect that you have answered in haste. We will meet seven days from now at Nottingham. I thank you for your counsel."

A week later, the judges reassembled in front of the king. Regardless of their personal feelings, in Nottingham the answers were exactly the same and the judges put their seals on the documents. Once again they were sworn to secrecy.

Richard had his answers and for once he felt unfettered. After submitting to counsellors and uncles and unwelcome advisors for all of his minority, this was his first step toward asserting himself. Unfortunately, his triumph was to be short-lived, for just like the myth of Pandora's jar, he was about to release a terrible menace threatening his barons and the monarchy itself. For in dredging up the terrible word *treason*, Richard was destined to drive his enemies to desperate measures and prove his undoing before the year's end.

225

PART 3

DEGRADATION

CHAPTER 1

With a loud crack of thunder, the shutters burst open, followed by a gust of rain that blasted sideways into the room.

"Damn it, man! Fix that thing!" shouted Thomas of Woodstock, Duke of Gloucester, as his servant rushed over, ducking to stay dry. He fumbled at the handles, pulling first one then the other until he finally forced the shutters to meet. Pushing the bolt through, he gasped, sliding off the window sill.

"I told you to fix that," grumbled the duke. "If those books got wet I'll have your head."

Wiping water off the table, the servant bowed before slipping out of the room. Thomas went over to the shelf, inspecting his manuscripts. He nodded, relieved. Those volumes cost a fortune, since he had paid for a whole scriptorium-full of monks to create them.

Gloucester's main residence, Pleshey Castle, was known for getting the worst of the weather, perched as it was on top of the largest motte in England. Nonetheless, it served its purpose; just north-east of London, it was located close enough to the city to get there in one day and far enough away to be left alone. But the fortress needed so much work to keep it from falling apart.

Thomas closed the book, putting it back on the shelf. He would just have to be satisfied with what he had, since his own brother John of Gaunt had destroyed his chance to make a fortune. It had all been planned so perfectly; his wife Eleanor and her sister were heiresses to the vast Bohun inheritance, and after great effort, eleven year-old Mary had been persuaded to join the nunnery. This would release her half of the inheritance to Eleanor, and Thomas would finally acquire the means to support his estate. The last thing he expected was for Gaunt to snatch the girl away—while he was on the continent, at that, doing the king's business—and marry her to his son Henry of Bolingbroke. What gall! Now that Mary was out of their reach, their plans were totally ruined. Lancaster had swelled his great patrimony to enormous proportions, while Thomas—the lastborn of Edward III's sons—might as well have been called Lackland like his ancestor John. He languished at the mercy of the exchequer for annuities, and more often than not the treasurer was hard pressed for cash and he had to wait. Thanks to his puerile nephew Richard, he finally gained the rank he was entitled to, but even so it came with cash subsidies and not landed resources, which he desperately needed. If it wasn't for his wife's inheritance—her half—he would be in very poor shape financially. Even Pleshey Castle was part of her patrimony.

To make matters worse, he had to compete for local leadership with that upstart, Robert de Vere, whose main seat was also in Essex, a mere fifteen miles away. Everyone noted the rising star in Richard's court, and the country gentry gravitated toward his hated rival. Just to add more insult, Richard was constantly rewarding de Vere with income-producing grants like castles and wardships and towns. And for what? He may be Earl of Oxford, but de Vere had shown no talent for anything except increasing his own favor with the king. Whereas Thomas knew that, like his brother the Black Prince, if *he* were given a military command, he would easily secure a powerful following of his own and increase his prestige. Too bad the king was intent on a negotiated peace with France. Where was the glory in that? With such a warlike ancestry, what went wrong with his nephew?

The storm which battered the castle didn't help his mood any. When a knock came at the door he whirled around, annoyed at the interruption. "What do you want?" he growled.

His valet peeked in. "You have a visitor, your Grace."

"A visitor on a night like this? Who is it?"

"Robert Wickford, the Archbishop of Dublin."

"Wickford? What could he possibly want?" Thomas ran a hand across the back of his neck. "Oh, very well. Bring him in."

Gloucester was a practiced courtier and knew when to put his personal feelings aside. As the archbishop was ushered into the room, the duke kissed his ring, bidding him welcome. Wickford pulled off his dripping cloak and handed it to the servant, followed by his hood.

"Come, you must be chilled to the bone. Sit here, by the fire." Gloucester pushed an armchair near the hearth and gestured for some wine. He sat down on the other side.

The archbishop gratefully lowered himself, sighing as he leaned back a moment, then came forward again, rubbing his hands together. "I bring news of such import that even this terrible weather could not keep me away." He looked aside at the duke, wanting to make sure he was making an impression.

Despite himself, Gloucester was intrigued. "What news is this?"

"The king—"

"What's he done this time?"

"He has called together six chief justices to deliberate on the proceedings of the last Parliament."

Gloucester let out a grunt of disgust.

"I have written down the questions," Wickford went on. "They all concern the king's prerogative. And whether or not Parliament is permitted to act against his will. Or without his direction. And whether he can dissolve Parliament at his pleasure."

Thomas picked up a goblet from the servant's tray and Wickford did likewise, waiting for the duke's response.

"I assume the king got the answers he was searching for."

"Oh yes. That and more. They declared the chancellor's impeachment in error and revocable."

"We can take care of all that."

The archbishop hesitated.

"What, man? Get on with it."

"Well," Wickford took a long draught of wine. "They declared that anyone guilty of these trespasses against the king's royalty should be punished as traitors."

"What!" Gloucester sprung to his feet, throwing his goblet into the fireplace. "That little bastard has gone too far!" He started pacing while the other quietly sat, watching him. "Damn, his father would have knocked some sense into him if he had been alive. What have we come to when a spoiled, ungovernable child can wield such power?"

"I would dare remind you that Richard is twenty years old."

231

"And acts like a fool!" He paced some more before sitting back down. "All right, let us consider exactly what happened. Where did this take place?"

"The first conference was at Shrewsbury. Then a week later, he repeated the questions at Nottingham."

"Hmm. Why did he do it twice?"

"I believe the king wanted to demonstrate that the judges were not acting under duress."

"They were the same judges both times?"

"All but one."

"And they used the word 'traitor'?"

"Ah, the distinction was purposeful. They said the guilty should be punished as traitors, not that they *were* traitors," said Wickford, priding himself on his legal knowledge.

"Small comfort."

"It is a fine difference, but a difference, nonetheless. By speaking so, they skirted the precise definition of the Treason Act of 1351..."

"Which defined traitors as those who attacked the king directly, aided the king's enemies or levied war against the king in his realm. Since our recent acts of Parliament were directed against the king's friends—"

"They were therefore not treasonous, as per the Statute."

"However, my nephew seeks to redefine treason—"

"Which brings us back to the terrible days of Edward II—"

"God forbid!" Thomas stood again and started his pacing. King Edward's rein was infamous; he encouraged his favorites— the Despenser father and son—to run rampant throughout England. They illegally seized lands, tortured and imprisoned their enemies, and murdered their victims—among other atrocities. The potential parallels between Edward II's favorites and Richard's favorites rose before him like a specter.

Wickford sighed. "There is one more thing..."

Gloucester stopped, his back to the archbishop.

"One of the questions referred to 'the person who sent for the Statute concerning the deposition of Edward II'."

The wind pounded the windows as Gloucester gasped, appalled. He turned, staring at Wickford as if seeing him for the

232

first time. Both men knew this was a direct attack on Thomas. "Is this person to be punished as a traitor, then?"

The archbishop nodded, reluctantly.

"Then there is no turning back is there? We must retaliate before it is too late."

Gloucester surveyed the room, hopeful that his associates would come to feel the urgency that drove him to call this secret meeting. The Archbishop of Dublin had agreed to attend and was sitting quietly off the side. Richard, Earl of Arundel was poking the fire, trying to take the chill out of the room. Among them, Arundel was closest to him in attitude and aspirations; he had often complained to Thomas about the king's willful behavior and the need to keep him under control. His outburst at the Salisbury Parliament was as accurate as it was shocking. He was right: the kingdom lacked good government and was going to rot.

Arundel's new son-in-law, Thomas Mowbray, was sitting at the table nursing a mug of mulled wine. Once a favorite of the king, Mowbray strained his relations with Richard by marrying Elizabeth, the daughter Arundel. Richard's loss was their gain; as Earl of Nottingham he brought more prestige to their ranks.

The Earl of Warwick was inspecting Thomas's new gauntlets which he had specially made in Milan. "I must say, this is exquisite," he said, bending the fingers. "The articulation is perfect." Thomas nodded, pleased. He wondered if he would be needing them soon.

Henry of Bolingbroke was just coming in—the last person they waited for. Since he was administering the Lancastrian estates during his father's absence, it made sense to include him in any important negotiations. Perhaps his intentions would become obvious; Thomas hoped so, since he hadn't had much opportunity to sound him out. He strode up to his nephew, taking his hands in his own. "Thank you for coming. How's your boy, my namesake?"

Henry's face lit up. "Walking already. He's the sweetest, most charming child. His mother thinks he looks exactly like you."

"Ha. Poor thing. Come, Henry. We are most anxious to get started."

Once the men were settled, Gloucester gestured for Wickford to join them. "The archbishop came to me the other night with the most disturbing tidings which have implications for all of us. You can tell them best in your own words."

Wickford stood slowly, weighed down by the significance of his report. As he related the news, the others watched him first with disbelief, then with alarm. When he finished, they sat very still, staring at him.

Finally, Arundel shifted his weight in his chair. "Why are you the only one telling us this?"

"The judges were all sworn to secrecy." His voice shook with the answer.

"And you?"

"Yes. As a witness I was also sworn to secrecy. But I could not live with myself if this distortion of the law was to instigate proceedings against the king's critics."

Gloucester handed them each a copy of the judges' questions. "Archbishop Wickford has put this together for us. Read it well; these questions are directed against us." This wasn't exactly true; Henry of Bolingbroke had not attended the most recent Parliament. But at the same time, he could easily find himself the object of the king's unpredictable fury, just like his father was.

"I thank you, Archbishop Wickford, for your timely warning. It would be better for you if you did not witness the rest of our discussion."

Wickford was more than happy to get away. He uncomfortably took his leave and was quickly forgotten.

Gloucester suspected that his associates did not need much persuading. "The king will bring this up next Parliament. Of that I am certain. Given his temperament, he wouldn't stop at trying us for treason." For a second a chill ran down his spine.

Arundel scowled. "The pup doesn't have enough serious support."

"Can we take the chance?"

Warwick was still reading the document. "If this comes to trial, we could lose everything. Many of our ancestors were stigmatized by the trials of Edward II. Only the Treason Act of 1351 protects us."

234

"Then we shall bypass it, like the king did."

"Ignore it, you mean?"

"If we must!" Gloucester fought his impatience; Warwick was always too moderate. "What we must do is finish what we started. The Commons are with us, at least for now. We must push our agenda through Parliament and rid the kingdom of these intolerable favorites. They poison the king's mind and enrich themselves at our expense. We must clean house and replace Richard's bad counsellors with those willing to govern with the country's best interests in mind."

"And ours," interjected Arundel coldly. He was not one to mince words.

Thomas glared at him for a moment. "All right. Since we dare not attack the king, we can remove his supporters. We can isolate the king and thus render him harmless."

"And how to you propose to remove them?" Arundel prodded him, already suspecting the answer. "We can't impeach them all."

"Oh no. We need something more permanent than that. We will use Richard's own example and appeal them of treason."

"All of them?" Henry was shocked into speech, though he had intended to remain aloof.

Gloucester studied him appraisingly. *He was inscrutable, this one.* "Why not? Once we begin, we'll have to see it through to the end or else find ourselves destroyed. Given an opening, the king will exploit it for all that he is worth." He paused, studying his co-conspirators. They all looked down, considering the implications. "Take heed. I say the king is unfit to rule. There is no knowing what impulsive measures he might take against us. He needs to be guided by the great lords of the realm, appointed by Providence to uphold the liberties of the people. It's happened before. King John and the Magna Carta. Henry III and the Provisions of Oxford—"

"Edward II," said Arundel.

"It hasn't gone that far. Not yet."

"Might I remind you that those others did not end well," Warwick said.

Gloucester frowned at him. "Only because they did not go far enough."

All had much to think about and agreed to meet in one week's time at Harringay Park, just north of London. As they were leaving, Gloucester put his hand on Henry's shoulder. "Are you with us?"

Henry pursed his lips. "I must consult with my father. Rest assured, I will certainly do nothing against you."

The other nodded; it was pretty much what he expected. So far, Henry had stayed as much out of politics as he could. Thomas almost envied his freedom. "Well, if anything untoward happens in the interim, we may call on you for help."

Nodding uncertainly, Henry shrugged into his cloak. They both knew that day would probably come well before Gaunt would have time to answer.

On November 10, Richard returned to London, nine days ahead of the expiry of the Great and Continual council. He was accompanied by all his favorites, and had made many plans concerning how he would take over as soon as the council was dismissed. As he entered the city of London, the mayor and aldermen and important citizens came out to greet him, dressed in red and white. Together they formed a cavalcade and proceeded to Westminster. The monks had laid out carpets from the palace gate to the church of St. Peter, meeting Richard and his entourage and leading the way so he could make his devotions before retiring. This was encouraging. By all indications London was with him.

The following day he sent out a summons to Gloucester and Arundel to attend him immediately. It was another two days before the first answer came. Richard was in council when the message was delivered. Simon opened it and frowned, passing it to the king. "It is from Arundel."

As he read the missive, Richard's face turned bright red and he put the letter on the table, covering it with his fist. "Arundel has refused to come," he said in a low voice. "He said he mistrusts the mortal enemies at my side, and dare not approach for fear of arrest. Well, I will not disappoint him."

Richard turned to Henry Percy, Earl of Northumberland. "Sir Henry, You are the senior earl here. I order you to Reigate to arrest Arundel and bring him to the Tower."

Northumberland took his time getting up from the table; he hoped someone would intervene. No one did. Bowing, the earl left the room and was soon riding south with a small retinue.

The king turned to Robert de Vere. "We might as well be prepared. I fear my uncle and his confederates are preparing an offensive against me. I need you to go back to Chester and raise my army. I require the protection of my good Cheshiremen."

Robert stood, straightening his back in as military a gesture as he was capable of. "You can depend on me," he said.

Richard put a hand on his arm. "Stay a bit. I will prepare letters under my seal commanding the muster." He turned to Nicholas Brembre. "Do you think I can count on London to support me?"

Nicholas frowned. "It is a difficult question to answer. Those men are motivated by their own self-interest—especially Mayor Exton. They will probably try to wait to see who is in the ascendant."

"Perhaps we can persuade them to swear an oath of loyalty to me?"

"With the proper incentive, perhaps we can."

"I'll have to be satisfied with that, for now. Arrange that for me, Nicholas. Summon them to meet me tomorrow." He turned to the others. "What do you suggest?"

Burley stood, leaning over the table. "Perhaps this would be a good time to ask the King of France for advice."

"Much as I would like to do so, I think that should be a last resort. It's good to use as a threat, though." He winked at Burley, a wicked smile on his lips. Then he turned to Michael de la Pole, usually the last to offer advice.

"I fear," the ex-chancellor said slowly, "we may be forced to treat with the lords. In the end, they can call on large retinues and you have none. Save what Robert can summon." He turned to de Vere. "Yours is a great responsibility. The king depends on you."

The lookout at Reigate castle had very good eyes. The sun was just a sliver to the west, and the feathery clouds glowed pink and orange, promising a gorgeous evening. But the lookout didn't have time to appreciate the sunset; coming down the main road from London, he could just distinguish the banner of a blue lion rampant on a gold background.

Running from the parapet walk, he banged on the door of the castle steward. "Armed soldiers approaching!" he cried. "I do not know the coat of arms."

A groan and scrape of furniture assured him the steward was getting up. He ran back to his observation post, where the approaching party was close enough to count. Luckily, there weren't enough men to challenge the castle garrison. He turned as the steward approached, adjusting his belt.

"I see a large retinue, nothing more," he said, pointing.

The other squinted. "Damn! It's Percy. What's he doing here?" He turned to the lookout. "You had better get the earl."

Anxious, the man bolted down the steps. As it turned out, the steward did not have to wait long; Arundel had already finished his supper and was on his way to the parapet.

"This is not good," the earl grumbled. The two of them watched quietly as the soldiers approached. Finally the leader pulled ahead, pausing just on the other side of the moat. It was Henry Percy himself.

"Are you visiting as friend or foe?" Arundel shouted.

Percy stood in his stirrups. "Neither, Lord Arundel. I come on the order of King Richard, who commands your return to London."

"For what purpose?"

"To answer why you refused his previous summons."

"You must be foe, then, Henry Percy! Knowing the king, you come to arrest me!"

Percy hesitated. He was not enthusiastic about this mission. "That is for Richard to decide."

"I will not put myself into his power! You will have to take me by force!" Arundel turned to his steward. "Summon my garrison. Let them show themselves."

As Percy studied the outer walls, Arundel's soldiers lined the parapet, spears silhouetted in the failing light. Their numbers were already double his own, and Henry knew there had to be many more inside. This was a waste of time. He had done his duty; he hadn't the men to attack the castle. Lifting his hand in salute, he turned his horse and rode back to his retainers.

For a moment Arundel watched him with satisfaction. Then he turned to his steward. "At least I know which way the wind is blowing," he said. "I will ride with thirty men. Tonight. I will join the Duke of Gloucester and the Earl of Warwick at Harringay Park. Put out a summons to my levies. Send one hundred men to meet me at Waltham Cross. Replenish the garrison here. Send to my castle at Holt and tell them to observe any suspicious activity in Cheshire. The king has been spending too much time there. As soon as I know more I will inform you."

The earl had a thirty-mile trip ahead of him, but he was so incensed that his anger sustained him through the night. His party crossed the Thames and made their way to Harringay, where he knew that Gloucester and Warwick had already gathered with their armed retinues. Gloucester welcomed him with open arms.

"Finally. We are all together." He waved an arm over the encampment. "More of the landed gentry are joining our ranks every hour. Get some sleep, Richard. Tomorrow we will move on to Waltham Cross, where I expect Thomas Mortimer to be waiting for us." Mortimer was uncle to young Roger, the 4th Earl of March and heir presumptive to the crown; he was fiercely protective of his seven year-old nephew's rights. He was also an intimate friend of Richard Arundel.

"Good. We can use his strong arm."

After a few hours' sleep, Arundel was ready to move on to Waltham. It was becoming clear that they had roused more support than they dared hope, and it was beginning to feel like they had a good chance of forcing the king to comply with their demands. As promised, Mortimer was waiting for them at Waltham.

Commandeering the town hall, the lords settled down to formulate their strategy while their reinforcements grew. "There will never be a better time than now to lodge an appeal against the king's advisors," Gloucester began, taking charge of the meeting. "We must strike at the worst offenders now and worry about the rest of them later. The king has prepared the way for a treason trial. I say we accuse his favorites of treason first. Starting with that canker de Vere, may he rot in hell!" He had to pause, taking a deep breath, for he had not yet gotten over his rage at his sister's humiliation. "I would throttle him with these two hands for divorcing my poor Philippa." The others watched sympathetically while he clenched his fists. He took another breath, shaking his head. "Robert de Vere," he went on, "most definitely. Sir Robert Tresilian, for persuading the judges. Sir Michael de la Pole; he is the most dangerous of all. Sir Nicholas Brembre who holds too much influence in London." He glanced around. "Who else?"

"Archbishop Neville of York," said Arundel. "He has joined the king's court party. He has betrayed us."

"Five appellees. Let us put it in writing."

Their discussions took most of the afternoon, and they were only slightly surprised to discover that a delegation had arrived from the king. By then, their objectives had been worked out, and they were almost relieved to get things moving.

Interestingly enough, the new arrivals were all members of Richard's hated continuous council—not his personal advisors. The king knew his choices would be agreeable to those assembled, and he wanted to avoid further alarm. In walked William Courtenay, the Archbishop of Canterbury followed by the others. Their status and authority were enough to demonstrate that the king understood the gravity of the situation.

The councilors were offered wine and refreshments, though the tension in the room was inescapable. Finally, Gloucester stood. "My lords, we have this to say to the king. We have taken arms to deliver him from his five traitorous advisors: Robert de Vere, Robert Tresilian, Nicholas Brembre, Michael de la Pole, and Alexandre Neville. These men are isolating King Richard from his true friends and councilors. We can see that the kingdom of England is in danger of destruction by these traitors unless a speedy remedy is applied."

The archbishop stood as well. "This is most disturbing, my lords. We beg you to put aside your armed retinues, for they will do more harm than good."

"Your Grace, we cannot do this. We mean to press our suit."

"And how will you proceed to do so?"

"We have composed a proclamation—an appeal of treason for those five dangerous men who pretend to be the king's friends. We submit this document into your care."

Gloucester handed a parchment to the archbishop; ribbons attached to the lords' seals dangled from the bottom.

His hand trembling, Courtney studied the document before looking at the duke. "You really mean to go through with this?"

"There is no other way."

"Then I must arrange a meeting with the king. Will you come to see him?"

"He must guarantee our safety."

"Then I will endeavor to do so."

It was to be three days before the Lords Appellant—as they were henceforth to be known—rode to Westminster to meet the king. In those three days Richard tried every approach he could think of to persuade the citizens of London to support him. He cajoled, he made promises, and when that didn't work he even demanded they raise a militia—only to be told that they were not warriors and were unsuited to fighting. He made a declaration that no one in the city was permitted to sell provisions to the Appellants' army, though it seems few paid attention. He attempted to gain the support of Northumberland and other nobles, only to be told that though their loyalty was unchanged, they refused to fight for Robert de Vere.

Frustrated, defeated, King Richard summoned his loyal friends to a private conference. Robert had already gone to Chester to raise troops; the other four attended the king, in no good humor.

"We have done all we could," Richard said, almost in tears. "I fear I cannot protect you."

Expecting nothing more, the others remained silent. Richard turned toward Archbishop Neville. "You, at least, can expect protection from the Church. The Pope will not allow you to be harmed."

Rubbing his chin, Neville nodded. "Yet it would be best if I stayed as far from Westminster as possible. With your permission, I shall return to York forthwith."

"Yes. You should go. Please give me your blessing first."

The archbishop stood, making the sign of the cross over each in turn. "I will pray for you. For all of you." Gathering his robes, he left the room as quickly as his dignity would permit.

Richard sighed. "This is terrible. What am I going to do without all of you?" He took Michael's hand in his own. "You have been with me as long as I can remember. You have always watched after my best interests, and now I can't look after yours."

Michael smiled sadly. "Bring us back when you can. For now, I will go to the continent. Perhaps my brother in Calais can help me."

"Godspeed, Michael." Richard wiped his eyes as his old friend and advisor bowed and left. There was no such affection between the king and Tresilian, and the Chief Justice was anxious to disappear. He, too, bowed and slipped away, leaving Richard alone with Nicholas Brembre.

"And you?" Richard said sadly. "Am I to say farewell to you as well? You have been my staunchest supporter and I owe you so many favors I don't know where to begin."

Nicholas shook his head. "They have nothing to condemn me with. What treason have I done? No, sire. There is much for me to do here. I stay."

"Oh, Nicholas." Richard's relief was palpable. "With you beside me, how can I fail?" They both knew that his words were empty. But Richard took heart; between Brembre's efforts in London and de Vere's mission to raise an army, perhaps there was a chance he would still prevail. He had to believe it. What was his alternative?

The best Richard could do for his friends was to declare that the appeal should be referred to Parliament. This would give them time to safely flee the country, and, though he kept his thoughts to himself, it would give Robert ample time to raise an army and march on London. The three Appellants, appearing at

Westminster accompanied by 300 men-at-arms, were nonplussed at the king's decision but dared not object since he promised to take all parties—both accusers and accused—under his protection. The Appellants weren't entirely sure how many of the lords still supported Richard and weren't ready to put it to the test. The date for Parliament was fixed for February 3. It was a small victory for the king and he meant to make the most of it.

CHAPTER 2

"How many men have we retained?" Robert de Vere removed his gloves and handed them to a servant before sitting and holding up his dripping boot. Another page hurried over, kneeling and tugging at the heel while Robert held out a hand for someone else to give him ale.

Thomas Molineux, Constable of Chester castle, leaned against the wall next to the fireplace. "We have 500 men on active duty plus another 1500 waiting to be called up."

"That won't be enough." Robert took a deep draught and held out his mug for more. "We need at least a thousand more before marching on London; I'm hoping for two thousand more. The king is in serious danger. I have letters with the king's seal commanding the local sheriffs to raise men. I doubt not that they will respond."

"How much time do I have?"

"A month, no more. I hope to reach London before Christmas."

"I will start on the Welsh border and work my way back to Chester. With you organizing the castle garrison and gathering provisions, I can concentrate on raising your levy."

De Vere nodded in agreement when a decidedly female voice interrupted his thoughts. "You've made it back! Welcome, my lord!"

He whirled around in his chair, his face flushed with pleasure. "Agnes. I couldn't get here quick enough. The sight of you makes me forget all my problems."

Grimacing, Molineux turned away. He gestured for his knights to follow him.

Robert had already forgotten his constable. He rose, taking her in his arms. "My dove. I thought of you every day." He pulled back just far enough to look in her eyes, pushing aside a lock of blond hair. "I have much to do, but not until tomorrow. Tonight, I must make up for all those lost days."

She smiled sadly at him. Though the life of luxury agreed with her, she felt isolated away from the queen's court. "Tell me all about it," she said, putting an arm through his. "I only hear partial tidings."

He sighed. "I don't even know where to start. Come, show me what you have done with our bedchamber."

Robert may have enjoyed his homecoming, but in many ways being parted from Richard was more stressful than being away from his new wife. He knew that he was the cause of much conflict between the king and his lords, and when Richard's letter reached him about the appeals, he nearly despaired. Everything depended on him and his army. The fact that he had never seen battle in his life didn't help matters any; at least he was fortunate in Molineux, who was as accomplished as he was experienced. It was said that at his nod, the whole province obeyed. His influence was wide and men responded to his call.

By the second week of December, Robert was proud that he commanded more than four thousand men thanks to the efforts of his constable. Archers comprised a large proportion of his force, and he felt that in numbers, at least, he had nothing to be ashamed of.

Richard Earl of Arundel slammed the door, interrupting the supper of Gloucester and Warwick. He sat at the trestle table and reached for a piece of cold meat pie, taking a huge bite then washing it down with a draught of ale.

"Hungry, I see," said Gloucester. "What kept you?"

"That damned de Vere. I was just talking to my messenger from Holt Castle. He has been observing activity on the Welsh borders. There is no doubt. De Vere is raising an army."

The other two stopped what they were doing and stared hard at him; Thomas Mortimer and the lesser lords in the room drew closer. Arundel finished his pie and wiped his hands. Gloucester was the first to speak. "Then King Richard has broken his oath of protection. It was all pretense. He needed time to gather an army while we waited for Parliament."

"With de Vere as his commander? We would be greatly shamed if that pup caught us unprepared." Arundel threw down his napkin. "He has merely played into our hands. Or perhaps he will die on the battlefield."

Gloucester was still fuming. "The king has proved himself unworthy to rule. He does not deserve the crown." Now it was the turn of the other two Appellants to gape at him, astonished. He was speaking treason and there were no two ways about it. Too late, Gloucester caught himself. He coughed, hiding his chagrin. "There are other sons of Edward III."

Their great respect for Gloucester and his ruthlessness kept the others quiet for a moment, though it would be no exaggeration to say that their thoughts flew to John of Gaunt in Portugal, still striving to maintain a hold on his Castilian title. But John was over there and Gloucester was over here. After a moment Arundel nodded his head, pursing his lips. He turned to Warwick. "There are grounds to justify what he is saying."

Warwick stood, stepping away from the table. "Nay, our quarrel is with Robert de Vere, not the king. We need to keep de Vere away from London at all costs. We must find him and block him, even if it means fighting other Englishmen."

Recovering his composure, Gloucester readily agreed. "Yes, you are right, of course. And now let us send to Henry of Bolingbroke and Thomas Mowbray. I think they will come over to our side. Let us go north of the city and gather our forces. We can meet at Huntingdon in one week's time, and there make our dispositions."

Events proved Gloucester right. Bolingbroke felt no love for Robert de Vere and saw the threat posed by his actions. He agreed to meet the others and Mowbray followed his lead. On the 12th of December the Appellants—now numbering five—held a council of war then moved west to Northampton and the midlands, dividing their forces to surround de Vere.

For the first time in his life, Robert de Vere felt like a real soldier. His breast plate was polished to a high gloss; his pure white palfrey was well-bred and strong, absorbing the long distances with a smooth ambling gait. His favorite black war horse was tied to the wagon storing the rest of his armor. Thomas Molineux rode beside him, tall and sturdy, and the steady tramping of feet from behind comforted him.

If he had known that the more experienced Appellants had sent out a slew of scouts who were tracking his exact whereabouts, he surely would have been less complacent. But he had his own scouts and so far, nothing was amiss. However, this was soon to change. The clouds, which hung low all day, seemed to hug the earth as the sun went down, and he heard, rather than saw, a lone horse galloping his way. Breaking through the fog, the man was almost upon them when he pulled his mount to a halt.

"My lord," the man gasped. "They are coming. Gloucester and Warwick are blocking your way to Northampton."

"Damn," hissed Molineux. "How far away are they?"

"Half a day's march," the scout said.

"I was afraid of this. We don't want to fight them unless we must. Sir Robert, we have to turn south. If we take the Foss Way toward the Cotswolds, we can continue on until we cross the Thames at Radcot Bridge. If we follow the river on the southern bank, we can keep it between us and their army all the way to London."

Trusting to Molineux's experience, Robert agreed. They reached Stow-on-the-Wold the night of the 19th—a high and windy spot perched atop Stow Hill. It was there that the other scouts converged. "The Earl of Warwick is at Chipping Camden," said the first. "Gloucester is at Moreton-in-Marsh," said the second, coming in right after him. Robert turned to the third. "The Earl of Arundel is at Witney, blocking the road to Oxford," the man stated.

Molineux paced from one to the other. "That puts Gloucester and Warwick behind us and Arundel to the east. I don't like this at all. They are pushing us toward the Thames whether we like it or not."

"We don't have much choice," Robert muttered. "If we keep pressing forward, we can reach the river by tomorrow night. Hopefully we'll have enough time to cross before they catch up with us."

Molineux sighed. "I don't like this at all," he grumbled to himself. "We can only afford four hours' sleep. I'll tell the men."

Robert watched him stalk away. If his captain was this concerned, he knew they were in trouble. A gust of wind pulled the corner of his tent out of the ground and a soldier rushed to secure it before any more damage was done. Robert tugged his cloak tighter around his shoulders, wishing he was back in Chester. This soldiering was vastly overrated, he decided. If they got of this alive, he would promote to Molineux to overall commander and let him keep all the glory.

Before the sun was up, they started on their way. The air was just below freezing and the fog wrapped around them, causing a fine drizzle that froze to naked tree limbs and blades of dry grass. All day they slogged past fields dotted with sopping wet sheep, and their boots turned the road into mud.

As the afternoon drew on they were getting close to the Thames; on their left they passed the forest surrounding the market town of Bampton, which everyone knew was near the river. Encouraged, they picked up their pace even as the mist turned to heavy fog and they had trouble seeing what was in front of them. At times like this a soldier's ears take over as his eyesight diminishes, and from behind they detected the muffled clatter of an armed force. The jingle of harnesses, the occasional snort, the subdued but unmistakable tromp of hooves drew closer every minute.

De Vere raised a hand, bringing his troops to a halt. He turned to Molineux. "Draw the men into battle formation," he said. "Raise the standards of the king and St. George. If it's Gloucester, we will face him now before the others catch up."

Nodding, the other drew his horse around. There was no need for secrecy now and the trumpets sounded, blasting their challenge into the fog. The archers took the front line, ready to release their first burst before falling back behind the infantry.

"It is Gloucester," Molineux growled. "He caught up with us."

As Robert blinked in alarm, a herald rode forward from Gloucester's army. He drew rein, addressing the Cheshire army rather than its leader.

"My master the Duke of Gloucester supports the king as his liege man," he cried in a clear voice. "He does not wish to fight you unless you intend to stand by the traitors to King Richard and England."

One of the Cheshire captains stepped forward. "At the king's command and for the protection of the king's person we ride with the Duke of Ireland. We do not wish to offer support or give encouragement to traitors."

"Damn it, man! That is what you are doing. The Duke of Ireland has been legally appealed of certain treasons. Return home and proceed no further if you want to save your lives."

Up to this point, the Cheshiremen had been steadfast enough, but Robert could see that they were suddenly losing heart. Kicking his horse, he rode along the front line.

"Gloucester seeks to confound you! Do not heed his treacherous words. We serve the king! Gloucester marches on London to imprison King Richard!"

Back and forth he went, his voice rising higher in panic. He stopped in front of Molineux then turned around as his constable pointed a sword at their own archers. Almost as one, the men were holding up their weapons in supplication.

"We had better take what troops remain loyal and run for the bridge," shouted Molineux.

Nodding, Robert urged his mount forward. "Follow me!" he cried. "My faithful men, follow me to the river!" Not bothering to wait for response, Robert fled, leaving his uncertain army—and his baggage wagons full of gold and supplies—to the tender mercies of the Duke of Gloucester. Molineux was right behind him, along with a small force who preferred fighting to surrender. Robert would have found slim consolation in knowing that Gloucester kept his word. He stripped de Vere's army of its weapons and let them go home in peace.

For once, Robert was grateful for the blanket of fog. It wasn't far to Radcot Bridge; he hoped the poor visibility would hinder pursuit. For a moment, he thought they would escape, but of a sudden he drew rein, aghast at the scene before him.

Instead of finding a path to safety, he was blocked by tree trunks and rubble piled across the road, while an armed retinue sat astride their war horses under Bolingbroke's coat of arms. Bolingbroke! The rest of Duke Henry's men were busy with destructive work, smashing the stone arches of Radcot Bridge with mallets and hammers. By now there was only enough width for one man to cross—forget about an army.

Robert may have been disconcerted, but Molineux had his wits about him. "Charge!" he shouted, raising his sword and driving forward, dashing past the reluctant de Vere. His men followed in tight formation. Hesitating for only a moment, Robert went after them, drawing his sword and shouting encouragement. His constable clashed with the leading soldiers blocking the bridge; they traded blows that rang fiercely through the thick haze. Alas, after a brief exchange, Molineux fell from his horse, only getting back to his feet with difficulty. One of Bolingbroke's knights charged him, swinging a war hammer against his breastplate. Again and again he struck, pushing Molineux into the river; the constable found himself on the defensive and couldn't recover. "Thomas Mortimer, you bastard," he gasped, recognizing the man's colors.

Robert was close enough to hear, but he was too busy defending himself to be of any help. Swinging wildly at a mounted horseman, he just nicked the man's leg armor when an ally came up from the side, driving a spear into the horse's flank. Shrieking, the destrier reared up and Robert pulled out of the fray, just missing the flailing hooves. Bringing his mount around, Robert saw Molineux knee deep in the river, still defending himself.

He knew they were finished. Robert's men were already retreating, and some actually leaped into the river. Without another thought, de Vere spurred his horse and raced along the shore, hoping to cross at the next bridge—while behind him, Thomas Mortimer insisted that Molineux come out of the water or else he would order his archers to shoot.

"If I come out," gasped Molineux, "will you spare my life?"

"I won't promise it. You will either come out, or you will soon die."

"If it must be, then let me climb out and fight so I can die like a man." As Mortimer didn't respond, Molineux stumbled forward, trying to keep his balance in the mud. After two short steps, his enemy grabbed his helmet and pulled it from his head; with his other hand he quickly thrust a dagger into Molineux's eye.

Falling into a bloody heap, the Constable of Chester was quickly forgotten while the victors searched for Robert de Vere. In all the excitement nobody paid much attention to a solitary knight dashing downstream along the river. After all, they knew the next bridge was guarded, so why bother to chase him?

By now, Robert had only one thing on his mind: get to the safety of Windsor Castle. Oh, if only Richard had come out in person like he had promised in his last letter. With him in the field, the Appellants would have been exposed for the traitors they really were! But now was not the time for regrets. The Duke of Ireland was a hunted man, and his only hope was the protection of the king.

The next crossing over the Thames was at Newbridge. Robert rode directly there then dismounted, leading his horse quietly along the edge of the woods. It was to no avail. A score of archers paced back and forth before the bridge, ensuring that none would pass their barrier. Robert had trouble containing his panic; he immediately mounted his horse, kicking it into a gallop and dashing east, disregarding the need for quiet. As he flew across the road leading to the bridge, he could hear shouting and a scramble to follow him. Luckily, he had spent much of his boyhood in this shire and knew of a rope ferry at Bablock Hythe where the river was narrow, though deep, and the waters were fairly still. With a last burst, it was a race to safety of a desperate sort, for if the ferry was on the other side, he would have to swim for it.

Alas, after skirting water-meadows and avoiding marshy patches, when he finally passed through a row of tall poplars and reached the waterside, he knew his luck had come to an end. Bolingbroke's men were somewhere behind him and the ferry was out of reach. Untying his saddle bag and dropping it on the ground, he tore off his gauntlets, threw away his sword, and spurred his horse into the river. Taking a great leap, the animal swam with powerful strokes while Robert clung to his mane, praying to God and weeping with frustration. The water was

251

freezing and the horse was tiring quickly, but after what seemed like hours it found footing on the far shore and scrambled to safety.

CHAPTER 3

The king's chamber at Windsor Castle was a sad, quiet place this night, just three days before Christmas. Unlike his usual habit of filling the room with candles, Richard's mood was so dark he blew most of them out, and his servants crept around him like mice, trying not to be seen. Simon Burley and Queen Anne sat nearby, waiting for him to move; both were at a loss for words though they occasionally spoke to each other. It had been two days since the last letter from Robert, and everyone sensed that something had gone wrong.

Richard finally stood and walked to the window. Below in the bailey, he could see his sentries walking back and forth, lit by flickering torches against the wall. A few flakes of snow dropped lazily to the ground. Leaning on the window sill, he watched with interest as someone was let in through the gate, escorted by two guards who treated him familiarly.

The king stiffened. He knew that walk. It was Robert. Alone.

Hurrying to the door, Richard opened it himself, listening to the footfalls coming up the tower stairs. In the shadows he saw Robert's head, hung low in defeat. As he reached the door Robert stopped, staring at the king. His eyes were anguished. The guards bowed and retreated while Richard stared back, unable to break the silence. His friend was disheveled, unshaven, dressed in some sort of peasant garment.

Words were inadequate. Richard stepped back and de Vere practically stumbled into the room. He was so dirty the king was reluctant to touch him but Burley rushed over, putting an arm around Robert's shoulders. A servant pulled up a bench near the fire and Robert sat down heavily.

At first de Vere stared at the floor; someone shoved a cup of ale into his hand and he took a deep draught before looking again at Richard. "I failed you."

Blinking back tears, the king pulled his chair closer. "Gloucester?"

253

"Gloucester, Arundel, Warwick, Bolingbroke, and I think Mowbray was among them."

"Bolingbroke?" Richard shuddered.

"He's the one who stopped us at Radcot Bridge. He was waiting for me; they were smashing the bridge as I approached. With the others behind us, pushing us into a trap. I see it now. They were blocking my way to Oxford, then they blocked the road back to Chester. I had no other way to go but south to cross the Thames."

"What happened to my army?"

"They surrendered! Gloucester accused me of treason and they believed him! The cowards."

"They surrendered? All of them?"

"Only a handful stayed with me all the way to Radcot Bridge. We were too few to resist Bolingbroke. I knew they were after me and I escaped."

"What about Molineux?"

"They drove him into the river. I doubt whether he survived."

Richard sat back in his chair. "This is armed revolt."

With a cry of anguish Robert threw himself to his knees. "Forgive me, sire! I am desolate."

"Shh. Shh. Get up, Robert. You need a bath and clean clothes." Gesturing for someone to help, Richard leaned forward. "But you are not safe here. I will give you letters of introduction to the French court. You must wait for things to settle down before I can bring you back."

Nodding, de Vere meekly followed the servant. He clearly wasn't himself. Richard watched with a frown until the door closed. Then he turned to Anne.

"My dear, we are not safe either. If the Appellants are truly victorious, God only knows what they might attempt. Tomorrow we move to the safety of the Tower."

"I'll start packing tonight." She stood, kissing him on the cheek.

He gave her a quick smile before gesturing to Simon, bringing him closer. "Nicholas Brembre will help us. We need to close the gates of London against the invading armies; I don't want to see another hostile force. The Tower is well stocked with

254

arms, but I do remember that we need to repair at least two canons."

Burley nodded in agreement. "I will start out at once. We should be able to stay ahead of them." They spent some time planning their next move and Simon departed, leaving the king alone with his secretary. They were still writing letters when Robert returned, looking presentable though no better in spirits.

"I must take my leave." He started to kneel when Richard stopped him, leading him over to the window. He put an arm through Robert's.

"My heart is breaking," the king said. "It was bad enough when Michael left. Now, to see you go—"

"It is better for you. I know that much of this trouble is because of me."

"I care nothing for that!" In defense of his friend, Richard's voice took on a harsh tone. "They may rot in hell for all I care!"

Robert smiled sadly. "I would that it was so easy. Ah, if we were only simple knights, our friendship would bother no one. But for you, every move, every statement attracts criticism. And since they can't attack you, their judgment falls on my head. Though I would bear the burden willingly, it's not enough to save you from their onslaught."

"Oh my friend. What will I do without you?"

"Your dear queen will stand by you. She is inviolate."

Forgetting his dignity, Richard took Robert into his arms. When they pulled apart, there were tears in his eyes.

"You will bring me back when you can," said Robert. "I will be all right. If you would send a safe-conduct to Agnes, I won't be entirely alone in my exile."

"I will do so," said Richard, resigned. "There is a horse ready for you in the stables." He watched quietly as Robert gathered his things and paused at the door, an arm around his pack.

"Fare thee well, my King. I hope to see you again in this life."

"Speak not thus," said Richard to the closing door. "Godspeed."

Burley was right in assuming the Lords Appellant were not in a hurry. Intent on celebrating their victory, the lords paraded their armies through Oxford and continued on to St. Albans, where they spent Christmas Eve and Christmas Day drinking and feasting. Richard and his court, safely lodged in the Tower, were greatly subdued; since the king kept company with the bishops of Ely, Hereford, and Winchester, he spent his Christmas in holy contemplation.

On St. Stephen's day, December 26, the Appellants marched their army to London. At first they camped at Clerkenwell, just north of the city walls—for the gates were closed against them. But that didn't last long. Although Nicholas Brembre did his best to secure the city against the lords, in the end he was overruled by the mayor and leading guilds who opened up negotiations. After much back-and-forth, the Appellants agreed to spread out their forces around the city walls. Mayor Exton promised that provisions would become available to the armies so long as *they* agreed to behave themselves. Brembre found himself arrested and thrown into prison.

Richard had to accept that he was under siege. Indeed, he could see the army from the Tower; it was beginning to feel like the Great Revolt all over again. Except that this time, he had no say in the matter.

Richard tried to make light of his waning support in London. "Let the army languish until they run out of food," he said to his uncle of York, who was kind enough to attend him. "Then I can negotiate from strength."

York, whose beard was showing plenty of grey and whose walk revealed the stiffness of arthritis, sat heavily before the king. Neither ambitious nor covetous, York was the uncle Richard trusted the most, for he was willing to negotiate both sides with equal simplicity. *At times like this*, Richard thought, *a lack of zeal will take us farther than the most emphatic persistence.*

But this time, even York was doubtful. "I think we had best not depend on that," he said slowly. "The lords have shown themselves to be most persistent. No, I think we should send a delegation to meet the leaders. They will be expecting as much."

"Is there no other way?"

York shook his head sadly. "You have nowhere else to go. Do you want them to lay siege to the Tower?"

Fortunately, neither side wanted to drag this out. It was difficult enough to control thousands of hungry and bored soldiers waiting in the depth of winter. There was no way to stop more from joining the ranks every day. That was all well and good; they were necessary to prove a point. But beyond their obvious show of strength, they could turn into a nuisance. Or worse.

Richard finally consented to a deputation; he insisted that it be at the Tower. The Appellants agreed at once, though they were concerned that the king might be laying a trap for them. Exasperated, he offered to let them bring 200 men—or however many they wanted—to reconnoiter and make sure all was safe. This created another delay, but finally the lords were satisfied.

Next to the chapel in the White Tower, Richard was seated in the council chamber under a short canopy. While waiting, he studied his St. John the Apocalypse tapestries, thinking that this room was a most appropriate setting for the upcoming interview. The Duke of York entered from the corner staircase, followed by the three bishops who had negotiated with the lords. They climbed into the dais to stand behind him. Other councilors gathered along the far wall, having come in through the banquet hall.

York cleared his throat. "They are here. Each one of them has brought one hundred men and they have locked the gates behind them."

Richard sighed. "Five hundred men to enforce their will on one king."

There was no answer to Richard's plaint. The king nodded, giving his knights permission to announce the lords. As they waited, the uproar from the inner ward filled the room; it sounded like the soldiers were barely kept under control. Ignoring the ruckus, the five Appellants came up the stairs; each one paused before entering the room. They did not kneel; rather the five of them stood in front of the throne, dressed in full armor. Each wore a jupon with his own coat of arms. Gloucester was the tallest, his black eyes flashing fire; he hadn't shaved for days and his scruffy chin added to his ferocity. In contrast, the shorter and stouter Arundel glared at Richard with those disconcerting pale blue eyes.

257

The Earl of Warwick tried to appear impassive, but Richard noticed that he kept glancing worriedly at Gloucester. The two newcomers, Bolingbroke and Mowbray, stood off to the side as though they were not entirely in harmony with the proceedings. Richard wondered if he could exploit their differences.

"Well, you are here," the king said. "What is it you want with me?"

Gloucester took the lead. "We are here to hold you accountable for breaking your word. You made an oath of protection and yet you sent letters to Robert de Vere commanding him to bring an army to London. Do not deny it!" He held up a parchment. "We have it here! Sealed with your own hand! Your precious duke left it behind when he fled from Radcot Bridge."

Richard flinched at the first verbal blow. He hadn't realized that his letters fell into enemy hands. The lords already had him at a disadvantage.

Gloucester was too absorbed to savor his triumph. He had only just begun. "What we have to say to you would be better delivered in private. We would see you alone."

Pushing himself up, Richard resisted taking one last despairing look at his uncle of York. He understood that any shame would be best hidden from witnesses. Sighing, he walked toward the chapel.

"Here," Richard said, gesturing them forward. "This will serve us well."

St. John's chapel used to be a comforting place—before the Great Revolt. Now, Richard associated it with the murder of Sudbury, since it was here that he was seized by the rebels and dragged to his death. Lit by candles only on the main floor, the high ceiling receded into the gloom. But there was enough light for Richard to see the determination on the Appellants' faces. Feeling petulant, he sat down on a first row bench.

Gloucester walked in front of him, still brandishing the damning letters. "We repeat our demands. We demand the arrest and imprisonment of Michael de la Pole, Robert de Vere, Justice Tresilian, and Archbishop Neville. Sir Nicholas Brembre is already imprisoned."

Richard shivered. He hadn't realized that Brembre was taken. He raised his head, pursing his lips. "You may arrest the others if you can find them," he snapped.

Ignoring his remark, Gloucester went on. "For the honor and the good of your kingdom you will remove from your palace the tale-bearers, flatterers, malicious slanderers, and useless people who disgrace your sovereignty and you will replace them with others who will be more honorable—"

"You overstep your authority!" Richard cried.

"By God we do not! You have surrounded yourself with sycophants and they must be cast out!"

"I will cast no one out of my household. How dare you attempt to make such demands?"

"You forget who is *en puissance* here!" Gloucester shouted. "We decide who is to stay and who is to go."

Blinking, Richard shrank back for a moment. Arundel took a step forward.

"That is not all. We order you to arrest and bring to trial the following traitors: your seneschal Lord Beauchamp of Holt; your confessor Thomas Rushook; Sir Simon Burley, constable of Dover Castle; Sir Thomas Tryvet, Sir Nicholas Dagworth, Sir James Berners, Sir William Elmham, Sir John Salisbury—"

"You seek to eliminate all my chamber knights! Their only crime is their loyalty to me—"

"Your clerks, Richard Medford, Richard Clifford, and John Lincoln. We also appeal Justices Robert Belknap, John Holt, William Burgh, John Lockton, John Blake, and John Fulthorpe."

"They only obeyed my commands! They are not culpable."

"There are others we shall merely banish; they are a drain on the crown's financial resources."

"Enough!" Richard leapt to his feet. "This is unendurable. You seek to remove all my supporters, all my advisors—"

"Yes. All of them." Gloucester put his face next to Richard's; the king stepped back involuntarily. "You have misgoverned the realm with impunity. You have been misled, deluded, misguided by those who only want to advance themselves. They took advantage of your youth—"

"Oh, not that old refrain! You have overused that device."

259

"They will be cast out!"

"Never!"

Letting out his breath in disgust, Thomas turned his back on the king. He looked at Bolingbroke, jerking his head at Richard. "Show him."

Richard turned from one to the other. Henry came over to him, daring to put his arm through the king's, and led him to the window. They stood together, observing activities in the inner ward. Rowdy soldiers had set bonfires in the open space and amused themselves—some practicing their swordplay, some throwing dice, others passing around a wineskin. All wore their armor.

"Cousin," said Bolingbroke quietly, "they may be enjoying themselves right now, but make no mistake. They support our cause and will help us keep the peace."

"Your peace," said Richard bitterly.

"If necessary."

"And I am to give up everything."

Henry shrugged. "We are here to make an understanding."

"Oh, I understand. I understand all too well." He pulled away and went up to the altar, wrapping his hands around the edge.

"I am your king," he said to the room. "My household is my own. My advisors are my own. You may not assault my prerogative."

Gloucester whirled around. "*When* will you understand? You have no power. You have no support. You have no army. You have no say! If you do not comply, you have no crown!"

There. It was said. Suddenly subdued, Richard seemed to collapse into himself. He gaped at Bolingbroke who walked away from the window. He turned his eyes to Mowbray who stood with his arms crossed. He blinked at Warwick who gripped his sword. He couldn't bring himself to face the others. He shut his eyes.

"It happened once, not too long ago." Gloucester's voice cut the silence like a steel blade. "Remember that there is a full-grown heir to succeed you."

Despondent, Richard failed to see Henry jerk his head in surprise.

260

"You cannot do this," the king said, though his conviction had fled.

"We can and we will. We will do what we must."

Richard gasped then caught his breath. Gloucester curled his lip. "Remember what I said. The game is over. You have lost. Submit or face deposition."

He turned to leave; Arundel and Warwick followed without a word. The other two hesitated for a moment.

"Henry, Thomas, will you sup with me?" the king said weakly. "I would have your company."

Arundel swung around, ready to object. But Henry had already turned his back on the departing lords. He clearly intended to follow his own inclinations and there was not much the others could do about it.

It was rare for Richard to dine alone—especially without the queen—but he needed to regain his self-confidence. The fewer witnesses, the better. The only interruptions were the servants, and since this was an informal meal the three of them were mostly undisturbed.

Richard sipped his wine, peering over the edge of the goblet at his cousin. "I thank you both for staying with me this evening," he began. "I feel like a king under siege."

Henry grunted briefly. "Our uncle Gloucester can be most persuasive."

Mowbray smiled bitterly. "You should try having Arundel as a father-in-law." His jest was lost on Richard who frowned at the thought. He hadn't forgiven Mowbray for that betrayal.

Catching himself, Richard tried to lighten up the conversation. "How fares your father?" he asked Henry. "I heard that he had caught dysentery at Benavente."

Henry sighed. "It was a terrible summer in Spain. My father recovered, thanks be to God. But between that and the plague he lost over three hundred knights and squires, including Burley's nephew Richard and Northumberland's younger son Thomas." They all crossed themselves. "Father returned to Portugal, and it is said he is arranging a marriage between my half-sister Katharine and the Infante."

"I wish your father well, though I do miss him terribly." Richard couldn't repress a grimace, for in truth he understood that if Gaunt were here, none of this might have happened. The duke was the only person strong enough to resist an attack against Richard's prerogative. "My magnates blame me for not pursuing the French war."

"They wish to see England regain the old glory," said Mowbray.

"I would that it were so simple!" The king took his time sopping up the gravy. "It's been more than thirty years since Poitiers. Thirty years of failures and ruinous expense. How many more losses before we can accept peace?" He didn't expect an answer and didn't receive one. The others ate as though concentrating on their meal.

"I know I am a disappointment to many," Richard grumbled. "I'm not a fighting king, they say. Only a fighting king can rule, they insist. But I see nothing wrong with peace! I would think that people should prefer keeping their sons at home rather than sending them off to die. Glory. Pah! What glory is there in a *chevauchée*, reducing the French countryside to a burnt-out ruin?" Richard sat back, putting down his knife. "And why do they insist on going to war when there is no money to pay for it? Just think how long it took for your father to raise a fleet to take him to Portugal. We have no navy and we must acquire transportation at the expense of our shipping trades. It's not worth it."

Richard's attitude bordered on heresy to hardened soldiers. But his guests knew better than to object. At least this kept them from straying back into discussion about this evening's business.

Slim chance! The king looked sideways at Henry, trying to decide how far he could rely upon his cousin's wariness toward Gloucester. "Henry, does our uncle refer to Mortimer as the full-grown heir to the throne—or did he mean himself?"

Henry nearly choked on his food. "I do not presume to speculate," he answered with a sharp glance at Mowbray.

"Hmm." Richard tore off a piece of bread. "You may need to guard against him, yourself."

262

Henry stopped chewing. The king knew he had his cousin's attention.

"My grandfather's entail is not widely known," Richard pursued, despite the confusion on Mowbray's face. "Gloucester could seek to circumvent it altogether."

"Entail?" Thomas said.

"Ordering the royal succession along male lines." Richard hated the thought of his crown descending on Lancaster, but today he found the entail a useful tool. "That cuts Mortimer out. Of course, Anne is still young and we hope to see a son of our own."

"Of course, of course," Bolingbroke said.

"But Henry," the king said, pouring wine into his cup. "In helping me, you help yourself."

The other coughed. "How so?"

"Think about it. Keep our bulldog uncle under control, and I will be in a better position to advance the interests of you and your father."

"You have always advanced our interests," Henry choked out.

Richard was bemused; his cousin actually seemed at a loss. "Would Gloucester?" he said softly. The other took a sip, neglecting to answer. Richard knew when to stop.

By the time they finished, the king had recovered his composure and he even accompanied them to the door, smiling and nodding as they took their leave. It wasn't until he found himself alone that his mouth trembled and his eyes watered. He looked out the window at the clamorous soldiers, left behind to guard him. *How long would he remain a prisoner?* He put his forehead against the glass and closed his eyes. His thoughts were a jumble and he couldn't conceive any way out of this predicament.

Most of the candles had burned down and Richard turned to the stairs, up one story to the queen's chambers. He knocked lightly before letting himself in. Anne was waiting for him, sitting by the fire with her embroidery.

"Oh, my dear," she cried, dropping her needlework and holding out her arms. Forgetting his dignity, he rushed over to her and fell on his knees, sobbing into her lap. She stroked his head, cooing soft sounds. It tore at her heart to see him like this. "It must have been terrible," she murmured.

Taking a deep sigh, Richard put his arms around her waist, burying his face in her bosom. They stayed like that for a moment until he stirred, sitting beside her on the bench. Gently, he touched the edge of her embroidery.

"It's a white hart," she said, opening it up. The hart had a gold crown around its neck.

"Maybe you should attach a chain to its crown," he said. "That's what I feel like. A king enchained."

Anne held it up, tilting her head. "That would make a splendid badge for you." Richard said nothing and she hesitated, frowning. "What did they do?"

"They threatened me with deposition if I don't do their bidding."

"What!" She took his hand, the embroidery forgotten. "That is impossible!"

"I would that it was. They may have the power to do so. They have the army, not me," he added bitterly. "Oh Robert, I should have met you in the field instead of waiting for you."

Anne pursed her lips. "There's no helping that now. What did the Appellants want with you?"

He took a shaky breath, on the verge of tears again. "They want to arrest my advisors. My clerics. The justices. My chamber knights. Simon Burley."

"Simon! Whatever for?"

"For his loyalty to me. They seek to destroy everyone I trust. They want to rule in my stead. Oh, it's so much worse than the Parliament last year!"

"What will you do?"

"What can I do? I refused, and my uncle declared that I would lose my crown if I persisted." His eyes were haunted as he blinked at her. "Like my great-grandfather."

It was *not* impossible and they both knew it. "Would you like me to stay with you tonight?" she asked quietly.

Nodding, he picked up her hand and kissed it. "At least they can't take you away from me. You are my best and only hope."

Henry of Bolingbroke was not a man to take insult graciously. And Gloucester's behavior was bordering on insult. Richard's question had echoed his own. Just who was he referring to when he threatened to replace the king?

After dining at the Tower, Henry was in no mood to return to his own quarters. He and Mowbray rode directly to Gloucester's town house and were satisfied to see that no one had retired yet—in fact, all three Appellants were still there. Plotting, in all likelihood. The servants let them in and Henry stood at the door pulling off his gloves while the others turned from the table.

"Ah, there you are," said Thomas, beckoning them over. "Had a nice supper with the king?"

Henry frowned. "It was not terribly pleasant."

"What did he say?"

The other shrugged. "Nothing of consequence. He was shaken."

"I would certainly hope so," laughed Arundel shortly. "It's time he understood we are resolute." He moved over as Mowbray took a place next to him.

Sitting at the end of the table, Henry leaned forward to grab an empty cup. As he lifted it a servant poured some ale. The others watched him uncomfortably as he drank; they didn't know where to start.

Henry finally put his ale down. He cocked his head. "The king wanted to know who you were referring to," he said finally. "A full-grown heir. I wondered the same thing."

Thomas cleared his throat. "I think we've had enough of Richard's rule. He has proven himself unworthy of his great position."

"Unworthy." Henry twirled his cup. "And who is worthier?"

"Why not the son of a king?" Gloucester said, almost defensively. "We are in a position to compel that boy to step down."

"We?" Henry raised an eyebrow. "Aren't you putting the cart before the horse?"

Gloucester stood and began pacing. "All right. Let us come out and say it. We can dethrone him. Now. There will be no better time. We have Richard at our mercy and there is nothing he can do about it."

"And put you in his place?" Henry's voice was not cordial.

Thomas whirled around. "Any why not? I am the better warrior. I am more acceptable to the Commons, more deliberate..."

"You forget yourself, uncle." They stared at each other, one on his feet, the other sitting tensely at the table. "You are not next in line."

"Does it matter? My brother Edmund wouldn't want the responsibility. Your father has other interests. He already has a crown."

"But I do not."

It was as though they were the only two people in the room. They stared at each other before Warwick broke the tension; he was ever the moderate. "What about Mortimer? I thought Richard favored him as his heir."

"Another boy? We don't need another boy king."

"That is not for you to decide," Henry retorted. "Or are you so sure of your position?"

Gloucester made a deprecating sound. "We must strike while the iron is hot! This is our moment."

"And I say it is not," Henry objected, finally standing. "Who is going to tell my father that his interests were passed over? How do you think he will react?"

Eyes flashing, Gloucester turned toward the fire. He stood before the hearth, taking an iron and thrusting it through a burning log. A shower of sparks flew up the chimney.

"Then we must bend the king to our will."

CHAPTER 4

The last day of the year, 1387, Bolingbroke and Mowbray rode to the Tower which had been surrounded by their men since that terrible night. Richard was ready to meet them and he sat on his throne, pale and sullen, though the words he spoke were civil enough for a man whose command had been shattered. Richard was relieved when the newcomers removed their hats and bowed. At least they still recognized him as king. However, there was a limitation to their obeisance; Henry quickly stood, tucking his hat under his arm.

"Most gracious sovereign, much work needs to be done and we request your presence at Westminster tomorrow so we may begin our writs for the upcoming Parliament."

Richard felt his anger boiling to the surface. He hadn't given Henry permission to speak! But he bit back his indignation. During these last few lonely days of introspection all was coming clear. He finally understood that his own behavior was responsible for the predicament he found himself in. All those fits of temper, thoughtless remarks, and reckless commands had damaged his authority. From now on, he was determined to be more circumspect. Never again would he allow himself an outburst that could be turned against him. He would be calm, steadfast, and determined. He would keep his own counsel. He would make his enemies relax their wariness; he'd convince them that he was subdued. Only then would he take back his kingship and recast it in its proper magnificence like in the days of Edward I.

Forcing himself to stay calm, Richard closed his eyes for a moment before fixing his gaze on his cousin. "All right. I am prepared to acquiesce to the lords' wishes and to be guided by their wholesome advice—without prejudice to the crown."

Henry nodded. "On the morrow, then. We will be here at first light and accompany you." Bowing slightly, he turned and left, followed by Mowbray. When the door closed, Richard accepted a

267

goblet from a servant; but after taking a sip he threw it after them, spewing wine all over the floor.

On February 3, 1388, Parliament opened in the king's White Hall at Westminster. A huge crowd of all different estates waited in attendance, from great lords to common knights. The king sat above them all while Chancellor Thomas Arundel stood before him, facing the assembly. Richard stared at the chancellor's back, hating that this man had already replaced Michael de la Pole, one of the Appellees destined to be condemned. The king knew the results of this trial were already a foregone conclusion—and yet he had to suffer through this whole travesty of a parliamentary court, so his enemies could force through their uncompromising agenda. He would resist where he could and hoped to save his friends from execution—or worse. The horrors of a traitor's death should not be visited on political rivals, but Gloucester was capable of any atrocity.

Richard's preoccupation was interrupted by a blast of trumpets, announcing the entry of the Lords Appellant. As all attendees craned their necks to see better, the huge double doors flew open. The five great lords stood in the entrance, all dressed in cloth-of-gold, arms interlinked to form a long solid line. As one they marched ahead, eyes forward and mouths set, their regular footfalls echoing against the walls like distant thunder. Stopping before the king, they fell to one knee, heads bowed. Then they stood and separated, taking their seats across the hall—with the exception of Gloucester, who hadn't moved.

After the chancellor declared the session open, Gloucester stood; he had knelt long enough. "Sire," he started, his voice ringing through the room, "I understand that there are those among my enemies who told you I have plotted to seize the throne. I come before you to clear myself of this charge, for I only have your best interests at heart and sincerely strive for your reform."

Before Richard even had a chance to respond, the chancellor spoke for him. "The king holds you innocent of any attempt on the crown. Now, will the royal clerk read the appeal of treason against Robert de Vere, Michael de la Pole, Archbishop Neville, Robert Tresilian, and Nicholas Brembre?"

It took two hours to recite the appeal, which was filled with 39 separate articles. The same old accusations were dredged up. Richard's supporters were accused of giving him bad advice, estranging him from his loyal councilors, encouraging him to waste the treasures of the realm, urging him to betray Calais to the French. They were held responsible for the questions to the Judges and for keeping Richard away from the continual council. They were charged with bribery, corruption, frustration of justice, and encouraging the king to use military force against the Appellants.

To Richard, few if any of the charges could be construed as treasonable. Regardless, the trial moved relentlessly forward. Over the course of the next week, the only thing he could do was question the validity of the appeal at all. It did not fit in with either civil law or common law, and even Gloucester's picked judges agreed with the king that the procedure was most irregular. However, this was merely an inconvenience; determined magnates could always find a way around the law. After much discussion the Appellants declared that the defendants were of such high status, the only court qualified to confer judgment was Parliament itself. Parliament's law was to supersede the law of the land. Never mind that this was totally unprecedented.

Now that preliminaries were out of the way, the Appellants proceeded to push through their agenda. After a brief one-sided trial, the Speaker stood, holding out a scroll.

"The Lords and Commons of Parliament declare Robert de Vere, Michael de la Pole, Justice Tresilian and Archbishop Neville guilty *in absentia.* They are to be sentenced to death and to forfeiture of their lands—all except for Neville, who will be turned over to the Pope for punishment. The rest are to be hanged and drawn as befitting the traitors that they are."

Richard was appalled. He leapt to his feet. "My Lords! You overreach yourselves! I did not assent to these judgments! How can these men be accused of treason when I do not recognize these charges as such?"

The chancellor turned calmly. "Sire, these judgments are in the hands of Parliament."

"Am I only to be an observer, then?"

"That is the decision of Parliament, sire." Chancellor Arundel spoke as though to a child. Richard sat back down, his stomach churning. His only consolation was that Robert and Michael, at least, were safely out of reach.

But for his brave Nicholas Brembre, this protection didn't exist. He was the only Appellee left to bear the brunt of the Commons' antagonism.

The former mayor did his best to retain his dignity when brought before the judges. "I request the assistance of counsel," he stated, "before I respond to your charges."

The chancellor shook his head. "Request denied. Counsel is not permitted in an appeal trial."

Brembre pursed his lips. "Then I request the opportunity to prepare answers for the charges brought against me."

The chancellor shook his head again. "Permission denied."

There was nothing for him to do but throw back his shoulders and plead not guilty to all the charges. Every time he denied an accusation, the Commons grew more and more belligerent.

"We have further special crimes to be laid to your account," Chancellor Arundel stated, reading from a document. "First, that you undertook to murder the forty deputies of the Commons in 1386, when they planned to meet with the king at Eltham—"

"That is a total fabrication!" cried Brembre. "There was no such plot. Mayor Exton spread those rumors to discredit me."

Arundel ignored the outburst. "Secondly, you are accused of making a prescription list of 8000 Londoners to be executed."

"Impossible," shouted Brembre.

"And made a special block and axe to murder them!"

"Another lie!" Brembre was shaking with rage.

"Thirdly, that you attempted to raise London in arms to defeat the lords and myself and put us to death—"

"That is not true!"

"Fourthly, when you were mayor you plotted to change the name of London to Petty Troy and have yourself declared duke—"

"I object!" shouted Brembre. "Whoever had charged me with these things, I give witness that I am ready to prove by combat that these accusations are false!"

270

At that, all five Lords Appellant stood and flung their gauntlets to the floor. Arundel's voice was the loudest. "And we give witness and offer ourselves ready to prove by battle that these same things are true."

Most of the Commons jumped to their feet. Another gauntlet landed on the floor, then two more, then from every directions gauntlets flew—like snow, someone said—and covered the ground before the astonished defendant. Later chroniclers stated that more than 300 gauntlets were cast against him.

The officials put their heads together then called for order. It took some time, but finally the room settled down. "The petition is denied," said Chancellor Arundel. "In accordance with civil law procedure, ordeal by battle is only permitted when there are no witnesses."

Grumbling ensued, when to everyone's surprise, King Richard stood. The clerk pounded his staff. "I have never known Sir Nicholas Brembre to be a traitor," he said, turning to the right and to the left. "He has always served me fairly and well. I say he is not guilty of these charges, nor have I ever known him to plot against the citizens of London."

The Commons started shouting back at the king, too excited to restrain themselves, even in his presence. Shocked into silence, Richard did the only thing he could think in protest. He pushed past the chancellor and marched out of the hall, ordering the guards to shut the doors behind him.

Sighing in defeat, the chancellor beckoned the Appellants forward. Kicking the gauntlets aside, they approached him for a consultation. Gloucester and Arundel shook their heads, Warwick raised his arm in contradiction, and the other two listened, their hands clasped behind their back. Finally they came to an agreement. Chancellor Arundel turned to the assembly.

"We have decided to refer this question to a special committee for investigation. We call on the Duke of York, the Earls of Kent, Salisbury, and Northumberland as well as eight barons to be selected. Tomorrow they will examine the charges against Sir Nicholas Brembre and make their decision."

When Richard later heard of the announcement, he was encouraged. Surely these lords could think for themselves. They

271

were no cowards to be intimidated by the Appellants. He had registered his protest; on the morrow he would attend once again.

On the following day, after due consideration, the committee selected the Duke of York to speak for them. To a quiet Parliament, York stood. "We have investigated the charges and have determined that we cannot find that Nicholas Brembre has done anything to deserve the death penalty."

As expected, the chamber broke into chaos. Men stood and shook their fists at the duke. The chancellor shouted for order. Gloucester was remonstrating with his brother. But in the midst of all this disorder, a page had entered the room and was whispering something in Bolingbroke's ear. The earl quickly spoke to Mowbray who leaned toward his father-in-law who tugged Gloucester's arm. Startled, the duke interrupted his harangue while Warwick listened in. Gloucester jerked upright as though struck by lightning. "Chancellor Arundel. We request an adjournment," he said. Then, without waiting for an answer, the five of them dashed out of the room.

All arguing ceased at their sudden departure; those closest to the door followed the Appellants and after a moment many others did the same. The chancellor had his hands full demanding order. "What has happened?" he asked the clerk. "Go find out."

The Appellants had good reason to be excited. A crowd was already gathering outside a house that had a wall adjoining the palace. Gloucester pushed his way through the shouting throng. "Where did you see him?"

Someone pointed to the roof. "He was there. It was Justice Tresilian sure enough. He was leaning against the gutter and watching the lords go in and out of Parliament. Once he knew we saw him, he disappeared." Others agreed with the man. "I would know him anywhere," another said, "even through his disguise."

Gloucester pounded on the door, demanding entrance. After a minute, someone answered, putting his eye to the opening. But the duke was already pushing his way inside, practically knocking the unfortunate man to the floor.

"Where is he?" he roared. The other backed up, catching himself from falling. Gloucester grabbed him by the hair, drawing a dagger. "Show us Tresilian or I'll cut your ear off."

Terrified, the man pointed to a cloth-draped table. Mowbray pulled up the tablecloth and reached underneath, dragging out a ragged beggar with a thick wiry beard, a torn brown tunic, and red shoes. He hauled the old man to his feet with a grin. "Well, well. What we have here!"

"Tresilian!" Gloucester proclaimed, not bothering to hide his satisfaction. "You've been watching us all the time! Well, I hope you learned something." He jerked his head at two guards, who seized the Chief Justice by both arms. "Open the door."

As the barons exited the house with their prize, the gathering crowd broke into howls of glee. Guards surrounded the Appellants as they pushed their way back toward the Parliament hall, tugging their none-too-willing captive who was shouting to be released. A quick blow to the side of his head stopped the pleading. Things were getting out of hand; roused by all the excitement, the crowd was turning into a mob and they kept rushing the guards, striving to lay their hands on the unfortunate prisoner. Swords were drawn and a few in the throng were slapped by the sides of blades before they decided to pull back.

Richard was still in his throne as the Lords entered the chamber. "We have him! We have him!" shouted Gloucester as they propelled Tresilian to the platform still occupied by Brembre. As the Commons stood and gloated over the new development, Chancellor Arundel quickly ordered the ex-mayor to be returned to his confinement. Brembre strained to look back at the Chief Justice as he was escorted from the room; Tresilian still struggled to be released. Firmly deposited at the bar, he turned in desperation toward the king. But Richard couldn't help him; clutching the arms of his throne, he bit his lip, saying nothing.

Seeing that he would get no help from the king, Tresilian threw off his panic and tried to comport himself like the Chief Justice that he was, though he was far from dignified in his ridiculous beggar's garb. "These proceedings are illegal!" he declared. "There is no appeal process in Parliament!"

Ignoring his objection, Gloucester turned to the room. "Chief Justice Tresilian has been found guilty of the 39 articles of treason and condemned to death." He faced around to the defendant. "You have been sentenced *in absentia* and therefore you have no

273

defense." The snarl on his face was enough to deter Tresilian from further objections. "Take him to the Tower of London, so that execution may be carried out on his person."

There would clearly be no more business this day. The chancellor declared this session at an end.

Stepping aside, Gloucester watched in satisfaction while the same guards seized the unresisting defendant and marched him outside. The Lords Appellant followed, and the chamber emptied out; almost everyone wanted to witness the destruction of this "hanging judge" who would always be remembered for his cruelty after the Great Revolt.

It was hard for Tresilian to retain his dignity while tied hand and foot to a hurdle, hitched to two horses. Snorting, the animals started forward on their long trip to the Tower, led at a walking pace while the lords mounted their horses and rode beside them. A great crowd of commoners and lords, walking and riding, accompanied them; most jeered at the prisoner, while others laughed and joked as though going to a revel. Every furlong or so the horses were halted—out of consideration of charity, as was customary—and a friar stepped close in case the condemned wanted to confess anything. But Tresilian stubbornly shook his head, which only tended to confirm his guilt to the witnesses. When they reached the Tower they untied him; he peered up at the gibbet then jerked forward as his captors pushed him off the hurdle. The guards held the restless throng aside as he prepared to walk the rest of the way.

With a scream a woman broke from the crowd and threw herself on him, crying out and begging for mercy. "My husband, save my husband. He has done no wrong!" For a moment Tresilian let out a sob as she wrapped her arms around his neck and kissed his cheek. She tried to hang on as a soldier dragged her back—catching her as she fell into a faint. Groaning, the condemned man lowered his head and trudged up the hill.

At the foot of the gibbet Tresilian hesitated until they goaded him with sticks. Slowly, he ascended the stairs. On the platform, he refused to acknowledge the curiosity seekers and stared at the White Tower. The executioner climbed up a ladder, noose in hand, as they prodded the prisoner up a second ladder. The hangman leaned on the gibbet, watching. "I've killed many of your victims," he said, spitting to the side, "but none have given me as much pleasure as you." He tightened the noose around Tresilian's neck and climbed down. The crowd waited, expectantly. At a nod from Gloucester, he twisted the ladder away and the first victim of the Appellant's revenge dropped heavily to the end of the rope, kicking for a minute then twirling back and forth as he slowly suffocated. The crowd cheered.

After enough time had passed to entertain the onlookers, Gloucester nodded at the body. "Go cut his throat just to be certain he is dead," he said to the executioner. Holding out his hand for an additional coin, the hangman was happy to oblige.

As the Appellants rode back to Westminster, Arundel nudged his mount next to the duke. "A fine predicament the Lords have put us in. What are we to do about Brembre?"

Gloucester grimaced. "He has got to go. We must find a way." He glanced at Warwick. "What do you think?"

The earl scratched his head. "Perhaps we should rely on his enemies to condemn him. He certainly has enough of them."

"Hmm. The guilds. Let us summon two representatives from every major guild in London. Let us question them as to our accusations. Did he really draw up a prescription list? Did he prepare a special block and axe for their execution? Did he really try to make himself duke of Petty Troy? Yes, you are right. We're not the only ones who want him dead."

The following day, Brembre's trial resumed. As per their plan, the Lords Appellant summoned guild representatives and asked their damning questions. But once again, they had miscalculated. The draper guilds denounced Brembre while the victualler guilds denied the accusations. Brembre had just as many loyal friends as he had enemies.

Richard stood at this point. "You cannot prove your case against Sir Nicholas Brembre. I move that you dismiss him immediately."

Richard of Arundel stood. "I request a moment's discussion with the chancellor." Still lusting for blood, the Commons rumbled in his favor.

"Sire, the earl has the right to a consultation," said Thomas Arundel. Since the two Arundels were brothers, the king knew he was outmaneuvered. Frowning he sat and watched while the lords advanced and whispered their request. Finally, the chancellor straightened.

"The Lords Appellant request the presence of Lord Mayor Nicholas Exton as well as the aldermen and the recorder of London." The named persons were present, and the consultations began at once.

The mayor was the first to be questioned. Once again, Gloucester did his best to intimidate. "Lord Mayor, you have heard the accusations. Is Nicholas Brembre guilty?"

Exton was not a happy man. Although he was a supporter of Gloucester, he was first and foremost a London man and owed his loyalty to his city. He didn't like Brembre, but that was no reason to give in to pressure. "I would say," he started slowly, "that on the balance, he is more likely to be guilty than not." This was not the answer Gloucester wanted, and he glared at the mayor before moving on to the first alderman. However, the precedent was set and every alderman answered in exactly the same way.

Gloucester's patience was at an end. The last man to submit to his questioning was the recorder of London who duly followed the mayor's lead. "Come man," the duke said, leaning on the bar, "surely you have an opinion. Is Nicholas Brembre worthy of the extreme penalty of the law?"

Regarding the other witnesses, the recorder pursed his lips. "Well, if he is in fact guilty, and if his offenses are really treasonous, well yes, then the penalty should be death."

"There you have it!" Victorious, Gloucester whirled toward the Commons and pointed his finger in the air. In no time at all, Nicholas Brembre was declared a traitor and sentenced to execution. Just like Justice Tresilian, he was tied to a hurdle, dragged to Tower Hill and hanged. Witnesses were later to say that he gave great penance and begged God for mercy, and many along the way prayed for him.

Richard was shattered. Nicholas had been on trial for four days and the king had been sure that it would be impossible for the Appellants to find a way to condemn him. But now he saw that truly his enemies had taken the law into their own hands and would stop at nothing to destroy his friends and supporters.

The king wasn't the only one shaken by the results of the appeals. The lords recognized that this process had too many irregularities and too many complications. From then on, they would have to be content with the impeachment procedure. Although the defendants might be allowed to testify and the king's written signature would be required for the death penalty, the last thing they wanted was a repetition of the Brembre fiasco.

The next men to go were John Blake, Tresilian's clerk, and Thomas Usk, the man who tried to hold London for Richard the end of last year. They were quickly found guilty and executed. Next, the six judges were found guilty, but the Archbishop of Canterbury and other clergy interceded for them, and they were outlawed to Ireland rather than killed. They were the lucky ones. The real targets were four of Richard's inner circle: Sir John Beauchamp of Holt, the king's steward; Sir John Salisbury, who negotiated with the French for the king; Sir James Berners, whose worst offense seems to have been his friendship with the king; and most importantly, Sir Simon Burley, Richard's vice-chamberlain.

A two week break then a recess for Easter allowed Richard to garner support for his friend and tutor, though he was soon to understand that the Commons were just as inflexible as the Appellants. To this the king had no recourse. But he had to try. Many of the lords favored Burley—the Duke of York among them—and even Bolingbroke showed signs of uneasiness. Richard hoped their influence carried some weight with the Commons.

Inexorably, the trial continued. On the 12th of March, all four defendants were led to the bar at the same time to face their impeachments. Sir Simon, who was ill, was obliged to lean on the arms of his nephew Baldwin and his friend Lord Cobham for support. Even from across the room, Richard could see that his old tutor had lost much of his strength; for the first time Burley slumped like an old man. Normally so tall and sturdy, today he hung his head and stared at the gathering through half-closed eyes. Richard suppressed a shudder.

Sixteen articles of accusation were brought up against the four knights, mostly a repeat of the earlier charges. The prisoners were denied the ability to defend themselves—either verbally or by right of arms. In addition, they were accused of "counselling, aiding, and abetting" the five original Appellees, and helping them escape.

Gloucester had much more to say. "We accuse Sir Simon Burley of three additional offenses. First of all, he abused his position as Constable of Dover and Windsor. Secondly, we accuse him of filling the household with Bohemians to the great impoverishment of the realm. Thirdly, we indict him for making illicit use of the Great Seal."

Richard stood, incensed—his intentions to keep quiet forgotten. "I object!" he cried. "This is false and malicious! The Bohemians you so wickedly bewail serve my queen! And he never had access to the Great Seal! Of that I can swear!" Gloucester turned away, but Richard wasn't finished. "These allegations are trifles! The real reason you are attacking Simon Burley—along with my other chamber knights—is their loyalty to me. Anyone can see that."

"Sire," Gloucester answered, "it is our conviction that they have misled you, deceived you, suborned you to perform their will—even to the point of attacking us, your loyal servants."

Richard stared at him. "Are you saying I have no will of my own?"

"I am stating that these men are very experienced in the ways of the world."

This was too much for the Duke of York. For weeks he had listened quietly to the arguments; unlike his brother he was not by nature a choleric man. But now, he had had enough. He stood up before Parliament and demanded the floor; due to his rank, no one denied him.

"These knights all have flawless reputations. I have known Sir Simon Burley these forty years," he declared, pointing at the defendant. "He has always been loyal in his service to the king and realm. Anyone who wishes to deny this, I will myself prove my point in personal combat!"

At this, Gloucester stamped his foot. "And I say that Burley has been false to his allegiance and I am willing to prove this with my own sword arm!"

For once York showed the mettle he had often been accused of lacking. His face turning a deep red, he took two steps toward his brother. "You are a liar and a scoundrel!"

"Perjurer! I challenge you!"

"You evil plotter! Murdering innocent men!"

By now they were shouting in each other's face and it looked like they would soon come to blows. Alarmed, Richard dashed onto the floor and placed a hand on each uncle's chest, pushing them apart. "My lords, my lords. Restrain yourselves. This is not meet."

The king's uncles stood glaring at each other, chests heaving. Finally Gloucester turned away, grumbling in disgust. Now Richard had the floor and decided to use it. He turned to the Commons.

"My countrymen," he reasoned. "I beg you to reconsider. These knights have been loyal servants and deserve to be heard. Some of these charges are false; others are not treasonous."

The chancellor suspected that no one would be able to respond to the king and save himself from future harm. Banging his staff once again, he shouted out, "Take the prisoners back to the Tower."

Not waiting for the defendants to be taken back into custody, King was the first to leave the hall. But Richard did not go far. He sent a messenger to the three Appellants to converse with him privately; he still hoped to win over Bolingbroke and Mowbray and didn't want to involve them in this discussion. The Appellants were reluctant; they knew Richard was going to remonstrate with them, but there was no way they could evade his summons. Gloucester was still angry from his altercation with York; nonetheless, he couldn't afford to antagonize his nephew further. "Where does he want us to meet him?" he growled at the messenger.

"The king suggests the bath house behind the White Hall," was the answer.

"Very well. Tell him we will come." He turned to the others. "He doesn't want witnesses. That's good. Neither do we."

Richard was pacing the floor when the lords came to meet him. He, too, knew this was a delicate moment. "My lords," he began, "I want to truly understand why you insist on the execution of Simon Burley." He stared at Gloucester.

"Sire. We have already presented the sixteen articles."

Richard shook his head. "There has to be more than this. You know the temper of the Commons. What is their complaint?"

"All right. They feel that he has enriched himself at the expense of the exchequer which means they must make up the shortfall with more taxes." Richard frowned. This was a common complaint.

Gloucester went on, "They accuse him of laying his hands on the Leybourne inheritance by improper means, thus cheating the intended recipients of King Edward III's last will."

"Go on." Richard was not ready to admit his own participation in that unfortunate but necessary enterprise. He had to reward the vice-chamberlain somehow for all his years of service, and he planned to make it up someday. Still, that was old news; it had happened ten years before.

"He is accused of trying to sell Calais to the King of France for his own benefit. He attempted to despoil St. Thomas Becket's shrine and carry off the treasures to the safety of Dover. He plotted with the French to capture the island of Thanet, and he ordered the people of Sandwich not to leave the city on pain of imprisonment, whereby he could keep the island for himself—"

"These accusations stink of spite and malice! I do not believe a word of it."

Gloucester paused, taking a deep breath. "You know, sire, that Burley has used your chamber knights to erect a barrier against the rest of us who only seek to help you. He has turned you against your advisors."

"Is this the best you can do? I see no cause for capital punishment here. I see the jealous rancor of frustrated courtiers."

"You see? Of course you see! It just shows how much you are under his influence," Gloucester said.

Richard was about to respond, but he knew that anything he said would be turned against him. Pulling his cloak tighter about his shoulders, the king strode to the door. "I implore you, for your sake and my own, do not seek this man's death." Not trusting himself further, Richard departed.

The three exchanged worried glances. "What can he do to us?" asked Warwick.

"Nothing. That's all bluster." Arundel didn't sound as convincing as he meant to.

"We'll just have to make sure that we impose an oath of loyalty after all is done, so that no one can overturn the verdicts."

"What if they use the procedure against us in the future?" Ever the moderate, Warwick was still uncertain about their methods.

Gloucester frowned at him, wishing he would stay silent. "We will make sure the rulings from this Parliament are not construed as precedent. They will stand for this Parliament only."

Shrugging, Warwick conceded. What else could he do?

But this wasn't the end of the matter. For three weeks the king refused to sign Burley's death warrant. In the meantime, controversy continued to go back and forth between the Commons and the Lords—all the Lords favoring Burley, that is. By now the discussions were about sparing the life of the accused. The Commons clamored for the death of Burley, deaf to any arguments which were uttered by those of all ranks, from the Duke of York all the way down to Richard's household clerks, willing to risk their necks to put in a good word for the vice-chamberlain.

Finally, after much hesitation, Henry Bolingbroke stood—to the amazement of the king and the wrath of Gloucester. After a moment, Mowbray stood with him. "My lords," Henry said, "I am of the opinion that Sir Simon Burley does not deserve the death penalty. By all means, remove him from the offices he now occupies. But do not debase yourself by this disgraceful verdict which reeks of partisanship." The last words had to come out at a shout, for before he had finished the members started hooting and booing at him. For some minutes he continued to holler at the

crowd before giving up and sitting back down. He ignored
Gloucester's furious glare.

The next morning, when the Appellants were sitting in the
judges' chamber awaiting the beginning of Parliament, Gloucester
couldn't restrain himself. "I cannot believe what you did," he spat
at Bolingbroke who sat at the other end of the table. "You could
have ruined everything we have worked for."

Henry casually picked an apple from a bowl. "Everything *you*
have worked for. It would not be a great exaggeration to say I do
not agree with your policy of extermination."

Gloucester stood, leaning over the table. "Don't you
understand? If we let them live—even one of them—they will
come back and destroy us!"

"Sit down uncle, please. If we pull their teeth, they cannot
bite." Just to emphasize his statement, he took a bite out of the
apple.

"As long as Richard lives, we are not safe unless we render
him powerless."

"And thus we should prove ourselves more disgraceful, more
ignoble than the king could ever be. No, my Lord, I do not fancy
such a reputation."

"Henry, you are committed to this course of action. As are we
all."

An uncomfortable pall fell over the room; they jumped when
the door flew open and the queen entered, holding up the edge of
her mantle. Richard was right behind her. Guiltily, the men stood.
She gestured for them to sit. "No, my lords. It is I who must kneel
to you." To their great dismay, Queen Anne fell to her knees
before Gloucester. "My Lord, I beg you, with all my heart, to
spare the life of Sir Simon Burley. Do not impose this terrible
penalty."

Richard moved over to the fireplace, leaning against the
mantle in disgust. He was clearly against this show of humility.
But Anne didn't care. This was all her idea.

"Simon Burley was the man who brought me to England
when I was just a frightened girl. He has been my staunch ally and
my dearest friend. Please, I beg you. Do not take him from me." A
tear ran down her cheek.

After his first astonishment, Gloucester turned away. She grabbed his hand, putting it against her wet face. "He is not the traitor you accuse him to be. He is loyal, and true. See how the king mourns." She kissed his hand, but he carefully withdrew it, trying not to insult her.

"Take pity, Lord Thomas. I beg you not to do this thing."

How Gloucester endured this woeful behavior was more than anyone in the room could fathom. The chroniclers were to state that she spent three hours on her knees, but how could that be possible? It was certainly long enough to be remembered throughout history, much to his discredit. After an uncomfortably long demonstration of her abject humiliation, he finally reached his limit. "You had best save your prayers for your husband," he said roughly, "for he stands in great need of them."

Stung by this remark, Richard came over and lifted the sobbing queen into his arms. "Have you no shame?" he retorted.

Still sitting, Gloucester turned to the king. "I will tell you this one last time. If you do not sign the warrants, you will face the same fate as Edward II. Do not take my warning lightly."

Richard looked in panic at Bolingbroke but his cousin was studying his fingernails. Why wouldn't he? Henry had nothing to gain from helping his beleaguered king.

Silently cursing his opponents, Richard whispered in Anne's ear. "Come from this terrible place."

Back in Parliament the arguments went on as before and still Richard did not give in, though even he knew he had run out of options. But fate was about to take a hand. Another storm was brewing that nobody had anticipated.

The members were arranging themselves for a long afternoon's debate when a small group of representatives from Kent were introduced into the hall. They came forward as a knot of men, uncomfortable before this commanding assembly but determined to have their say. Their leader stepped forward, bowing before the king.

"Sire," he began, "we are representatives of your loyal citizens in Canterbury, Dover, Maidstone, and the counties in Kent. All this time we have been waiting for Parliament to pass judgment on Sir Simon Burley. We charge him with imprisoning people without cause. We are here to accuse Burley of harassing the servants on his manors, of threatening tenants at harvest time and imposing heavy fines as though they were rebels. He is guilty of these crimes and more! Why does Parliament tarry?"

The sudden uproar in the room was so loud, Richard couldn't hear himself think. The Appellants wasted no time joining their voices to the accusers.

"The Appellants brought them here to stir things up!" someone shouted.

"We did nothing of the sort!" retorted Gloucester. "We knew nothing of these delegates!"

"Liars! You seek to spread more outrage!"

"Burley must pay for his crimes!" the Kentish leader insisted. "My countrymen are ready to rise up in rebellion if our demands are not met!" He shook his fists in the air.

"Those are the same men who led the Great Rising! The Rebels!" Others repeated the words, and the shouting diminished to a murmur as the ugly conviction took hold. The specter of the Peasants' Revolt rose up before them; no one wanted to repeat that debacle. The chancellor banged his staff on the floor until order was restored.

King Richard stood. "We must investigate the truth of these accusations," he said. "I suspend this session until we are better informed."

For once, his wishes were obeyed. Riders were sent out to discover if the delegates had truly represented the temper of the south. The Great Revolt was only seven years in the past; just thinking about it chilled the blood of every member in Parliament. Would they be any more able to resist tens of thousands of angry protesters than they were in 1381? Today's rebels weren't likely to trust the king's promises a second time.

Late that afternoon, after giving it much thought Richard decided to visit Simon at the Tower. In his heart he feared that this latest turn of events would prove the death knell to his resistance. It was only fair that he should see his old friend one last time in private, much though the prospect pained him.

Simon was lodged in Beauchamp Tower, a spacious accommodation reserved for high-ranking prisoners. Richard had himself announced, giving Simon enough time to prepare. The guard opened the thick wooden door and Richard ducked slightly to enter the room; he blinked a few times while his eyes got used to the gloom.

"I'll order you more candles," the king said awkwardly.

Simon was trying to get up from his writing table, but Richard forestalled him. "No, please old friend. Sit back down. I know you are not well."

With a sigh, Burley relaxed. "I feel better this week. I can get around on my own again."

Richard frowned. He wasn't so sure. He pulled up a chair to the table and brought a candle closer. "You are very pale."

"I expect so. I don't get much sun these days."

"Yes. Well." This was absurd. He had known Burley all his life. "Simon..."

"I know, Sire. My position is hopeless. The Appellants demonstrated that when they murdered Nicholas Brembre."

Richard put his face in his hands. "I am so helpless. I cannot protect my lowliest clerk, much less my vice-chamberlain."

"No, no. Do not carry on so. None of us expected them to go so far. They have distorted the law, twisted the statutes to conform to their own malicious schemes. They are implacable."

Blinking, Richard reached for the other's hand. "I promise you, Simon. They will live to regret this despicable behavior. I shall avenge every single death, every humiliation they impose on me and my loyal followers."

"Beware, Sire. Do not do anything that will unseat you. They are too strong right now, but in time they will lose their accord—especially their unnatural partnership with the Commons. Once you regain the confidence of Parliament, the Appellants will lose the upper hand." He hesitated, closing his eyes. "Of course, it will be too late for me."

Richard's mouth trembled and tears ran down his face. "Here you are tutoring me again," he said, his voice breaking. "Simon, I am afraid we are beaten. This afternoon a delegation from Kent threatened violence if you are not condemned. Everyone is afraid of another Great Revolt."

Burley sighed. "My old malcontents. Then I am truly damned."

"I am without recourse. I can no longer delay signing their cursed warrants."

"Sire, dry your tears," Simon said, getting up and coming around the table.

Richard rose and put his arms around his old friend. "What am I to do without you?"

"Protect yourself, my Lord. There is nothing more I can teach you. But please, don't let them treat me like a traitor. I am ready to die, but let it be with dignity."

Coughing out a last sob, Richard let go and turned away. "I promise, Simon. May God be with you."

Burley watched as the king went to the door and summoned a guard. Turning, Richard gave him a look that reminded him of the ten year-old boy who had left his father's sickroom for the last time. Only now, he was the one who would be dead, leaving his young charge unprotected and vulnerable.

Richard was as good as his word. As he had feared, the Kentishmen had spoken the truth and the south was seething with unrest. In the blink of an eye all dissention in Parliament melted away, and Richard reluctantly agreed to sign the warrant, provided that Burley was granted the privilege due to a knight of the garter: the block rather than the gallows.

On May 5, Sir Simon Burley, his hands tied behind his back, walked the length of the king's Highway to Tower Hill where he met his end. Hopefully he died quickly and painlessly. The chroniclers are mute on that point.

CHAPTER 5

A week later the other three chamber knights followed Burley to the block. The Lords Appellant—who complained so bitterly about squandering royal monies on unworthy favorites—were awarded by Parliament 20,000 pounds for their "great expenses in saving the kingdom bringing the traitors to justice". Apparently sated in their bloodlust, they released the rest of the prisoners on their promise of good behavior. Most of them were exiled from court, and it was likely they went away gladly, happy to save their own skin.

All that remained was to appoint a new Committee to oversee the king's personal affairs, while the Lords Appellant would be entrusted with the actual government of the realm. The Committee, consisting of the Earl of Warwick, the bishops of Winchester and London, and two knights were to attend the king continually for the rest of the summer. What were they afraid of? Richard had no fight left in him after his devastating humiliation. He had lost every friend, every advisor he ever had. His regality had been taken away, and he was threatened with deposition every time he tried to assert himself. He had no supporters, no army, no authority.

Richard and Anne retired to Sheen, where they could leave their nettlesome wardens in the palace while the king and queen sequestered themselves on the island of La Neyt. For the first week Richard said very little; he sat in a window seat gazing at the river for hours at a time, only stirring when a servant brought food or drink. Even then, his favorite dishes ceased to please him and he ate sparingly, picking absently at his food. At first, Anne merely watched from a distance, unwilling to distress him further. But after a few days she sat next to him, picking up his hand, stroking his face, until finally he seemed to notice her for the first time.

287

Blinking, he brought her fingers to his lips. "You've been so good to me," he said softly. "How could I have survived without you?"

Anne fought back her tears. "They've taken everything from you. At least Robert and Michael are safe."

He sighed. "I may never see them again. They are as good as dead to me."

Dropping her hand, he stared out the window again. The air rumbled with distant thunder and he leaned his head against the wall, staring at the swirling dark clouds. Had he forgotten her presence so soon?

She came back later and persuaded him to walk in the garden. "I think the rain won't come until later tonight. Come. Let me get you a cloak," she fussed. "There's a chill to the air this evening, but the flowers are so beautiful in this light."

Nodding, he stood at the door, waiting. She arranged a cloak around his shoulders and he took a deep breath, taking in the spring air. "It feels wonderful," he said, despite himself. "I wish Simon was here. He always loved this time of year."

They took a few steps outside and she bent over, sniffing an iris blossom. "I remember he used to cut the purple ones for me. They were his favorites."

"Really? I never noticed." His voice was expressionless.

"He was the kindest, most considerate man I ever met. Aside from you, my dear."

He took her hand, holding it in both of his. "Be patient with me, sweet Anne. I am bereft and know not what to do." The sat on a little bench, listening to the river. "I'm so overwhelmed with guilt. I could not save any of them."

"It is not you who are to blame. It is those terrible men who were eaten up with envy."

He gazed hard at her, wanting to believe.

"They grumbled and complained because they were losing influence. They would not rest until their wicked pride was satisfied. You had no choice in the matter." Usually so mild, she amazed him with her vehemence. "They had no plans beyond purging your household. Let them try what they will. They will fail, mark my words."

288

Heartened by the queen's reassurance, Richard ventured an uncertain smile.

"All this time they have blamed your youth," she pursued. "But you won't be young forever. What will they do then?"

He laughed shortly. "I'm twenty-one now. How much longer should I wait?"

"You will know. You need time to make yourself whole again. And we have many things to consider. And when the time does come, you will be ready to assume your patrimony."

"And you will be with me."

"Until the day I die."

Almost a year to the day after Simon Burley was led to his death, Richard summoned the Great Council to meet him at Westminster. Although in that year he had no one to advise him, his natural intelligence held him in good stead. He was wise enough to know that there was no legality to the Appellants' new rule. Technically, the authority of the continuous council ended in November of 1387, and in their arrogance the Appellants neglected to arrange for its renewal in Parliament. He knew that their failure to provide for the defense of the North was largely responsible for a major invasion from Scotland just a few months before. The humiliating defeat at Otterburn, where Hotspur and his brother were taken prisoner and held for ransom, cost the country a great deal of money. Richard saw that the Appellants were no better at ruling than the people they so violently ousted. And, most important of all, John of Gaunt was soon coming home; by now, Richard concluded that he could use his uncle as a bulwark against those who opposed him.

On May 3, 1389, Richard attended the Council dressed in a specially-made robe quartered with the royal coat of arms. His crown was polished until it sparkled in the light. He wore a pair of gloves made from the finest doeskin. As he entered, they all stood and waited for him to place himself at the head of the table. He nodded first to the right and then to the left as the lords sat.

Almost all were here: Thomas Arundel, the chancellor, sat next to his brother Earl Richard. The Duke of Gloucester was impatiently searching through a stack of papers. Warwick sat quietly at his side, tapping a finger on the table. Bolingbroke and Mowbray were absent, for they had lost all interest in governing after the Merciless Parliament was over—as it was now called. But Richard had invited others to attend more moderate in their political leanings. His half-brother John Holland sat smirking at Gloucester; Archbishop Courtenay along with the bishops of Hereford, Exeter, and Salisbury added a sense of stability, and the Duke of York could be depended on to remain steadfast. Northumberland's loyalty could be counted on, and his brother Thomas had proven most useful. Richard nodded to himself, satisfied.

After some opening statements, the king took over the meeting. "I ask you, my lords," he began, "how old do you think I am?" He gazed directly at the Duke of Gloucester.

His uncle glanced at Arundel before clearing his throat. "Um, I would say twenty, sire."

"Actually, this last January I turned twenty-two. Now, I put it to you, my lords, that I am entitled to the rights which the meanest heir in my kingdom acquired on attaining his majority. Would you not agree?"

Caught by surprise, the members of the Great Council mumbled that indeed, it was both his right and his duty to take upon himself the responsibilities of sovereignty.

"You know very well that for the last twelve years I have been ruled by others. I have been allowed no part in the decisions that have cruelly oppressed my people with grievous taxes. I could do nothing without permission from my guardians. Henceforth, with God's help, I will endeavor to bring peace and prosperity to my kingdom. Starting right now, I appoint whosoever I will to my council. I will transact my own business and make my own decisions."

The council members sat in complete silence, more stunned than indignant. With these well-considered words, Richard had just released himself from all responsibility for past shortcomings in the government. *He* wasn't accountable for deficiencies during his minority. *They* were.

Richard held out his hand toward Thomas Arundel. "And now, as my first step, I order that the chancellor shall surrender to me the great seal. And you, Thomas of Woodstock, Duke of Gloucester; you, Richard FitzAlan, Earl of Arundel; and you Thomas Beauchamp, Earl of Warwick, I thank you for your past duty and no longer require your services."

Richard II, King of England, had at last come of age.

END OF BOOK ONE

AUTHOR'S NOTE

Richard II has proved to be one of the most enigmatic kings in the Middle Ages. Just like that other Richard (III, as we know him) his reputation was demolished by the person that usurped him. Historians are destined to muddle through documents that have been altered or written by hostile chroniclers. They must search for missing records and interpret passages written by survivors anxious to curry favor with the new king—or at least escape censure. It doesn't help that there is such a wide range of conflicting opinions about him.

In the course of my research I discovered the immense value of academic articles that focus on a particular subject (the site Jstor.org is invaluable). For instance, after the 1384 Salisbury Parliament there is a scene where a Carmelite friar accused Gaunt of plotting the murder of the king. Richard immediately ordered his uncle's execution but was talked out of it, whereupon he allegedly went into a frenzy "like a madman" and threw his hat and shoes (or cloak and shoes) out the window. Many historians took this at face value; however I always had a problem with it. I just couldn't see the king throwing a hissy fit and hurling his shoes out the window. Well, imagine my surprise when I discovered an article entitled "An Alleged Hysterical Outburst of Richard II" by L.C. Hector which addressed this very scene. According to Hector, there was an error in translation from the original Latin chronicle, where the order of the passages was taken wrong. It wasn't Richard who threw his cloak and shoes out the window; it was the friar who did so in order to fake insanity so Gaunt wouldn't persecute him. Now it all made sense, and this is the interpretation I chose for this book. But you can see how easy it would be for a misunderstanding to stain the character of a historical person. Richard's biography is full of value judgments against him; I wonder how many were manufactured?

When Edward III died the ten year-old Richard was crowned king without a regency; apparently many of Gaunt's contemporaries were convinced that the duke aimed to seize the throne for himself, and this was preempted by crowning the boy as soon as possible. This resulted in a series of councils that took control of the government in Richard's name, which goes a long way toward explaining why he found the Commission of 1386 so onerous. By then he was nineteen years old—past the age where his grandfather Edward III was crowned. I think we find that overall, many of his early difficulties came from the attempts of his uncles and other magnates to control the king as long as possible. His elders thought he was too young and inexperienced to reign, but I wonder whether many of Richard's early "transgressions" were in the category of a frustrated young man struggling to assert himself. His kingly prerogative was taught to him at an early age, and yet no one seemed to respect him— except his inner circle of friends and advisors. And there's the crux of the matter.

The more Richard surrounded himself with trusted followers, the more shut-out the magnates felt. They were not getting the patronage they deserved due to their rank. And once Richard raised Robert de Vere to the marquisate, many of them were even outranked by this undeserving favorite. It was said that the king's inner circle restricted access to these outraged nobles, and I don't think it would be a stretch to say Richard actively disliked most of them. As with Edward II, hostility boiled over and once again the king found himself outfaced by his powerful barons. Alas, they had an armed following and Richard had nothing but his loyal friends who were unable to save him any more that he was able to save them.

Because they were accused of treason in the events leading up to the Merciless Parliament of 1388, three of the five original Appellees had fled to the continent. The chroniclers tell us that Robert de Vere sailed to the Low Countries, where he had already deposited a large sum of money with the Lombard bankers. Richard wrote to the French King Charles VI, requesting a safe-conduct for Robert which was granted, permitting him to live in Paris where he stayed for about a year.

Michael de la Pole escaped to Calais, where he presented himself to his brother, the captain of Calais Castle. His head shaven, dressed like a Flemish poulterer, Michael must have been a sad sight. Alas, brother Edmund preferred loyalty to his job above loyalty to family. He turned Michael over to William Beauchamp, the governor of Calais who promptly sent him back to London. Richard was most wroth at Beauchamp and allowed Michael to escape again; the exile took refuge in his family lands at Hull. When things got too hot for him, he escaped to Dordrecht and from there to Paris where he met up with de Vere. Michael died in Paris on September 5, 1389, only four months after Richard declared his majority.

Robert moved on to Louvain in Brabant (Belgium), where he joined Archbishop Neville. The archbishop, who had spent some months in the north before attempting a Channel crossing in a small boat, was captured off Tynemouth in mid-June, 1388. He was kept in the custody of the mayor of Newcastle until the end of November, when he escaped to Louvain. While Neville was in Belgium, the Pope translated him from his see in York to the Avigonese see in St. Andrews; this was about as undignified a situation as he could imagine. But since he spent the rest of his life in exile, perhaps it mattered little. Neville served as a parish priest in Louvain, where he died in May of 1392 and was buried in the church of the Carmelites. In the same year Robert was fatally wounded in a boar hunt; Walsingham tells us he died in "anguish of mind and pitiable poverty". Three years later, Richard was to bring his embalmed body back to England, where he gave his old friend a touching funeral.

The history books are silent about Agnes de Launcekrona, the queen's maid of honor whose love affair with de Vere caused so much strife. It was suggested that she returned to Bohemia or even followed Robert to France, though no one knows for sure.

One thing is undeniable: Richard's first crisis, the Peasants' Revolt, was managed so bravely by the fourteen year-old King that everyone saw him as the epitome of his famous father, the Black Prince. It was a terrible pity that this early promise was eclipsed by later foibles that were blamed on his youth and inexperience. Or was he just caught in the crosshairs of a changing society that no longer played by the same rules as in his father's days? The government was deeply in debt when Richard was crowned in 1377; over the previous decade the French wars had only produced one debacle after another. The great commanders were either retired or dead, and the next generation of eager warriors had few opportunities to distinguish themselves in glorious battle. They naturally blamed the king for his disgraceful peace policy, forgetting that wars could bankrupt the exchequer and after the Peasants' Revolt the country had little stomach for additional taxes.

Once Richard took the reins of government into his own hands, England settled into a quieter phase, and the country experienced peace and prosperity.This lasted seven years, "a veritable doldrums to chronicler and historian alike...There was no war with France, and the political executioners were unemployed," as stated by Harold Hutchison. Although Richard broached the subject of bringing back the exiled appellees in the early days, he was so vehemently denied that he quickly backpedaled; his friends' untimely deaths removed that issue. Nonetheless, Richard was not the type to forgive and forget. And when the time was right, retribution had its day.

Author's last note:

I changed Simon Burley's elevation as constable of Dover and warden of Cinque Ports from Jan 5, 1384 to after he was denied the earldom of Huntingdon. All other sequences of events I attempted to follow as closely as I could, given the occasional disagreement of our sources.

BIBLIOGRPHY

Armitage-Smith, Sydney, JOHN OF GAUNT, Endeavor Press Ltd, 2015

Barker, Juliet, 1381, THE YEAR OF THE PEASANTS' REVOLT, The Belknap Press of Harvard University Press, Cambridge, 2014

Costain, Thomas B, THE LAST PLANTAGENETS, Doubleday & Company Inc, New York, 1962

Dobson, RB, THE PEASANTS' REVOLT OF 1381, Macmillan Press, 1970

Given-Wilson, Chris, THE ROYAL HOUSEHOLD AND THE KING'S AFFINITY: Service, Politics and Finance in England 1360-1413, Yale University Press, 1986

Goodman, Anthony, THE LOYAL CONSPIRACY: The Lords Appellant under Richard II, Routledge & Kegan Paul, London, 1971

Hutchison, Harold F. THE HOLLOW CROWN, A Life of Richard II, Methuen, London, 1961

Jones, Dan, SUMMER OF BLOOD, The Peasants' Revolt of 1381, William Collins, London, 2009

Jones, Richard H. THE ROYAL POLICY OF RICHARD II: Absolutism in the Later Middle Ages, Basil Blackwell, Oxford 1968

McHardy, A.K., THE REIGN OF RICHARD II From Minority to Tyranny, 1377-97, Manchester University Press, 2012

Oman, Sir Charles, THE GREAT REVOLT OF 1381, Greenhill Books, London, 1989 (first published in 1906)

Pierce, Patricia, OLD LONDON BRIDGE, Headline Book Publishing, 2001

Saul, Nigel, RICHARD II, Yale University Press, London 1997

Steel, Anthony, RICHARD II, Cambridge at the University Press, 1962

Tout, Thomas Frederick, CHAPTERS IN THE ADMINISTRATIVE HISTORY OF MEDIAEVAL ENGLAND; THE WARDROBE, THE CHAMBER, AND THE SMALL SEALS, Manchester at the University Press, 1920

Tuck, Anthony, RICHARD II AND THE ENGLISH NOBILITY, Edward Arnold Publishers, London, 1973

Made in the USA
Coppell, TX
12 March 2021

51664386R00184